Praise for
and the Wic

"Steamy, romantic, and surprisingly tender, Lynda Aicher's *Bonds of Trust* is a great place to start for those wanting to add some spice to their romance reading. A strong start to a new series."
—Roni Loren, *New York Times* bestselling author of *Not Until You*

"*Bonds of Trust* is a beautifully detailed erotic romance.... The intense sex, building in both passion and deviance, is not only perfectly in balance with the love story but also deeply sensual. It is this perfect harmony of narrative and eroticism that makes a book that will leave you extremely satisfied."
—*RT Book Reviews*, 4½ stars

"Aicher's first contemporary erotic romance [is] appealing to readers bridging the gap between mainstream romance and *Fifty Shades of Grey*.... This title will appeal to fans of the works of Lora Leigh, Maya Banks, or Sylvia Day."
—*Library Journal* on *Bonds of Trust*

"This is an excellent read. Kendra's growing relationship with Declan rings true, with all of the triumphs and low points of real life."
—*RT Book Reviews*, 4 stars, on *Bonds of Need*

"This book was even better than the first one in the series."
—*Fiction Vixen Book Reviews* on *Bonds of Need*

"Lynda Aicher's Wicked Play books are solid erotic romances featuring BDSM relationships.... I can't wait for more books in this series from this author."
—*Romance Novel News*

"This is a rare book that can make you laugh and blush at the same time."
—*RT Book Reviews* on *Bonds of Hope*

"Everything about this book just worked for me."
—*Smitten with Reading* on *Bonds of Courage*

"I would recommend these books to [Cherise] Sinclair fans as something equal and just as intense."
—*Fiction Vixen Book Reviews* on *Shattered Bonds*

Bonds of Trust
& Bonds of Need

LYNDA AICHER

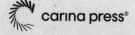 carina press®

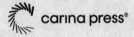
carina press®

Recycling programs
for this product may
not exist in your area.

ISBN-13: 978-0-373-00277-1

Bonds of Trust & Bonds of Need

Copyright © 2015 by Carina Press

The publisher acknowledges the copyright holder
of the individual works as follows:

Bonds of Trust
Copyright © 2012 by Lynda Aicher

Bonds of Need
Copyright © 2013 by Lynda Aicher

Bonds of Trust Epilogue
Copyright © 2015 by Lynda Aicher

www.CarinaPress.com

Printed in U.S.A.

CONTENTS

BONDS OF TRUST

To my faithful Beta Readers, Val and Cindy, who gave me the confidence boost when I needed it the most. And a special thanks to Lori, my email angel and dear friend, who is always there to lift me up when things get rough.

To my friends and critique partners Sue, Paula, Jenna and Kim for the support, feedback and brainstorming that let the stories evolve.

To my editor Rhonda Helms, for loving the stories, making the books stronger and teaching me so much along the way. And Angela James for believing in me and making this series happen. Working with the Carina Press team has been such a pleasure and I'm so grateful to see these books in print and reaching more readers.

And as always, to my family, for understanding my distractions, dealing with late dinners and cheering me on the whole time.

PROLOGUE

"Do you like bondage?"

"I don't know."

"Spankings? Whips? Floggings?"

"I don't know."

"Exhibitionism, being a slave, serving a Master?"

"Again, I don't know."

"Golden showers, enemas or any other classification of water sports?"

"What?" Cali Reynolds gasped then shuddered. Water sports? "God, no."

The long-haired co-owner of The Den paused in his barrage of questions to eye her intently. He braced an elbow on the desk and leaned in, assessing her, the blue polo shirt tugging across his shoulders, his muscled biceps flexing. Seth Mathews was the last obstacle she had to pass before she could be granted membership to the exclusive club. He gave a half smile at the expression of pure disgust that had to be on her face.

"There are members here who do enjoy those activities,

Ms. Reynolds," the man said. "These are standard interview questions. I hope your opinions wouldn't be so blatantly displayed in the presence of those who do like those things."

She winced. Her hands clenched in her lap and she hoped the large desk between them hid the action. "I didn't mean any disrespect. It's just not for me."

He nodded then glanced at the paper on his desk, making a mark on the page. He appeared younger than she'd expected, maybe late thirties, but his age didn't hinder the authority he exuded. "What *are* you looking for, then?" He studied her, missing nothing.

She swallowed, her stomach knotting into a state of sickly pain. "I don't know, exactly," she answered, her face heating with embarrassment. She tore her gaze from his and stared at her lap. She picked uncharacteristically at the small hangnail on her thumb, wondering if the straight-cut black slacks and purple sweater set had been too conservative for this interview.

He sighed, the pen clattering against the desk as he tossed it down and leaned back, crossing his arms over his chest. "Then why are you here? The Den is the most exclusive BDSM club in the Twin Cities. If you don't know what you want or like, then why come here?"

She snapped her chin up, desperation snaking into her voice. "Because you *are* the most exclusive club. I have to get in here."

"Why?"

Cali ducked her head, tucking her hair behind her ear, using the habitual move to calm herself. Why, indeed. "I'll never try this anywhere else." She waited for him to respond, but he didn't. So she continued, filling in the silence with the truth. "It's taken me a very long time to understand what I desire. Just as long to *accept* that what I crave sexually is way outside the box of normal. And even longer to do something about it. This isn't a game for me, if that's what you're thinking."

He picked up the pen, letting the object flip absently between his fingers. "Why now?"

"If not now, then it's never." She took a deep breath and hoped he believed her, because it was true. This was her one and only chance of safely getting what she secretly fantasized about. She couldn't risk the exposure by going anywhere else.

He sat forward. "Why do you think you're a submissive if you've never participated in any submissive activities?"

"How did you know you were a dominant?" she fired back. He obviously was and she was tired of his game. Of the questions and disbelief. She wasn't going to be intimidated into walking out because he doubted her intentions. "How did you discover what you liked and wanted without experiencing them? I bet you didn't know for sure. No one can. So if inexperience is the only thing keeping me from getting into this club, then I ask you, how else am I supposed to learn?"

He stared at her and this time, she didn't flinch away. She'd thrown down the challenge and she wasn't backing down. Maybe he'd toss her out or maybe, just maybe, he'd throw her over the desk and spank her for her defiance. Her gut dropped at that thought as a wave of heat flashed through her.

Either way, she'd have an answer.

After a minute of tense silence, a slow smile curled over his sensual lips. He stood, his large frame towering over her as he extended his hand. "Welcome to The Den, Ms. Reynolds."

ONE

Inhale, exhale. Two simple, reflexive actions that seemed almost impossible for Cali to execute. Breathe. She had to forcibly remind herself oxygen was necessary. But then, she could hardly hear her own thoughts over the pounding of her heart.

It'd been four days since her final interview. Four days to digest and stew on the fact that she'd been granted membership to the exclusive sex club. She'd be mortified if anyone ever found out she was here. Just the thought of it had her swallowing back her dinner.

They won't, she reminded herself. She could fulfill this side of her life without anyone knowing.

She forced herself to look around the small room in an attempt to focus on something besides her increasing anxiety. The space was tastefully decorated in deep burgundies and greens. The black leather love seat where she sat was positioned across from two matching chairs. A waiting room that with its warm tones and expensive furniture was more suited for a corporate office than a sex club.

What was she waiting for?

Had the club decided to revoke her membership before she'd even started? Then why did she spend the last half hour listening to all of the rules being repeated to the small group of new members like herself? It didn't make sense. No one else had been excluded, pulled aside and singled out.

She'd gone through the interviews, both on paper and in person. Paid the exorbitant membership fee. Completed the new member checklist filled with questions that made her cheeks flame and her heart race at the images they conjured. Submission, spanking, bondage, anal play, voyeurism, exhibitionism—*oh God*, she had to think of something else.

She forced another slow exhale, the breathing technique doing little to instill the calm she sought. The utter silence of the room was an added torture. No piped-in music or even the insistent ticking of a clock to distract her mind. She'd been left alone with her thoughts, nerves and a barely restrained instinct to flee.

Abruptly she stood, hesitated then immediately sat back down. She cursed silently, berating herself for the show of nerves. Shifting, she moved to tuck the strands of her sleek bob behind her ear, but her hand stilled when she touched the unfamiliar tumble of curls instead. Like the mini-skirt and low-cut blouse she wore, the loose curls flowing untamed around her head were an extension of this other side of herself. The side that seemed so very, very dirty. So wrong.

But desperately ached to be free.

She dropped her hand and clasped it tightly with the other, refusing to fidget. Refusing to run or panic or any of the other things they were probably hoping she'd do. If this was a test, she wasn't failing.

Determination reasserted, she breathed a little easier. She would get through this. It might have taken her forty-four years, two grown kids and a divorce to get here, but she wasn't turning back now.

Tonight, she would once again have sex with a man.

Jake McCallister leaned back in his chair and kicked his boots up to rest on the edge of the desk. The silent action felt off, missing the persistent creak he was accustomed to hearing. Shifting against the shiny leather for a comfortable spot, he wished for his old eyesore of a chair that had fit his body perfectly.

Too bad the garbage truck came that morning.

Sighing, he closed his eyes for a quick break before the night began. Before the crowds arrived and forced their expectations on him. Two minutes. That's all he wanted. Two minutes of silence to rest his mind.

The door to his office swung open, the booming rock music from the main floor pulsing into the room. "Hey, Jake," Seth called out as he strode into the office. "Do you have the file with tonight's newbie info?"

So much for two minutes. Jake opened his eyes and sat up, his boots thumping on the wood floor. He shuffled some papers around on his desk until he found the folder his business partner was searching for. It was First Friday, the one night a month new members were officially introduced to the club. "Here," he said, holding the folder out to Seth. "Do you have the assignments done?"

All newbies were paired with an employee their first night to show them around and answer any questions. It was both a courtesy and a precaution, with no obligation from either party. Still, they took care in assigning the member escort, as those matches often ended the night together—in one fashion or another.

"For the most part," Seth answered as he glanced at the

list. "There's one I'm having a hard time with. I was hoping you would do another interview and verify my choice before we send her out."

Internally, Jake groaned. "When?"

"In fifteen minutes."

"Let me guess," Jake said as he leaned back in his chair and thought about the new client list he'd just handed to Seth. "It's the forty-four-year-old divorcee looking for a little adventure but having no idea what she's getting into. Desperate to hang on to her youth after her husband dumped her for a younger woman, she thinks our club will validate her desirability and boost her self-esteem."

Seth shut the door cutting off the music and took a seat. Not a good sign. "You know I would have denied her membership if there was any indication she wasn't serious about the lifestyle." He shot Jake a reproachful glare before continuing. "On the surface, it seems a lot like what you just described, but I can't pin this one down. There's an element of almost virginal curiosity about her that doesn't fit with her age."

"So do the interview yourself."

"Can't. I have an appointment at ten and I've already done the prelims. I want a second opinion."

"What about Dek?" Deklan Winters was their third business partner. The three men had started The Den five years ago on an idea, a desire and barely enough cash to open the doors.

Seth leaned forward, resting his forearms on his knees. "You're the 'people person,' Jake. You can figure her out faster than either Dek or I can." He furrowed his brow and tilted his head in consideration. "Why are you dodging this?"

"Why did you wait until now to let me know?"

Seth sat up. "We always get a second opinion when in doubt."

Jake's gaze darted to the wall of video screens. Every room

in the club had a security camera. No exceptions. The club had a reputation to uphold. The three men had worked hard to establish The Den in the BDSM scene and it was currently on the top of the Twin Cities list. But they all knew the list was as fluid and quick to change as a river bed during the spring thaw.

Discretion, safety and exclusivity kept them on top.

"Fine," Jake responded as he scanned each screen in a practiced rhythm, absorbing every action, from the clients playing in the private rooms to the Scenes taking place in the Dungeon. "Give me her information and I'll take care of it." He glanced back to Seth. "Who have you matched her with so far?"

Seth extracted a sheet from the file and handed it over before he leaned back, his shoulders relaxing at Jake's agreement. Seth ran a hand through his hair, the straight, brown locks combing through his fingers before they fell back to brush over his shoulders. Jake noted the telling actions. For some reason, this client had Seth flustered.

"Marcus," Seth replied in answer to Jake's question, his knee bouncing in a rapid beat of contained energy. "But it's not feeling right. Nothing against Marcus, he's one of our best Dom's, but my gut tells me I'm missing something."

"Like what?"

Seth's lips compressed in a brief line of frustration. "Shit," he exhaled. "I don't know. That's why I want you to meet her." He stood abruptly and paced across the room to the minifridge, yanked the door open and stared inside before slamming it closed and turning back to Jake empty-handed. "She's not typical. The interviews I've had with her just don't fit with the divorced cougar looking to feel better about herself."

Intrigued now, Jake examined the details outlined in the

client dossier. The puzzle of one Ms. Cali Reynolds was becoming more attractive than he wanted it to be.

Over the last few months, he'd felt the restlessness returning. That inescapable, persistent itch to move on. His five-year commitment was up at the end of December, and he knew he'd be leaving. Seth and Dek, his de facto brothers since they'd bonded dodging fists and abuse in a foster home together, had made him promise he'd stick with the club for five years. Knowing him and his wanderlust a little too well, it was the only way they'd agree to go into business with him.

He didn't need to be pulled into client issues when he was quietly trying to disentangle himself from the club. Hence, his reluctance to do the interview. But he couldn't dodge the task without making Seth suspicious.

Not when both Dek and Seth were already looking for departure signs.

Jake picked up the head shot then studied the full-body shot. "She's very attractive." He glanced up at Seth, who was watching him a bit too intently. "Are you sure her age is correct?"

Seth frowned, crossing his arm over his chest. "Like Dek would mess that up. Everything in her file has been validated. Like always." Membership was strictly monitored and all applicants had to pass a rigorous interview and background check before membership was granted.

Jake flashed an apologetic smile. "Right. I'd place her at least ten years younger by her photos." The blonde in the pictures had the face and figure of a woman in her early thirties. Hell, she looked better than a lot of women did in their twenties.

"And you look like you're crowding forty?" Seth scoffed. "Come on, Jake. You, of all people, should know how deceiving appearances can be."

"Touché." People constantly assumed Jake was younger

than he was. He pulled his attention from the soulful green
eyes in the picture and tossed the papers back on the desk. "Is
Marcus doing the meet and greet then?"

Seth nodded. "I told him to take Ms. Reynolds to Lounge
One when he was done with the basics." He turned to leave
but paused before he opened the door. His lips quirked in a
mischievous smile. "Let me know how it goes with the cougar."

Jake laughed, a reflexive bark that burst from his gut.
"Right. She looks and sounds more like a kitten. I'll be surprised if she doesn't run from the club in blind fear once she
sees the action up close and personal."

"Don't be so sure." Seth opened the door, letting the noise
enter in a smooth rhythm of drums. "I told you, there's something about this one."

He left before Jake could respond. A quick exit was the only
way Seth could leave and still get in the last word.

Damn.

Jake picked up the headshot once again. A submissive? She
had the doe eyes, but they were sharp and filled with intelligence. Not that subs were stupid, but most had that eager,
need-to-please expression when they were at The Den. Her
hair was styled in an efficient bob that grazed her shoulders.
Not a strand out of place. Pale pink lipstick complimented
her creamy skin and highlighted the cupids-bow arch of her
upper lip that was curled in an almost shy smile, contradict-
ing the edge in her eyes.

Intriguing.

He turned to the security screens, his gaze hunting down
the mystery woman. A lone blonde sat in Lounge One, her
back to the camera, showing her stiff spine and a tumble of
curls that moved softly as she swiveled her head to look around

the room. Her face was hidden from view and he leaned to the side in an unconscious move to get a glimpse of her features.

He jerked away when he realized what he was doing. *What the fuck?*

Jake tossed the photo on the desk and stood. He flexed his fingers, working out the residual ache left over from his earlier appointment. A regular who enjoyed being spanked after work before she headed home to her boyfriend. Her end-of-the-work-week tension release.

He chuckled under his breath. Too bad she couldn't have an honest conversation with her boyfriend about what she desired. But then, the stigma around BDSM prevented a lot of people from openly admitting what they wanted, needed in their lives. It wasn't just about sex, either.

Not that most people understood that.

It wasn't his problem. Half the draw of The Den was the forbidden aspects of what it offered. Aspects he enjoyed both exploiting and encouraging.

He ran a hand over what he thought of as his Dom outfit. The expected black leather pants and black shirt that most Doms wore at the club. It was part of the image, another expectation he fulfilled, even though a truly dominant nature did not require specific clothing.

The facade was just one more thing he was tiring of.

A tight smile curved over his lips as he left the room, the persona of the Dom settling comfortably on his shoulders.

It was time to perform.

TWO

The almost imperceptible click of the door opening echoed in the still room. Cali whipped her head around, her focus anchored to the entrance. Her breath hung in her lungs, her spine stiffened with the tight clenching of her stomach muscles as the moment lapsed into a tense second of expectation.

This was it.

A tall, dark-haired man stepped into the room, closed the door and moved with a purposeful stride to stand before her. He had a lean build that showed solid muscle under the tight shirt and form-fitting leather pants. His head-to-toe black clothing only served to emphasize his commanding presence and aura of authority. Without question, he was a Dom.

His lips thinned. "Ms. Reynolds?" His deep voice tumbled over her, sending a quickly concealed chill down her spine.

"Yes," she answered hesitantly, not knowing if she should stand and meet his gaze or kneel and stare at the ground. What was the protocol? Going with what she knew, Cali stood and extended her hand. "I'm Cali Reynolds."

The man looked her over in an almost critical fashion before staring pointedly at her extended hand. With a slight curve to his lips that didn't quite make it into a smile, he clasped her hand in his much larger one. "Ms. Reynolds, I'm Master Jake. Welcome to The Den."

His grip tightened, his thumb caressing the back of her hand in a sensual stroke. Instantly, tingles of sensation whispered up her arm straight to her nipples, which stiffened in urgent desire.

Licking her lips, she once again stifled her response to the intriguing stranger and kept her poker face in place. This immediate attraction she felt had to be due to her prolonged sexual dry spell. But then, that was exactly why she was here.

Her stomach ached, the anxiety building with each step closer to achieving her goal. Could she really go through with it?

"Have a seat." Master Jake released her hand and motioned to the love seat. "I'm one of the owners of The Den, and I'd like to talk to you before you proceed into the club."

That didn't sound good. "Is there a problem?"

"No." He took a seat across from her, leaning forward in the chair, arms resting on his legs, hands clasped in an intense, aggressive pose. "Why are you here, Ms. Reynolds?"

She shifted back into the couch, an unconscious move to put more space between them. "Please, call me Cali, and I believe what I want is obvious." She met his gaze and refused to cower. "I answered all of the questions Mr. Mathews asked in my screening interviews. Is there still more?" Please, please don't let them reject her now. Not after she finally had the courage to do this.

"I have a few more," he replied. "What specifically are you looking to get out of The Den?"

"Sex," she boldly stated, proud of her ability to answer without blushing.

"What kind of sex, Cali?" He said her name in a low, taunting way that made her stomach clench and her throat dry. Not to mention the rush of desire that pooled between her thighs.

She crossed her legs, lifted her chin and refused to turn away from his hard, calculating gaze. "The kind that makes me come."

Again, a small quirk of a smile curled over his lips before it flattened once more. Gone as fast as it came. He leaned back in the chair and crossed an ankle over the other knee. His dark hair was long, but not so much as to be classified as unkempt. It brushed across his forehead and curled slightly on the ends. Cali imagined it would be the perfect length for gripping when she came.

That thought had her squirming, just slightly, against the soft leather of the love seat. His eyes, a clear gray that was both pure and sinister when paired with his dark hair and bronzed skin, flickered as he registered her movement. Apparently, nothing got by the man.

"There are all kinds of sex that can make you come, Cali." Again, with the purr of her name. "Can you be more specific? At The Den, we cater to a wide range of lifestyle choices. Where, exactly, do yours lie?"

This time, she had to look away. It had been so long since she'd talked openly about sex, it was incredibly hard for her to trust anyone with her desires.

"Cali, look at me." His voice was low and commanding. He waited until she complied. "There's no wrong answer here. No judgment either. You obviously came to The Den for a reason. It's my job to see that you get what you want. I can't do that if you're not honest with me."

He was right. Of course, he was right. But that didn't make it any easier for her to talk about it.

Inhaling slowly, she stared at her hands and gathered her courage. "Honestly..." she began.

"Look at me," he demanded again, his voice stronger, more insistent.

She immediately responded, her body tingling in a rush of shivers. Why?

"Now, continue. And don't look away again."

Was she doing something wrong already? But she didn't even know what to do. "Yes—" She paused then continued, based on instinct. "Sir. If you want honesty, then I have to say I don't know what I want. I only know what I long for."

"And that is?"

Her heart raced. It was the moment of truth. Time for her to admit her desires out loud and hope he didn't laugh. "For someone to take control. To know intuitively what I want, sexually. To drive me crazy without me needing to direct the person. I want a man who will take me to the edge, make me beg for more until I don't think I can take any more, and then give me more." The loud drum of her heartbeat thundered in her ears.

"Are you a submissive?"

"In my real life, no." She tilted her head and assessed him for a moment, keeping her gaze on his as he'd directed. "Here, I think so."

"Would you like to explore that?"

Would she? "Yes, since giving up control is part of what I just defined." She thought for a moment before quickly adding, "But I don't want porn BDSM."

He raised one dark eyebrow. "Explain."

This time, it was incredibly hard to hold his gaze. That penetrating, mesmerizing gaze. "I researched before I came here. The internet is a wealth of information and I know a lot of it is staged and exaggerated. However, there are things I watched that didn't appeal to me at all."

"Such as?"

She swallowed her embarrassment, her clasped hands clenching. "Degradation of any kind, especially public. Fisting and…being peed on is blatantly disgusting to me. And I'd probably be a horrible slave, as I'd feel more embarrassed than satisfied by being forced to lick someone's boots."

He nodded, his face remaining completely neutral. "Have you ever engaged in any kind of submissive or bondage play? In your marriage or otherwise?"

Her eyes closed. "No," she whispered.

The silence held in the room as she waited for his next question. When none came, she opened her eyes to see him watching her with the same intense patience he'd held before.

Control.

He was slowly, subtly taking control and that realization made her insides melt.

"Why?" he asked.

A very simple question with an impossibly hard answer. At least, for her to admit. It was so much easier to evade. "Does it matter? I thought I answered all of these questions in the checklist."

His eyes narrowed, his lips thinned as if he was annoyed or angered by her answer. "In all the research you did before coming here, tell me, what is *the* most important and essential thing between a Dom and sub?"

She knew this. Had read about it but didn't really understand it. "Trust," she finally answered, her voice just barely reaching an octave over a whisper.

"Then tell me," he said just as softly, only *his* voice held the hard edge of steel. "Does it matter?"

"But you're not my Dom," she hedged again, irritation starting to bubble in her gut. Why was he grilling her?

"True," he conceded. "But if you can't speak honestly with me, someone who's here to help you obtain what you want, then how will you be honest with your Dom? And, more importantly, why would a Dom want to pair with someone who won't answer the simplest of questions?"

She glanced down, his sharp gaze just a bit too insightful for her to handle at the moment.

"Look at me, Cali."

There it was. That calm command that had her inhaling against the flash of burning desire rushing through her system. Her heart hammered once again as she lifted her head and followed his directive.

"Answer the question," Master Jake ordered. "Why haven't you engaged in any kind of submissive play if it's something that interests you? Your application states you were married for twenty-two years. Playful bondage between married couples is very common."

And there was the question. That one she avoided at all cost, but he wanted an answer. Master Jake had cut to the chase and got to the heart of the issue in less than five minutes of conversation. Her face grew warm as she prepared to answer the question.

Honestly.

"Because my husband wasn't interested in sex," she finally admitted. The lingering anger, pain and resentment made her answer come out as a clipped challenge. A dare for him to believe her.

He watched her silently for a moment, her admission wavering between them in limbo between belief and doubt.

"And that hurt you," he stated.

"Yes," was all she could say. So much went into that one

simple answer. Relief, shame, grief and much, much more. Her throat tightened, the ache causing her to swallow against the rise of tears. She'd never admitted any of that to anyone.

To have this man, this stranger, not only believe her, but understand how her husband's indifference had affected her was almost too much to handle when coupled with everything else she was tackling tonight.

Abruptly he stood and extended his hand to her. "Come with me. I'll show you around The Den."

Relief rushed through her in a wave of mixed gratitude. She wasn't being kicked out and he'd stopped before she was pushed over the edge. As if he was already in tune with her. She placed her hand in his and stood on shaky legs.

His hand closed around hers and infused her in warmth, his free hand lifting to tilt her chin until her eyes met his once again. "Trust me, Cali."

Her name. That repeated use of her name in that deep, rolling voice of his was her undoing. Her skin tingled where he touched her, her body flushed with heat at the contact. Right then, she felt like she would do anything he asked. Anything to please him so he didn't leave her. Who was this woman who now possessed her body? Where was her backbone, her strong, controlling nature that ruled every aspect of her life?

It was resting quietly beneath the desire to let someone else lead for a while. He was offering her the freedom to let go and trust that her needs would be taken care of.

On a shaky breath, she answered the only way she could. "Yes, sir."

THREE

The hard beat of alternative music pounded through the room, the vibration carrying up her legs through her spiked heels. The air, however, vibrated with something much more substantial, yet invisible.

Sex. Desire. Lust.

It was everywhere. In the sway and grinding of bodies on the dance floor, the hooded looks and heated touches between couples and the blatant wanting that was etched in so many faces. She'd never been anywhere where sex was so openly displayed and exchanged without actually revealing anything. It made her pulse accelerate and her skin flush.

Master Jake led her effortlessly through the dimly lit main floor, the crowd seeming to part in unspoken respect of his authority. She caught a number of raised eyebrows, a few speculative gazes and even one or two scowls before they were concealed. She focused on keeping her face neutral and her chin up.

There was power in rising above. She'd learned that the hard way.

The dance area was the first room everyone entered and was packed with a variety of people dressed in anything from G-strings and leather to silk and diamonds, including more than a few collars and leashes. The diversity only testified to the wide range of clientele The Den catered to.

Cali did her best not to gawk, but her gaze couldn't stop roaming. There was so much to observe and she knew from the tour during the application process that this was only the first room.

The rooms beyond this one became increasingly more explicit. The big red doors in the back served as the barrier to the voyeur and exhibition rooms just beyond. A fully equipped Dungeon took up half of the second floor, and the third floor was filled with private rooms for members to reserve.

The slight pressure of Master Jake's hand at the small of her back kept her grounded. Next to him, she felt safe. Everything seemed just a little less overwhelming with his tall form protecting her.

Yes, protected. That's exactly how she felt. A sensation so lost she couldn't remember the last time her ex-husband had made her feel that way.

"Would you like a drink?" Master Jake spoke into her ear. The warmth of his breath tickled the small hairs on her neck.

Her mind scrambled for coherent thought. Was that all it took to turn her on? Warm breath on her neck? Was she so sexually starved that even that innocent action made her knees weak and her pussy wet?

She stared into his silver eyes and forgot his question.

"Alcohol is only served in this room if you need it," he reminded her. "Otherwise, we can continue on to the other areas of the club."

"No, thank you," she finally replied. Although a shot of liquid courage was enticing, Cali wanted all of her faculties

coherent for whatever the evening brought. This was definitely a night she didn't want to forget or blame on inebria-
tion. It was a choice, a monumental one that she wasn't going
to hide behind an excuse.

"Shall we continue?"

Continue. Was she ready for this? "Yes."

"This room is exactly what it seems. No open sex or nudity is allowed. Hence, the permission of alcohol." He guided
her toward the red doorway at the back of the room. He nodded at the large man standing at the door before the bouncer
opened it and let them through. "Anyone who's inebriated
is not allowed to enter the other sections of the club. It's for
their safety and ours."

They stood in a long hallway with numerous closed doors
and a stairway at the end leading to the second level. There
was a couple making out at the bottom of the stairs oblivious
to anything around them, their bodies wrapped around each
other, moans trickling down the hall to spike her imagination and her desire.

"Is there any place you'd like to start?" Jake looked at her,
his gaze seeming to catch her every thought.

She swallowed, her dry throat giving her a moment to find
her courage. Finally, she reminded herself that this was why
she was here. She wanted sex. Plain and simple.

Or maybe not so plain and simple.

She smiled at that thought and found her voice. "I think
I'd like to watch for a while."

The back of his hand brushed down her cheek, an approv-
ing smile curling over his lips. "Very good."

She flushed, the heat spreading up her neck and over her
face as the praise of his approval warmed her.

"Do you still trust me?"

Did she? "Yes, sir."

"Then allow me to decide."

And with that, he guided her down the hall to the last door on the right before opening it and escorting her inside.

Jake led the seductive Cali Reynolds to an empty space along the wall near the front. The room was crowded, the few remaining seats were at the back, but he wanted Cali closer to the action. Intuitively, he realized he was testing her. Finding her limits—her unspoken, possibly unrecognized, desires.

He didn't probe into why he was doing so or when his decision to take on the role of Cali's escort had been made—a job he hadn't personally done since the club first opened. But she was too intriguing to turn over to Marcus, or any other Dom for that matter.

No. For some inexplicable reason, he wanted to define and shape her needs himself. It had been entirely too long since such a captivating sub had been offered to him. His protective instincts had flared as a surprising partner to his desire to top her. And with it, a possessiveness he refused to acknowledge. He was a professional Dom. Contracts only. He didn't do possessiveness or ownership.

Yet his gut tightened at the mere thought of keeping Cali to himself. Of her submitting to only *his* commands. There was something within her clawing to be free. And damn if he would let anyone else discover it.

He stood by the wall and tucked Cali in front of him until her spine pressed against his chest. He snaked his arm across her abdomen, keeping her hips tight to his pelvis, his cock snug against her lower back.

She stiffened at the contact.

"Relax," he murmured into her ear. "Just watch the show and don't think. This is about feeling." The light scent of soap, mixed with a hint of musky perfume, invaded his nose and he took another deep inhale of the heady blend.

She gave a slight nod, but her muscles remained tight and tense.

"Trust me," he commanded. "This is about you. I won't violate the trust you've given me. Remember that."

Cali's body relaxed a tad, and she turned her head until her cheek brushed against his. "Yes, sir," she whispered.

His free hand tightened into a hard fist as he straightened and fought to control the urge to yank her from the room and demand she submit to him. But it was too soon for that. She wasn't ready.

He would wait.

Or she would run.

The lights rose on stage to highlight a man and a woman in an intimate embrace. Jake immediate recognized both parties. Paul and his wife, Trisha, had been members for over three years. They were both in their late twenties and enjoyed the aspects of public displays. Their shows were often sensual and erotic without getting extreme. Their reputation accounted for the packed house.

They would be a great introduction for Cali.

Her breath hitched, her attention focused on the couple as Trisha's silk robe slipped from her shoulders to pool at her feet. Her nipples stood out hard and rosy beneath the thin lace of her pink bra. Trisha had a toned, but sensual body with large breasts and curved hips. Tan all over, her auburn hair curled down her back in waves of taunting copper. She was a beautiful woman who fully understood the power her body held over others.

Paul dipped his head and nipped one of Trisha's nipples with his teeth. She moaned and tossed her head back as her husband slowly worshiped the nub before disposing of her bra and taking the naked nipple back into his hungry mouth.

Cali slowly relaxed into Jake. Whether it was intentional or not, he didn't care. He absorbed her weight and stroked his hand across her firm stomach over the silk of her black top.

"How do you feel?" he asked her.

She inhaled, her chest raising a tempting vision of her breasts over the edge of her top before they receded on the exhale. "Fine," she breathed.

Paul had worked his way down his wife's stomach and was removing her matching lace panties, adding slow nips and licks as the material slipped down her legs. A second man entered the stage, walking up behind Trisha, allowing her to lean on his bare chest while Paul finished removing her panties.

Cali gave a low gasp, but her ass swayed imperceptibly against Jake's hardening cock, as if she couldn't prevent the movement from happening. Jake smiled and let his tongue trail a light line of desire over the shell of her ear.

"Would you like that, Cali? To have two men worship you?"

She shivered but didn't pull away.

On stage, Paul hungrily licked and sucked at his wife's shaved pussy. One of her legs was thrown over his shoulder, her upper body supported by the second man, who massaged her breasts and pinched her nipples with large hands. Trisha's moans echoed through the room, blending with the erotic sounds of Paul's actions. Her hands were buried deep in her husband's hair as she held his head tightly against her sex.

Cali's hand came up to grip Jake's forearm, but she didn't stop his slow, sensual movements over her stomach. It was as if she were searching for something to hang on to, to keep her grounded. And she'd reached for him. Good.

"Do you find that hot?" Jake breathed into her ear. He let

his other hand smooth up the side of her leg, watching her reaction, measuring her submission.

"Yes." The barely spoken word escaped between open lips.

She looked so passionate. Her profile revealed hooded eyes and pink lips wet and open. Her breathing was labored, like she was working to keep her growing arousal in check. Her hair curled temptingly in a loose, alluring halo of blond silk that made her features appear as soft and inviting as her hair. So very different from the straight, no-nonsense bob in her profile picture.

The short, tight skirt she wore showed off long legs accentuated by the three-inch heels. Her nipples pointed sharp and tight through the thin material of her top, and his fingers ached to pinch them. To tweak and play with them until she begged for more.

Just like she said she wanted.

Straightening, he pushed her away then guided her to the exit. She snapped her head around to catch the action on the stage. Obviously, she was still enthralled.

"Why'd we leave?" she asked once they were in the hallway. Her eyes sought his.

The outright lust and curiosity pooling in the green depths had him backing her against the wall, his lips hovering just inches from hers. Her eyes widened, her mouth parting in shock, but she didn't fight him.

Fuck. Where the hell was his control?

"This was only one room, Cali," he told her, stepping away, his gaze dropping to the rapid rise and fall of her chest. "There's much, much more to see before the night is over."

"Oh." She cleared her throat and licked her lips, "What do you recommend next?"

She was going to kill him. And she didn't even recognize

the power she had already. She was a heady mix of innocence and desire, timid and strong.

Holding her hand, he led her up the hall to another closed door and yanked it open. They were greeted by the sinful rumble of a long, unmistakable moan.

Cali stalled as they stepped through the door, her hand rising to cover her lips as she viewed the sight of a couple fully engaged in sex on stage.

Jake grinned.

Training Ms. Reynolds was going to be so fucking fun.

FOUR

Cali was on fire. Her blood had turned to molten lava long ago, her bones slowly melting in the current of fiery liquid flowing through her system. She was so aroused, so incredibly turned on that she was almost ready to beg Master Jake to take her.

To throw her down and fuck her right there in front of everyone.

It wasn't like anyone would care.

They had progressed through each of the downstairs rooms, the stage Scenes increasing in decadence, creativity and outright displays of sex until she ached for release. Oral sex, multiple partners, Doms and subs—at some point her mind had disengaged as she'd watched the Scenes until she'd finally let the last of her inhibitions go. She let herself respond to the acts on stage and to Master Jake behind her, touching her, stroking her skin, whispering dirty thoughts and desires in her ear.

A long time ago, in another failed attempt to perk up their nonexistent sex life, she'd talked her husband into going to a stage show when they were on vacation in Amsterdam. The

Red Light District show had been nothing like these. There, the performers were obviously paid actors, or whatever they were called. The show had seemed so mechanical, the actions stiff and routine. It lacked emotion and had left her feeling empty.

The Scenes at The Den were filled with undeniable passion. Master Jake had explained that the rooms were open for members to reserve. It was one of the fetishes they catered to—exhibitionism. And in return, voyeurism. The desire of the performers to be on stage came across in the honesty of emotion simmering over the crowd.

It had been shocking and incredibly erotic to watch what was usually a private, intimate exchange between a couple—or more. To witness the decadence and arousal up close and personal had excited her more than she ever imagined possible.

"How do you feel, Cali?"

The deep timber of Master Jake's voice rippled over her delicately balanced senses, almost pushing her over the edge.

She gasped then slowly released the trapped air. "On fire… sir."

The last bit slipped out unconsciously. Her body—no, her mind—responded to that simple word as if it were an aphrodisiac. So much power held in one syllable.

Sir.

But it wasn't the word alone. It was also him. The man who held her close had slowly, gently taken control of her desire. Made her want not only him, but what he offered her.

"What do you see?"

On command, her gaze drifted over the activity in the large open room on the second floor. The Dungeon. Her desire-fuzzed brain tried to focus. Long forgotten were her insecurities and hesitations of earlier. What did she see?

"Sex." Everywhere. In different forms. At different stages. "Masters and subs. Acts of dominance and submission."

His firm, controlling hands drifted up her sides and across her front, pulling her tight against his hard body. His hard cock. Her head fell back against his shoulder, the muscles in her neck incapable of holding the weight.

"Details, Cali."

Really? How? Her brain could barely form logical thought at this point. She was a mass of over-sensitized nerves and he wanted her to talk. Logically.

What she saw was not porn BDSM. Not even close.

Just like the stages, everything in this room was real. Powerful and honest.

"Cali."

God. Her name had never sounded so erotic. He held her captive by her name alone. The soft, throaty purr was edged with varying levels of desire, command and authority.

"I see lust in every form," she finally managed to say.

Erratic emotion-filled moans, grunts and whimpers filled the air with tension and expectation. The repeated hiss of a whip snaked through the noise in a consistent pattern of demand. In contrast, the deep smack of a paddle echoed off the walls like thunder on the edges of a storm.

She licked her lips and inhaled, getting a dose of the unique blend of sex, leather, sweat and the misplaced hint of lemon that cloaked the space and seemed to cling to the heat of the room. She forced herself to focus. She wanted to answer him. Someplace, deep inside her, she needed to answer him.

"More."

She squirmed in his arms, his erection rubbing across her lower back in an erotic dance of invitation. She couldn't hold still. Was incapable of simply standing there. Details, he'd said. She could do details.

"In the far corner, a woman is strapped, stomach down, to a bench. Naked," she said in an almost clinical way. It was the only way she could get the words out. "Her legs spread. Ankles and wrists bound. Restrained. A man behind her is spanking her with a wooden paddle." Cali stopped to breathe, the air escaping her chest in shallow gulps.

"What does her face say?"

The woman's head was turned toward them, her eyes half opened. Her mouth parted in a silent gasp. The emotions on her face were clear.

"Ecstasy," Cali whispered in amazement as the realization fully registered. Even though she was being paddled, her bottom a bright, startling red, the woman looked beyond content.

"Describe another Scene." The order, though spoken low, was still commanding.

She scanned the room, glossing over a man in a stockade, a woman gagged and bent over a pommel horse, a dildo strapped between her spread legs, before Cali stopped. "A woman cuffed to a cross...a St. Andrew's cross, I think," she mumbled as she desperately dug into her internet-learned lingo. "Blindfolded. Her nipples are clamped and weighted. Her stomach and thighs are striped in pink and red marks. A man is on his knees licking her...pussy."

It felt wicked just saying that word. Especially when they were surrounded by sex and the heat of Master Jake's body pressed into her back. He was touching her, but not *touching* her. God, she ached for him to rub *her* pussy, her breasts.

"And what does her face tell you?" Master Jake murmured into her ear.

Even partially covered by the blindfold, the emotion on the woman's face was clear. "Bliss. Need." *Trust*. For some reason, she couldn't say the last one out loud.

"And the Dom—what do you see on his face?"

Cali forced her gaze away from the alluring face of the sub and focused on the man who was now standing before the tied-up woman. He had rugged features that would normally be classified as interesting, but not traditionally attractive. But right then, his expression held Cali captivated. Her knees weakened, and she was thankful for the strong arm of Master Jake holding her against him.

"I see tightly held control and…reverence," she managed to whisper. That was the most fitting word she could think of. The Dom stared at the sub not in condemnation or scorn, as she'd seen on the bad porn clips. Instead, there was true respect and lust on his face.

"Do you see the difference?" Master Jake traced the under curve of her breasts with one finger, a teasing caress that taunted her with its proximity without actually touching where she craved. "What happens at The Den is honest. It's open and involves deep levels of trust that only heightens the exchange and ultimate release that's achieved."

She did see it. Felt it. And God help her, she wanted it.

His breath caressed her neck, his lips brushing over the sensitive juncture where it met her shoulder. "What do you want?"

Did she have the nerve to say it? Now? When it was openly presented to her? Her head dropped forward, her gaze landing on the scratched surface of the polished wood floor. "I already told you," she answered, her defiance rekindling with her embarrassment.

He nipped her skin, a chastising snip that caused her heart to race. "Do you still trust me?" The hard bite of his voice matched the tightening grip of his hands on her waist.

Why did she? She didn't even know the man. But for some strange reason, with this, she did. More than she'd trusted her ex-husband in many, many years.

"Yes," she finally managed to say.

She felt his chest compress with the slow release of his breath. He held her so close to his front that she could feel his muscles tense, his chest move, his cock twitch. Every movement, no matter how small, was amplified by her over-sensitive nerve endings until she felt like she was a part of him.

He straightened and turned her around. He kept her tucked tight against him, causing the hardened tips of her breasts to rub almost painfully over his chest.

"Look at me, Cali."

Yes. Look at him. Obediently, she lifted her gaze in a slow ascent that was killer on her blood pressure, but she couldn't force her eyes to go faster. From the tantalizing bob of his Adam's apple as he swallowed, over the firm square chin, past the equally firm but inviting lips to finally meet his deep, silver eyes.

"Let's go upstairs."

Upstairs. To the third floor, full of private rooms for individual use. Anticipation mingled with anxiety and sat like a rock in her gut. The moment of decision not so easily made. She was way too old and cautious to go into anything blind. No matter how much she wanted it.

"What will you—" she swallowed, "—we do?"

"Only what you want," he reassured her. His fingers traced an intimate line down the edge of her jaw. "We'll discuss details upstairs. Remember, a Dom/sub interaction is all about negotiation and honesty. No pressure. No expectations. It's you who holds the power. I'll only give what you're willing and able to receive."

He made it seem so simple. Safe.

His fingers tightened on her jaw. "But *I* want to see you beg. I want you aching for a release that only I can give you. I want you tied up and bowing to my desires to get yours." His eyes darkened to a deep gray and were filled with all the passion and need he expressed. His look, his words triggered that deeply buried longing she'd denied for so very long. A tremor raked her body as she fully accepted that she could have this.

A high-pitched wail reverberated through the room and surrounded her with the pure pleasure of the seemingly tortured sound. She wanted that even if she doubted she'd ever find it. Even if the very thought of actually reaching it both enticed and scared her senseless.

And Master Jake was offering it to her.

"Yes." Cali breathed. She licked her lips and nodded, attempting to put some conviction into the movement. She could do this with him. More importantly, she wanted to do this with him. It was now or never. "Let's go upstairs."

His boots thumped low and hollow across the hardwood floor, projecting an ominous feel to the thick tension cloaking the small room. Jake walked a slow circle around Cali, touching her shoulder, stroking her arm, inhaling her scent that had turned deeper, muskier with her arousal. She shivered at his touch, but her body was once again stiff, her nerves seeming to resurface now that they were alone.

Jake had purposely requested one of their less intimidating rooms. This one contained nothing shocking outside of an unobtrusive spanking bench along the far wall. Everything about the space spoke of seduction with a subtle hint of dominance, the primary item being a large bed with black sheets and iron headboard. The cuffs attached to both ends of the bed were tucked away and all the toys and other equipment were hidden behind the closed door of the armoire.

"What do you want, Cali?"

Jake would keep asking her that question until she answered. They would only proceed if she had the courage to

voice her desires. Her hesitation, and almost immediate defensiveness to his direct questions, told him she needed to
overcome the fear—or maybe it was shame—she seemed to
associate with her needs. Otherwise, she would be filled with
self-loathing and recriminations in the morning.

She'd come to the club willingly, asking to be dominated
without fully understanding what that meant. Her courage
called to him, even as her natural submissive tendencies began
to show. The way she melted under his touch, how she automatically followed his commands as she began to trust him.
They were like lures, reeling him into her charms until he
was unable to pull away.

Despite her hesitations and obvious inexperience, the mysterious Ms. Reynolds had him completely enthralled. The odd
mix of courage, tempered with vulnerability, made her far
more enticing than the young twenty-somethings who came
into the club, brazen and cocky in what they thought they
wanted, or even his seasoned clients who knew exactly what
they wanted. She was like an exquisitely wrapped present just
waiting to be stripped of the bows and ribbons to reveal the
hidden prize beneath the tightly held pretense.

She stood before him, illuminated by the light strategically
placed around the edges of the room. Her hands were clasped
tightly in front of her, her chin lifted, shoulders back, but her
eyes refused to meet his despite his instructions.

He grabbed the back of her hair and gave a soft, but firm
tug. Her head jerked and her gaze flew up to meet his.

"Look at me and answer my question. What do you want?"

Her eyes widened, the green depths deepening as her pupils dilated more.

"Answer, or we're done."

After a brief, tense pause, she spoke. "I told you, I don't
honestly know." Her cheeks flushed. "I want a man to make

me come. No vibrators. No toys. I want…" Her gaze darted away from his, but with a tug on her hair it returned. "I want a man's touch. His control. His confidence in owning my body and giving me everything I want. I want sex that is also about me…not just him."

A good start. He could give her that. Easily. But he sensed there was more. "And…" He let the question trail off.

She swallowed, her lips working as she gathered her courage. "I don't know," she admitted, the honesty projected in both her voice and eyes. "My sexual experience is so embarrassingly limited that I don't honestly know what I want outside of what I just told you. I don't know what I like or don't like because anything outside of vanilla sex has never been given to me." She sucked in a breath of air like she was shocked at the admission.

Jake clenched his free hand behind his back, the hidden action his only break in the calm, controlled facade he displayed. The desire to do exactly as she asked was so overwhelming it took everything in him to hold himself still.

"Very good," he reassured her as he released her hair and massaged her tender scalp before moving his hand to her chin. "Your honesty will be rewarded. But first, let's set some boundaries for this Scene."

The tension in her stiffly held shoulders immediately subsided with the slow release of her breath. "Yes," she said, the relief communicated in her eyes.

Idly, his thumb caressed the soft skin on the underside of her chin. His only contact with her at the moment. "Let's start with what excites you," he said gently. "When I ask you about something, answer me honestly. No moderating your responses. Do you understand?"

Her lips compressed, her muscles tightening once again. "Yes."

"Good." He rewarded her by rubbing the pad of his thumb over the lush skin of her bottom lip. Her eyelids drifted down in a sensual half closed flutter. "Does the thought of bondage excite you?"

A pause. "Yes."

"Blindfolds?"

Her eyes closed like she was testing the thought. "Yes."

"Nipple clamps?"

Her eye flew open, followed by a long pause. She licked her lips. "Yes."

"Anal play?" He knew the answers from her application, but she needed to respond. To verbally admit to what she wanted.

"Yes." Her replies were getting softer, barely spoken.

"Spankings, flogging, whips?"

A hesitant, "Yes…I think. Some."

"Threesomes or more?"

A deep inhale held then slowly released. "Maybe."

"Public displays?"

"I…don't know." She chewed her lip, her gaze finally darting away before returning to meet his. "Maybe. But not tonight."

Her breathing was now erratic, her fingers so tightly clenched together that her knuckles were white. Her cheeks were flushed an attractive shade of pink, but her spine was still stiff and straight. The questions were obviously hard for her to answer.

"And dominance. Will you submit to me, Cali? Are you willing to follow my commands, to let me lead you through the Scene?"

"Yes…sir." The quiet, hesitant tone of her voice was negated when she turned her head to force his thumb to rub over her chin. An act he would not tolerate with another sub. But with her, he let the small insubordination pass.

"Thank you," he said, swiping his thumb over her lip once again. "For that, I'll let you choose your reward. What do you want?"

Her tongue slipped out to touch the pad of his thumb, the action at once daring and teasing. Again, he let the act pass, more captivated by her courage than angered by her aggression. He held still and let her play. The barely there stroke tingled over his skin, testing his own tightly held restraint.

She challenged him in a way no one else ever had and he was letting her get away with it. For that reason alone, she screamed of danger. Any other sub would be gagged and bound for such defiance. But with Cali, he couldn't find the will to stop her, let alone punish her.

"Can I kiss you?"

Her soft request tore through him and hardened his dick to an almost unbearable degree. He kept his face neutral, withholding his shock and subsequent desire.

He didn't kiss subs, especially clients.

The very nature of the act was too personal, too intimate. All of his regular clients knew this and would never dare to ask. No good sub would ask for something so personal. He should deny her and define the act as one of his boundaries, like he always did.

But he didn't. Instead, for reasons he couldn't fathom, he found himself giving a short, sharp nod. He was certain his voice would give away too much. Show the sudden longing coursing through him to feel her lips on his, to taste her.

Tilting her chin, Jake dropped his head and brushed his lips over hers. He made it deliberately light, a temptation more than an assault. His restraint was as much for him as her. Her lips were as soft as they looked and, for the first time in years, he wanted more.

She sighed and strained forward, seeking a stronger touch,

more contact. Abruptly he backed off and she followed before she pulled away and peered at him with questioning eyes.

"Are you ready to proceed?" he asked, trying to regain control of the situation. Of himself.

She inhaled and released the air slowly. "I want safe words." She glanced down then returned her gaze to his. "I read about those."

He smiled, an unwarranted sense of pride burning in him. She was new to this, but she wasn't stupid. "Of course. Do you want your own or the traditional red, yellow and green?"

She thought on it for a moment. "Red, yellow and green are fine. Red means stop, yellow slow down, green go. Right?"

"Yes." He dropped his smile and stepped back. "Does that mean you want me to continue?"

She gave a slight nod.

"I need the words, Cali."

She looked down and closed her eyes. This was it. She might run. Right here, right now, after all of the progress they'd made. But she had to come willingly, completely, or not at all.

He waited, the silence extending around them in lengthening waves of tension. Finally she opened her eyes and raised her head until her gaze held his. The green of her eyes had darkened to emerald gems, her lips slightly parted and slick from being licked.

The moment lengthened until she said, "Yes." The scarcely spoken word echoed through the empty quiet. With more conviction, she gave him a half-smile and finished. "I want to proceed."

His tight muscles loosened with the release of her words, but he didn't let her see that. Internally, the relief he felt at her agreement was both foreign and disturbing. Externally, he retained his composure and gave a sharp nod. "Good." He stepped forward and cupped a hand around the nape of her neck. "That deserves a reward."

Before she could respond, he leaned in and kissed her with all the desire and need that had been building in him since she'd stood and extended her hand in introduction. She moaned and opened to him, her tongue meeting his in an instant duel of longing. The hint of mint mixed with the heat of her mouth, drawing him in deeper. His fingers threaded through her hair, the soft strands encouraging him to hold on, to yank her close and savor the moment, but he drew back, leaving them both wanting.

Their breath mingled in shortened pants in the small space between them. He slid his hands down her sides then under her shirt, letting his palms rest against her warm, silky flesh. She flinched at his touch, her stomach muscles contracting sharply before they slowly relaxed.

"Remove your top." Her eyes flashed, and he struggled to keep his voice even. "I want you naked."

Her lip was immediately sucked between her teeth, but she didn't pull away. He took a step back and watched. Would this be where she balked?

With shaky hands, she grabbed her shirt hem and followed his orders, removing the top and letting it drop to the floor.

The Scene had begun.

FIVE

The air whispered over her heated flesh, the cool edges barely registering against Cali's flushed mind. It was all she could do to stay standing. To remain focused on what Master Jake was saying to her.

His touch was both firm and soft as he stroked his hands over her skin. She bit her lip to contain the whimper that threatened at the back of her throat.

"Don't," he commanded, his grip flexing on her sides. "Don't hide what you're feeling from me. I want to hear everything. Every sound, every moan, every desire you feel. Understand?"

She exhaled, a small wheeze escaping with it. "Yes...sir."

He walked behind her, never releasing contact with her body. It was his touch that held her there. In the room. The simple pressure on her chin, the brush of his thumb over her lips, the slide of his palms down her sides—not once had he stopped touching her since the Scene began. It was as if he knew she needed that.

Like he understood her.

After being physically starved for touch for years, he was providing her with the intimacy she craved. The actual act of sex was secondary to the connection he was building. She wanted what he offered, but it was her own personal fear of everything he embodied and represented that made her legs tense, ready to bolt. Her senses were in overdrive, her base survival instincts in a fight or flight mode.

This man, Master Jake, owned his sexuality and desires without shame. He was decadence and freedom rolled into one delicious package.

And he scared the shit out of her.

Not him exactly, but how he made her feel.

Everything about him, from his looks to his actions to the way he touched her, made her knees weak and her mind reel. The whole experience was so much more than she'd expected. More than she'd wished for, and they were still clothed. If she was being honest, it was the intensity of the feelings and desire he stirred within her that she truly feared.

His warm breath fluttered over her bare shoulder as his hands smoothed down her back and deftly unclasped her bra. "You have beautiful skin." His hands came up to push the bra straps down her arms until the garment landed on the floor next to her shirt. Her nipples were already tight with desire, the physical ache for touch bordering on unbearable. "Before the night's done, I will touch every inch of you."

A noise somewhere between a whimper and a moan escaped from her lips. Never in her entire life had she felt this turned on, this overwhelmed, this desired by a man.

By anyone. Period.

His hands moved down her back before his fingers edged under the waist of her skirt. They moved back and forth against her skin in a silent foreshadowing of what was next.

"Remove your skirt, Cali."

She swallowed but complied without hesitation this time. With smooth fingers, he undid the small clasp at the back, eased the zipper down, then helped her push the material over her hips until it pooled at her feet.

"Panties too."

The order sent shivers down her spine, but once again she obeyed. She was helpless to deny anything he asked. He'd taken complete control of her body and was bordering on owning her mind too.

The lacy material fluttered against her skin before it landed at her feet. She released a shaky breath, feeling completely exposed. Naked except for her heels, she was bared both physically and emotionally.

And still he touched her.

Kept her there. Grounded. With him.

In the moment.

Callused, roughened fingers ran over her hips, down the sides of her thighs, back up and over her buttocks. Constant motion that focused her senses and her mind on nothing but him and the hot trail of fire that followed his touch.

"Beautiful," he whispered before he took her hand and guided her toward the bed.

The very large bed that was the obvious focus of the room.

She'd been surprised and relieved when they'd first entered the room to see both the bed and the lack of other domination equipment. Again, Master Jake had known what she needed.

He turned her to face him, the back of her legs bumping against the smooth cotton of the bed sheets. He lifted her chin with one finger until her gaze met his once again. "What are you feeling?"

Talk about an impossible question to answer. Her hands fidgeted at her sides as her mind scrambled to process an answer. "Scared…exposed…" There was more, but did she dare to tell him?

"What else? I want to hear it all."

How did he do that? She swallowed and pushed on. "Flushed, excited…like I'm going to die if you don't touch me soon." The admissions made her heart race; her blood pumped through her over-sensitive body in heated waves of longing.

He smiled, a devious, yet sensual curve of his lips that had her almost begging for everything he had to offer. "Where, exactly, should I touch you?"

Damn him. "Can't you figure that out?" she snapped, irritation forcing her voice to deepen. She didn't want to direct him. She'd told him that. Her desire faded to disappointment. She took a step, ready to leave.

"No." His hands tightened on her shoulders, his body coming flush against hers. His eyes narrowed, cooling in their intensity. "Unless you use your safe word, I won't allow you to run."

"Then stop talking and just do something," she demanded, caution forgotten with her rising frustration.

"Is that what you really want?" he challenged. "To be thrown down, paddled and taken blindly?" His hand landed with a sharp slap against her naked ass, forcing her to stumble into his chest and gasp in surprise. "Or do you want this?" He stepped back an inch, just enough for his hand to snake between their bodies and skim over her sensitive nipple.

She moaned at the touch, the reaction impossible to hide.

"And this," he said, right before his mouth covered hers. His lips were firm and demanding, crushing over hers with authority. His tongue entered her mouth, engaging hers in a desperate battle. He tasted like chocolate and felt like heaven to her starved senses. He owned the kiss and she was helpless but to follow his lead.

Her mind fuzzed, her head spinning with unleashed desire. She reached for him, her hands grasping his bare arms in a failed attempt to stay grounded. A nail scraped over her nipple, teasing the nub with just a hint of pain, and she arched into him, seeking more. Abruptly he pulled back, his hands coming up to frame her face. His breathing was deep and labored, much like her own.

"Tell me I'm wrong." His eyes were filled with challenge as they held hers.

Which one did she want? One was distant, less emotional. The other could break her. But there was really no choice. It was all or nothing, and she wanted it all.

She slid her hands up his arms until her fingers laced in his dark hair. It was soft, thick and felt exactly like she had imagined. She tugged his head down until his lips were just a breath away for hers.

"I want this," she breathed then crushed his mouth to hers in a kiss filled with everything she'd missed in the last ten years. It was the touch, the contact, the mutual desire that she craved.

He'd been right. Again.

He broke the kiss but held her close, captured in his arms and by his gaze. "Stop fighting me, Cali." His low voice stroked over her skin like another touch.

"Yes, sir." Again, the only possible answer.

He stepped back, his hands sliding down her arms until they clasped hers. "Sit down."

She nodded and slowly lowered herself to the edge of the bed, the sting on her bottom reminding her of the choice she'd made. His hooded gaze scanned her before he kneeled and removed her high heels. His touch was gentle, caressing. Each act of tenderness reeling her into his web of trust.

His palms smoothed up her legs, spreading them apart as he

skimmed over her knees and up her thighs. He stared pointedly at her exposed pussy before a half-smile curved his lips. "You waxed." He looked at her, a daring gleam in his eyes as he stroked a finger over the smooth flesh. "For me?"

Her cheeks burned, but he'd asked for the truth. "For tonight, yes."

"Perfect." A simple statement that fired her blood even more. He stood and reached for the bedside table, opening the drawer and removing a black silk scarf. He turned back to her and held the cloth up. "Tonight is about trust. You'll trust me to put this on you."

A blindfold. She shouldn't, she knew that. She'd just met this man. But it didn't matter what she should do. Those thoughts left her long before she'd entered The Den's door. In reality, she shouldn't be doing any of this.

"Yes."

"Good," he murmured before he reached down and pinched one of her tight nipples. The shot of pain and passion fired through her instantly, causing her to gasp then groan. "Turn around."

Nipple throbbing, she slid on the bed until her back was to him. The material covered her eyes, sending her world into darkness. She shivered, not from the cold, but from the sheer vulnerability that descended on her with the lack of sight.

"This deprivation will heighten the rest of your senses," Master Jake said into her ear. "It'll keep you focused on what's important. Not what I'm doing, but how it makes you feel."

His large hands cupped her breasts. Finally. She pressed into the touch, which felt so good. He kneaded the flesh before he caressed her nipples, stoking each peak into an even tighter, harder nub. Another moan rose from her throat as the sensations swamped her.

She did want this. Needed this so very much.

His hands left her breasts and she whimpered in desperation for them to return. "Shhh," he soothed as he guided her to lie on the bed. The sheets were cool and soft under her back. The heat of his body flanked her side and she leaned toward it, seeking what he could provide.

He grabbed her wrists and dragged them over her head. "Should I bind you, or will you hold on?" He wrapped her fingers around a bar, holding her grip against the cold, hard metal of the headboard. He was giving her a choice. Did Doms do that?

Confused, Cali fumbled for an answer. "Hold… I'll hold on."

"Don't let go until I say you can."

Her fingers flexed around the metal. "Okay."

His lips touched against the tender flesh of her inner arm, then down, next to her breast. She jerked toward his touch, but he was gone. Then his hands were there, skimming down her stomach and leg until he gripped her ankle.

"I'm going to bind your legs." He kissed the inside of her ankle before he drew it to the side and wrapped a padded cuff around it. "This will keep you open to me." He quickly did the other, leaving her spread wide. She tested the bindings and found she had some give in the straps that let her move and bend her legs, but not close them.

She had never felt so blatantly exposed in her life. But despite her position and obvious subservient pose, she didn't feel vulnerable.

No. She'd felt more vulnerable fully clothed with her ex-husband, trying to understand why he didn't want her. What did she lack that had made him so resistant to having sex with her—his wife?

"Beautiful," Master Jake said, the low purr of his voice caressing her heightened senses and bringing her back to the moment. "You look absolutely beautiful." His hands moved up her legs. "Open. Waiting." He nipped her inner thigh, his hair brushing against her skin, causing goose bumps to race over her legs. "Responsive," he breathed against her wet pussy.

The sudden flash of warmth made her inhale, her breath sticking in her lungs as she waited and hoped he'd kiss her there. She twisted in frustration when he moved up her body, his lips trailing kisses over her hip and stomach until they reached the valley between her breasts.

She struggled against the sheets, her fingernails biting into her palms as she gripped the bar in a death hold. "Please, Jake," she begged. "Please…" She just needed him.

"Please what?" His breath was hot, his mouth hovering over one of her aching nipples.

She inhaled, and the fresh shampooed aroma of his hair flooded her nostrils. He smelled of rain and man, the scent blending with the heat of the room and the desire of her body.

"Lick me," she managed to say. "Kiss me, touch me." She wasn't picky right then.

Her head snapped back on the mattress when his mouth covered a nipple. God. *Yes.* Finally. His hot mouth sucked and licked at the hard bud before his teeth grazed over and then clamped down. The sharp spike of pain meshed with the pleasure and made her arch into his mouth. Her legs hitched in reflex before he let go and soothed the ache with a slow lap of his tongue.

He shifted and repeated the process with her other nipple. His mouth was the only part of him that touched her, but she felt surrounded by him. His heat was over her, near her, and she wanted to feel all of him.

The sounds of him working her nipple became intimate and erotic as her senses strived to accommodate for her loss of sight. Each touch, every noise was amplified into an over-whelming crescendo of sensation.

"More," she begged now, her voice hoarse. "Please." She felt no shame in begging. Not with him. He would give her what she craved. It was so freeing to be able to ask for what she de-sired and know she'd get it. Because Jake would give it to her.

She trusted that.

In answer to Cali's request, a finger trailed through her pussy. A slow caress from bottom to top that made her pelvis thrust and reach for more. His touch was smooth, skin against skin, a sensation she'd never experienced. She'd been too em-barrassed to wax down there before. But now, the uninhib-ited contact was amazing.

"Yes," she panted. "That, please."

He chuckled, the low rumble vibrating against her breast as he moved his mouth down her body. "Do you want that?" he asked, his finger making another swipe through her pussy. "Or would you prefer this?" The hot, wet tip of his tongue re-peated the same path as his finger and her hips shot off the bed.

"That," she croaked. "God, definitely that." She moaned and shivered in response to the sudden warmth. It had been so long since she'd felt any kind of heat and wetness down there, she almost came from his one simple touch.

And then he was gone.

The bed shifted and he moved off the mattress. She ached for him to return. Her mind faltered at his sudden absence.

"What…where'd you go?" She strained to hear his move-ments, turning her head in an attempt to catch a sound. Any sound. Her grip on the headboard loosened and all the doubt and mistrust started to descend on her.

The light trace of something soft tickled down her chest and around her bellybutton. She jerked away, clenching the bar. He was still there.

"Trust me, Cali." His voice was deep and tender, so intimate in the darkness that surrounded her.

The object returned. The scent of leather invaded her nose, teasing her with the image of a flogger as the individual strands flirted over her nipples then up the length of her leg, only to disappear. *No.* A light touch against the sole of her foot, the inside of her knee, down her side. *God.* The tantalizing, teasing strokes where everywhere, but nowhere she really needed them.

Then the strips landed in a hard, sharp slap across her stomach. She jumped at the unexpected action, surprised at the sting of pain and even more shocked as the heat radiated downward to warm her pussy. Her hands loosened on the rail, but his grip was immediately there, clamping over hers.

"Don't let go." The hard edge in his voice made her hands clench on the bar before he backed away.

Her entire body was tense with expectation. What would he do next? Her breath was labored, her lip clasped between her teeth as her muscles tightened once again in wait. There was a small clicking noise, followed by the hushed rustle of material and the thread of a zipper. Was he undressing?

"Jake?" she tentatively spoke into the silence.

The whisper of softness against the heated flesh of her pussy had her panting and clinging to the edge of an orgasm. She was so ready to tumble over, every nerve ending just waiting for one more touch.

"Not yet, Cali," Jake ordered, his warm breath caressing her ear. How'd he get there? "Not 'til I say so."

Really? A groan escaped from deep in her throat. A sound of protest and desire mixed with desperation. Then he kissed her, hot, searing lips against hers. The surprise of the attack as potent as the kiss itself. His tongue warmed her mouth and rolled with hers in a passionate demand.

She strained for him, her hands slipping off the bar. Immediately his lips were gone, his hand gripped tightly around hers. "I told you not to let go." He guided her fingers back around the bar. "Hold on or I'll bind you. Can I trust you?"

Trust. There it was again. "I'll hold on," she said and added a small, "Sorry, sir." And she was. She didn't want to lose his trust. It was suddenly as important to her as the acts they were doing together.

His touch was gone again, leaving her empty and aching once more. Her lips tingled from his kiss while every other part of her body throbbed for his touch. The mattress pitched as his weight returned. She was so tuned in to him that she swore she felt his heat, knew he was there, crouched between her legs.

She heard the slow, deep pants of his breath that he seemed to be struggling to control and hide. She bit her tongue to keep quiet. To wait for him as he told her to do. The anticipation increased her desire.

Several long seconds later, she was rewarded. He closed his mouth over her aching pussy in another sudden attack that constricted every muscle in her body. She cried out. She heard the sound echo in the room without realizing she'd let it go. The response was automatic, one she couldn't have withheld if she'd tried.

But she didn't want to.

She wanted Jake to hear it all. Just like he'd ordered.

This time he didn't leave. His tongue heated her smooth flesh then flicked against her waiting clit. She jerked as he repeated the touch and inserted a finger into her. The combination almost unglued her.

"Please, Jake," she begged. "I'm going to come."

"Not yet," he demanded, his voice carrying a tone of reprimand. "Wait 'til I say."

Another finger entered her wet channel. She whimpered while thrusting her hips into the intrusion and the hot warmth of his mouth. A sharp inhale caught the tangy sent of her arousal, of what he was doing to her. She needed more but at the same time was almost afraid of the aching flood of yearning building within her. His tongue circled her entrance, taunting her with the possibility without fulfilling the promise. With his expert touch and knowing way, Jake held her at that point, the very edge of what she could endure while he fondled and licked her repeatedly.

His lips closed around her clit and this time he sucked. Hard. Pulling on the sensitive flesh until she cried out against the blend of pain and pleasure on the overstimulated bud. Her skin was hot and damp, her body flushed, her mind incoherent.

All she knew was his mouth, his fingers, his touch on her. Him.

His teeth scraped over her aching clit and she clung to the edge with a flimsy hold. His fingers withdrew from her, leaving her feeling empty. For one brief second he pulled away completely, depriving her of all touch.

"No," she cried, arching toward him.

Another second, filled only by her raspy breath.

Finally, a harsh, "Come, Cali," ground against her mind as his fingers thrust into her and his mouth clamped over her clit. And she flew, obeying the command without hesitation, crashing through the climax on wave after wave of pure sensation.

Her mind shattered with her body, her muscles tensing and clenching as she gasped for breath and reached for still more until she thought she would die from the continued wave of heat and bliss that exploded within her. Slowly she descended, shivering as he moved away. She was at once relieved and lost when his touch receded.

Her fingers were still fastened to the bar, tight and cramping from the frantic hold. Her lungs heaved for air, the sound loud and harsh in the quiet room. The quick, unmistakable ripping of foil shot through her, immediately bringing her body back to life and putting her mind on alert. Her head jerked in the direction of the noise, her lips parting in a silent plea for what it meant.

"Yes, Cali," Jake confirmed. "I'm going to fuck you."

Her body fired once again at his words. "Yes," she panted. "Please. Fuck me, Jake."

Who was this person begging for sex? Wanting more of everything he'd given her? She wasn't certain, but right then—in that moment—she loved her.

SIX

She was unbelievable.

Cali was real. Honest. Truly magnificent in her response to everything he'd done to her. There was no act or pretense behind her emotions. What she showed was one hundred percent real. Not what she thought he wanted to see, but what she was truly feeling. He was certain of that.

She trusted him enough to give him everything.

And it turned him on until his dick throbbed with the need for release. *Damn.* He couldn't remember the last time he'd been so hard. The last time he'd ached to fuck a sub. There were only a few of his long-term clients he did that with. He definitely didn't with a new sub. One who wasn't even a contracted client.

Control. He was supposed to be in control, but he felt anything but that. The blindfold had been as much for him as her. He didn't want her to see how she was affecting him. Didn't think he could keep his emotions from showing.

He stared at her now, bound, spread and trembling. *Fucking beautiful.*

She was sleek and toned but with enough curves to be real. Her breasts were high, firm and proportioned, with stiff, rosy nipples that were as sensitive as the rest of her and begged to be sucked and plucked. She was rounded where she was supposed to be, which Jake liked so much better than the gaunt and starved look so many women in the club strived to maintain. A woman was meant to be soft. Inviting.

Tempting.

Jake moved onto the mattress, his sheathed cock straining for her warmth. She jerked, a gasp escaping her parted lips, making him bite his own lip to stay silent.

Deprivation was part of his dominance over her. It was what Cali needed that night to make every sensation that much more intense and powerful. After keeping her grounded with his touch, he removed it until she begged to have it back. He was certain she'd been expecting something different. More blatant and hard-core. Which was why he'd gone the other way.

Watching her submit to this more subtle approach to dominance was even sweeter. Making her want him, what he alone could give her, was the ultimate turn-on. Any Dom could whip her, order her to submit. But not every Dom would take the time to earn her submission and she was too inexperienced to understand the difference.

Jake only wanted what she'd give him. What he earned. He'd push her, eventually. But first, he needed her trust.

He ran his hands up her legs and felt her muscles contract under his touch. He swallowed a groan as he braced himself over her, careful to avoid touching her. Her skin gleamed in a fine sheen of sweat that matched his own. He dipped his head to let his lips brush against hers then leaned back.

"God, Jake," she pleaded as her head lifted to follow him, her lips seeking his. "Please. Touch me."

He inhaled in satisfaction before slowly lowering his body,

using every muscle he had to control his descent onto her. First his legs, then his pelvis and finally his torso until he touched her skin to skin, head to toe. It felt amazing.

Cali felt amazing.

She sighed into his weight, which he kept balanced on his forearms to keep from crushing her. He kissed her shoulder and she stretched her neck to give him more room. She tasted like salt and sin.

Just like her pussy had. A taste that still sat on his tongue, teasing him with the lingering flavors.

"I want to touch you," she said softly, her grip loosening on the bar.

"No," he barked and watched her fingers tighten once again. "Trust me."

His dick was hard and aching where it rested between the juncture of her thighs. Directly against her hot, wet pussy. So close to what they both wanted, but not quite there. It was a tease, another touch that tested his control while depriving her. He moved his hips and let his erection slide up and down against her wetness. She moaned, her hips arching in an attempt to increase the touch.

He stopped. "No, Cali."

She stilled, her chest heaving under his.

"Trust me."

She licked her lips and nodded.

Damn, she was incredible. She had all the instincts and desires to be an incredible sub.

It was tempting, very tempting, to want so much more with her.

He clenched his teeth and reminded himself that this was just a Scene. One night. That was all. He had no claim to her. But for the first time ever, that thought angered him.

He nipped her shoulder, his teeth nibbling a trail up her

neck to her ear. "Trust me to fuck you better than you've ever been fucked. To give you everything you've ever wanted out of sex. And then more." His low murmur of words sent off a shiver that he felt go through her entire body. She was so ready for him.

"Yes," she panted, turning her head to kiss his jaw. Her lips were soft, butterfly light against his rough skin. "Just do it soon."

He swallowed a chuckle. A perfect sub, she was not. But then, he'd had plenty of 'perfect subs' and they all paled in comparison to Cali. A sharp thrust of his hips brought the whimper he sought from her. But it also cost him another thread of his control. He had to have her soon.

He inhaled and let her musky scent infuse him. He licked the shell of her ear before moving to her lips. Her tongue met his stroke for stroke, her passionate response raising his own until he almost forgot it was a Scene.

Forgot where he was.

He positioned his hips, kept her tongue entangled and her mind distracted until he was poised and ready at her entrance. He yanked his mouth from hers and looked at her. Her lips were red, swollen and parted—waiting. Her chest heaved with deep, heavy breaths, her hands clenched tightly to the bar over her head.

The sight nearly sucked the breath out of him.

At that moment he wanted to see her eyes. To fully see her expression as he entered her.

Fuck.

Not giving himself time to think or give in to the foreign feeling, he arched his back and thrust his hips, impaling his rock-hard cock into her waiting flesh.

The groans echoing in the room was equal parts his and hers. She felt even better than he had imagined. Her hot warmth encased him and he gritted his teeth to hold still, to let her absorb the feeling.

To make her beg for more.

Sweat beaded on his neck and trailed in rivers down his back from the struggle to withhold the instinct to move. She squirmed under him, hips flexing against his.

Then finally, he got what he wanted.

"Jake, please," Cali gasped. "Fuck me."

Would he ever.

He felt like heaven. *Damn*. It was amazing to have a dick in her once again. Actual warm, heated flesh. Not a toy. Not a battery-operated anything.

But a man.

Yes. She rejoiced at that sensation alone. He was big, and she felt so incredibly, wonderfully full. Mentally, she almost came when he entered her. The realization that her seven-year dry spell was over was enough to make her convulse in release. But she didn't want it to end so soon.

No. She wanted this to last for as long as possible. He had no idea how truly important the night was for her. Monumental in so many ways, it felt like the very foundation of her life was being ripped open and redrawn.

"Move, Jake," she begged. "God, please, please move."

Her body was crawling with the need for more. That empty, undefined sensation that there was something much bigger and better just out of reach and she wanted it. Now.

"Patience, Cali," Jake gritted out. With a control that bordered on maddening, Jake slowly drew his cock out then pushed it back in.

Her muscles rippled around his hardened flesh, sending waves of tingling awareness through her entire body.

"More." She wiggled under him, trying to feel more, get him to move more.

He stopped. *Damn it.* "Who's in control here?"

He was, of course. She was ready to curse at him, the expletive poised on the tip of her tongue and prepared to exit. But she bit it back, retaining *her* control.

He pulled out, exiting her body. *No.*

"Fuck you," she panted, unable to stop herself now. "You're in control. Complete control, so just fuck me." She wouldn't cry, she swore to herself as she squeezed her eyes closed. The blindfold was suddenly a huge blessing. He didn't need to see how his actions affected her.

She would not be that vulnerable again for anyone.

"Easy, Cali," he breathed into her ear. "I'll give you what you want."

Her heart raced, her emotions a riot of mixed information vacillating between what her mind said and her body felt.

"Focus. Stop thinking and feel." His mouth closed around a nipple, giving it a hard bite then teasing it until she cried out in a mix of pleasure and pain. "Have I let you down yet?"

"No," she consented.

Immediately his cock reentered her, driving all the way in with one hard plunge.

"Yes," she cried out, aching for movement. But she stayed quiet when she longed to beg. Held in her frustration and felt her desire rise, the contained words just one more thing bursting to break free. The combination did exactly as Jake had said.

It made her want it all. Made her feel ready to explode.

He scooped his arms under her, cupping around her back and lifting her torso against his. Her arms and legs ached to encircle him. To hold him tight and not let him go. He fastened his mouth on the sensitive juncture between her neck and shoulder and finally—finally—he moved. A slow, steady pace of thrusts that made her body sing.

Her head dropped back and she reveled in the pleasure. A moan grew from the depths of her chest and was released on a long, low exhale. His mouth found her nipple once again, the hot, wet moisture and following bite firing straight to her pussy.

"Jake," she cried. His name was the only coherent thought she could make. Everything else was focused on how she felt. Exactly as he'd wanted. The rustling of the sheets as they moved, the low rasp that came from Jake with each drive, the hot, slick wetness of their bodies as they rubbed together. Every sound, every touch added to the swirling feeling of combustion igniting within her.

A deep, guttural grunt echoed in her ear as Jake increased the pace, his rhythm becoming harder, more urgent. "Cali," he groaned. The hint of desperation in the single word eased into her like a small river of hope.

The deep, musky smell of sex and sweat and Jake surrounded her—them. She was so close, her body tingled everywhere, even her toes. She could feel the build, the rising crest like a wave slowly climbing to a height and holding right before it broke and crashed upon the rocks below.

And again, as if he could read her mind, he read her body. Suddenly his hand was there, in between them, his finger rubbing over her aching and swollen clit, pressing hard with the thrust of his cock.

"Come for me, Cali."

Instantly she flew. Her mind completely blanked behind the darkness as every nerve and cell in her body spasmed and convulsed into another mind-shattering orgasm.

Vaguely she recognized that sound was coming from her mouth, but it was a mix of incoherent words, whimpers and probably curses. Then she felt him tense, along with a series of quick hard drives that ended in a deep, guttural moan of his own.

Cali was lost in the moment.

She writhed against him, sweat making them sleek and smooth where they rubbed each other. The muscles on his back bunched and strained through his release, the ripple of movement running against her palms in an erratic rhythm.

Slowly her muscles relaxed, her mind returning to conscious thought as she struggled to once again catch her breath. Their heavy pants mingled in the air, and then the blindfold was gone. She blinked, letting her eyes adjust to the dim light and come into focus.

What she saw stole the breath she was desperately trying to regain.

Jake was watching her with an intensity that crossed into intimate. The chiseled angles of his face were relaxed. His eyes searched hers, looking for something she was incapable of comprehending. Sweat soaked the ends of his hair and one lone bead of moisture ran a lazy trail down the side of his face.

"You let go," he stated quietly, but a lazy curl of his lips softened the curt statement.

It was only then she realized her arms circled his shoulders. His skin was hot and smooth under her hands.

"Sorry," she whispered, the moment too intimate to break with noise.

He gave a low chuckle. "A perfect sub, you're not."

She shrugged, unable to define if his comment was a reprimand or a praise. "I've never been one before. I have no idea what a perfect sub is," she told him honestly. "But I liked everything you did." She licked her lips, her hands running lazy circles over his back. "Thank you."

His gaze held hers, his mouth thinning briefly before he

shifted, pulled out and rolled away, deftly removing the condom and disposing of it. She shivered, a reflex to the sudden absence of his heat. He stood and efficiently moved to undo the cuffs and release her ankles, tenderly stroking and rubbing her feet and legs to restart the circulation.

The second she was free, Cali curled to her side and tried to process all she was feeling. All that had happened. She blinked hard, forcing back the sudden threat of tears. Where were they coming from?

His chest pressed against her back before his arm circled her, tugging her against him. He tucked his arm under her head then forced her to relax against it until she was completely encompassed within his warmth. She felt almost cocooned in safety.

Which only pushed the tears closer to the surface.

"It's okay," he murmured against her ear, his leg lifting to drape over hers. "The crash is normal. You've experienced a lot. Don't be ashamed of the tears. Of what you feel. I've got you."

Yeah, he did. And that scared her even more than every act she'd committed since entering The Den. She wanted nothing more than to lay there protected in his arms. To fall asleep and wake up with him still surrounding her.

But this was a Scene.

That was it.

A short time of mutual interaction. Nothing more.

"I have to go," Cali mumbled as she pushed against his hold, struggling to sit. To get away.

He let her go and pushed up on an elbow to watch as she scrambled around the room for her clothing.

"There's a bathroom over there," he said, pointing to a door.

She gratefully took his offered escape and rushed to the safety of the small room. The second the door closed, she collapsed against it and dropped to the floor, burying her head in her hands. Oh God, what had she been thinking? She wasn't built for this. Nothing in her background had prepared her for how she would feel after. She'd been so focused on the event, she'd never stopped to think of the aftermath.

It wasn't shame she was feeling. No. She'd done nothing to feel shameful about. In fact, the entire Scene had been more intimate and normal than she'd anticipated.

What she felt was longing. For everything she couldn't have with that man in the room behind her. Jake.

After so many years of being physically starved for that emotional connection with a man, her body and mind were screaming to stay there with him. To let him touch her. Protect her.

She had to get out of there before she lost it completely.

Pushing to her feet, she quickly redressed. A passing glance in the mirror over the sink made her cringe and halt. Her hair was a mess, her face flushed, her lips red and swollen, her eyes dark and hungry. She looked like she'd been thoroughly fucked.

And she had.

Crap. Doing what she could with her fingers, she tamed her hair down and then dampened a washcloth to press over her heated cheeks and neck. Calling it good, she braced herself to reenter the room.

To face Jake.

She'd act cool. Normal.

As if the entire evening hadn't rocked her world and left her floundering at the bottom of an emotional hole she had no idea how to get out of.

Jake got dressed, his clothes feeling itchy and uncomfortable as he waited. It took every ounce of willpower to keep still.

He didn't pace over a sub—a woman he'd met only hours ago. He was always concerned that they were fine after a Scene, that they'd gotten what they desired, but he definitely didn't worry about them.

Worrying meant attachment.

Cali had come to the club seeking a Dom, searching for an experience, and he'd given her that. Simple as that.

Fuck. It wasn't that simple, and he knew it.

Everything about her was different. Something he'd sensed when he'd met her. Even Seth had picked up on it.

Shit. Seth.

Realization smacked him hard between the eyes. Jake had been set up by his business partner. It all made sense now.

Anger rode front and center on his emotions. That asshole. Seth had been way too cagy, dodging Jake's questions and practically pushing the second interview with Cali on Jake. That bastard had done it on purpose.

If Seth was hoping Jake would form an attachment with a sub and stay, it wasn't going to work.

The low click of the door opening brought his attention back to her. Cali. He hardened his resolve and refused to play into the vulnerable look she was struggling rather poorly to cover. She lifted her chin and gave him a quick nod.

"Thank you," she said, her voice level and strong. "I'll be going now."

She moved toward the door but he stepped in front of her, stopping her quick exit. Damn, what was he doing?

"Are you okay?" he found himself asking. He was only finishing the Scene, he tried to tell himself. Making sure she left safe, sound and unhurt.

"I'm fine," she reassured him, her attention focused on the floor.

Every inflection of her body told him she wasn't. But that

wasn't his problem. Physically, she was unharmed. And she was refusing his comfort. His job as a Dom was done.

But his honor as a man wasn't.

He tilted her chin up in a now familiar move until her gaze met his. "Cali, I know you're not telling me the truth."

She stiffened, eyes going wide before she recovered and thinned her lips against whatever she'd been about to say.

"I can't force you to talk to me," he said, his tone crisp but gentle. "But don't leave here feeling bad or ashamed of anything that took place. Everything that happened between us was open and consensual. No shame."

She nibbled her lip and slowly nodded. It was almost like she was afraid to speak. Afraid to let out whatever she was keeping so tight inside.

And that was her choice. Whether he liked it or not.

"Thank you for giving me your trust tonight. I hope you got what you came for." Jake stepped back and forced himself to open the door. "I'll see you out."

"That's okay," she rushed to say. "I can find the way." Cali hurried by him, brisk strides that bordered on a run, but she was too controlled to do so. She was halfway down the hall before she stopped and turned back. Her eyes were dark, her face displaying the vulnerability she struggled to hide. "Thank you, Jake," she said so quietly he almost didn't hear her. "The night was beautiful. Everything I wanted." Then she turned and disappeared down the stairs.

Out of his life.

Every instinct told him she wouldn't be back. She'd had her night and now she was gone.

Fuck. Why did that make him feel so empty?

And why the hell did he care what she did?

Damn it. He hated feeling like this. Doubt and uncertainty were not his game. He'd trashed those emotions long ago, learning the hard way that anything that left you feeling helpless and vulnerable also left you exposed.

He quickly picked apart the evening, dissecting each step, every interaction until he came to one resounding conclusion.

Seth was a dead man.

SEVEN

Cali stumbled up the stairs in her condo. Just a few more feet. Another step. That was all. She crossed the hallway, staggered into her bedroom and finally let her knees buckle. Collapsing onto the edge of her bed, her body sagged as all the strength and focus that had taken her from the club and allowed her to drive home dissipated.

She stared numbly at the beige carpet, not really seeing it. Her hand shook as she raised it to brush her hair behind her ear and let go of an equally quavering breath. Fisting her tangled curls, she tightened the hold until the tug of pain on her scalp forced her to double over in a silent shudder of emotion.

She'd done it. She'd gone to a sex club and had erotic sex with a stranger. Sex that had been more intimate and personal than she ever had with her ex-husband.

Peter. Just the thought of him made her groan. She didn't want to think about him. Not now.

Not when she felt so good after being with Jake.

Cali rocked where she sat, moving in the soothing motion as the tension invaded her muscles. She couldn't lie to herself;

she'd loved every moment with Jake. Wanted more of what he gave her, of how he'd made her feel.

Her nipples tingled just thinking of his deep voice as he'd commanded her to trust him. To submit to his desires. Giving over control to him had been so easy. Almost too easy.

With Peter, asking for anything sexually had only led to guilt because she knew she wouldn't get it. It had always resulted in disappointment and frustration for both of them. Ultimately, he made her feel ashamed of her desires.

Not with Jake.

She could see herself becoming addicted to what he'd given her. To the feelings he'd stirred. But mostly, to the warm cloak of protection that had wrapped around her and calmed her inner angst when she'd let go and trusted him. And he hadn't let her down. No, he'd exceed all of her expectations.

Cali let the strangled groan escape her tight throat and squeezed her eyes closed. Now that she'd had a taste of what submission under the hands of an experienced Dom like Jake could be like, she wanted more. The reality was better than any of her deepest, dirtiest dreams.

Fantasies she never shared with Peter. The man she should have been able to share everything with. It was easy now to look back at her marriage and see all of the errors they'd both made. She was just as much to blame for the distance that had grown between them over the years. He might have have pushed her away, shunned her sexually, but she was the one who'd stopped fighting for the passion. Complacency on both of their parts had led to their eventual divorce.

A divorce she'd accepted as inevitable years before she'd finally asked for it.

Years she could have insisted on marriage counseling, or tried harder to breach the growing gap that had settled between them. It was when she'd stopped trying, though, that all intimacy between her and Peter had died. The simple fact that he hadn't care enough to instigate it had been the final blow.

It'd been a one-way street that she'd gotten tired of traveling.

And now, she was on a new road. One she didn't think she had the courage to continue down.

Cali swore into the silence, the sudden noise bouncing off the walls to smack at her. She released the grip on her hair and slowly straightened, swiping at the tears lingering on her cheeks. She inspected her rumpled outfit, the sexy one she'd bought specifically for that night.

It was doubtful she'd ever wear it again.

The sex had been amazing. But Jake was right; it was the connection she craved. The control he exerted over her would feel empty without the bond that went with it. One he'd cultivated so subtly that she'd been snared before she realized the trap had been set.

He'd made her feel special, safe, for the first time in years. But she couldn't romanticize it. She was just another sub to him, nothing different. And it was doubtful that he'd want to pair with her again. Not someone as old and inexperienced as her. Hell, he owned the club. He could have any sub he wanted, whenever he wanted.

A spark of jealousy tightened her gut with surprising force. She puffed out a small laugh. Obviously she wasn't a random-sex kind of girl. And after experiencing submission with Jake, she couldn't see herself with any other Dom. She certainly couldn't go back to his club and let her desire override her pride. She was way too old to live in a world of illusions and dreams, and lusting after an unattainable Dom wasn't on her list of humiliating behaviors to model.

Yet she couldn't help but wonder where Jake would take her if they paired again. Would he push her more? Strap her to a bench and spank her? Or would he use something else on her, like a crop or even a whip? Take away all her control…

Cursing again, Cali jerked to stand and forced her legs to move toward the bathroom. What she needed was an icy cold shower to wash away the night and the emotions it'd stirred up. She'd tried. She'd gone after a dream, had been daring for once in her life. She could check it off and call it good.

Now, if she could only wash away the memories of Master Jake, maybe she could move on and put the night behind her. Forget her kinky desires and go back to life as usual.

If that were even possible.

The door crashed against the wall, the sound pounding through the room, causing the man behind the desk to flinch then duck his head when he saw Jake. The fucker practically admitted his guilt with that move.

"Something wrong?" Seth tried to act cool, leaning back in the chair.

"Cut the shit, Mathews." Jake slammed the door closed behind him and stalked over to brace his hands on the desk. "You set me up."

Seth cocked a brow and frowned. "Don't know what you mean. Set you up how?"

"With Cali," Jake bit out. He pushed from the desk and spun to pace the interior of the small office. His frustration hadn't cooled in the hours since Cali left and the club finally closed. Instead, it had brewed and festered until he was now ready and itching for a fight.

One with fists would be nice.

"Cali?" Seth questioned. He leaned forward to rest his elbows on the desk in an awful attempt to look confused. As if the man didn't know exactly who Jake was talking about.

"Don't fuck with me. I'm not in the mood."

Seth leaned back and raised his hands in a gesture of truce. "Not fucking with you, man. What's your deal?"

Jake exhaled sharply and closed his eyes, giving a silent count to ten, the practiced attempt at forced calm having zero effect. He fisted his hands on his hips to keep from striking his long-time friend and business partner.

Soon-to-be ex-business partner, that is.

"Where's Dek?" If Jake was dropping his news, he wanted to do it once, with both men in attendance.

Seth cocked his head, eyebrows furrowing as he tried to follow the change in topic. "He went home. You know it's his night to head out early." Seth pushed the chair back, the wheels giving a protesting squeak before he stood and came around to lean against the desk. He crossed his arms over his chest and nailed Jake with a hard glare. "What's wrong?"

"You fucking in my business, for one," Jake growled.

"How? What did I do to 'fuck' in your business?"

"Don't play stupid. You practically shoved Cali at me."

The confused look on Seth's face hinted at honesty. "The newbie cougar I asked you to interview tonight? Her?"

Jake gave a nod, a tint of clarity starting to penetrate the edge of his red haze of anger to show just how irrational he was acting.

"What the hell?" Seth gave an angry shake of his head. "Second interviews are standard on First Friday if any one of us requests it. Club policy. Nothing more to it."

Was Jake overreacting? Damn, it had all seemed so clear earlier. "Then what was wrong with her application that warranted a second interview?"

Seth shrugged. "I didn't say there was a problem with the application. If there was, it would have been rejected. I only asked for another opinion on placement. I told you that. Despite her age and divorced status, she didn't come across as a real cougar." He ran a hand through his hair. "So, did Marcus fit for her?"

"No," Jake said too quickly. *Shit.* What was wrong with him?

Seth grinned but wisely kept his mouth shut.

Jake turned his back to his friend and moved to lean against the far wall. "I escorted her myself. Marcus is a fine Dom, but Cali needed something different."

"Something you could provide her?"

Jake ignored the hint of doubt—or was it mocking?—in Seth's voice. "Fuck you. I did my job. Something you should try doing."

"Right," Seth scoffed, his hands bracing against the desk. "I'm not the one looking to bail on the business in three months."

And there it was. The real elephant in the room. The one all three partners had been dancing around in anticipation of the looming December date.

He turned, his attention darting to the wall of security screens currently displaying the cleaning crew as they scrubbed and sterilized the place, preparing it for the next day's business. He noted that a few of the third-floor rooms were still occupied, reserved by members for use until morning.

Jake finally met Seth's sharp scrutiny. There was anger in the deep brown eyes. But he also detected the hidden hurt. That bit of betrayal Jake always saw whenever he took off. It didn't matter if he gave fair warning of his departures, because someone was always hurt when he followed his gut and moved on.

His anger faded behind the guilt he'd been trying to avoid. "It's not like you didn't know I'd leave," Jake said as he tried to push off some of the responsibility. "There was a reason you made me sign the five-year contract."

Seth's lips thinned, the tight line doing nothing to detract from the sharp angles that attracted so many to him. After a tense minute he sighed, his shoulders sagging with the release of the tension. "Shit. I'd hoped I was wrong."

"So I just confirmed it for you," Jake stated. No sense in leaving the possibility open now that it was out.

Seth nodded, a simple signal of acceptance. "You have to tell Dek yourself," he said after a pause, then smiled. "I'm not stepping in that shit."

Right. Dek. Jake had to smile as well. Of the three men, Dek was the most volatile. Part of the reason the man headed up more of the behind-the-scenes portions of the club. Dek was a security guru and had personally installed every camera, lock and alarm in the building. He also saw to the security staff, recruiting bouncers from his extensive and sometimes scary list of acquaintances from his years in military special ops.

"Yeah," Jake finally agreed with a snort. "Can't talk you into being there?"

"Hell, no. Your shit, your wading."

Too true. But it didn't make the prospect of doing it any more enticing. "I'll take care of it this weekend." Might as well get it over with so they could all deal with the changes that would need to be made. "This doesn't mean I'm dropping everything, Seth."

The other man gave a non-committal shrug and moved to sit behind the desk once again. "But you'll be gone. Like it or not, that means changes for all of us. And for the club too."

Damn, Jake wouldn't let the guilt sway him. He would only damage things more if he stayed. "Sorry."

The curt apology wasn't enough. It was never enough, but it was all he had to offer.

"Look, I need to finish the books before I head up tonight,"

Seth said dismissively as he turned toward the computer screen and clicked the mouse. "We can finish this discussion after you've talked with Deklan."

Jake bit his tongue and nodded. There was nothing left to say. He left the room, the soft tapping of keys following him into the hall before the door closed and cut off both the sound and the man.

It held a finality that he wasn't quite ready for. There were still three months before he could leave. Three months to make the other men understand.

Shit. Jake thumped his fist against the wall. Not only had Seth forced him to play his hand before he was ready, the other man had completely avoided answering Jake's questions about Cali.

Double fuck. When had he ever let Seth beat him in a verbal sparring match?

Never—that's when. Jake was truly off his game to let that happen. And who was to blame for that?

The image of one Cali Reynolds leaped unwanted into his mind. Her body spread naked and waiting on a sheet of black that made her skin look like caramel and cream. His dick hardened instantly.

Damn. It was definitely time to get the hell out there.

He was becoming too comfortable. Too settled. Wanting and wishing for so much more than he could have. It was time to go before the shit landed. It was better to control his own destiny than let it hit him from behind.

He rubbed his hands over his tired eyes, trying once again to focus his mind and temper his thoughts. With a sigh, he moved down the hall toward the back storage area. He opened the door and flicked on the light. The room was littered with broken equipment, the standard cleaning supplies and other random stuff that got shoved into the room. But the area along

the back was his workspace. Nobody put anything there without his permission.

He walked past the junk and let the wood and grease smells
of the workshop calm him as he went through the process of
getting his tools and turning on the bright work lights. He
was currently in the middle of two projects: a modification to
a pommel horse he was still tinkering with, and a more complicated revolving cross that would allow the sub to be bound
and then positioned at various angles by the Dom.

The simplicity of working with the wood and metal soothed
him in a way few other things did. He was in charge of the
equipment at The Den. He loved the challenge of taking standard stuff and making it better, tweaking it until it suited the
needs of both Dom and sub. He took special requests, thought
of his own and repeatedly hunted the internet for new ideas.
It was just one more thing that distinguished The Den from
other clubs.

Working with inanimate objects was way preferred to dealing with his emotions. Wood and metal didn't talk back, didn't
disappear and leave you to fend for yourself. No, the materials
would meld and form to his control until it became exactly
what he wanted. Sometimes they would struggle and fight,
resist his vision, but the end product was always his.

Right now he needed to lose himself in the work. To stop
thinking and just forget, before heading upstairs to his loft.
It wasn't like sleep would be happening anytime soon. Not
when thoughts of Cali Reynolds continued to haunt his mind.

EIGHT

Jake fisted his hands on his hips and waited, the plain white door before him the last barrier of protection from the anger he had to face on the other side.

Or was it really the disappointment he was dreading?

The door swung open—it was time to wade the shit.

"Hey, Dek," Jake said, trying to remain casual. "You busy?"

Deklan grunted then turned and walked back down the hallway. The fact that the door remained open was Jake's signal to follow the man. There'd been a number of times the door had simply closed in his face—a very effective, nonverbal *fuck off*.

A small part of Jake had been hoping for the closed door, if only to put this off.

Stepping into the condo, he shut the door and took a deep breath. It wasn't like Dek would physically hurt him. That wasn't the problem. No, Deklan had much better ways to make a person feel like a minuscule piece of shit without having to raise a fist. Often without saying a word.

Jake walked down the hall into the living area. No matter how often he was there, he was always mildly surprised at how sophisticated the room looked. Decorated in rich browns and blacks, the abstract artwork and polished silver sculptures strategically placed around the room spoke of a complexity Deklan rarely showed to anyone. Immaculately clean, if it weren't for the large flat-screen hidden behind the closed doors of the maple entertainment center, he'd swear he walked into the wrong condo.

"Beer?" Deklan asked from the kitchen.

"Sure."

Jake crossed the room and took a seat at one of the leather bar stools that sat beneath the counter separating the two spaces. The inclusion of a physical barrier between them was a deliberate move on his part.

Dek twisted of the top of the beer and handed it to Jake. After taking a drink of his own, Dek gave him a level stare. "So?"

Right. A man of few words, Dek always implied more into everything he said.

"So," Jake said. "You talk with Mathews?"

"Every day. You?"

Jake hid his smile behind his beer bottle. The man wasn't going to make it easy for him. Not that he blamed Dek. At six foot five, Deklan Winters didn't have to make anything easy for anyone. Six-two himself, Jake never felt overly intimidated by his friend, but Dek could definitely make a man squirm.

As the oldest of the three men, Deklan took the role of big brother and protector seriously when it came to Seth and Jake, which also made disappointing him that much harder.

Jake let the cooling fizz of the beer run down his throat. "Dick."

Dek cupped himself and gave a profane tug. "Yup, got one." He lifted an eyebrow. "You?"

"You should know. You've seen it enough." The club didn't allow for modesty.

"That inferior piece of equipment you carry?" Dek snorted. "That hardly counts."

Jake smiled, some of the tension leaving his shoulders. The familiar banter settled the bundle of knots that had formed in his gut. "Not all of us need to carry a fucking Uzi to feel like a man."

"No. Only the most skilled get the Uzi." A devious smile curled over Dek's lips.

"Oh, really? I thought it was only those who need to over-compensate for their lack of skill who required an Uzi?"

Dek grunted. "Lack of skill, my ass." He took another swig of his bear then set the bottled down and leaned onto the counter. His beefy arms spread wide, showing the strength and muscles that bulged under his T-shirt. Dek had lost none of his military-earned physique since he left the service six years ago.

It'd been at Dek's post-military party that the three friends had crafted their plan for The Den. Their mutual interest in the more extreme side of sex sprouted from their teen years, when the three boys had found a safe haven in a BDSM club, of all places. The club proprietor gave them a place to sleep, income for cleaning the club and, most importantly, a sense of safety. All with the strict rule that none of them could partici-pate in any club activities until they were eighteen and legal.

Jake glanced over his shoulder and nodded toward the closed doors of the entertainment center. "No football?"

Dek shook his head. "Packers have a bye." Being a Green Bay Packer fan while living in Minnesota Viking territory could be a dangerous prospect for a less confident man. He leaned in. "Why are you here, Jake?"

Direct. The man was always direct.

Unable to hold Dek's searching stare, Jake stood and grabbed his beer to the stand beside the tall windows of the sliding glass doors. He leaned against the wall and took in what appeared to be a party of sorts happening in the courtyard behind the condo.

Jake had avoided this conversation for two days. It was Sunday afternoon, and they both had to be at the club that night. It was better to get everything out before they all met again.

"I'm leaving when my contract's up in December," Jake finally admitted. After a tense bit of silence, he turned to look at Dek, who hadn't moved from the kitchen.

"Figured that," Dek grumbled before he shifted to cross his arms over his chest. "So?"

No give whatsoever. "Thought you should know."

"Thanks."

"Look, Dek—" Jake started then stopped. What could he say? "It's nothing personal. I just need to move on."

Dek thinned his lips and nodded. That was it.

"Nothing else?"

The man lifted a shoulder in a dismissive shrug. "Nothing I say will change your mind. Right?"

Jake gave a reluctant nod.

"Then there's no need to say more."

"No hard feelings?"

"Of course there are," Dek answered honestly, shooting the verbal dagger at Jake.

He cringed as he absorbed the impact of the words. "Anything I can do to change that?"

"Stay."

Right. "Can't do that, man."

"Why not?"

Jake sighed. He took a drink of his warming beer to stall

for time. How did he possibly explain it to Dek? To anyone? "I just need to move on. It's time for something different."

"Running again?"

"What?" Jake stiffened, getting defensive. "I'm not running."

Dek tossed his empty bottle into the recycle bin. "Seems that way to me." He reached into the fridge and pulled out another beer, silently lifting and offering one to Jake. Jake shook his head and Dek closed the fridge. "It's what you always do."

"What the fuck are you talking about?" Annoyance was quickly replacing anger.

Dek opened his beer and took a drink before he answered. "Every time things get too settled, going too smooth in your life, you bail."

"Fuck you."

"Just telling you what I see."

Jake held his retort and turned back to face the window. What the hell? He didn't run. This was exactly why he hated telling people he was moving on. They always tried to analyze him and find a reason for his simple desire to do something new. Christ. Couldn't anyone ever just accept that?

He felt Dek behind him, not that he'd heard the man move. Dek had the stealth thing down.

"Your parents died when you were ten, Jake. How long are you going to keep running from that?"

What the fuck? Jake straightened, tensing at the harsh accusations. "That's hitting below belt, asshole." He clenched his teeth to keep from saying more. It would only prolong the conversation.

Deklan stood silently behind him, obviously waiting for Jake to continue.

Refusing to give in to his anger and Dek's intimidation tactic, Jake focused on the party outside. A cluster of tables decorated with white linen table cloths and small vases of red roses occupied the far end of the courtyard. There were about thirty people mingling around, eating food from the short buffet table and drinking. He imagined some sort of background music played from the iPod docked to speakers on the far side of the gathering. It seemed so quaint and normal.

"Not invited to the party?" Jake asked Dek, opting to change the subject.

"I was. Didn't go."

"Why not?"

"Why?"

Jake huffed out an agreement. It was hard to have a separate personal life, given the business they were in. The questions always came about what he did for a living and if he answered honestly, the inquisitor inevitably paled and found someone else to talk to. Well, the nice ones did. The rest gave some sort of scathing putdown before they huffed off in rigid superiority.

"What's it for?" Jake asked, his curiosity piqued. And damn, this topic was way safer than the last one.

"Hell if I know." Dek shot him a look like Jake had grown a second head. Dek stepped up and slid the door open before moving onto the small patio. The sounds of a John Mayer tune mingled over the air with the low chatter of voices.

Jake followed Dek out to lean against a wood support beam for the deck overhead. He took in the intimate gathering and felt just a little bit of longing. The assembled group gave the impression of closeness, laughing and talking about nothing, probably. When was the last time he'd done that? Just hung out with people, friends, and shot the shit on a Sunday afternoon? It was a gorgeous fall day, the sun high with a slight breeze that held just the edge of chill and hinted winter was coming.

"Do you ever want to join them?" Jake asked, not exactly sure where the question came from.

This time, Deklan's glare guaranteed Jake had definitely sprouted a second head. "Uh, no."

Of course not. "Maybe you should."

"Why?" The incredulous tone in Dek's voice indicated his complete incomprehension of Jake's conversation. After all, ex special ops men and Doms did not mix well in condo courtyard parties.

Yeah, why? "Because it's good to have outside social activities," he said lamely.

"That's what The Den is for." Dek shot Jake another glare that would have a wise man dropping the conversation.

Jake was seriously starting to doubt his intelligence, because he pushed on. "And what about outside of the club? Would it really hurt to be nice to your neighbors?"

"I'm nice to my neighbors," Dek objected. "Why the lecture? You're the one bailing on the friends you do have."

And he scores. Jake cringed and straightened to set his empty bottle on the patio table. He glanced back at the little party, taking another scan of the happy group. Living above the club was convenient, but it didn't allow for neighbors. The more industrial neighborhood setting lacked social amenities, such as courtyard parties and backyard barbecues.

"You can have my loft over the club when I leave," Jake offered. "It'll get you away from this social hell."

Dek gave a noncommittal shrug. "Kind of like it here."

"Minus the people."

Dek grunted and emptied his beer in one long swallow. "They're not so bad if you don't talk with them."

Jake chuckled, having to agree with his friend on some level. He shifted to move back inside when a flash of blond at the edge of the gathering caught his eye. He stopped and stared, narrowing his eyes in concentration. Could it be her? What were the odds?

The woman in question was sitting dressed in a sleeveless, green dress that hugged her curves and rode high on her thighs, showing off her shapely legs. She tossed her head back, laughing at something another person said, her hair bobbing in waves against her shoulders.

She looked different. Refined and sophisticated, like the image she projected in her profile picture. Not at all like the soft and sexy woman he'd fucked two nights ago.

His breath stuck in his chest as he took her in. This wasn't the first time he'd seen members outside of the club. Hell, he saw them all the time. But this *was* the first time he'd ever reacted this way. The graceful movement of her arms as she talked with others, the light smile lifting her lips, the genuine laugh he could pick out over the crowd of noise all worked together to spike his interest and set his dick throbbing.

Jake stepped back into the shadows and reached blindly for his empty beer bottle, intending to retreat into Dek's condo. His hand knocked the bottle and sent it tumbling off the table instead. He made a hasty grab for it, missed, then swore as the bottle shattered onto the cement. The crash of the glass echoed across the courtyard and rang like a car accident to his ears.

He cringed and glanced up, afraid he'd see her staring at him.

"Deklan Winters," a voice called out. "Is that you hiding over there?" An older lady flamboyantly dressed in a bright floral sundress better suited for a Florida retirement community was waving and strolling toward Dek's patio.

"Good afternoon, Mrs. Jennings," Deklan said politely and added a smile that surprised the shit out of Jake. "A lovely day, isn't it? Just like you."

The rotund lady blushed and waved a dismissive hand at him. "You're so kind to flirt with an old fart like me. And it's Edith," she said as she stopped at the edge of the patio.

"How many times do I have to tell you that?" She patted his beefy arm in a grandmotherly gesture. "Now, what are you doing over here all by yourself? There's a party going on and I insist you join us." With more courage than most men, the lady grabbed hold of Dek's hand and began to pull the much larger man into the courtyard.

Dek's deep, genuine laugh shocked Jake even more. It was a sound even he didn't hear very often, but this five-foot two-inch whirlwind of energy had managed to provoke the reaction in less than a minute. Amazing. Jake had to make a physical effort to close his gapping mouth as he watched the exchange.

"But, Edith," Dek said kindly as he slowed to a stop. He gave her hand a gentle pat where it gripped his. "I have company." He tilted his head in Jake's direction.

"Oh." Edith perked up and leaned around Deklan to observe Jake. Her lips rose in an almost devious smile before she turned back to Dek. "And who is this handsome man?"

Dek's back straightened before he sputtered, "He's a *friend*, Edith. That's all." The big man turned to Jake, an actual spark of amusement in his eyes. "Jake, this is Edith Jennings, the unofficial social director of our condo complex."

Jake smiled and stepped forward, unable to escape without seeming like a complete ass. He extended his hand. "Nice to meet you, Edith. You must be a something of a social magician if you can get this man to join a party."

She grabbed Jake's hand and gave it a pat. "Oh, I haven't managed that yet. But there's always today." She smiled at the two men, her fluff of white hair bouncing around her head in a careless sprig of curls. "Come on, what will it hurt?"

Jake wasn't sure about Deklan, but he had an inkling it could hurt him a whole hell of a lot. Before he could extend his apologies, Dek nailed him with a smile that left his gut at his feet.

"You know, Edith," Dek said with a deceptively friendly tone, "I think we'd love to join the party." Dek gave Jake's back a harder-than-necessary slap. "Jake here was just saying how fun it looked."

Jake choked on his retort, the joyous spark in the conniving Mrs. Jennings' eyes making him bite back what he really wanted to say. Instead, he plastered on his practiced smile and gave a laugh. Two could play at this game. "So right, Dek." Jake leaned in to Edith and spoke in a conspiratorial fake whisper. "Dek was just confiding how he was feeling lonely here and was too shy to approach his neighbors."

The look of horror that flashed over Dek's face before he schooled his features was worth any future repercussions.

Edith's eyes widened at the juicy piece of gossip. "Well, we'll just take care of that." She promptly situated herself between the two men, looping an arm around each of theirs, and started to move toward the party. She seemed completely undeterred by the fact that the top of her head was over a foot below theirs. Instead, she lifted her chin and preened like a debutant leading the catch of the season into the ball. Or catches, as the situation warranted.

"Come along, gentlemen. We have a party to attend," Edith said in a voice that didn't allow for protest, the strength in her small form an additional surprise.

Over her head, Deklan shot him a glare that guaranteed hideous retribution later. Jake laughed and did his best to shake off the tingle of warning sliding down his spine. There was nothing he could do now.

Against his better judgment, he was going to meet the lovely Ms. Cali Reynolds once again. And this time, she wasn't slipping away.

NINE

"A toast," Evan boomed as he stood and raised his glass. "To Lacey and Paul."

Everyone immediately followed suit, the couple in the spotlight sporting the open smiles of untarnished love and endless hope.

"May your life be filled with love and your dreams filled with happiness," Evan said. "Congratulations on your engagement."

Soft rounds of agreement followed as the small gathering of friends gave heartfelt words of support and encouragement to the couple. Lacey glowed, the rosy blush of dreams coloring her cheeks, the shiny new diamond glittering in the sunlight. Paul, her fiancé, held her close to his side, his strong arm tucked possessively around her shoulders. Pride and devotion stamped on the hard lines of his face.

Cali smiled politely and unclenched her fist, careful to ensure nobody noticed the act. She didn't want her cynicism to spoil the festivities. Light notes of music drifted over the breeze, filtering through the courtyard. A burst of laughter, deep and robust, snapped over the low murmur of conversation.

"Aren't they lovely?" The low voice close to her ear jerked Cali from her observations. She sucked in a breath but held her smile as she peered over her shoulder at her neighbor, Allie.

"New love is always lovely," Cali agreed, fluttering another quick look at the happy couple.

Allie gave a soft snort. "Spoken by the woman who so recently told me love is an illusion easily shattered by reality." She plopped down in an empty chair and gave a sardonic lift of her sculpted brow. Her wide mouth wrinkled in amusement that matched the spark of her coffee-colored eyes.

"I did." Cali nodded, pausing to take a sip of her water. "And I believe that. But new love is nice to watch." She looked over at Lacey and Paul, who still touched each other with that freshness of needed contact. Cali was truly happy for them. "And who knows, maybe their love will meet with a gentle reality."

"Right." The sarcasm wasn't lost as Allie reached across the table for the open bottle of Merlot and refilled her glass. The thirty-seven-year-old lawyer had her own opinions on love and marriage that weren't that far from Cali's. She stared at Cali's water. "You're not drinking today?"

"No. I have work to do later."

"On a Sunday?"

"Yeah." Cali glanced away from her friend's penetrating stare. "The owner of the book store is going out of town and wants to review some numbers before she leaves." Cali took care of the bookkeeping for a few of the local stores. What had started off as a favor to a friend ten years ago had grown into a profitable business. She was always mildly surprised at the number of people who could open and run a business but had no idea how to manage their accounts.

Allie shook her head, her curly hair bouncing around her shoulders. "Life of the self-employed is not as glamorous as everyone makes it out to be."

Cali nodded in agreement, even though she really loved the control self-employment gave her.

"Of course," Allie continued, the sarcasm still heavy in her voice, "life as a wannabe law partner isn't all that great, either."

"They're still giving you the run around?" Cali asked, referring to the law firm where Allie worked.

Allie gave a dismissive shrug and took a drink of her wine. "Whatever. There's not much I can do short of leaving and starting my career over. But hey, this is a party and we're supposed to be enjoying ourselves on this gorgeous day."

Cali studied the clear blue sky and smiled wistfully. Having a seventy-degree weekend in October was a bonus Minnesotans didn't take for granted. She smoothed a hand over the tiny wrinkle in the skirt of her fitted dress and wished she'd taken the time to re-iron it before the party started. But she'd been running late and had promised Evan and Edith she'd help set up the courtyard. Evan, of course, took care of most of the planning arrangements, but Cali was the execution person.

And every detail was perfect.

It was relaxed, nice and exactly what she needed to keep her thoughts off her own problems.

Moving into the condo complex was one of the best decisions Cali made after her divorce. Ending her marriage had been difficult. And getting out of the house and the neighborhood filled with families and memories a necessity. No one understood why she'd divorced her husband. But then, no one understood just how lonely and empty she'd been behind the facade of suburban soccer mom extraordinaire.

Being sexually ignored by your husband wasn't something you shared with your neighbors. As if they'd even believe that her perfect husband hadn't touched her intimately in over seven years.

It was way less shameful to let them think she was having a mid-life crisis. And maybe she was. However, she preferred to think of it as a mid-life correction.

Cali shifted in her chair then stood. She rubbed a hand over her churning stomach at the thought of the "correction" course she'd taken two nights ago. She hid the telling action by moving around the table to pick up empty plates and cups.

"Do you need some help?" Allie asked without moving from her relaxed slump against the plastic patio chair.

"No, you're fine."

"Good. Because I'm almost drunk enough to make another pass at the hunky Mr. Montgomery over there." Allie tilted her head and stared at the man in discussion.

Cali laughed and followed her friend's gaze. Yes, Carter Montgomery was a handsome man. Tall, dark and sexy pretty much summed him up. His midnight hair and contrasting crystal blue eyes, paired with a body toned and hardened by diligent gym time, made him a prime piece of eye candy at the pool.

He definitely came across as a man who knew his way around a bedroom. But then, looks didn't guarantee performance. And a guaranteed performance was what Cali had sought and obtained. She felt her cheeks heat at just the thought of her night at The Den. With Jake.

She glanced at Allie to see if she'd noticed the blush, but the woman appeared to be lost in her own musings. A glaze of pure lust had fallen over the sharp angles of Allie's features and Cali wondered if she'd looked at Jake like that. Until two nights ago, she'd buried lust beneath responsibility, motherhood, expectations and denial.

"Good luck," Cali said with a chuckle as Allie got up and

made her way over to her target. Cali glided between the tables with her pile of trash, keeping her smile in place. She dropped her items into the garbage then went over to the buffet table to start on the cleanup there.

"Cali, darling," Evan called as he sashayed over to her side and slid an arm around her shoulders. "Stop your puttering and enjoy yourself for once. Mingle, laugh, have fun with the rest of us." He tugged her away from the table. Short of digging in her heels and causing a scene, Cali was forced to go with him.

"I'm fine," she insisted, but gave in and looped an arm around his trim waist. "I was just taking care of some of the mess."

"And the mess will still be there when the party's over."

"True, but there would be less of it if you let me do some cleanup now."

"No can do, sugar," Evan emphasized with a back and forth swing of his finger. "Little Miss Details is having fun today instead of hiding away behind the guise of cleaning up or organizing or whatever other detail you always find to stay busy."

"I do not."

He halted and shot her a look of sarcastic disbelief. "Darling, I dare you to sit down for one hour and simply enjoy yourself."

Cali resisted the urge to rub her hand over her stomach as it cramped up once again. She smiled tightly. "I do enjoy myself. I just believe in maintaining the mess instead of compiling the work at the end. There's nothing wrong with that."

"Down, girl," Evan said, pulling her into a gentle hug. "That was not a criticism." He leaned back and gave her a tender look. "I just want you to stop playing mom and start being the attractive, single lady that you are."

Cali found herself blinking back tears. Evan, in his gentle but direct way, had summed up her life in a nutshell. But he didn't need to know just how close he was to nailing the truth or how lost she was in figuring out how to do as he suggested.

"I think Richard's searching for you," she evaded and pointed to Evan's partner, who was gesturing for Evan to join him. Evan and Richard lived in the corner unit adjacent to hers and had instantly welcomed her when she'd moved in last spring. Both men were in their late thirties, openly gay and completely committed to each other.

Which made them safe and easy for her to befriend.

Evan tossed his head in an unsuccessful attempt to move his blond bangs out of his eyes. The overlong hair always managed to lop back over his brow and dust enticingly across his dark, girl-envy lashes. His blue eyes sparked when he watched Richard and his lips softened into a gentle smile reserved for that someone special. He sent his lover a quick wink then turned his attention back to Cali. "He'll be fine," he said. "The question is, will you?"

She wrinkled her brow and scoffed. "Of course I will." She would be. She was always fine. The real question was, would she ever be better than fine?

"When are you going to start dating again?" he prodded.

Date? Just the thought of it made her mouth dry and her stomach heave. The last person she'd dated was her ex-husband twenty-five years ago. College sweethearts, they'd married right after graduation and dove headfirst into family life.

Dating was something her kids did in college. Not her. Even the thought of it made her sick with that strange sense of been there done that.

"Evan," she said with a sigh. "I know you mean well, but honestly, dating is the last thing I want to do. I just ended a twenty-two-year marriage. If I'd wanted a man in my life, I would have stayed with my ex." And what would Evan think of her if she told him all she wanted right now was sex? Hot, forbidden sex with Master Jake, to be exact.

But then, that wouldn't be happening again, anyway.

"Then maybe you need a lady." Evan's immediate laugh and tight squeeze let her know he was joking. "Just kidding. But promise me you won't spend the whole afternoon cleaning up after everyone."

"Promise," she said, leaning over to give him a light kiss on the cheek. "Thanks for caring."

"Are you trying to steal my man?" Richard said, a joking smile on his face as he tugged Evan into his arms and gave him a kiss.

Cali laughed. "Not a chance of that happening. Evan is one hundred percent committed to you. Even if he is the best-looking man here."

Evan blushed, causing Cali and Richard to laugh even harder. The man really was handsome in an innocent, boy-next-door way. "Stop it," he admonished, shooting them both daggered glares from under his lashes. He pointed a finger at Cali. "You, go and have some fun. And you—" he grabbed Richard's hand, "—come with me before you get distracted by those two boy toys Edith is toting to the party."

Cali laughed as Evan dragged a willing Richard across the courtyard toward their condo.

She checked her watch then turned to see what Evan was talking about. What she saw stopped her heart and froze her breath. She couldn't move. Couldn't think.

Could not breathe. Not even a little.

Strolling across the law on the arms of Edith Jennings was not one, but two talk, dark and totally stunning, yet danger-ous-looking men. Both dressed in jeans and T-shirts, they towered over Edith, making them appear even broader and almost menacing compared to her tiny form.

And one of them was, unquestionably, Master Jake.

TEN

Fear froze Cali in place as a ramble of questions raced through her mind. How could he be here? Why was he here? Would he tell everyone what she'd done? With him?

Oh, God. This couldn't be happening. Her heart fluttered into panic mode. She'd gone to the club to keep her actions a secret. So she wouldn't have to deal with the recriminations that would surely come if anyone knew what she'd done. She did *not* pick up and have sex with strangers. No matter how gorgeous they might be.

The proper Ms. Cali Reynolds did not do *that.*

"I agree totally," Allie purred in her ear. "I can't stop staring myself."

Cali jolted out of her state of abject horror mixed with denial, afraid the guilt was displayed all over her face.

She yanked her gaze from the approaching trio and glanced at Allie. She was gawking at the two men with absolute lust and adoration in her eyes. A feeling Cali could totally relate to in that moment, if she overlooked the stark fear curling through her.

"Where did Edith find those two gorgeous hunks of men?" The newest voice was filled with blatant awe. Kendra, another neighbor, draped an arm over Cali's shoulders and pulled Cali's attention back to the two strangers. "I sure hope Newman's up for the challenge," she added with a laugh. Newman was Edith's husband of forty-seven years.

"Kendra," Allie snapped in disgust. "Do *not* spoil such a vision with lewd thoughts like that."

"Just saying—"

"Stop," Allie insisted, shooting the other woman a look of pure disgust. She reached behind Cali and smacked Kendra on the back of the head in a move reminiscent of the Three Stooges. "I do *not* need thoughts of Newman and Edith doing the dirty in my head." Allie gave a shudder and Cali cringed in full agreement.

Kendra shrugged and asked the question they all wanted to know. "So, who are they?"

Cali licked her lips as she crossed her arms over her chest. Was it a defensive or strategic move? With her nipples tightened into aching nubs, she wasn't really sure. Of course, there was no way in hell she was telling the women she knew one of the men.

Her cheeks flamed just thinking of how she knew him. She would die of mortification if the other women found out. If any of the people there found out.

"Hey, Mom."

Cali turned in shock at the shout of the familiar voice. Her eyes widened as she saw her daughter step out of her condo and head toward the party. *God, not now.*

"Stephanie," Cali said with more force than she intended. She walked away from the other women and cut off her daughter's approach. "What are you doing home? Is something wrong?"

Stephanie gave her a hug. "Nope. I just needed to grab some books for a research project." She stepped back, her dark ponytail swaying behind her. "Who knew I'd need to reference my high school books to do it?" Her laughter was light and real.

Cali sighed in relief and smiled. At nineteen and twenty-one, her two children had taken the divorce with a mixture of maturity and confusion. Logan, her son, had covered his angst behind a stiff facade of indifference. But Stephanie, the younger of the two, had been openly angry and hostile when they'd first been told.

Not that Cali blamed her.

The last year had required immense amounts of patience and emotional reassurance to earn back this easy relationship with her daughter.

"You never know, do you?" Cali answered with forced casualness. Every muscle in her body was stiff with anxiety and attuned to Jake's location. She could hear his deep laughter as they reached the party and Edith began to introduce her guests around.

Her daughter, evidently, was drawn to the rich sound as well. Her mouth gaped open as she ogled the two men. "Who is that?"

Cali cringed internally but glanced in the direction Stephanie was staring. "I don't know," she answered dismissively, fully intending to turn her back to the distraction.

But at that moment, Jake lifted his gaze and met hers dead on. An instant shot of heat and adrenaline fired through her body. Recognition flashed across his face and he smiled, a gleam of sexual appreciation dropping into his eyes.

"Oh my God." Stephanie grabbed Cali's arm either in shock or awe. "Do you see the way he's looking at you?"

Cali cleared her throat and turned her back on Jake to smile at her daughter with what she hoped was an expression of cluelessness. "What do you mean?"

"He was practically eating you with his eyes."

"Oh, he was not."

Stephanie shot her a look of disbelief. "You are so clueless."

Grateful her daughter bought her act, Cali didn't care if Stephanie thought she was so naïve. "You're just imagining it. I'm too old for him."

Her daughter's eyes almost bugged out of her head at that statement. "*Mom.* I wasn't suggesting you should go after him. God—don't talk like that. My mind can't take the thoughts. Ugh." She gave a fake shiver. "My mother does *not* have sex."

Cali dropped her head, her gaze landing on the polished toes of her daughter's feet, the shame once again flushing through her. If only her daughter knew just how close to the truth she was. She licked her lips and relaxed her features. She forced a light laugh and reached up to put an arm around her daughter's shoulders in an attempt to guide her toward the condo.

"I think the way it goes is my *daughter* does not have sex," Cali said, turning the conversation around. "Even if she does think she's old enough to be giving her mother advice on the subject."

Stephanie fumbled for words, the flustered shock causing her face to turn a deep pink. "I was not giving…I mean…I don't…" She looked away, her shoulders slumping in defeat as she let herself be led away from the party. "Sorry." She sighed. "I'm just not used to thinking of you that…way."

Neither was Cali. On both accounts. Sometimes it was hard to believe her baby was deep into the age of sexual activity. Cali gave a quick glance around to ensure their privacy. "As long as we're on the subject, I hope you're using protection."

Her daughter's blush deepened to a bright red. Even though

they'd talked openly about sex since her daughter was old enough to start asking questions, the embarrassment of discussing the topic with her mother was obviously still holding strong.

"Yes, Mother. We don't need to have that conversation, again." The sulk in her voice was reminiscent of her eight-year-old one.

"Good," Cali said, letting the subject drop. They were almost to her patio, their escape made without dramatics. Cali was suddenly grateful for the excuse her daughter's appearance provided. No one would think anything of them leaving the party. "Is there anything else you need for school?"

She felt the relief rush through her daughter's shoulders. "No, the book was—"

"Cali, dear." Mrs. Jennings' voice rang across the courtyard.

Cali's gut clenched as she continued forward ignoring the call. But her daughter stopped and turned.

"Cali, you're not whisking Stephanie away before I can get a hug, are you?"

Withholding a sigh, she turned with a smile on her face to see Edith fluttering over to them. Stephanie laughed, moved toward the woman and stooped to greet her with a warm hug.

"Hi, Edith," Stephanie said, a bright smile on her face. "How've you been?"

"Oh, I'm fine," Edith fluffed off. "The question is, how many men did you have to fight off this week?"

"Edith," Stephanie implored with an eye roll.

The other woman laughed, having earned the reaction she was seeking. Just as quickly, she shifted her attention to Cali. "Where are you running off to? Come here, I've got someone for you to meet."

Cali blanched. "I need to see—"

"This will only take a minute," she insisted, grabbing Cali

and Stephanie's arms and ushering them back across the court-yard before further objections could be raised. "I have the most handsome men for you to meet. You never know—one of them might be your next Mr. Right, Cali."

Stephanie gasped in time with Cali's deep inhalation of breath. The sudden paling of her daughter's face matched the hard knot of dread sitting in Cali's gut. Edith, however, appeared to be oblivious to the tension she was causing.

This had all the makings of her worst nightmare come true. How in the world was she going to pull this off? Before she could dwell on the thought for too long, Cali found herself standing before the one man she thought she'd never see again.

The one man she told herself she never wanted to see again—especially with her daughter present.

The one man whose silver eyes sparked with acknowledgement and something deeper, more sensual than could possibly be considered polite. Would he say something? Would he out her to everyone here? Mortify her in front of her daughter and friends?

Suddenly, with a clarity that almost knocked her flat, Cali realized everything she'd risked for her one night of passion. Her reputation, her respect, her standing among everyone she knew.

Most importantly, her daughter's love.

And all of it was poised on the needlepoint of this one man's discretion.

What, dear God, was he going to do?

Jake kept his gaze locked on her as Edith approached with his prey. Cali. His gentle nudge and inquisition to their social abductor as he'd watched Cali's attempted escape had worked exactly as he'd hoped. No matter how casual she'd made it appear, Jake knew Cali was attempting to run once again.

This time, he wasn't inclined to let her go.

"Cali, dear," Edith chirped. "I'd like you to meet Deklan Winters, who lives over in H-twelve but has been too shy to attend any of our other gatherings."

Jake stifled a laugh behind a choked cough as he watched the indignation rise over Dek's face. Deklan, shy? The man was going to kill Jake for this.

"And this is his friend, Jake," Edith continued, oblivious to the discomfort spreading among the small group. The tension jumped from each member as if screws were being slowly tightened with each word.

Edith leaned into Cali and added with a stage whisper, "Not his *friend* friend, like Evan and Robert. Just a guy friend. So they play for your team, honey."

Jake burst out laughing, unable to stop the reaction. Deklan shook his head, his lips thinned in an unaccustomed effort to hold back his words. The small grandmother of a woman had managed to both embarrass the two imposing men and lighten the mood in one quick moment.

"And this is Cali's daughter, Stephanie. She's a sophomore in college, so she's off limits to you two." Having given her admonishment, Edith patted Cali's arm before she hustled off, leaving the four to flounder in her wake.

The stunned silence that followed hung among the group as everyone apparently tried to figure out where to go after that whirlwind of an introduction. Jake watch Cali's eyes dart everywhere but to him. Her shoulders were stiff, her hands clasped before her in a pose that could be taken as polite or nervous. Her daughter had taken an extraordinary interest in the blades of grass beneath their feet, her cheeks a deep shade of red.

Jake extended his hand. "It's nice to meet you, Cali."

Her gaze shot to meet his. Finally. The green of her eyes

appeared pale and stunning in the natural sunlight. Her shoulders relaxed incrementally as she cautiously extended her hand. She was clearly afraid of something. The fire of awareness that zapped through him at the soft touch of her hand made his chest tighten.

What was it with this woman?

"Look, Mom," Stephanie said, turning her back to the men. "I've gotta run. I need to get back to school and work on that project tonight." She gave her mother a quick hug, forcing Jake to drop Cali's hand before he was ready to let go.

"Do you need anything else?" Cali gripped her daughter's arms, halting her quick exit for just a moment longer. She glanced at the men. "If you'll excuse—"

"It's okay," Stephanie injected, darting a quick glance at the men, sending her dark ponytail bobbing behind her. "You stay and have fun." She added a quick, "It was nice meeting you," to Jake and Deklan then took off, bolting out of the courtyard as fast as she could politely exit.

"I hope we didn't run her off," Jake said as they all watched the younger woman dart across a small patio and slip into Cali's condo. "I swear, we don't bite."

Deklan gave a snort as Cali's head whipped around, a mixture of shock and distrust on her face. Jake gave a polite smile and held her gaze. Her mouth opened, closed, then opened again as she floundered for a reply.

"Here you go, gentlemen."

Slightly annoyed at the interruption, Jake accepted the offered beer from a slender, curly-haired brunette with dark eyes that openly ate up both men. Edith had introduced them, but he'd forgotten her name when he'd heard it.

"Oh, Allie." Cali jumped at the intrusion. "You've met Jake and Deklan?" Her hands trembled briefly as she tucked a piece of hair behind her ear before she quickly clasped them once again.

"Can you believe Deklan was too shy to come out and meet us this whole time?" Allie rubbed a hand over the man's bicep in a gesture that was an apparent attempt at comfort but came across as blatant flirting.

Dek rolled his eyes and stepped away from the touch. Contact was not in the man's comfort zone.

Allie laughed, evidently not hurt or deterred by Dek's actions. "So, what do you men do for a living?"

The question was a basic conversational topic under the circumstances, but it was the one Jake always wanted to avoid. Dek raised an eyebrow and shot him a look that clearly said he wasn't answering.

Cali had stilled instantly at the question. Her lips were clamped between her teeth as she waited. Jake took quick note of the honest fear flashing in her eyes. Did she really think he'd out her? Here?

He took a drink of his beer, not tasting the liquid at all. He processed his newest revelation and buried the anger that rose at the thought that Cali trusted him so little. After the night they'd shared, all the work he'd done to build up her trust in him, she truly feared he'd tell everyone about that night. What the hell?

Jake gave Allie a stiff smile. "Dek and I are partners in a private business."

"Oh? What kind of business?"

"A private one," Jake responded flatly, the hard edge indicating the conversation was closed.

Allie lifted her eyebrows and glanced at Cali. "Okay." She took a drink of her wine and Jake watched her brow furrow behind the glass as she gave Dek a sidelong perusal. Clearly, she did not intend to let the subject drop forever.

Thankfully, or not, Edith arrived at that moment to drag them over to meet some more people. Like they hadn't been paraded around enough already. "You have to meet Lacey and Paul," she chattered. "This is their engagement party, after all. They are such a lovely, young couple. So in love. Have you ever been in love, Deklan?"

The man in question choked on his beer. Jake helped him out, giving a few hard swats to the back that earned him yet another death glare.

Jake positioned himself so he could continue to watch Cali. She'd turned away from them and pretended to listen to the nosy brunette. She gave an absent nod, but her eyes kept straying his way. Quick, circumspect glances that showed where her attention really was.

On him.

Right where he wanted it. He didn't question why that pleased him so much. Not now. Not when one night with Ms. Reynolds was far from enough. No, he wouldn't let her run again.

Excusing himself from the current conversation, Jake followed Cali as she moved to the buffet table and began consolidating food and cleaning away empty dishes. He brushed against her, an innocent glide of his arm along her back as he passed by on the way to the garbage can. She stilled for a second before continuing at her task.

Oh yes, the attraction was there. But then, he'd known that. The contact was a reminder to Cali.

He dropped his empty bottle into the recycle bin and turned to her. "Do you need some help?"

"No, thank you." She kept her voice polite and her head down. "Please, go and enjoy yourself."

"What if I'm not enjoying myself?"

She stopped and closed her eyes before straightening to look at him. Her smile was stiff, her eyes shuttered. "Then maybe you should leave."

Jake leaned over, grabbed a stack of piled trash and spoke low. "Like you did on Friday?"

She winced and gave a quick scan around. "Don't," she said sharply. "This is my life. Please—" Her lips thinned and she appeared to struggle with the next words. "Please don't mess with it."

He tossed the trash in the garbage before giving her his full attention. "I have no intention of messing with your life." He shoved his hands in his pockets to keep them from reaching out to her. To comfort her—a foreign thought in itself. "I only want to give you what you need."

Her eyes searched his face, her tongue sweeping out to wet her lips. "I don't need anything from you."

Jake let his grin show. She really was an awful liar.

Cali looked around again then shoved past him to another table and efficiently collected empty plates and cups. Her hands stilled when he added a dirty napkin to her pile. "Why are you here? Are you following me?"

He chuckled. "No. I'm not following you. Deklan really does live here. He's the third business partner in the club. The only one you hadn't met. I was visiting when the lovely Edith insisted we join this little soiree." He grabbed half of the collected trash and followed her over to the garbage, tossing his pile into the bin. "Are you running from me?"

"W-what?" she stammered as she grabbed a clean napkin and wiped off her hands. "Why would I do that?"

"Why indeed?" he answered, managing to inflect question and not the rising frustration he was feeling. "I'll see you next weekend. Right, Cali?"

Her eyes widened, the shock and desire displayed before the doubt and recriminations pushed them out.

He stepped closer and pitched his voice low. Intimate. "No shame. You promised."

She closed her eyes and shook her head. But she didn't back away.

"Look at me."

She complied immediately. Beautiful.

"When you come back, ask for me." He had her full attention and she didn't reject his assumption. "I'll ensure you get what you want. Just like last time." He turned and took a step away. "And, Cali." He waited until she met his gaze. "I know you want it."

Her eyelids dropped in lust, or anger—he wasn't certain, but he didn't wait to find out. He strode across the courtyard to Deklan's condo. There was no need to make polite small talk anymore. He'd achieved his goal, for better or worse.

Cali Reynolds would once again be his.

ELEVEN

She was crazy. Absolutely certifiable. She had to be, since she was waiting there. Again. What was she thinking, coming back to The Den?

Two weeks of bitter internal debate and more than a few pro and con lists later—ones where the cons heavily outweighed the pros—she found herself back where her body wanted to be, even if her mind said she shouldn't.

It was a clear case of desire trumping logic.

No excuses.

She simply couldn't stop thinking about the way Jake had made her feel. Of how much she wanted to feel that again. With him.

The music thumped hard and loud through the large main room. People were crammed into every corner, her small space next to the bar a coveted spot she'd scored only because the bouncer had escorted her there and told her to stay.

"Can I get you something, sweetheart?"

Cali turned to the bartender and gave a polite smile. "Just water, please." She was afraid she'd immediately slam anything stronger, and liquor was something she didn't need. Wanted, but didn't need right now.

She thanked him when he set the glass on the bar then shifted her attention back to the room. She smoothed her hand down the side of her short dress, resisting the urge to give the hem a tug. Even in her sexiest, most revealing outfit, she felt seriously overdressed. And this was the room where nudity *wasn't* allowed.

"You came."

The statement was purred into her ear a half second before his warmth melted into her back. His arm moved possessively around her stomach and pulled her tight to his length. All of the stiffness and doubt drained from her as she relaxed within his strength. "Yes."

Jake.

She knew it instinctively without turning to see him. His voice—low and commanding. His touch—strong and confident. His scent—clean and masculine. They were all programmed into her system. She didn't try to mask her reaction. She was too committed now to act coy or disinterested.

The courtyard incident had shown her just how much she had to lose. Her being here was anything but a game. She definitely wasn't going to pretend otherwise.

"Are we playing tonight, Cali?"

She swayed against him in time to the music, her ass rubbing his hardening erection. "Yes."

Instantly she was flipped around, her front crushed against the solid wall of man who held her. She gasped in surprise before his fingers found her nipple and squeezed. Hard. This time she gasped in shock, her reflexes jerking her away from him, but his other arm held her tightly in place.

"I lead." His steel eyes met hers. "Agreed?"

She stopped resisting as the pain shooting from her nipple morphed into an ache for more. "Yes, Jake." *God, yes*. A small part of her railed against that answer. The part of her that was used to controlling everything. Of *having* to control everything. Women were supposed to want independence, not submission.

But Cali wanted more than anything to submit once again to this man. Master Jake.

"Come with me," he said as he released her nipple. The blood rushed into the abused tip, making it throb, causing the other nipple to feel neglected. "Tonight you belong to me."

And that was exactly what she both wanted and feared.

Jake didn't mess with warm-ups tonight. He led Cali straight to the third-floor room he'd had on permanent reserve for the last two weeks.

The door to the private room had barely closed behind him before he had her pressed to it, his mouth crushing hers. She tasted so good, a flavor he now craved after years of denial. Her hands gripped his shoulders, her mouth opening wider as her tongue engaged his. He pushed his fingers through the curls of her hair and held her head still.

She moaned, turning soft and compliant against him. He yanked his lips from hers and stepped back while he still could. He took her hand and hauled her to the center of the room. Her small gasp let him know she'd examined the space.

She hesitated, her steps faltering slightly.

He faced her. "Rules, Cali."

Her bottom lip was tucked between her teeth, but she nodded.

"Safe words. Tell them to me."

She swallowed. "Red—stop, yellow—wait, green—go."

"You'll use them if needed."

"Yes," she whispered and looked down. Her hand flexed

in his, the small twitch another giveaway to the nerves she tried to hide.

The two weeks he'd waited had only increased his longing to have her. Add to that the repeated digs both Seth and Deklan were giving him over his decision to leave, and his frustration was like a tangible, unreachable itch under his skin. It was like Cali had known the perfect way to get to him.

And no one got to him.

Tonight she would get what she wanted. His way.

Anticipation flooded his system, but he pulled it back. Banked it behind the hardened wall that gave him distance. The Dom had to be in full control tonight.

"Remove your clothes, Cali. And place them on the desk." He pointed to a small bureau positioned next to the door before he stepped back, crossed his arms and waited.

She scanned the room and he watched her eyes track to the spanking bench on the right, the cross against the far wall, the swing hanging from the ceiling, then over to the open doors of the armoire displaying the array of whips, paddles, floggers and other equipment. Her cheeks paled then flushed. And still, she'd not moved to follow his order.

"I think—" she started.

He stepped forward and cupped the back of her neck, cutting off her words. He held her gaze, the green depths dark and frantic with need-laced fear. "Trust me. You did before."

His breath stuck in his chest as the feelings flowed across her face. A quick shuffle of emotions he would have missed if his attention was not glued to her. He let his thumb caress the soft skin of her cheek and she pushed against his palm, seeking more.

"Yes, Jake," she finally said. "I trust you."

He exhaled, the relief an unexpected sensation. "Good." He stepped back. "Now, your clothes, Cali. And no more hesitations."

TWELVE

Cali stared at the floor, the polished gleam of the hardwood highlighting the intricate patterns made by the grain. Nature's art displayed at her feet.

The stupidity of her thoughts forced a smile across her lips. She really was losing it. The entire scenario had her feeling disjointed. As if the normal part of her, the part that was her for most of her life, was suddenly gone. In her place was this woman standing before a Dom in a BDSM club, waiting to get spanked or whipped or whatever this virtual stranger wanted to do to her.

And both her body and her mind ached for it.

Yes, the frank display of equipment initially startled her. There wasn't a bed in this room. Not even a couch. And that made it real. This Scene was going to be very different from last time. She might be a little naïve, but she wasn't stupid. He was out to prove something, only she wasn't exactly sure what that was.

Yet, she still wanted it. Wanted Jake to lead her.

Control her.

Taking a deep breath, Cali raised her arms and pulled down the side zipper on her dress. The material loosened before she caught it and slid the dress down her legs. She resisted the urge to hide behind the garment as she folded it then moved to set it on the dresser he'd indicated. The dress hadn't allowed for a bra, so all that remained were her skimpy lace underwear and heels.

She peered at him over her shoulder. "Everything?"

"Everything."

Taking another fortifying breath, she slipped out of her shoes and slid her panties off. She willed herself not to blush. After all, he'd seen everything before. But this felt so much more exposed. She was clearly the vulnerable one here.

Exhaling, she pulled her shoulders back and moved to stand before him. Keeping her eyes on him, she slowly lowered herself to her knees and clasped her hands behind her back before she let her gaze fall to the floor.

His inhalation echoed through the room and made her flush with warmth. She hid her smile of pleasure behind the fall of her hair. If he thought he could throw her off by playing the hard-core Dom role, then she could reciprocate. She hadn't spent hours researching this topic for nothing.

She might be the submissive, but she still had power. Pleasing him gave her that.

His fingers trailed through her hair as he moved around to stand behind her and straddle her legs. "That is beautiful, Cali."

The caress of her name matched the subtle stroke of his finger along her jaw line, a line of heat following the touch and melting through her. Her breathing deepened and she fixated on that. On each breath as it pushed air through her lungs.

His deep voice was pitched low and washed over her from his position above and behind her, forcing her to focus on his words. "You will do exactly as I say tonight. No speaking unless I ask a direct question. Your orgasms are mine. You will not come unless I say you can." His hand fisted in her hair, yanking her head back.

A startled gasp escaped as she stared up at him.

"Do you understand?"

His features were cut and hard on his face. His neck muscles stood out in tension as he waited for her answer. It was the reverence and passion she saw in his eyes that enabled her to answer.

"Yes, sir." The soft reply was barely over a whisper but seemed to rock the otherwise quiet room.

She caught the slight flare of his nostrils before he released her hair and stepped away. She let her head drop forward as she held her breath and tried to slow her racing heart. His boots thumped across the wood to the armoire. She closed her eyes and focused inward, but he was back before she could catalogue her thoughts.

"Stand."

She responded, rising swiftly if not smoothly to her feet before she even realized what she was doing. His pleased smile stifled her mental objection and warmed her.

"This way," he said, pivoting to stride to the spanking bench. "You responded to the sight of this last time. Tonight, we'll see how you respond to the act."

Cali swallowed, her throat seemingly starved for moisture. Unable to rub her damp palms against the material of her dress, she kept them clenched behind her and walked to the bench. The piece of equipment was mounted on a platform that raised it about three feet off the ground. It took only a quick calculation to realize the added height provided better access. For the Dom.

The understanding brought another flush of arousal. She

bit her lip to hold back the sound that wanted to escape. He couldn't see that her stomach was tied in knots or that her heart thundered in her chest. No, she wouldn't let him know exactly how terrified and excited she was.

But he could see her tight, pointed nipples. He stepped close and rubbed his palms over the aching nubs. He bent and sucked first one then the other into his hot mouth—a quick, teasing action that made her legs weak and her nipples impossibly hard.

"I'll take care of these soon," Jake said, stepping back and positioning her until she was kneeling on the thick pad of the bench. "Lay forward and grab the handles below."

This was it. Her mind tried to rebel one last time before she stretched out on the thin padded bench extended before her. Jake adjusted her, spreading her legs, scooting her bottom back until her ass hung off the end and she felt completely exposed. He strapped the padded cuffs attached to the bars around her wrists and ankles, trapping her to the bench.

Locking her in place—for him.

Her legs quivered, a quick flash of heated desire that shocked her with its intensity from something so simple. Did that make her a freak? She turned her head to the side and tried to quiet her nerves, to focus on how the leather bench was cool and smooth against her front. And how the soft fur lining of the cuffs felt too kind for their purpose.

"One more thing, Cali," Jake said, kneeling beside her. He smoothed her hair away from her face so she could see. In his hand was a set of nipple clamps attached with a chain like she'd seen on the woman on the St. Andrew's Cross.

She inhaled, the distinctive smell of the leather bench rushing up to distract her from the increasing tangle of fear and anticipation warring within her.

The bench she lay on was just wide enough to support her

torso but thin enough that her breasts hung over each edge, making her nipples easily accessible to Jake. He reached for her breast and she closed her eyes. She bit her tongue and resisted flinching when his fingers plucked at the tip. He played with it for a moment, urging the flesh to pucker and bud even tighter until she felt a moan rising in her throat.

The metal was warmed from his hands and the bite instantaneous. She hissed and tensed at the sudden pressure and shot of pain radiating from her nipple. Her hand jerked in an attempt to remove the offending object, but it was halted by the cuff. She could do nothing but focus on the strange pinch and ache that was both painful and enticing.

She cried out when his fingers tugged on the other nipple. She'd been so intent on the new pain she hadn't realized he'd moved. Soon, both clamps were in place and she groaned at the sheer unaccustomed ache spiraling from her nipples. She pressed her forehead into the leather padding on the bench, all of her attention forced to her breasts, making her forget about her earlier discomfort at being exposed.

"Beautiful," Jake said in her ear. He tugged on the connecting chain, which pulled on both nipples and made her groan again. "And this is only the start."

Cali blinked her eyes open and panted in an attempt to catch her breath. The throbbing eased some, but the rest of her body was completely sensitized. The air brushed against her open pussy, reminding her she was spread open to him and wet.

More than that, she realized she was aching for more. The lower half of her body felt neglected and ignored. She wiggled on the bench, swaying her bottom into the air.

Jake chuckled, a low, sensuous rumble before the sharp slap of his hand bit against her ass. The smack of skin against skin masked her cry of surprise.

"You'll wait for me, Cali." Another slap on the other cheek, and the stinging burn fired across her skin, merging to spread down her ass toward her pussy. "Hold still."

Cali complied. Rationally she knew she should be fighting this. Resisting, using her safe word, running the hell away. But the other her was marveling in the burn as the pain blended with excitement and warmed her entire body.

"I'm going to spank you now." His hand caressed her ass where he'd just hit her. "I want you to count them. Out loud."

Count? Right. She licked her lips and forced out a, "Yes, sir."

"Jake."

"What?" Her mind tried to process what he meant.

"Yes, Jake," he said.

Her thoughts were too jumbled to understand the difference, but she repeated his command. "Yes, Jake."

She swore she heard him growl, but then all her focus went to the sharp smack of his hand against her tender flesh. "One," she remembered to say, even as his hand hit her again. Her eyes were closed now and she huffed out the next number. He alternated cheeks, hitting first one then the other in a consistent rhythm that had her anticipating when and where the next strike would come.

Her muscles relaxed, her death grip on the handles eased and slowly she floated into the act, giving herself to Jake.

The counting kept her focused, the stinging pain kept her there. But even as the burn built with each slap of Jake's hand, the heat spread downward along her pussy in a completely unexpected way until she found herself lifting her ass to meet his hand. Her breathing was labored, each number becoming more forced and breathy as she continued to count.

"That's it," Jake said, pausing to caress her burning cheeks.

The light touch ignited flames across her sensitive nerve endings. "What number are we on?"

God. She couldn't think. Her brain fuddled to remember, but her mind could only process how she felt. On the strange blend of pleasure and pain that flew from her nipples to her ass to her now wet and needy pussy.

"Cali." Jake's sharp command drew her back. He'd asked a question. She was supposed to answer.

"Sixteen," she mumbled, hoping it was right.

"Wrong." The censure in his voice was emphasized by the hard thrust of his fingers in her aching sex.

She gasped—the intrusion was sudden and felt so incredibly good. But then it was gone. Like his mouth on her nipples, it was only a tease. The whimper that left her mouth was a sound she couldn't remember ever making before. She pushed her bottom back as far as her bonds would let her, a silent plea for more.

After a moment of nothing, no words or touch from Jake, Cali angled her head to look at him over her shoulder. His hard gaze caressed her as completely and thoroughly as if he'd run his hands over her. Her body tingled and ached until she gave in and said the words now screaming in her mind. "Please, Jake. Please, touch me."

A scowl marred the smooth lines of his forehead before he answered. "You owe me ten more for losing count."

A shudder wracked her body. She had no idea if it was in anticipation or fear. "I...I don't know if I can," she finally managed to say.

Then he was there. Tight against her legs, his big palms rubbing over her flaming skin. "You can." One hand moved between her legs to tease her clitoris. The touch, as light as it was, shot sharp waves of pleasure through her body, making her hands clench and her toes curl. She strained against her bonds, tense and ready to come.

And he was gone.

She collapsed against the bench, every muscle weak from unfulfilled release. Never, in all her fantasies, did she ever expect this intense and complete loss of logical thought. Right then, she could only feel and would do anything to reach the end. Anything to please Jake and find that shattering fulfillment he dangled so elusively before her.

"Are you ready, Cali?"

No. Yes. *God*. She closed her eyes and whispered, "Yes, Jake."

She stiffened once again in expectation of the coming strike. He surprised her when he crouched next to her, pushing her tousled hair off her face. Her eyes flew open and her lips parted in a silent gasp. Then his mouth was on hers. All hot, probing and commanding as he controlled the kiss the way he controlled her body.

His tongue battled with her own, and she leaned toward him as much as the restraints would allow. She wanted to touch him. To feel his skin beneath her hands and against her body. He withdrew and she tried to follow until she was unbalanced and tilting precariously on the bench.

"Stop." His hand on her back halted her movement and he repositioned her until she was safe from sliding off the edge. The leather was slick and sticky beneath her, which she only now noticed. Like the cool air brushing over her heated skin and the musky scent of sex and arousal hanging heavy around them.

Jake stepped behind her. "Ten more."

Crack. The pain seemed to ricochet through her an instant before the sound rang in her ears. *Crack.* The heat raced over her skin and fired down to her aching, wanting pussy. *Crack.*

She squirmed on the bench, unsure if she was trying to get away or get closer.

"Let go, Cali." Jake's word came to her in a fog, distant yet clear. "Don't fight it. Let it take you."

Let it take her.

"Stop resisting. You're thinking too much. Let go. Feel."

Thinking? She *couldn't* think—that was the problem.

Crack.

Damn. Her body was alight with sensation. Every nerve ending, from her throbbing nipples to her aching ass, quivered. *Crack.*

It hurt. She couldn't do it. She bit her lip to hold back the whimper. *Crack. Crack.* She cried out, the release of sound like a valve on a tea kettle. Her body flew, her mind blanked and she floated. *Crack.* She drifted, the pain obliterated in the quiet plane of her mind.

Crack. The nipple clamps were suddenly removed and she arched against the instant throb in each tip as the blood rushed into the swollen buds. Before she could think—*Crack.* A hard smack directly to her tender, exposed pussy. Fire—hot, threatening, inviting, chased her to the edge until she panted in desperate need.

"Please, Jake," she begged, not caring how it made her sound.

"Who can give you what you want?"

"You," she panted, not even hesitating. "Only you."

He flicked her clitoris. "Come for me, Cali."

And God, did she. One long, hard plunge over the edge that sent her sailing to a level of bliss she'd never dreamed of. She let go and rode the wave of pure pleasure that shook her to her core. Her back arched, her eyes clenched shut, the sharp intensity of sensation tensing her muscles as it rippled through every cell in her body.

Seconds, minutes, hours later she became aware of strong hands caressing her wrists and ankles as the bindings were removed. Still, she couldn't move. She was both exhausted and sated in a way that made her smile but prevented movement. She was content to just lie there.

Incoherent sounds drifted to her. The squeak of the cabinet hinges, the scrape of a chair against the floor, the clump of boots over the wood. Distantly she felt the tenderness in her bottom, the tingling of her nipples, the dampness between her legs. She was able to comprehend then that she was still lying spread open on the bench, even though she was no longer tied down. Some portion of her mind registered that this should embarrass her. That she should move.

But she didn't want to.

Fingers caressed her hair. Strong, attentive fingers that brushed her temple and curled around her ear. She forced her eyes open.

Jake.

The man who'd turned her world upside down for the second time. The one who did this kind of thing for a living.

The moisture built in her eyes before she even realized what was happening. And then, it was too late to stop. The tears spilled over and ran down her face—silent testament to the range of turmoil bursting in her chest.

His eyes were gentle, concerned as they tracked the tears before he reached to wipe them away. An action that only made more tears spill out. She took a shaky breath and he stroked her hair, the comforting act so gentle and contrary to the man he was just moments before.

Who was he, really? Would she ever know? Did she want to?

It took less than a second for the answer to come. Yes. Against her better judgment, she wanted to know this man.

Jake. Not the Dom, but the man who could master her one second and soothe her the next. The man who seemed to know this side of her better than she knew herself. Who could push and lead without smothering her. Any man who could do that was worth knowing.

But her mind put a crashing stop on the wayward thoughts with a dose of reality.

This was just a Scene.

THIRTEEN

"Come here, Cali," Jake said softly as he eased his arms beneath her lethargic body and lifted her off the bench. He cradled her and she curled into him as if she wanted to disappear.

He let her.

His boots echoed through the space when he moved to the armless chair he'd positioned in the middle of the room. He sat down and adjusted Cali until she was straddling his legs, her head tucked against his shoulder. He kept his arms wrapped around her and was mindful of her tender bottom. She'd be sore for a while, as unaccustomed as she was to being spanked.

His fingers smoothed her hair and he found himself whispering soothing words into her ear. He felt a wet spot growing on his shirt where her tears continued to fall. This was normal, he reminded himself. A typical crash for a sub after finding subspace and coming with the intensity Cali had.

Normal.

But he couldn't seem to find the distance *he* normally had in this instance. Every reaction had wound him in tighter until he'd been so turned on, so tuned into her that any possibility of detachment was obliterated. With her he experienced something besides power. For the first time ever, he felt the intimacy on a level that went deeper than base trust. There was a connection that threatened every emotional wall he'd ever constructed. But with Cali in his arms, in his control, he felt a vague and foreign sense of peace.

He kissed her shoulder, the light hint of salt tempting his tongue. He moved his hand over the damp skin of her back, the other tangling in her hair to hold her closer.

"It's okay, Cali," he murmured against her ear. "Let it out."

Her shoulders shook as she listened to him. He held her until the sobs quieted and her body stilled against his. Her arms were curled under her, crushed between their bodies. He felt her push against his chest.

He tightened his hold. "No." She stilled. "You don't get to run this time."

She inhaled, the skin on his neck tingling against the sharp hiss of her breath. But she remained in his embrace. He continued to caress the heated skin on her back, slow, soothing passes until her muscles relaxed and she sagged against him.

Time passed, but he had no concept of how long they sat like that. Eventually, her heart rate returned to normal, the soft beat thumping against his chest. He reached down next to the chair, pulled a tissue from the box he'd placed there and nudged it into her hand.

She took it, a small laugh vibrating against his shoulder. "Thank you." Her voice was hoarse and throaty from the extended cry. "Did you think of everything?"

"That's my job." He didn't tell her that this, right here, was more than his job.

She leaned back slightly and wiped at her tear-streaked face then blew her nose. She puffed out a laugh. "Not so attractive now, huh?" She wadded the used tissue in her hand and attempted to bury her face into his shoulder.

He didn't let her hide this time. "Wrong," he said, holding her away from him. He framed her face and pushed her hair back until he could see her eyes. "You are more beautiful to me now than you have ever been."

She looked down, obviously not believing what he said. Her face was blotchy, her eyes puffy and red, her makeup smeared, but that's not what he focused on. What drew him to her. It was her complete and total trust and submission that knocked his knees out from under him.

"Look at me."

She complied instantly, her eyelids lifting a half second after he spoke. *Beautiful.* He caressed her jawline as he took in the swirl of emotions held in her eyes. Fear, confusion, desire and there—trust.

"You were fantastic," he reassured her. "You gave me your trust. That's beyond gorgeous to me."

She sniffed and her fists clenched against his chest, but she held his gaze. Did she believe him? Did she really understand how her submission affected him?

For the first time ever, he wanted a sub—Cali—to understand.

"You gave yourself to me. Trusted me to lead you. To give you what you needed, even when you didn't know what that was." He took a low breath to steady himself. "Watching you find your space, to reach that place where pain and pleasure blend until that's all there is… Seeing you give in to the feeling and knowing I brought you there. The moment you flew, I followed."

The words didn't seem enough. Didn't seem adequate in explaining what he felt. But her mouth parted and she lifted trembling fingers to brush over his lips. She searched his eyes, hunting, he was certain, for the truth of his words.

"Why *do* I trust you?"

The question was rhetorical, an internal thought that slipped out. He stayed quiet and let her ponder, focusing on the light rub of her fingers over his lower lip. On how the touch both tickled and enticed him and oddly drew his attention to her lips. He suddenly wanted nothing more than to suck her fingers into his mouth.

Before he could act, she withdrew them.

His gaze flashed back to hers, but he only caught a glimpse before her mouth covered his. The kiss was hot and searching. Need poured from her and he met it with every thrust of her tongue. Her hands fisted in his hair and pulled until the pain made him flinch, but he let her.

He responded to her aggression with instant arousal. His dick throbbed beneath his pants, hard and aching for release. In her.

Cali wasn't just a client.

In truth, she hadn't been since he first heard his name roll off her lips. Not sir, but Jake. Spoken in deference and passion. And she'd done it without thought or calculation. The honesty of it had echoed through him and struck at the facade he held to. The same barrier that was pushing him to leave. To move on.

She was the only one in all his years in the BDSM world who had ever used his name during a Scene. For the first time ever, this was personal.

Cali rotated her hips and ground against this erection. He bit his tongue and resisted cupping her ass. A fraction of his mind was still able to remember her flesh would be too sore for his grip. Instead, he clenched her hips and held her down as he thrust upward.

It wasn't enough. "Touch me," he gritted out.

Instantly her hands were at his waist, undoing his pants and reaching inside before he could halt her. Not that he wanted to. Her fingers closed around his cock and stroked. One hard tug up and down his length, and he almost lost it.

What the fuck?

Gasping a breath, he leaned forward and devoured her nipple, the sweet bud hard and silky beneath his tongue. She cried out under his attack, the nub obviously still tender and sensitive from the clamps. He eased his attention with a haggard breath and shifted to the other nipple.

She resumed her caress of his cock. Each stroke slow, but firm, almost like she was exploring his body by touch. But then, she was. It was the first time he'd allowed her to touch him. Her thumb smoothed over the sensitive top, stopping to probe the opening and collect the spilled pre-come. He arched his hips, thrusting his cock into her fist. He grunted his need against the damp flesh of her breast.

He moved his mouth to the juncture of her neck and bit down on the tender flesh. She flinched then tilted her head, giving him more room. He used his teeth to hold her in place as he lifted his hips and worked his pants down his legs. She continued to rub his cock, her movements increasing with the freedom from his pants.

"Jake," she panted, her warm breath caressing his ear. "I need you."

He let go of her shoulder and reclaimed her mouth, if only to stop himself from agreeing with her. He needed her.

Blindly, he tore open the condom packet he'd snagged from his pocket. He started to roll it on, but she pulled back to push away his hands and slowly rolled the rubber over his cock herself. Even that basic safety precaution became erotic under her exploring hands.

He groaned, his body an inferno that was unbearably close to igniting. He moved his hand between her legs, seeking her core. She was wet, hot and ready for him. He circled her clit and she pushed into his touch with a moan. He let his fingers entered her, hard strokes of preparation she didn't need.

"Please, Jake. I'm going to come."

"No, Cali." He knocked her hand from his cock and positioned himself at her entrance. "Not 'til I say." The words tore from his throat as he struggled to hold himself back. He fisted her hair and forced her to look at him. Her eyelids hung heavy over eyes that had turned a deep emerald green. Her lips were parted and her chest lifted with each breath. *So fucking beautiful.*

"You're mine." He held her gaze, forcing her to understand. "When you're here, you're mine." Her eyes drifted closed, but a hard tug on her hair had them open once again. "Tell me you understand."

She wiggled her hips, seeking what he withheld from her, her wetness coating his hand as he held his cock firm.

"Please, Jake," she begged.

He bit his tongue in an effort to stay in control. "No, Cali. Not until you agree."

"To what?" Her words stroked across his cheek in complete innocence.

"If we finish this, you're my sub."

She stilled.

"You will obey only me. No other Dom will touch you without my permission."

Uncertainty flashed in her eyes and he felt her retreating. *Fuck, no.*

"Trust me." He rubbed the tip of his cock along the hot opening of her pussy. She gasped and tipped her head until her forehead pressed against his. Her breath brushed his face in quick, deep gusts. He knew he was pushing her, but he couldn't let her go.

"Trust me," he whispered against her lips. "You belong to me." He tensed, waiting for her answer. Never had one word been so important in his life.

But then, he had never wanted anyone as badly as he wanted her.

FOURTEEN

"Yes."

The simple word slipped from her lips almost without her permission. She whimpered as the logical side of her battled against her need to comply. To give him everything he wanted.

"Look at me and say it again." Jake pulled on her hair, forcing her head back until she could look in his eyes once again. "Tell me now."

His gaze drilled her, the gray depths darkened to a burnt ash and flashing just as hot. Moisture beaded his forehead, creases marring the smooth span, denoting his tension as he waited for her. He was everything she should run from.

He was everything she craved.

It was just sex, right? This was just about sex. He'd said 'here.' As in, the club. She could agree to that. There was no harm in that, right? No one would ever find out.

"Yes, Jake," she finally said. "I'm your sub."

He released a long, guttural groan and shoved into her in one hard plunge. She bowed her back, his thick, rigid cock filling her. She clenched around the intrusion, even as he started to move. He gripped her hips and pushed into her in strong, demanding pumps.

She rode him, clutching his flexing shoulders until her nails bit into the muscles. She stretched her toes, finding leverage from the floor to make each stroke longer, deeper. The sound of skin slapping was at once obscene and intimate and blended with the non-verbal noises they were both making. He pulled her closer, forcing her nipples to rub against his chest. The tender tips screamed in shock with each brush against his shirt, the sharp pricks of pain bringing her to the edge. Sweat streaked down the side of her face, their movements becoming disjointed and frantic in their race to the end.

"Please, Jake," she remembered to ask. "I need to come."

He made a rough, harsh sound that was close to a possessive growl. He thrust again, harder and deeper as he ground his hips into her. He grabbed her hair and watched her. "Come for me, Cali."

The sheer intensity of the moment exploded within her. She cried out, completely gone as the storm crashed around them. He made one last, deep drive that lifted her feet from the ground. Then his arms were around her, his mouth at her neck, and she was lost to everything but the pleasure consuming her.

She came back to her senses in a series of short realizations— she was exhausted, she needed a shower, she was wrapped in Jake's arms. His breath was warm against her neck and he smelled of man and sex. But most prominently, she felt protected and cherished.

Her eyes flew open at that thought. The truth of it shocked her. She had never expected that to be one of the emotions that would come with entering a BDSM club. If anything, she had expected the opposite.

Both times now, she'd felt more cherished and cared for than she had in many years. She blinked rapidly, refusing to give in to the damn tears again. One big cry a night was more than enough.

His fingers combed through her hair and she shivered. Goose bumps formed up her arms and back, despite the inferno of heat simmering inside her.

"Cold?" Jake's voice vibrated against her ear as it tumbled through his chest.

"Not really," she answered. She let her hand run up his chest to rub across the hard plane of his pecs.

He cursed, a low, sharp bite she probably wasn't supposed to hear.

"What?" She tensed and tried to push back to see his face.

He tightened his arms and held her firmly against him. "No bed," he said with a half chuckle.

She relaxed and resumed her exploration of his chest, the relief rushing through her. That was all. For a second she'd feared he'd changed his mind. Or had regrets. Did she?

"Do you have other subs?" she asked, the question shocking her even as she spoke.

His muscles constricted under her fingers, his hands stilling on her back. Nerves once again claimed her as she realized how important his answer was to her. Maybe she didn't have a right to ask the question. She didn't know the protocol, but she knew she didn't want to share.

"No," he finally said. "You are my only sub." But the connection that had felt so tight and intimate moments ago was suddenly gone.

She sat up, peering into his eyes. "What am I missing?"

He stared at her, his lips thinning in contemplation. He palmed the back of her neck in a move that smacked of possessiveness. One she should reject but found she couldn't. "I'll notify my clients that our contracts are terminated."

She pushed back the sense that there was something important she was missing, but she couldn't place what it was.

He pulled her closer until his lips were just a breath away. "This is an exclusive arrangement."

A flush of pure excitement warmed her at the finality in his voice. He belonged to her too. She swallowed, the heat of his lips so temptingly close to hers. "Okay."

His kiss was full of promise and commitment. For her it was acceptance. The sealer on a deal made in the height of passion, but it felt completely right. It was a deal she never would have made at any other time. She knew that to the depths of her repressed soul.

It was the other her who had agreed to his demands. The other her who was aggressively kicking back all of the nagging doubts and recriminations the real her was shoving forward.

He drew back, disengaged himself and lifted her off his lap. The floor was cold beneath her feet, a fact she hadn't noticed before. She wrapped her arms around herself and watched as he grabbed some tissues and used them to remove the condom and clean up.

She chuckled. "More than one reason for the tissues, then?"

He caught her eye and grinned. "Never know when you'll need them."

"Kind of like the condom?"

"Hell, the condom is standard dress code." He stood and pulled up his pants in one motion. He glanced at her, intent and serious as he finished dressing. "You should know that. Safety is mandatory here."

She studied the floor, embarrassed at her misstep. "Of course it is. I never thought otherwise."

He lifted her chin, forcing her to look at him. "I'd like you to come with me."

"I thought I already did." She couldn't resist the come-back, but the smirk left her face when she saw that he wasn't laughing with her. Everything, from his eyes to his voice to his stance, spoke of how serious the statement was to him.

Was this her first test? More importantly, did she trust him enough to follow without question? She'd trusted him with her body, but this was something very different and felt much more significant.

Could she do it? Could she not?

FIFTEEN

Cali took a deep breath and dove in. "Okay."

Something flashed in his eyes, a quick insight into him before he blinked and it was gone. What was it? She wanted more than anything to see it again. To know what it was.

He let her go and crossed to the bathroom. He returned with a black silk robe and held it out to her. It finally dawned on her that she was still naked. Her nudity hadn't even crossed her mind. That's how comfortable she'd become with Jake. Already.

It seemed so fast. But felt so right.

Too right.

She turned and slipped into the offered garment. He reached around and tied the sash for her, his strong hands brushing and caressing her abdomen. He engulfed her with his strength, his arms surrounding her and pulling her within his protection. The feeling soaked into her and warmed her in a completely different way than the sex had.

He kissed her neck then took her hand and led her to the

exit. He stopped to pick up her discarded clothing before he opened the door and reclaimed her hand.

She paused and took one more breath before allowing him to lead her from the room. Her heart raced as she followed him down the hallway, away from the stairway that led to the second floor.

It was on the tip of her tongue to ask where they were going, but she bit back the question. Trust. If she trusted him to tie her down and spank her naked ass, then she could trust him to keep her safe. Easier said than done, but she kept her mouth shut and silenced her doubt.

A part of her acknowledged she was placing too much faith too soon in someone and something she'd only just begun to know. But she'd waited forty-four years to feel this…free. To stop worrying and simply trust that someone else would take care of the details.

It was somewhat counterintuitive that in giving up control, instead of feeling enslaved she'd finally found freedom.

She didn't want to be anal and repressed any longer. Maybe she'd get burned, but at least she could say she jumped. She tried.

She dove in headfirst for once and felt more alive than she had in years.

She smiled at the warmth and contentment that settled in her gut and soothed through her. She would revel in that feeling for now.

What in the hell am I doing? Jake's mind hammered with reiterating words of judgment. He was asking for trouble. No, make that begging to be dropped-kicked and nailed in the nuts for this.

It made no logical sense. But here he was, unlocking the door and leading Cali into his loft.

His private space. A place that had never been graced by a sub.

Fuck.

But he didn't want her to leave. Not yet. Not when she could still run. And although the room downstairs had been perfect for the Scene, it didn't have a bed.

And a bed was where he wanted her.

"Is this your place?"

An innocent question. She was good at those. "Yes."

Her steps faltered, her eyes going wide. "Oh."

At least she seemed to get the importance. Done dwelling on his actions, Jake led her through the open space of the living area to his bedroom. He set her clothes on his dresser and moved to the master bath. He took a towel out of the cabinet and turned to her. "Take a shower. I'll be here when you get out."

She seemed a little startled, the whole deer-in-the-headlights thing. He tried to remember that this was one gigantic new step for her.

He cupped her face and lowered his voice. "You'll feel better after a hot shower. Your muscles will be sore tomorrow and the heat will help." He gave her a light kiss. "Now, go. I'll be here."

A smile curved over her lips before she twisted away and did as he said.

"Put the robe back on when you're done," he told her.

She gave him one last look filled with questions as he left and she shut the door.

He released a quick breath, ran his fingers through his hair then scrambled to get his things done before Cali got out of the shower. Hopefully she'd take a long one.

After a quick shower and change in the guest bath, Jake

grabbed his phone and sent a text to Seth. It wasn't often that Jake wasn't on the club grounds when it was open.

Sometimes it felt like it was the only place he'd been for the last five years.

The air in the loft was cool against his bare chest as he got out some snacks and made a tray of crackers, cheeses and fruit. He paused and surveyed the spread. Damn, when did he get so fucking domestic? That stirring in his chest pushed hard and he had to shove it back.

His phone beeped and he wiped his hands on his cotton lounge pants before checking the text message.

Seth: *WTF? You sick?*

Jake: *No. Busy.*

Seth: *With what?*

Jake: *Not ur biz.*

There was a pause before Seth's final text: *FU. Deets in morning.*

Great. Jake sighed, put down the phone and turned to the fridge.

"Is everything okay?"

Cali's soft-spoken question had him jerking back from the fridge. She stood in the doorway from his bedroom, her hair wet and curling around her freshly scrubbed face. He was pleased to see she'd followed his order and put the robe back on. The black silk clung to her damp skin in a way that made his imagination run wild.

He walked to her. "Everything's fine. How about you? Still okay?" He studied her face, searching for clues.

She nodded, but her lip disappeared between her teeth. He dipped and kissed her, tugging that lip into his mouth before he let her go. She gave him a tentative smile that spoke of the fine line she was balancing on.

He noticed the mark on her shoulder just visible under the

edge of the robe. He pushed the material aside and rubbed his finger over the deep purple bruise already blooming. "It looks good on you," he said, the claiming mark sparking the pride and ownership within him.

She jerked her head to see what he was talking about, but it was too close to her neck for her to see.

He gave her cheek a light caress then went back to kitchen, giving her the space he sensed she needed. Plus, it was important for her to come to him. He glanced back at her. "What would you like to drink? I've got wine, water, soda, iced tea."

She took a step toward the kitchen, swiveling her head to take in the room. The loft was the traditional open floor plan, containing high ceilings and exposed beams. The kitchen was in the far corner, decked out with high-grade appliances and marble countertops that still appeared as new as the day they were installed. Her face remained blank and he had to push back the question of what she thought of his place. Since when did he care?

"Do you have Coke?" Her soft question seemed loud against the emptiness.

"Got it." He grabbed two cans from the half-empty fridge and a couple of glasses from the cupboard. When he turned around, she was standing on the other side of the island, smiling. "What?"

She shrugged. "You surprise me."

He dropped some ice in the glasses, the clink of the cubes echoing around them, and popped open the cans. "Is that all? I take it you're someone who doesn't like surprises."

"No," she said, taking the glass he offered to stare intently at the hissing, disintegrating foam. "I'm just usually prepared enough to avoid surprises."

"Hence, the extensive internet research before coming to the club." Jake watched her as he took a drink of his soda.

She shifted on her feet before grabbing and nibbling on a cracker. "There's nothing wrong with being prepared." The defensiveness in her voice told him she'd battled this topic before.

"I agree. In fact, I'd have been disappointed if you'd come to a BDSM club knowing nothing about what you were walking into."

The rigidity left her shoulders and she relaxed against the counter. He could physically see the relief wash through her as the tension left her body to let the exhaustion show through. The night was catching up with her.

Jake grabbed the tray and his drink. "Come with me."

As he led her to his bedroom, the pad of her bare feet against the wood floors was his only indication that she followed him. He didn't turn around to check; it was assumed she would be right behind him. And it pleased him to know she was.

He set the food tray on the bed and his glass on the bedside table before clicking on the small lamp, the light casting a dim glow through the room. Taking Cali's glass, he set it next to his then arranged the pillows and sat on the bed. She accepted his extended hand and the mattress dipped as she kneeled next to him. He settled them both until she was positioned between his bent legs, her back resting on him as he leaned against the headboard.

Her skin was soft and smooth under his palms as he caressed her arms before gently tipping her head back until it rested on his chest. The wet tips of her hair brushed his skin, leaving a trail of moisture behind. He let his hands roam over her body, light touches meant to soothe and comfort.

She felt so good in his arms, next to him. The urge to keep her there, safe within his protection, roared up to nearly choke him with its sudden ferocity.

"What are you doing?" Cali asked after a moment. Her

muscles were slowly responding to his touch, her body sink-ing into his as she gave in to the safety he offered.

Reaching over, he grabbed a grape off the tray and held it to her lips until she accepted the fruit, her mouth closing around his fingers before he slipped them away.

"Taking care of you." He kept his answer low, the words spoken against her neck. The fresh scent of his soap filled his nostrils and his possessiveness flared. He loved his smell on her, wanted his scent on her. He inhaled again before he forced himself to lean back and give her another grape.

"I can feed myself," she objected.

He pushed the grape against her lips until they opened. "I know, but let me take care of you."

"That's what this is?" He couldn't see her eyes, but her voice was filled with question and doubt.

"What does it feel like to you?" Jake kept his voice neutral, waiting for her once again.

She twisted in his arms until he could see her face. She searched his eyes before reaching out to brush his hair off his forehead. The touch was whisper-light, but he could feel the imprint of her fingers through his entire body.

"It feels exactly like what I've wished for for so long." Her fingers grazed over his cheek to rub across his lips. She tracked the path, her thoughts appearing distracted by the movement. "It's hard not to doubt it when it's not at all what I expected."

"What did you expect?"

"Sex. That was it." She looked at him, fear and wonder shining in her eyes. "I don't know if I'm ready for this."

Neither did he. Jake let his fingers comb through her damp hair, intrigued by the gentle curls forming. She must force the softness out to get it as straight as she normally wore it. "This, what we're doing now, is just as much a part of BDSM play as the whips and paddles."

She curled into him, her head resting on his shoulder, her breast pressing into his chest under the silk robe. "I don't know what to do with this. I wasn't prepared for it."

"Then trust me and let me guide you." He pulled her close, wrapping his arms around her. "That's my job." One he hoped he didn't fuck up.

She remained quiet, no more doubts or questions surfacing from her lips. It wasn't long before he felt her relax and her breathing even out. Her exhaustion finally forced her mind and body to give in to the sleep it needed.

And he held her, inhaling the smell of his soap on her skin, absorbing the weight of her in his arms, reveling in the light strokes of her breath over his skin. The rightness of it surrounded him until his heart started to race in a sprint against the panic threatening to ruin the peace.

What am I doing? He reached over to click off the light, plunging the room into darkness. But the blackness did nothing to quiet his mind. He let his head thump back as it sagged under the weight of his thoughts. He shouldn't be doing this. He was leaving in just over two months. He had calls out to clubs along the southern coast, places that would take him far from here. He couldn't get close, couldn't risk the pain.

He was lying to himself just as much as he was lying to Cali. Because this—Cali in his arms, in his bed—was so much more than the standard Dom/sub connection made at the club. It was what most sought, but few discovered by simply coming to the club. It certainly wasn't what he'd been searching for or found in his five years of being there.

Yet here she was. Here he was.

And fuck, but she felt so right. Here.

His sub.

Cali Reynolds belonged to him.

And what exactly did that mean?

SIXTEEN

The warmth encased her. It was the first thing Cali noticed as her mind fluttered awake. She curled and arched into the hard body giving off all of the heat before she froze.

Where am I?

Her eyes flew open, her muscles stiffened, her mind immediately engaged.

"Hey." A deep voice rumbled behind her. "You're all right. Go back to sleep."

Jake.

Oh. My. God. She was in Jake's bed. Naked.

His lips brushed her shoulder, the soft kiss sending a shiver down her spine. His arm constricted against her stomach and pulled her tighter along his length. He felt so good. It felt so good to be in his embrace. To wake with his arms around her. To have him touch her.

Just hold her. Like last night.

She must have drifted to sleep in his arms. She hadn't intended on staying. Did he even want her to?

She should go.

She lifted her head, craning for a clock. The room was still dark, no light leaked in from the large windows in the room. He must have blackout curtains, considering the late hours he worked. From the doorway, she could see daylight playing in the other room, so it had to be past seven.

Like the rest of his loft, his bedroom was neat and sparse. The furniture was all clean lines and dark woods that fit the space but remained unobtrusive. The silk of the sheets caressed her skin and she noted he didn't spare on the luxuries. What he did own appeared to be well-crafted and expensive.

Unable to spot a clock without disturbing Jake, who'd apparently gone back to sleep, Cali settled into his arms and gave herself a moment to enjoy the feeling. She never imagined *this*—the almost overwhelming intimacy and closeness she felt so quickly with Jake—when she'd agonized about joining the BDSM club. Yes, she'd read about the trust and bond that existed between a Dom and sub, but this was so much more.

So much more.

And she'd agreed to be *his* sub. She still didn't really understand what that meant, but just the thought of it warmed her. If last night, if this right now was any indication of what being his sub would be like, then she'd gladly take the risk.

The faint jingling of a phone from the other room roused her out of her thoughts. Cocking her head, she listened again and her heart sunk to her stomach. *What time is it?*

Pushing away Jake's arm, Cali rolled out of bed and grimaced when she sat up. Her tender bottom reminded her of what she'd done last night, of what she'd allowed Jake to do to her. Ignoring the ache, she stumbled into the other room. The ringing continued and, as she feared, it was coming from her purse, which lay on the kitchen island.

Damn. She was supposed to meet Stephanie to go shopping. She sprinted across the open space and grabbed her purse, frantically digging for her phone. The ringing stopped as her hand closed around it. *Shit.* She snapped her head up and found the clock on the microwave, the green lights mocking her with their evil numbers. Ten o'clock.

No way. She never slept late. Never.

She jumped when her phone rang again, her fingers clenching around the now sinister object as the caller ID flashed on the screen. Stephanie.

Taking a fortifying breath, she answered in her most casual voice. "Hey, Steph."

"*Mom*," her daughter exclaimed, the volume forcing Cali to jerk the phone away from her ear. "Where are you? Are you okay?"

"I'm fine, dear. I just got—" What did she get? "Hung up. I'll be home in an hour, tops. Then we can head out."

"Where are you?" Cali grimaced against the accusation forming in Stephanie's voice. "I started to panic when I got here and you were gone, and then you weren't answering your phone. You don't do things like that."

Cali hugged her arm around her churning stomach, the chilly air directly conflicting with the flush burning inside her. "Sorry. I lost track of time." She fumbled for an excuse. "I had to run over to a client, who called in a panic over some misplaced invoices. Why don't you get a coffee, and I'll be home and ready to go in an hour? Promise." She put out a desperate prayer the diversion worked. Feeble as it was.

"You should've left a note."

Cali winced, the guilt layering over the one already clinging to her. "I'm sorry for worrying you. Go get a coffee and I'll be home soon."

The silence drew out over the line. Cali dreaded the connection her daughter was probably making. She literally sagged with relief when her daughter didn't push it further.

"Okay. Do you want your usual?"

Usual? Oh, coffee. "Yes, that'd be great. Thanks, hon."

Cali ended the connection, tossed her phone back into her purse and dropped her head into her palms. *Could she really do this?* The real her was standing in the light of day, naked in a man's kitchen, doubting she could.

Was this really worth the risk?

Warm arms snaked around her waist from behind, making her jump, the sudden presence of Jake startling her. He nuzzled the juncture of her neck, his breath hot on her skin as he pulled her against him.

"That Stephanie?"

"Yes." She closed her eyes, sinking into the comfort he offered. She couldn't resist a few more seconds of his warmth before the turmoil returned.

"Everything okay?"

"I have to go." She inhaled and forced herself to step out of his arms, the cold air surrounding her to reinforce her nakedness. Only Jake didn't let her run. He drew her back into his arms, his heat banishing the cold instantly. Cali had to force the next words out before she simply gave in and stayed there. "Really, Jake. I was supposed to meet Stephanie at ten. I need to get home. She's waiting for me."

Part of her reluctance to leave was the pure chicken part of her that didn't want to deal with the potential confrontation ahead.

"Then go." He dropped one last kiss on her shoulder and stepped back. Although his words were short, his voice held understanding. "I'll start the coffee."

She took the offered escape and hurried back to the bedroom for her dress. Since when did she walk around homes naked? She'd never, ever felt comfortable doing that around her own home with her ex-husband. Not in twenty-two years of marriage. Hell, she didn't even remember the last time Peter had seen her naked.

Yet she'd never once felt self-conscious in front of Jake, even though he'd remembered to throw on some pants before he'd left the bedroom.

It was just one more thing that made her stomach twist. She wanted this thing, whatever it was, with Jake. In truth, she needed it. For herself.

Regardless of what rest of the world might think of her. She needed to be Jake's sub.

If only to heal the chilling ache that filled her heart.

The aroma of freshly brewed coffee filled the space, the last spurt and gurgle of water hissing from the machine as Jake watched Cali step out of the bedroom. Her dress was slightly wrinkled and the damp ends on her finger-combed hair did little to remove the bed-rumpled look.

She sent Jake a crooked smile, her heels clicking on the wood as she walked over to him. "So is this the walk of shame?"

He straightened immediately from his lounge against the counter and met her halfway. "Absolutely not." He framed her face with his hands. "No shame. Ever, Cali. Do you understand? If shame is ever a part of this, then it's wrong." He leaned in and kissed her, the hint of mint letting him know she'd found the toothbrush he'd left out for her. "And this isn't wrong."

A smile formed on her lips. "Okay." Her hand covered one of his, pressing it into her cheek. "No shame." She stepped away and moved to the kitchen island. "Thanks for getting my purse and jacket. I'd forgotten about them." Jake had called down after Cali was sleeping and had her things brought up from the coat check.

"Do you want some coffee?" He already guessed her answer.

"No, thank you." She ducked her head, tucking her hair behind her ear. "I need to get home."

He held up her coat for her, letting his hands linger on her shoulders. "I'll walk you out," he said, gesturing to the door.

"You don't have to—"

"I do," he interrupted, taking her arm and guiding her toward the door. "Stop arguing."

She halted him as he reached to twist the lock. Her eyes were on the ground, her purse clutched in her hands. "What happens now?"

He smiled and tilted her chin up. An act that was becoming almost natural between them. One day, she would not be afraid to meet his gaze. "I'll see you tonight."

Her eyes widened as she inhaled. "I don't think I can."

"Do you have plans?"

"No." She stared over his shoulder. "I just don't think…"

"Look at me, Cali."

Her attention snapped back to him.

"You will come back here tonight. I expect to see you by ten." He couldn't let her run. The longer she stayed away, the more doubts would crop in until she talked herself out of coming back. That couldn't happen.

She licked her lips, the indecision clear in her eyes. "Okay," she finally whispered.

"I'll send you a package this afternoon. You will wear the outfit inside."

Her eyebrows shot up, the questions appearing across her face.

His Dom voice came on in full force as he explained. "You're my sub. Everything you do reflects on me. Your behavior, your appearance, your attitude are all a direct statement of me."

"I'm not your slave," she bit out, the fire in her eyes turning them bright green.

"No, you're not. But as my sub you will act as such while you're at The Den. If you can't agree, then this won't work between us."

Jake's heart pounded as he realized what he'd done. He'd given her an out. Maybe he wanted her to take it. Make it easier for him by forcing her to run.

"I've got to go. I can't process this right now." She spun away and he opened the door. Things weren't settled, but she hadn't said no. He'd give her time because pushing her right then would only force her into a decision or action they might both regret. Her shoulders were drawn back, her body stiff as he inserted his key in the elevator and hit the button for the ground floor.

When the doors opened into the private parking garage, Cali looked around in confusion. "Where are we?" She stilled. "How'd my car get here?"

He put his hand on her back and guided her out of the elevator. "I had it moved when I called for your purse and coat. It's safer down here."

She took a moment to absorb the information before she turned to him. "Thank you. That was kind." Her words were polite, but the firm tilt of her tone indicated she wasn't exactly pleased by his actions.

"What's wrong?" He stopped her when she tried to move away. "I won't let you leave here upset."

"Let me leave?" She closed her eyes and inhaled. She held her breath for a second before reopening her eyes. "I'm not used to this. I've been in control of my own life for, well, ever. Having you suddenly take over is not what I'm looking for. In the bedroom, yes. You can control what happens there. But the rest of my life is not open for you to run."

"I don't want to run your life. But I will see to your safety." He pulled her against his length. "Retrieving your purse and moving your car was for your security. Defining what you wear tonight is for your excitement, as well as your safety at the club. You are my *first* sub. Ever. Not everyone will take that with grace."

"What do you mean, your first sub? I assumed you've taken lots."

"Clients, yes. My own submissive, no." He lowered his voice. "You are the first."

"Oh." There it was again. That little sound that communicated so much more than the word itself. Her body softened as the fight left her.

He took that moment to reinforce his place in her life. He claimed her mouth in a fierce, almost violent kiss of possession. His body raged with the need to keep her close while his mind fought against what he was doing.

She opened to him, inviting him in without resistance. Her fight gone, she submitted to him stunningly. Taking everything he had without complaint.

God, she was beautiful.

He drew back, his lungs aching for air. She took gulping gasps of her own as her eyes searched his face. Without further words, he shifted and escorted her to her car. Her hands shook as she took out the keys and clicked the remote to disengage the locks.

He opened her door. "Expect my package, Cali."

She nodded and got in.

He stood in the chill of the empty garage long after the purr of her engine faded in the distance. His hands fisted at his sides, his bare toes turning to ice on the frozen concrete. That invisible itch flared into a full-on rash. Only, it wasn't urging him to run.

No. It was urging him to chase her. To keep her and not let her go.

Something he doubted he could do.

SEVENTEEN

Cali shut the garage door and hurried into her condo. The relief at not seeing Stephanie's car in the driveway was too great for words. She rushed into the kitchen, tossing her purse on the counter, and practically sprinted for the stairs to hit her bedroom.

She could do this.

"Hi, Mom."

Her sense of victory deflated at those two simple words. She stalled midstep on the stairs and cursed silently before schooling her features and facing her daughter. "Stephanie," she said pleasantly, as if she wasn't standing there, clearly wearing a rumpled dress from the night before. "I didn't see you in there. Where's your car?"

Her daughter's knowing gaze moved over Cali, shifting from her bed-messed hair, over her come-hither black dress, to the tips of her strappy stilettos in an obvious assessment of her attire. Stephanie's seat in the far corner of the family room provided her with a clear view of the entire downstairs.

This had been a deliberate stakeout. A calculated ambush that prickled against Cali's right to privacy.

"Where've you been?" The flat, scathing tone of Stephanie's voice left no doubt her daughter knew she wasn't returning from a morning meeting.

Cali straightened then calmly took the three steps down to stand at the bottom of the stairs. She kept her hand on the banister to stay grounded. The few seconds allowed her to gather her thoughts and regain her stability. "I can tell you obviously have that figured out and have formed a judgment. Even if it's not your business."

"Not my business?" Stephanie sprang from her seat, the defensively tucked arms splaying wide in an arc of frustration. "You're my mother. How can it not be my business?"

"Would you feel the same if I was waiting with accusations in your dorm room after you returned home from a night out?"

Her daughter stiffened, indignation flaring. "That's not the same."

Cali stepped forward, keeping her arms loose at her side instead of crossed tightly over her chest to mirror her daughter's posture. "How? I understand you care about me. But what I do in my own life is my business. Just like yours is."

Stephanie squeezed her eyes shut, her fists tightening in time with the pinched muscles on her face. "But you're my mother," she finally said, as if that explained everything.

"Yes. I'm your mother." Cali took another step forward, bringing her closer. "But I am also a woman with my own life."

Her daughter exhaled a tight breath. "I guess I'm not taking that very well."

Cali quelled her instant urge to apologize. "I understand it's an adjustment for you."

"Talk about an understatement," Stephanie scoffed, arms curling into a tight hold around her waist. She spun around and paced to stare out the window into the back courtyard. After a tense silence, she spoke again. "Can I ask who you were with? Is it someone I know?"

And how could Cali answer that question? A question she'd never anticipated. She cleared her throat. "No. You don't know him."

"Where'd you meet him?"

"Steph." Cali licked her lips, suddenly glad her daughter was looking away. "I'm not going to do twenty questions with you. I'm sorry I was late this morning. I never intended for this part of my life to impact you."

Her daughter gave a light snort, a clear sound of ridicule. "Yeah. Obviously." She turned away from the window to eye Cali. "Can I at least ask his name?"

Crap. She was damned if she did and damned if she didn't on that one. Not answering would only increase Steph's suspicions and distrust, while answering it could allow her to connect the dots. And her daughter wasn't dumb. She'd connect the dots.

"Jake," Cali finally answered. "Jake McCallister." A tidbit she'd only learned thanks to Edith. Did it say something about her relationship with him that she only knew his last name because someone else had told her? Yeah, it probably did.

"Jake?" Stephanie cocked her head, her hands propping on her hips as she followed the path Cali knew she would. "As in, the Jake Edith introduced us to in the courtyard? The man who was eating you up with his eyes? *That* Jake?"

Cali willed the blush to remain off her face, but she wasn't sure it worked. "Yes. That Jake."

"*Mom*."

"What? He's a nice man. I have a right to go out with nice

men." Yeah, go out. That's what they did. The duplicity was hard to pull off and she could only hope her daughter was too distracted with her own anxieties to pick up on Cali's.

Stephanie covered her eyes with her hands and took a deep breath, the ends of her ponytail falling forward to drape down her shoulder. Cali's motherly urge was to take her daughter in her arms and give her the comfort she so obviously needed. But she probably wouldn't welcome that right now. Not when Cali was the cause of Stephanie's distress.

"I still don't understand why you and Dad split." The barely spoken words were said behind the cover of her hands and Cali had to strain to hear them. "You two never fought. You talked, laughed, were friends." Stephanie dropped her hands and looked up, unshed tears making her blue eyes shimmer. "I still don't get it."

There was no way Cali could answer that with complete honesty. That had been the crux of the problem through the entire divorce. Her children were old enough to sense there was more to the problem than 'they'd just grown apart.' But there was no way she could articulate what really drove her to leave their dad.

And Peter had made sure everyone knew it was Cali who'd instigated the divorce.

"It happened. I can't explain it more than I already have."

Stephanie sniffed and made a couple of hasty swipes at her tears before they rolled down her cheeks. She stuffed her hands into the pocket of her hoodie, the action making her appear young and vulnerable. She hunched her shoulders and moved around Cali toward the front door. "I need to go."

"What about shopping? Isn't the formal in a few weeks?" They'd planned to look for a dress for Stephanie's sorority's formal.

"I'll take care of it," Steph said around another sniff. "I just can't do it today. Sorry." The last bit was mumbled as she hastened toward the exit.

"Stephanie." Cali waited for her daughter to still. Steph's hand perched on the doorknob. "My dating isn't about hurting you. I love you—" Cali stopped to swallow back the tears bulging in her throat. "I would never do anything to intentionally hurt you or Logan. You know that, right?"

A long silence hung between them filled with all the pain, anger and unanswered questions that had fractured their relationship since the divorce. Cali bit her lips, blinked back tears and fisted her hands to keep from reaching for her daughter. She couldn't handle the rejection she knew the touch would receive.

"I know." Stephanie opened the door, keeping her back to Cali. "I love you too." Then the door clicked shut, cutting off the words and her daughter.

Cali moved stiffly to the bottom of the steps before she sank down, her legs giving out as the strength drained from her. The fact that the conversation had been inevitable didn't ease the guilt or pain balled in her chest. The ache still came, and Cali's conscience still kicked at her for causing her daughter's distress. What kind of a mother hurt her own child? It didn't matter that it wasn't deliberate. She was supposed to protect and shield her daughter from pain.

Not cause it.

But short of remaining a hermit for the rest of her life, there was nothing more she could do. Stephanie would have to learn to deal with the fact her mother dated. More than that, her mother had a life outside of being just a mom.

She gave a short puff of derision as she removed her heels and pushed to her feet. Yeah, a life. Part of which she found disgraceful enough to keep hidden from everyone she knew.

What did that say about her?

The answer was one she wasn't willing to dig into. For the first time in years she felt physically and emotionally connected to someone. Someone who connected with her. And that bond, no matter how perverted or depraved it may appear to others, was strong enough to keep her tethered.

With everything she'd given up since the divorce, this was one thing she couldn't force herself to let go. Jake was hers. Being his sub was about her. For her.

Some may see it as selfish, but as long as no one found out, it would be her guilty pleasure. One she would continue to indulge in.

No matter how much it threatened to hurt her, she knew she would return to The Den that night. To Jake.

EIGHTEEN

Her newest weekly package from Jake arrived at four, right in the middle of a quiet afternoon girl chat with her neighbors, Allie and Kendra. Cali quickly tossed the box into her office and dismissed it as work-related to her suspicious friends.

"Work?" Allie questioned, doubt heavy in her voice. "Must be pretty important to pay for a Saturday delivery."

"More coffee?" Cali lifted the carafe and motioned toward the two women, who both declined. She topped off her own cup, even though the brew now tasted bitter on her tongue. Putting on her most charming smile, she shifted her attention to Kendra. "So how's the new job going? Have you settled in yet?"

Cali prayed Allie would go with the change of topic. Cali couldn't discuss what was really in the package. Over the last month since she'd agreed to be Jake's sub, his special deliveries had become anticipated. A gift of some sort she was expected to wear that evening when she saw him. She now had several new outfits appropriate only for the club, a set of nipple clamps, a bullet vibrator that he owned the remote to, a pair of thigh-high spike-heeled boots and an array of sexy underwear.

It was at the point that she'd had to dedicate a special section of her closet just for his gifts. A back corner hidden behind her normal clothes, that is.

"Cali." Kendra's voice interrupted her thoughts. "Are you even listening to me?"

"I'm sorry." Guilt flushed her face. "I got lost in my own thoughts about work. That was rude of me. You were saying?"

Kendra eyed her, doubt clearly etched on her face. "Never mind. The new job is fine." She gave a dismissive wave with her hand and jumped to another topic. "How's Stephanie doing at school? I haven't seen her around lately."

"Yeah," Allie piped in. "Not since Paul and Lacey's engagement party. I guess school is keeping her busy, huh?"

Cali took a drink of her coffee and worked to keep the flinch of pain from showing on her face. "She's fine. Just busy at school. Getting home to see Mom is not on the top of her priorities. You remember how it was in college."

Allie laughed, a slightly sarcastic sound to it. "God. Once I hit college, I never went home unless a holiday forced me to."

If that was the only reason for Stephanie's avoidance, Cali would be fine. In truth, her daughter had barely spoken to her since the morning she'd caught her coming home from Jake's. She'd received a few text and email messages, just enough so she knew Steph was okay, but no phone calls or visits.

It was the silent treatment as a form of punishment. One Cali was taking because of the guilt that clung to her. She could only wait until her daughter came around in her own time.

Kendra glanced at her watch and stood. "I gotta get going."

"Date tonight?" Allie prodded, a speculative arch to her brow.

"No," Kendra dismissed a little too quickly. "Just need to get home." She pushed her chair in and made her way to the sliding glass door. "You guys have a good week. Same time next Saturday?"

"Sure," Cali answered. The three women had started their little afternoon chats a few months back in a completely unofficial way that had now become somewhat of a routine they all anticipated. Or at least Cali did.

Kendra gave a small wave and exited, leaving a slightly awkward silence in her wake.

"So what do you think is up with her?" Allie asked as she watched the other woman stroll across the courtyard to her condo across the way. "She's always so secretive about her life."

"I don't know." Cali gave a shrug. Secrets were not something she wanted to dig into. Not when she had so many of her own. "Maybe she's still settling into the area. It's not easy moving to a new city alone."

Allie sat back, her brow furrowed in contemplation. At that moment, Cali could see her friend's analytical lawyer mind ticking away behind her deceptively attractive face. "It just seems strange, like there's something she's afraid of."

"Aren't we all afraid of something?" The question slipped out before Cali could think to hold it back.

Allie gave her a sharp look. "Yeah, I guess so."

Cali stood and started picking up the empty coffee cups and dessert plates, the soft clinking of china echoing in the quiet room. She tucked a loose piece of hair behind her ear and made the quick trip to the kitchen sink, her hands full of dirty dishes.

"So, what are you afraid of, Cali?"

The question startled her. The dishes clattered into the porcelain sink. Cali tried to pull off a light laugh. "Spiders. You?" She turned to look at Allie, who'd followed her into the open kitchen to lean against the small island separating the kitchen from the breakfast area.

Allie assessed her, one full glance from head to toe before she gave a light snort. "Mice. Can't stand the furry little shits." She pushed away from the counter and moved toward the sliding door. "Call me if you ever want to talk about what really scares you."

With that dangling statement, Allie slipped out the door and disappeared into the early darkness of late fall.

Cali exhaled the breath she hadn't realized she'd been holding and leaned against the sink. Was she that transparent? She couldn't be, or else she'd never have kept her secrets for so long. Allie was just too damn perceptive.

But then, the exposure of her secrets had never scared her like they did now. It was one thing for people to find out her husband didn't want to have sex with her. It was a completely different thing for the same people to find out she was a submissive to the owner of a renowned sex club.

Yeah, it was the exposure of that little secret that scared the shit out of her.

"See anything that interests you?"

Jake ignored the question and studied the crowded dance floor, his eyes glancing but not holding on the sea of undulating bodies. He resisted the urge to check the time.

"No," he finally replied to Seth, who'd stepped up next to him on the small private balcony that looked down on the main floor. The music thumped and boomed in the expected rhythm of enticement.

"She coming tonight?"

"Who?"

Seth gave a snort. "Your sub. Or did you think that was still a secret?"

Jake clenched his fists before giving his full attention to Seth. "What makes you think I have a sub?"

Seth looked him over, his observant eyes searching. Jake held still, refusing to flinch. "Couldn't be the tempting Ms. Reynolds you've been rushing into private rooms for the last month. Or the fact that you've reassigned all of your clients. Or how about the strange car that's been in our private garage in the mornings?"

Yeah, how about that. Jake looked away, unable to hold his friend's penetrating gaze. Why was he keeping Cali a secret?

Seth turned to stare down at the crowd. Jake watched the man's profile, doing his own search for clues. Seth was the classic middle child, if the three men had been brothers. The one who tried to smooth things over and hold everything together. So what did that make Jake? The rebellious, irresponsible younger brother? Well, fuck.

Things had been stilted between the three men since his little departure declaration. "I've reassigned clients as part of my transition. You know that."

"Right. You going to reassign her too?"

"No."

The slight arching of a brow was Seth's only response before he looked back at the crowd. The tension vibrated between them, another beat that blended with the music in unspoken words and questions.

"I see Ms. Reynolds has arrived," Seth said low enough that Jake almost missed it.

He snapped his head around to stare at the entrance. There she stood, dressed in the outfit he'd sent over that afternoon, the one he'd chosen specifically to entice her. It worked on him as well.

His phone vibrated with the expected texted message.

Standing instructions had been left with the doorman on what to do whenever Cali arrived.

Seth chuckled and shook his head. "Does she know you're leaving?"

Jake tensed. "Why would she care?" He winced. That sounded cold even to his ears.

Seth leaned in, his eyes narrowing in contempt. "Because she deserves better than to be led into this life and then abandoned by you. You should remember how that feels."

"Fuck you," Jake gritted out, his hands fisting at his sides. "It's none of your business."

"It is if I'm the one who's left cleaning up after you." Seth gave him a scathing once-over before he stomped down the stairs and slammed out the door at the bottom.

Damn it. He didn't need this. Jake raked his fingers through his hair and cursed again. The anticipation and pleasure at seeing Cali was now diluted under the murky layers of anger and guilt.

Seth had no right to bring up his past. They didn't do that to each other. The three argued all the time, but there was an unwritten rule that the fucked-up and shitty pasts that had brought them together were never used against each other. Deklan had nailed him a month ago and now Seth was shooting low too. It pissed him off.

And they wondered why he was leaving.

His past had nothing to do with Cali. For that matter, his future was nobody's business but his. He didn't need Seth's scorn or righteous indignation. Hell, he didn't need any of this. He'd call back that club in Savannah and accept the job offer tomorrow. It was as good a place as any to disappear to.

Jake paced away from the rail, cursed and spun back. *Fuck.* He leaned against the metal barrier pressing his palms down hard enough to leave marks in his skin.

Then what *was* he doing with her? The thought of letting her go, of letting another Dom touch her, spiked his anger in a completely irrational way.

She belonged to him.

Yeah. He shook his head. Not if he was leaving—Seth was right on that.

So he'd prove them all wrong. Tonight would be the perfect time to change those assumptions. To prove to everyone that she could be his sub without the feral possessive crap that was clawing at him.

He pushed away from the rail, a plan in place. Tonight he'd begin the process of moving Cali to another Dom.

Even if it killed him.

NINETEEN

The bouncer's eyes flashed with appreciation as he helped Cali remove her trench coat. The outer garment was required for concealment as much as warmth. It still surprised her how much that simple acknowledgement of interest from other men stoked her arousal. It was the secret security and knowledge that she had nothing to fear from their interest that freed her to feel.

Because she belonged to Jake.

She rubbed her hand over her bare neck. Even without a collar, no one else would touch her here without Jake's permission. That thought alone made her feel protected and powerful.

She didn't even know if she wanted to wear his collar. She'd seen them on other submissives in the club and had never thought she'd be into that level of claiming. A visual tag of ownership that could be viewed as both empowering and demeaning, depending on who was looking.

Cali smoothed a moist palm down the seam of the strapless bustier, the leather soft and supple against her skin. The restrictive garment kept her from taking the deep breath she desperately needed, but the constriction reminded her of why she was wearing the outfit. Because Jake wanted her to.

She'd been led to an office this time and her attention strayed once again to the wall of screens that revealed every area of the club. Every area. The amount of visual information displayed so openly had at first shocked then stimulated her. The variety of Scenes and images shown blew her still vanilla mind. Gags and whips, bondage and blindfolds, couples, trios, hetero, homo—you name it, it was presented before her in full-colored detail. The breadth and scope of activity was what truly shocked her. She'd had no idea the extent of the club's offerings.

Did Jake participate in all of it?

Would he make her some day?

The thought was both frightening and tantalizing.

The sudden intrusion of the booming club music had her whipping away from the cameras, the guilt at being caught watching flushing her cheeks. Jake stopped in the doorway, his slow, admiring visual caress over her body heating her until she thought she'd melt.

"You look stunning." His voice washed over her with his gaze. She'd followed the instructions he'd included in his package, down to the last detail. It soothed her to know she'd pleased him.

"Thank you." She clasped her hands before her to keep from fidgeting with the hem of the impossibly short leather skirt. The urge to tug it down was almost irresistible.

He stepped into the room, the loud beat of music abruptly cutting off when he shut the door. His boots thumped as he moved in front of her. He wore black, as always, only tonight he had on a silk button-down shirt that made him appear dressed up.

He ran a finger over her throat, the light stroke sending

tingles of anticipation through her. She'd twisted her hair up tonight, as he'd instructed, leaving her neck exposed. His eyes followed the back and forth movement of his finger as it caressed her skin. He appeared contemplative, like he was uncertain about something. It was a look she'd never seen on him before.

"Are you okay?"

His focus shot back to her. "Why do you ask?"

"You seem, I don't know," she said, a little hesitant. "Worried." She reached up and rubbed her thumb over the creases etched into his forehead.

He jerked away from her touch, leaving her hand hanging awkwardly in the air. "I'm fine," he said, the sharp bite of his words a verbal slap at her concern. "Let's go." He grabbed her dangling hand and pulled her behind him out the door.

Surprised, she stumbled after him down the long hallway, trying to walk as quickly as possible, given the height of her heels and short skirt. What was up with him? He'd never treated her like this. Abruptly she stopped and yanked on his hand.

He spun, anger flashing in his eyes before he had her pinned against the wall, her wrists held tightly over her head. Her heart rate spiked, an instant flash of fear coursing through her.

"Do you question me, Cali?"

Yes. Right now she did. But she trusted him. Whatever was wrong, she trusted him not to harm her. "No," she finally answered, her gaze stubbornly anchored to his collarbone.

He inhaled and she watched his pulse pound short, sharp beats on his throat. "Good." He let her hands drop but kept them bound tightly in one of his. "You owe me for that act of insubordination. Now, let's go."

She followed him, head down, as he led her through the crowd of people filling the main floor. Was this a new test?

To see if she'd question his authority in front of others? She wasn't sure, but she knew enough not to do that. Her only concern now was to keep from angering him further. To ease the ball of angst settling in her gut. A sensation she hadn't felt since she'd agreed to be his sub.

"Good evening, Master Jake," someone called out as they passed by.

"Master Jake," another voice purred.

"Sir, sir," yet another voice begged. "Are you taking clients again?"

Jake ignored them all.

He finally stopped when they'd reached the second floor. His gaze traveled the length of the open room until it settled on an open piece of equipment. A slow, almost devious smile crept over his lips. Nervous fear rolled in her as he moved into the Dungeon, the open space made available for public displays of Dominance and submission. The room she'd only seen once.

Did he really mean to do a Scene here?

She stumbled, her heels catching against each other as she tried to process Jake's intentions. Up 'til now, they'd only done private Scenes. She didn't think she could do one in front of others.

Where anyone could see her.

Suddenly she was in his arms. Jake's warmth surrounded her. Protecting her.

"You can do this," he reassured her. His breath caressed her ear. "I want you to do this."

Her eyes were clenched tight as she willed her heartbeat to slow. The cries and moans filling the room blended with the thumps, smacks and hisses of equipment and the heady scent of arousal and sweat until it all roared in her head.

"Trust me," Jake breathed, stroking her back in gentle, soothing motions. "You need this. Trust me."

Again. Those two words. *Trust me.*

One breath. Two breaths. Slow, calming breaths. Not that she was even close to calm. But they helped.

He stepped back enough to lift her chin up so she could see him. "Same rules apply as always. Use your safe word and we stop now."

That knowledge alone finally seemed to quiet her nerves. She could stop this whenever she wanted.

"Okay," she said, his silver-gray eyes holding her steady. "Green."

The flash of approval was all she needed to follow through. The Scene prep proceeded quickly from there. Maybe it was the fog clouding her mind from the fear she'd banked back or the fact that it all felt surreal, like it was happening to someone else. But in what seemed like seconds, Cali found herself strapped, spread-eagle, to a St. Andrew's Cross on full display to everyone in the room.

"Eyes open," Jake ordered. "Focus on me, Cali."

She obeyed. "Yes, Jake."

He stood before her, toying with the front zipper of her bustier. The warmth of his attention contrasted with the cool, hard surface of the metal at her back and the stiff, scratchy leather cuffs on her wrists and ankles.

Her breaths were short and constricted within the confines of the garment. The slow rasp of the zipper precluded the cool flush of air that met her skin. Jake watched her reaction as her breasts were exposed to everyone. One gulping breath of air filled her lungs as the restriction was removed. Her muscles tightened, pulling on the chains binding her wrists until they clanged menacingly against their brackets.

"Beautiful," Jake said, the reverence clear in his low voice.

His fingers flicked over the nipple clamps she'd been wearing under the bustier. He took a second to tighten the screws on each clamp until the nubs were aching, the air only enticing them more. "You follow directions perfectly."

He gave a tug on the connecting chain, shooting twin bolts of pain from her nipples in a direct line of fire to her pussy.

"Safe words, Cali."

"Red, stop. Yellow, slow down. Green, go," she panted.

"And where are we now?"

"Green."

"Excellent."

Jake had removed her skirt before he bound her ankles, so only her skimpy, boy-short panties, which hid nothing behind the black lace, remained. Despite her exposure, she was amazed to realize she was still okay with everything. The location didn't change how her mind and body reacted to being bound. She was excited and turned on beyond her imagination. She was in his hands.

He would take care of her.

And with that knowledge, she let go.

"I'm using a flogger tonight. The marks will show red and bright against your pale skin. You'll look at them tomorrow and know I gave them to you." He rubbed the ends of the object in discussion up her leg in a teasing taunt that immediately had her wanting more. The anticipation made her pussy wet, while her mind relaxed, settling into the quiet space of acceptance. "You're going to beg me to let you come. But you won't until I tell you. You won't question me or resist me." He leaned in and spoke directly into her ear. "Make me proud, Cali. Show everyone what a good sub you are."

The biting sting of the flogger flicked over the tender flesh of her thighs, making her cringe. He'd used a flogger on her before, so the sensation wasn't new. But this one was sharper, the sting more intense than the flogger he'd used previously.

He stepped back and she blanked her mind, letting the feeling absorb her. It was easier to do than she'd thought. Sinking into the pain, letting go, was something she'd come to need.

"Why'd you come here?" The question yanked her from her zone, pulled her back to the moment. "Answer me." The command was followed with a snap of the flogger tails over her breasts.

She sucked in a breath, clenching tighter around her chains. He'd asked her a question. One she was supposed to answer.

"To find a Dom," she puffed out.

"But why?" Again, the bite across her breast, the tails clipping her sore nipples. "Why did you want a Dom?"

Why was he asking her this? "Because I wanted to be dominated?"

"Wrong." The angry retort was emphasized with an intense strike across her stomach. Her gut instinctively sucked in to get away from the attack, but it was already too late. "I want the real reason."

She tried to meet his eyes to see what he wanted from her, but he wouldn't look at her. His focus was completely on her body, on the pink strips patterned over her flesh. What did he want? Another strike, the pain intensified and cloaked through her mind, making it even harder to think.

"I don't know," she whimpered, her voice confused and weak. Her gaze flew around the room, as if she'd find the answer somewhere out there. But all she saw was a collection of intent faces all focused on her. On the Scene she was a part of. *Oh, God.* She felt the panic start to rise, the fear of being exposed clawing through her. What was she doing here?

Then Jake was there, blocking her view, meeting her eyes. "Focus on me." His intensity seared into her, restoring her calm. "You know the answer." He gave her one brief kiss, his warm lips brushing against hers in a touch of confirmation before he stepped back and sent another lashing over her stomach. "Answer."

Answer. The stinging pain buzzed through her senses, her nerves on fire from the flaying of the flogger. Answer. Why did she come there? "To be touched."

That was true. It rang true in her garbled mind.

"Good." The hiss of the leather straps gave a brief warning before they connected with her midriff. "Why did you want to be touched?"

She bit her lip—against the truth or the pain? She wasn't sure. Why was he doing this? Jake knew the answer. She'd told him the first night.

"Cali." The command bolted through her name.

She let her head fall forward, whether from shame or the simple inability to hold it up, she didn't know. "Because he wouldn't touch me," she whispered.

"Who's he?"

Who's *he*? Fuck him. He knew who *he* was. Jake knew all of this.

Swish, snap—another bite across one, then the other thigh. The endorphins were flooding her system now, merging with the pain to bring the wonderful floating sensation. She just wanted to float, not answer questions.

Suddenly her chin was yanked up, her eyes flying open with the action. Jake stared back at her, his eyes dark and narrowed with anger. "You're disobeying me." His words were spoken through a clenched jaw, his brow furrowed in a mix of disappoint and disgust.

Tears prickled in her eyes. The realization that she was the cause of those feelings stung worse than the bite of the flogger. "Sorry, sir," she whispered.

"Jake," he snapped, his grip tightening on her chin.

"Jake," she pleaded. "Sorry. Please."

His fingers loosened slightly. "Who's in control here?"

"You."

"Who do you answer to?"

"You."

"Then answer me, Cali." Stepping back, he lifted the flogger and brought it down over her breasts, her arms and then stomach. "Now. Or end it." His breath heaved, as heavy and deep as her own. His chest lifted in large draughts as he waited. For her.

She blinked rapidly to hold back the threatening tears. She wouldn't cry. Not here. Her lip quivered, her arms twitched, the tension strung tight from her grip on the chains. She could use her safe word. Stop the Scene. But she had to trust him. He was making her do this for a reason. One she didn't understand, but there must be one. She had to believe that.

"My ex-husband," she finally croaked. God, the shame. She wanted to die. Right there. Her eyes were closed tight against the ridicule she knew she'd see in the watching faces. Her lips were clamped between her teeth to keep the agonizing moan from escaping. The one that sat aching in the back of her throat.

"Good girl."

Smack, another bite of the flogger. And another. Jake continued with more strikes until her mind was floating back to the nowhere zone. Her muscles were beginning to relax once again, her hold on the chains going slack.

"Whose fault was that, Cali?"

What? She winced and snapped her head away from the question. As if she could deflect it by not facing it head-on. She struggled between the desire to ignore and hide from the question and the urgent need building inside of her to answer.

To do as Jake asked.

"Mine," she finally admitted, the guilty word leaking out between barely moving lips. The admission caused her knees to weaken until her arms stretched tight against the restraining cuffs.

"*Wrong.*"

The growling denial bracketed against her and she tried to push away. From him, his anger. But there was nowhere for her to go. No escape. What did she do wrong? Confusion engulfed her, dramatized by the stinging pain lacing her body and the mellowing rush trying to temper it all.

The sharp tug against her nipples made her gasp, followed by a low moan that welled up from deep in her chest. It sounded foreign, almost animalistic to her ears. Jake held the connecting chain of the nipple clamps in his fist, the slack pulled taut so the ends stretched the tender tips of her breasts. She arched her spine, trying to decrease the strain, until her head pushed back on the cross support.

The nipples-to-pussy connection struck again, the pain firing down to ramp up her need. Unthinking, she tried to close her legs to hide the wetness that soaked her panties. Chains clanked and rattled with the jerk of her ankles.

She couldn't hide.

In the next instant, her last protective barrier was yanked away in a violent tearing of material. She inhaled and straightened instantly, the action forcing the clamps to tighten and tug on her now-tortured nipples until black dots swam before her eyes.

"There's nothing left to hide behind. Now, think and give me the correct answer. Whose fault is it your ex-husband wouldn't touch you?"

The light, tickling stroke of the flogger brushed against her mound, so close to her wanting pussy. Close, but not touching, the gentle tease in direct contrast to the tight hold he still held on the nipple clamp chain. Her mind could barely function; all her focus was on her body, on the feelings Jake evoked in her.

She had never felt so vulnerable and exposed in her entire life. She shuddered, a ripple of reaction that went through from head to toe. A jerk on the clamps reminded her Jake wanted an answer.

If her first answer was wrong, what else was there?

"No one's?"

"*Wrong.*" The sharp reprimand was followed by the slap of the flogger over her now-exposed mound.

She whimpered and shook.

There was only one answer left to give. "His."

"Correct, Cali." Instantly her nipple clamps were removed. Blood flooded into the nubs to make them pound in rhythms of pain matching the beat of her heart. She screamed, unable to keep the releasing sound from escaping. She wasn't sure if the scream was for the external pain flowing from her breasts or the internal pain wrenching her heart. Then his mouth was there, lapping and soothing away the ache as he diligently attended to the sore peaks. The contrasting sensation was overwhelming, his attention reassuring.

His approval, topped with the hot moisture of his mouth against the diminishing pain, had her so close to the edge. She could feel the evidence of her arousal making its way down her inner thigh. If she had any humility left, she'd be mortified.

"Do you believe that?" Jake stared into her eyes, the force of his intentions staggering. "Do you believe his actions were his own and not something you caused?"

Did she? She couldn't think anymore.

"You are gorgeous, Cali. Beautiful. Giving." He was so close she could almost sink into him. Almost. "Anyone who could not see that, not appreciate that, is a fool. If you don't believe me, then believe them."

Jake stepped aside but held her jaw so she had no choice except to look at the crowd of people who now gathered around them three to four deep.

She recoiled, closing her eyes to hide, but Jake wouldn't let her.

"Look. Look at their faces, in their eyes, and tell me what you see."

Did she dare? Did she have the courage to face the ridicule, the scorn she would see there? She could call a stop, use her safe word and flee. Or she could obey Jake and see what he wanted her to see.

"Trust me," Jake said into her ear. "I would never, ever hurt you."

Doubt swamped her in hard, thundering echoes of fear built on years of neglect. She bit her lip, the tight hold on the tender flesh doing little to stop the trembling she was unable to control. Jake's grip tightened on her chin, in reminder or anger she didn't know. It didn't matter.

He was waiting on her. Again.

It was then she noticed the utter quiet surrounding her. Over the roar of blood and her pounding heart, she heard nothing. The background noises of earlier—the moans, whimpers, whip cracks, hand-slaps—were all gone. Why?

Inhaling one deep, courage-gathering breath, Cali opened her eyes. Immediately she started to shake, the chains clanking in an ominous rattle through the silent room. Panic engulfed her. Her skin chilled and her breath stuttered in and out of her lungs in shaky waves.

"Easy, Cali." Jake's voice. In her ear. Low, calm. His warm touch on her cheek. Grounding her. "Look at them. At their faces."

Look at them. At the sea of people who seemed to be closing in on her until she couldn't breathe. The faces blurred.
She didn't want to see them. Row upon row of scorn. Why
would she want to see that?

"Do you see the respect?"

Respect? The word cut through the chaos cluttering her
mind.

"The admiration?"

Admiration? How? She blinked, the faces taking form before her.

"The envy?"

Envy? Her? She blinked again, one long squeeze of her
eyes guaranteeing she'd see straight when they opened. A low,
stunned breath escaped her gaping mouth at what she saw.

"Reverence. Desire. All for you."

And it was there. Every word Jake said was etched into the
faces staring at her. Cali's gaze darted from one face to the
next, searching for the truth, unable to believe what she saw.
But it was all the same—men and women, Doms and submissives—it didn't matter. Every face showed nothing but…
acceptance.

Understanding.

Not a single face showed even a hint of judgment, or scorn,
or ridicule, or pity, or any of the negative thoughts that had
consumed her for so, so long.

"Tell me. Do you see it? Do you see what we see? What I
see?" It was the slight hitch of Jake's voice on the last question that broke her.

The first jagged sob lurched from her gut in a gasp for
freedom. The strangled noise cut into the silence with harsh
cords of anguish. *Oh, God.* It really wasn't her fault. There
was nothing wrong with her.

"Yes," she whispered with the next bubble of breath, the

admission almost lost in the warble of her voice. They saw her. Her mind rallied around that one clear thought. They saw her. *Her*. Jake saw her. And they still respected her.

They understood her.

They didn't judge her.

They wanted her. Jake wanted her.

Oh, God. Frantic, desperate, she jerked her head, seeking him. Seeking confirmation. "Jake," she choked out.

And he was there. Before her. Blocking out everyone and everything but him. The honesty and truth of everything he'd said blazing in his silver eyes. His touch the connection she needed.

"Yes," she said stronger, the tears trailing down her cheeks. "Yes. Yes. Yes." Each repetition of the word got stronger with her belief. "Jake." His name came out in a plea. She stretched toward him, begging for strength. For his arms to hold her.

Support her.

"You're so brave," he whispered, lips grazing hers in a teasing caress right before his jaw clenched and he took a brisk step away.

The loss of his heat chilled her, but she trusted him. Needed him.

"Marcus."

She jerked against the curtness in his tone.

"This sub needs relief. Can you assist me?"

Cali was too shocked to react. What did he mean? Her gaze shot from Jake to the tall, black-haired Dom she recognized from her first night at The Den. His dark, almost black eyes assessed her, a slow smile spreading across his lips.

"With pleasure, Master Jake," he said, stepping forward. "She's a beauty." His gaze traveled over her, leaving a cold trail in its wake. Cali shivered, searching for Jake's eyes as the other man asked, "What would you like me to do?"

"Lick her pussy," Jake bit out. "Tell me how good she tastes."

She tried to withhold the flinch, the instant reaction to flee. Jake's eyes narrowed, his features turning stony as he caught her movement. Of course she couldn't run, but could she do this? Let this other man intimately touch her here? In front of everyone—in front of him?

She wanted to ask him why. What was he doing? Did she anger him? Displease him? Disgust him? Was this her punishment for resisting earlier? They'd never talked about this.

About sharing her.

Marcus dropped to his knees, stroking her legs in a slow caress starting at her ankles. She looked down; she had to. Her eyes widened at the unfamiliar sight, the long, straight hair so different from Jake's. His touch was firmer, his palms smooth, not coarse and callused like Jake's.

She reminded herself that Jake wanted this. She was pleasing him in allowing this man to touch her. That thought alone had her body responding. For whatever reason, he wanted another man to pleasure her. Her muscles relaxed, the tension ebbing from her as she let go of the doubt. Warm breath brushed over her wet pussy, forcing a sigh to slip from her lips.

She lifted her head to find Jake, but his focus was locked on the other man. His lips were thinned in a grimace, his eyes smoldering with what seemed like rage. His arms were crossed tightly against his chest, his stance unbending. He appeared anything but pleased.

"Stop."

The harsh command rang through the room. Marcus froze, withdrawing his hands from her. Cali tensed.

Jake stepped forward, every movement a show of extreme control. Slow, firm, calculated.

Marcus eased back then stood, his focus on Jake. "Certainly, Master Jake." He moved away without another word.

Cali couldn't look at the other people still there. She could feel their attention, the silence stretching as everyone watched the Scene. Watched her and Jake. The air was filled with a strain that pushed at her and enveloped her in expectation.

Jake dropped to his knees. Her stomach muscles clenched against the sensation of his tongue as he traced the blazing lines of red patterns across her skin. She could do nothing but watch as he followed a path down to her pussy. Thoughts of anyone else in the room were gone.

At that moment, Jake was the only one who existed in her world.

Her eyes focused on the silky black strands of hair, the familiar curled ends wet with perspiration. His rough hands held her firm at the hips, fingers digging into her flesh and holding her still. The tip of his pink tongue flicked in and out of his mouth, leaving a trail of cooling moisture that sizzled against the fire of her skin.

She was on the edge, her body and mind both perched in expectation of the next touch. Of satisfying the cleansing need for release. She whimpered, uncaring of how she sounded. Uncaring of anything but the relief only he could give.

"Please, Jake," she begged, just like he said she would.

His gaze flashed up to meet hers. "You've earned this." The pride was openly displayed for her to see. And with it, all of the other emotions he spoke of. Acceptance, reverence, admiration, desire and something she didn't dare hope for.

He covered her pussy with his mouth in a sudden ferocity that shocked her. She gasped at the heat, the hot pulse of his tongue over her engorged and needy clit, the nip of teeth on the delicate flesh. He stretched his hands up to pinch her hypersensitive nipples.

"Jake," she pleaded, holding tight in anticipation, in the fight to retain the release threatening to tumble out of her.

Through the fog clouding her brain, she heard the words she needed. "Come for me, Cali."

And she did. Her muscles clenched, sound escaped her mouth, but she wasn't aware of what she said. Her world imploded, wave after wave of ecstasy rippling through her in a mind-numbing, full-body orgasm.

Her arms screamed in protest as she pulled them past their limits. Already aching and tired from their extended position held outstretched and over her head, the muscles quivered then gave out. Her body sagged and dropped like dead weight as the rest of her muscles followed suit and refused to work. Vaguely she was aware of the scrape of the leather against her wrists, the two points now responsible for holding her up. Then it was gone.

Strong arms circled her. She inhaled, her senses logging the subtle masculine scent of Jake. He had her. She was safe.

It was too much work to open her eyes. She didn't need to see to know Jake had her. The whimper that escaped her lips barely registered as the pinpricks of tingling pain coursed up her arms when her wrists were freed. Then hands were there, rubbing and kneading the muscles until the circulation returned and the ache eased.

And the whole time she could think of nothing but the strong chest she huddled against. Of the arms that circled her, holding her tight.

"You're okay, babe. I've got you."

He got her. In more ways than anyone else ever had.

She exhaled, the one long breath releasing the last of her doubts. The last of her reservations. But most importantly, that breath expelled the last of the self-recriminations that had plagued her for so many years.

Finally, for the first time in forever, she felt cleansed. Free.

In Jake's arms.

TWENTY

He held her. His exceptional sub who trusted him enough to bare and purge her deepest shame to a crowd of strangers. Who let another Dom touch her because Jake ordered it.

His chest ached, the odd rush of longing nearly taking him to his knees. He clutched Cali closer. She was curled in an almost fetal position against him as he cradled her limp form to his.

"I've got you," he whispered again into her ear, nuzzling the skin of her neck. The light, salty taste from her lingering perspiration a flavor he'd come to crave.

She mumbled a response, but coherent words had not returned to her. Did she understand how much his words meant? How much her complete submission, her trust, filled him?

He could barely comprehend it, so how could she?

One of the Dungeon Masters brought a robe and slipped it over her shoulders. Jake adjusted his hold until the material provided a modest covering and a layer of warmth.

"She's a treasure, Master Jake. Truly exceptional."

Jake gave him a stiff nod. She was.

"Should I have her clothes delivered to a room?"

"My loft." Jake's reply was met with only the slightest raising of eyebrows. The crowd had dispersed when the Scene ended, so his answer was for the Dungeon Master alone. If the man valued his job, that tidbit of information would not be shared.

"I'll deliver them myself," he answered before returning to his duties.

Jake moved from the room, Cali bundled in his arms, trusting him completely. A few people watched as he departed.

"She's amazing, Master Jake," one Dom praised as Jake passed. Others nodded in agreement. He caught the longing that lingered in the eyes of more than a few Doms and subs, admiration clear on every face. He clutched Cali closer.

At the edge of the room his gaze caught and held on Seth and Deklan. The two men stood side by side, watching him, a look of knowing on their faces. Jake refused to acknowledge them or the question silently conveyed across the space.

He looked away, his focus on his sub. His sub. Cali was more than just his sub. He'd proven that tonight. Exactly the opposite of what he'd set out to do. *Fuck*. He was so incredibly fucked.

Could he do it? Could he take the risk and do what his heart so strangely and desperately wanted him to do? He'd had a collar made on a fool's whim, one he hadn't planned on fulfilling. But after tonight, after Marcus…fuck.

Jake pushed back the flash of jealousy as he juggled his hold, eventually getting the door to his loft open. Cali's breathing had returned to a more normal level, but she remained impassive in his arms. He sat on the edge of the Jacuzzi tub in his master bath, settled her onto his lap and turned on the taps. She roused at the sound of the rushing water.

"Whatcha doing?" she mumbled against his collar.

He smiled. Her voice was so soft and trusting. Even after the mind-fuck he'd put her through. Even after Marcus. He dropped a kiss to the top of her head. "I'm taking care of you."

Her hum of approval was reinforced by her snuggling closer. His cock ached. His hard-on hadn't subsided since he'd seen her standing in the office decked out in the outfit he'd bought her. But it wasn't important. Denial of his own needs was all a part of being a Dom. Right now his submissive needed his care, not his dick.

He tested the water, made a few adjustments and reached over to pour a small amount of vanilla-scented bath oil into the water. Another luxury bought on a whim for her. Soon, the calming aroma filled the rapidly heating room.

"Cali." Jake nudged her, holding her arms to keep her from falling. "The water's ready."

She opened her eyes, her lids only rising part of the way. She gave him a sultry, tired glance before she curled her lips in a lazy smile. "I don't think I can stay coherent enough for a bath." She chuckled. "I'll probably drown."

He stroked her cheek before shifting her around until she was propped against the wall. "Then sit here while I undress."

Her eyebrows lifted and her smile grew. "I like the way you think."

A few minutes later they were both sinking into the warmth of the steaming bath. Her low moan of approval rippled through him as he held her against his chest. He wrapped his arms around her waist and she relaxed into his hold. She sighed, a deep sound of contentment.

"I agree," he said, relaxing into her as well.

He let her rest for a while, content to just hold her. To take care of her. The warm water would soothe her muscles and temper the sting from the flogging. He'd used a flogger with stiffer strips that left a sharper impact and heightened the intensity to get Cali past her fears. To take her mind away from what she was thinking and back to the basics of what she was feeling.

After a while, he shifted her in his arms until he could see her face. Wisps of her hair had fallen from the fancy ponytail she'd constructed, curling around her face in damp spirals. He lowered his lips to her ear and nipped at the shell before he said, "Tell me about it."

She stiffened, just a second, before once again relaxing against him. "Is this my Dom ordering me or my lover asking me?"

He gave a soft snort. Trust her to still question him. "Both. It's time to let it go."

"I thought that's what earlier was about."

"It was. Think of it as the release of the pressure valve. Now the rest needs to escape and be banished for good. All of that withheld emotion doesn't go away that fast or easily."

She sighed. "I don't know if I can. I've never talked about it with anyone before."

"Just talk. Pretend I'm not here and talk it out of you. Admit to your feelings and then let them go."

"Are you my therapist now too?" she asked with a smirk.

"No. I'm your friend. Someone you can trust to confide in."

She searched his eyes before she finally conceded, her voice low and hesitant. "I honestly thought I'd dealt with all of these feelings long ago. Accepted the issue was his, not mine, and moved on. But obviously I haven't."

"When did it start?"

She puffed out a short breath. "Basically, before we even married. Our sex life was never great, never wild or frequent even when we were in college, before kids." She looked away. "I told myself then it didn't matter. That the relationship we had was better than great sex. That I was lucky to have a loving husband, a good life, with someone I could talk to and who supported me. And it was fine for a while."

She paused, her fingers lifting to push distractedly at the water. She watched the ripples ring outward before she continued. "Eventually the neglect hurt. Many, many times I tried talking to him about it. Tried to come up with suggestions or ways to make him feel better, to work it out. Inevitably he would twist it around, and somehow it was my fault. I was too bitchy. I was too busy with the kids. I didn't respond to him. I, I, I...until it was just easier to let it go. To live without and take care of my own needs." She exhaled a defeated breath. "The longer I lived without, the less I tried, the less he touched me, the less we connected until we eventually co-existed, raising our kids like two friends living together. Not two lovers sharing their lives together. When the kids were both in college, there was nothing left for us to hang on to. There was nothing left for just the two of us."

Jake stroked her arm but remained quiet. He couldn't believe a man would reject her. What an ass. The guy had no idea what he'd missed out on.

"Do you know what the worst part is?" she asked, tilting her head to look at him. He gave a small head shake in reply. "The world assumes it's my fault. After all, society teaches us all men want and think about is sex. So if sex isn't happening in a marriage, then it's the woman who's at fault. With all of those stereotypes, how do you admit it's your husband who doesn't want you? Even then, it's still the woman's fault. It must be something she did to turn him off."

He rested a palm on her cheek. "It's not your fault. I thought we covered that downstairs."

She chuckled. "Yeah, we did. And I get that. Logically. But emotionally, it's taking longer to sink in." She quirked her lips up in a devious smile. "But I think it's been beaten into me now."

He leaned down and kissed her, a light touch of caring. "I wanted you to see what everyone here sees." He searched her face. "Was this need—the Dom/sub desire—a reason for your sexual problems with your husband?"

"No." She laughed and shook her head. "Well, maybe. Unknowingly." She sighed again. "I'd always wanted him to take control in the bedroom. The more he didn't, the more I wanted him to. He let me, almost made me by default, control every other aspect of our marriage. Couldn't he control one simple thing like sex?" The question was filled with the frustration she spoke of. She took a deep breath, the inner struggle clear on her face.

Jake rubbed her neck, gave her comfort but remained silent.

"The more frustrated I got," she eventually said, "the more I started to identify what it was, exactly, I wanted. What I truly fantasized about. It was a slow process, a gradual understanding that came with the isolation and loneliness. I stumbled across the concept of Dominance and submission through women's romance books, of all places." She laughed. "My desires just blossomed and grew from there until I got the courage to do something about it."

She reached for him, her fingers resting on the edge of his jaw, her eyes wide with her honesty. "Thank you, Jake, for giving me this freedom. For letting me experience this side of myself for the first time in my life. For making me feel desired and whole."

Oh, man. He was so fucked. Cali, in all her innocence and bravery, just gave him that drop-kick to the balls he'd been trying to avoid. No one had ever thanked him—Jake—for what he'd done. Master Jake had received hundreds of such courtesies, but they'd never extended to the other him. The simple man named Jake.

"It was your courage that did that," he insisted, hoping she believed him. "It was your own strength that brought you here. Despite your fears, you took the risk. You could have stayed in your marriage and continued to pretend everything was fine. Live half a life. Instead, you took the harder, riskier path in the hopes of finding what you really needed. Very few in this world are brave enough to do that."

"Some would call it stupidity," she tried to joke.

"And they would be the idiots." He wasn't going to let her brush this away. "Safety and security over happiness? It's a hard choice. It's not easy to give up what you know in the hopes of finding something better. What if you never find anything better? That's the risk most people won't take. Even if it means never being completely happy."

"Are you happy, Jake?"

And she nailed him. Internally he cringed, but he kept his expression neutral. He honestly hadn't thought of his life in those terms in a long time. Not until Cali had walked into it.

"I guess that's all relative, isn't it?" he tried to hedge.

She wasn't letting him off the hook that easy. "Does being a Dom make you happy? Do you like owning The Den? Having this world surround you all the time?"

Damn. He could ignore her questions. He *should* do that, but after the honesty she'd displayed and the trust she'd given him that night, he owed her better. He *wanted* to do better.

"Being a Dom is who I am. I realized early in my life that having control over others excited me more than was deemed normal. I didn't have a stable childhood. The control I found in dominance gave me the stability I craved. Being a Dom lets me be who I am without shame." Not an exact answer to her question, but it was more than he gave most people. More than he'd admitted in years. Jake edged her away from his hold and stood. "The water's cooling and you're barely staying awake."

"But what about you?" she asked, staring pointedly at his semi-erection.

He stepped out, wrapping a towel around his waist. "Tonight is about you, Cali. Not me." He helped her out of the tub, meaning what he said. The night was for her. His dick would deal.

He dried her off, taking care to rub cream into her tender nipples. They'd be sore for a few days after the punishment they took from the nipple clamps. He moved down her body, gently rubbing the cream over the stripes left from the flogger. The sight of his work burned a possessive trail through him. He'd marked her. Some were already faded and most would be gone in a day or two. In deference to her needs, he'd kept them light because he knew she didn't want the risk of exposure that came with lasting marks.

Jake settled Cali into his bed then left to lock up the loft. He found her possessions sitting nicely folded outside his door and brought them back to his bedroom. The sight of her curled on her side, her hand tucked under her cheek in sleep, stopped him in the doorway. The light from the bathroom spilled in to cut a sharp line down the bed, leaving it half in the dark and half in the light.

Of course, Cali lay in the light. How fucking cliché.

He set her clothes on the dresser and snapped off the bathroom light, plunging the room into darkness. What the fuck was he doing? He stood in the dark for a long time, unable to force himself into bed with Cali, yet unable to leave.

He was a fucking hypocrite. Telling Cali how brave she was to take the risk, to find her happiness. And here he was, too scared to grab what was right in front of him. Was it possible to extend this to something more? A growing part of him wanted to try. What would it be like to hear her laughter every day? To share takeout and watch movies until they fell asleep on the couch?

What he hadn't admitted to Cali was the fact he was tired of being *only* a Dom. Somewhere along this path, he'd lost the other side of him. The side Cali could give him back if he only dared to take it.

Dared to take the risk.

TWENTY-ONE

Cali stood at the bar. A smile warmed her face, the music drumming through her body. She inhaled and released the tension that had built up over the two weeks since she'd last been to The Den. The Thanksgiving holiday and family commitments had kept her away from the place she'd come to need.

Or was it the man she needed?

She'd been surprised when he'd asked her to spend the holiday with him. It'd been tempting to accept, but she couldn't skirt her obligations, and introducing him to her family wasn't an option. Not yet. They'd talked on the phone, something they did almost daily now. She was certain that wasn't part of a standard Dom/sub contract. The fact that she wanted to see him more—wanted to watch the old movies he said he liked or taste the Thai food from that restaurant he swore was the best—scared her.

What had started out as a "club only" thing had expanded to form the semblance of a relationship for her. He was a vital part of her life. Was it possible for him to be a part of her whole life? Did he want to be?

She took a drink of her water, the liquid cool in her throat. This was her first appearance since the public, soul-baring Scene she'd done with Jake. She couldn't help but wonder if any of the people looking at her now had seen her then. Was the woman in the blue leather wearing a collar one of the ones who'd watched her? Or maybe it was the blond Dom in black leather who'd seen her stripped, beaten and bared to all.

Two months ago, that thought—that fear—would have had her running from the club, her head hung in shame. But now, to her surprise, she felt nothing but pride. How was that possible?

She felt so strong. The simple knowledge that she could do something like that and thrive gave her a confidence that, to her amazement, she found carried over into her other life as well. Where most people would think that strange and bizarre, here she found understanding. Now she got it—there was power and strength in submitting.

In giving up control to Jake, she'd finally, truly found herself.

At The Den she found acceptance. A place where her desires were not seen as deviant, or forbidden, or disgusting. But as honest and okay.

She set her glass down and stretched her neck, searching for Jake. He usually didn't leave her waiting so long. His package today had included a strapless leather dress that just covered her ass cheeks and a black pushup bra and thong set. Written instructions defined she wear the thigh-high boots, her hair up and no jewelry. All of which she'd followed without hesitation.

She turned around, resisting the urge to hunt for him. The bouncer had told her Jake would meet her there and she didn't want to disobey. The music switched to another sultry tune and Cali let her hips sway in time to the beat.

A tall, dark-haired man stepped through the crowd and stopped in front of her. "Ms. Reynolds?"

Marcus. The Dom Jake had pulled into their last Scene.

Cali's heart stalled in unison with the drop of her gut. She hadn't planned on seeing the Dom again, especially without Jake present. She'd never been addressed by another Dom, let alone one who'd kneeled before her naked pussy. Embarrassment flushed her skin and she glanced down, uncertain of how to act. She might have been coming here for two months, but she was still naive when it came to all of the rules and intricacies of the BDSM world.

"Yes," she said, deciding to meet his gaze.

"I'm Master Marcus. Master Jake has been detained with new-member details." The man extended his hand. "He asked for me to escort you to a room. He has a special surprise planned for you tonight."

A special surprise? With Marcus? Cali licked her lips, her pussy clenching at the images her thoughts created.

After a brief hesitation, she placed her hand in his and allowed herself to be led to the second floor, where the Dom opened a door to the right she'd never noticed before. She paused for a second, uncertain of where she was being led.

The man stopped, having noticed her hesitation. "It's all right, Ms. Reynolds." He let go of her hand and stepped to the side, allowing her to fully enter the room. He stood in the doorway, keeping it open and letting her feel a little less trapped. "Master Jake told me to give this to you." The Dom handed her an envelope, her name written boldly across the front in a firm script she recognized instantly.

Cali slid her finger under the seal, her hands shaking just enough to make the simple task difficult. Finally she got it open and extracted the slip of paper. On it was written instructions from Jake to do as Master Marcus defined. That she could trust the Dom, and he was going to prepare her for the evening's Scene.

She inhaled a shaky breath and returned the letter to the envelope. Looking around, she saw the space seemed more like a backstage area than a domination room. It was fairly small, with a set of stairs leading up to what was apparently a stage. One she'd never seen before. What did Jake have planned?

She turned to Marcus, who stood waiting for her in the door. Was he a part of tonight's Scene? Did she want the other Dom to be?

"I don't suppose you'll tell me what he has planned?"

The man smiled and shook his head. "It's not my place. You have to trust your Master."

And she did. She was too far down this path not to. After the last Scene, he had her full trust. From the Scene, to the way he cared for her after, to the almost tender sex they'd had in the morning, he'd shown her just how much he cherished her. She felt it in a way her ex had never come close to.

Jake made her feel special. Cared for. Loved—a word that wasn't supposed to be in this vocabulary but loomed dangerously in her heart. She was foolish to think it, let alone feel it.

"Okay," she said to Marcus with a slight nod of her head. "Sir."

And with that, she was committed. Marcus smiled, a shine of approval in his dark eyes. He stepped into the room and allowed the door to close behind him. The click of the latch sounded a bit intimidating, but Cali stood still as the Dom approached. No other words were spoken as the man took the paper and envelope from her hands and moved behind her.

She heard a drawer open, something being shifted around. The drawer closed, and a door opened. Cali wanted to turn, to see what the man was doing, but she didn't. She stared at the floor, hands clasped tightly before her, and waited. Jake instructed her to follow Master Marcus and she didn't want to disappoint Jake.

A mask was placed over her eyes and she cleared her throat to cover the startled gasp. Her heart accelerated, but she held in her nerves. Once again, just like the last time a mask was used on her, her other senses kicked into overdrive to compensate for the loss of sight. The Dom's grip on her wrists felt cold as he pulled her arms behind her and cuffed them together.

"What are your safe words, Cali?"

She responded automatically. "Red, stop. Yellow, slow down. Green, go."

"Those words still apply. Use them if you need them."

Her breathing leveled out with that simple reassurance. She still had power. Jake wouldn't hurt her. Nor would he send somebody who would.

His boots clumped on the floor as she felt him move away from her. Then she heard the door open and close. The scent of his cologne, a deep, musky smell, lingered in the room, blending with the hint of leather and the lemon-scented cleaner.

She strained to hear other sounds. She thought she was alone, but she wasn't certain. The back of the room had been dark and there were the stairs leading up to a stage. Someone could have been up there. The waiting was making her mind race with questions and ideas. Strange, wild ideas that would have scared her not long ago or made her think she was borderline crazy for desiring such things.

Now, the strongest feeling she had was anticipation, not fear.

Slowly she began to hear voices. Low, murmured sounds that grew in volume and quantity until they echoed from the stage area down into her little room. She shivered when she realized people must be entering the room that viewed the stage. That could mean many things, but the most obvious was that they were coming to watch her.

Or whatever Jake had planned for her.

Another public Scene. That was certainly what it was. Why else would he have her wait here? She tried to mediate her breathing, taking calming breaths to ease the jitters and slow her racing heart.

She snapped her head around at the creak of the door opening, ears straining for an indication of who had entered. "Jake?"

No answer.

She heard the boots on the floor, felt a presence before her. The anxiety left when she caught his scent, the rich, earthy smell of Jake. She smiled and his lips drifted over hers.

"I've missed you, Cali." The husky words were murmured against her ear.

Goose bumps prickled over her skin at the flutter of his warm breath and the depth of meaning in his tone. He cupped the back of her neck and pulled her in for a deep, passionate kiss. Off balance, she stumbled against his chest, his arms holding her steady as the kiss went on. He tasted so good and felt so right. Only now could she truly acknowledge how much she'd missed his touch, his presence.

With one last sweep of his tongue against her lips, he drew back. He kept his hands on her arms until she regained her balance. Then his touch was gone.

"Do you like being my sub?"

"Yes, Jake," she answered, breathless. Fear trickled in for the first time.

"Do you trust me?"

"Yes, Jake."

"Would you like to remain my exclusive sub?"

"Yes, Jake." The desperation showed in her voice as she

started to worry. Where was he going with these questions? Was he going to leave her?

He grabbed her arm. "Then come with me. I have something special planned for you tonight."

"What?" she dared to ask.

"No questions," he said harshly. "Trust me, or use your safe word."

She bit her lip and looked down. She couldn't see a thing, but she hoped her posture gave him the answer he wanted.

Then he was leading her up the stairs. He kept his hold tight and the crowd stirred as Jake led her on to the stage. The voices slowly quieted until the click and thump of their boots was the only noise that reached her ears. She sensed the space, however big it was, was filled. The vibration of bodies, the shifting and fidgeting of a large group of people, prickled over her skin.

She was hot, burning under the feeling of hundreds of eyes on her. Jake stopped and turned her until she faced him, the audience to his back. He pushed lightly on her shoulders. Her boots creaked as she bent her knees and kneeled before him.

Suddenly her blindfold was gone. The briskness of the action forced her to blink several times as her eyes adjusted to the bright lights that lit up the stage and heated her skin like a summer day. Instinctively she wanted to look around. To see where she was and what was going on. But she kept her head down and focused on his boots in the position of a good sub.

"Beautiful." Jake's words caressed over her and she filled with pride, the act of pleasing him bringing her a contentment that still surprised her. She kept her eyes downcast and let the rest of the surroundings fade away. Her sole focus became Jake.

On what he wanted.

He stepped to her side, one lone finger running a path over her naked neck. He'd done this before, more frequently the last few times she'd been there. Then it hit her. What this could be, what this could mean. Starbursts of light flashed before her eyes and she struggled to ward off the sudden lightheadedness that made her sway on her knees.

Jake moved behind her, his finger following the curve of her neck until it reached the vertebra at the back. At this point, Cali couldn't have looked up even if Jake ordered her to. Her gaze was frozen on the scuffed planks of the stage.

A murmur went through the crowd. She couldn't make out anything distinctive, but then she couldn't hear much over the roar in her ears. Sweat beaded over her skin, and all of her senses were focused on the man behind her. What was he doing? Her fingers ached, sore from the tight grasp she held on them below the cuffs on her wrists.

Then she felt the metal against her neck, the links warm and firm as they pressed into her flesh. His knuckles brushed her skin as he fixed the clasp. Then his fingers circled her neck, outlining the collar in a possessive stroke.

His declaration to the world—she belonged to him.

Oh. My. God. There were too many emotions swirling within her to clearly identify what she was thinking. Jake had just publicly claimed her. She could feel every millimeter of the collar where it sat firmly against her skin almost as if it had the ability to choke her. But instead of restrictive, the collar was…comforting. She shivered, her inner turmoil calming.

Applause rippled through the auditorium, followed by a few catcalls and whistles. Then Jake was before her, lifting her to her feet and claiming her mouth in a hard, plundering kiss that was yet another declaration of ownership. He eased back. The possessiveness she saw in his eyes should have frightened her, but it was tempered by another emotion that she could have sworn was love.

Shocked, she couldn't breathe. More than his actions, the

collar—everything they'd done together—the silver shine of promise he was extending stunned her. Could she trust it? She trusted him, but could she trust what he offered?

"What's your color, Cali?"

His question for her alone. Even after his public display and declaration, he was giving her a choice. She never thought of herself as wanting this. But then, everything she'd found at The Den was different from what she'd expected. Better.

She wanted this. To be claimed by Jake. For everyone to know she was his.

"Green," she managed to whisper.

He inhaled a long breath, as if he'd been uncertain of her response and was now absorbing her answer. His eyes closed for a moment, only to reopen with his exhale. "You honor me," he said, his voice deep and rough like coarse sandpaper that prickled over her nerve endings, sending a shiver of pleasure down her spine.

Jake moved behind her and it was then she got her first look at the audience. The room was large, about the size of a small theater, and packed. The lights glared over the sea of bodies and Cali quickly ducked her head to keep from being overwhelmed.

He unlinked the cuffs but kept her hands held in his. She heard the unmistakable clank of a chain being lowered—the slow chink of metal from above foreshadowing what was ahead. Cali couldn't think anymore. Too much had happened, was happening, for her to process.

She was Jake's.

And his plans for the evening weren't done.

Jake shifted her arms to the front and reconnected the cuffs. Then Master Marcus was on stage, lifting her wrists to attach the cuffs to the chain lowered from the ceiling. Jake kept his hands on her hips, steadying her until the other Dom had her hands secured. Jake attached a spreader bar between her ankles. Tension increased on the chain, pulling her arms higher until she felt stretched from her wrists to her ankles, making it impossible to move.

Impossible to escape.

She kept her head down, unwilling or unable to look out at the crowd. She shook with anticipation, a touch of anxiety, but most prominently desire and pleasure. It'd been two weeks since she'd submitted to Jake. She let all of her other worries and fears melt away until there was only him.

It was freeing to let go. To place herself in his hands. To trust him so completely that the only thing she had to focus on was following his orders. Pleasing Jake.

"You belong to me, Cali." Jake's voice boomed over the air, echoing off the high ceilings and hushing the low conversations of the audience. "Who is your Master?"

"You," she answered.

"Who do you please?"

"You."

"Look," Jake ordered. "Look at the audience and see your admirers. Show them who you belong to."

She had to obey. More importantly, she wanted to. Jake owned her, body and soul, and she was helpless against it. Somewhere along the way, between the bondage, the spankings and the whips, she'd fallen in love with the compassion, the tenderness and the complete adoration he showed her.

She had fallen in love with Jake.

Fuck. She was beautiful.

Cali's body quivered, little shakes that were barely visible unless you were attuned to her the way Jake was. She followed his command and surveyed the audience. He saw more than heard the soft inhale.

His attention drifted to the collar around her neck. His collar. The silver chain shone brilliant against her creamy skin, the figure eight infinity links custom-made especially for her.

Because Cali would belong to him forever.

She owned him. Whether she knew it or not. He was as much a slave to her—to what she gave him—as she was to him.

He scanned the crowd, an audience of his peers, friends, employees and customers. He'd declared to all of them that Cali was his. Pride swelled in his chest. Cali was a magnificent sub. But more importantly, she was a magnificent woman.

His cock throbbed, hard and wanting in his leather pants, the sight before him pumping him full of adrenaline and lust. The short skirt of the leather dress had ridden up her thighs when he'd attached the spreader bar to display a tantalizing glimpse of her ass cheeks and the thin lace of her thong. With her arms stretched over her head, the strapless bodice had slipped down, revealing the upper curves of her breasts.

The dress needed to go.

Jake stepped behind her and slowly traced the line of the collar. "It looks perfect on you," he whispered. He watched the shiver race to her toes before he reached for the zipper on the back of the dress and slowly lowered it. Specially designed for easy removal, the zipper held the garment together much like a coat.

Goose bumps followed his fingers down her spine and spread across her back when he removed the dress. A murmur of appraisal and appreciation went through the crowd.

Jake tossed the garment aside and circled around to face his sub. Her face was flushed, her chest heaving in tight, little gasps, pushing her breasts up within the confines of the strapless bra. The black lace revealed tantalizing hints of her areolas beneath the thin material. Tempting, but keeping secrets.

His gaze traveled down the planes of her stomach, past the thin patch of lace covering her pussy to the smooth expanse of her thighs before they disappeared into the leather boots.

God, she was so fucking amazing. A thought that kept repeating in his head every time he saw her. But this, as she was now, was beyond words and description. Her head had fallen forward, her eyes once again on the ground, her submissiveness displayed for everyone to witness.

She was perfection.

Jake stepped forward, grabbed her chin and kissed her with all the passion and possessiveness he felt. She gave herself willing to him, moaning her pleasure before he dragged himself away. He cast a pointed glance to Marcus waiting in the wings, and the man brought out the paddle Jake had selected for the Scene.

Jake stepped behind Cali and took the paddle from the other man. He ran a hand over the smooth globes of her ass. "I'm going to spank you, Cali. You're going to take it without complaint."

"Yes, Jake," she answered immediately.

"What color are you?"

"Green. I'm green."

Cali couldn't see the paddle he held in his hand, but her muscles tightened in nervous expectation for what he had in store. Her trust was both humbling and exhilarating.

A silent hum of anticipation settled over the room, everyone waiting for that first crack of wood against flesh. Sweat beaded over Jake's skin as he stepped back and raised the paddle. He held it high for a second, dragging out the moment, heightening the suspense. He felt the collective gasp flow through the room as he lowered his arm and swung the paddle at Cali's naked ass.

The crack of wood against her skin echoed across the stage,

followed by Cali's sharp cry and the jerk of her hips as the impact shuddered through her. An assortment of groans and grunts of approval rippled around the room and added to Jake's high. Adrenaline raced within him, leaving a heady rush of power in its wake.

He let the paddle land again, the flesh of her ass turning a luscious shade of red. Cali whimpered a sweet sound that mingled between shock and desire. Her legs quivered, but she didn't complain. She simply waited for him. For more.

Jake hit her again, two quick paddles, one for each cheek. Then one more landed flat across both of the flaming mounds. The sweat rolled down his back now, soaking his shirt and dampening his scalp. Cali hung almost limp from the chains, her head resting against an arm. Perspiration covered her skin, making it shine in the bright lights of the stage.

He pressed close behind her, holding her against his chest. "You're mine," he growled into her ear.

"Yes," she breathed, completely compliant.

He stroked a hand over the skin of her stomach, feeling her muscles clench and tremble under his touch. Before them, the crowd shifted, agitated flutters accompanied by quiet sobs of want. They understood what Jake had. The treasure he'd claimed.

He smoothed his hands up to tug and twist first one, then the other nipple. She curved her chest into his hands in a silent plea for more. She was so close to her point, to finding the plane where pain changed to pleasure. He could tell by the sounds she made, by the tension in her body and the expression on her face.

Jake stepped away to rub his palm over her reddened ass. The skin was hot against his hand and she pushed into this touch. He ran a finger down her crack, snaking beneath the thong strap to find her wet pussy. A whimper left her throat when he entered her hot channel, thrusting into her flesh before he withdrew.

"Please, Jake," she begged, making his cock ache for release.

He hit her again, using the element of surprise to up the pain. Cali responded stunningly, arching forward with the blow of the paddle, her head dropping against her arm, her eyes closed and her lips parted as the breath left her body. One more hit would take her where he wanted her.

He stepped to the side. "What do you want, Cali?"

Her breathing deepened as she struggled to answer. "More… please," she finally said.

"More what?" Jake needed to hear the words. "Tell us what you want."

Her head dropped forward and he quickly moved to lift it back up.

"No shame," he demanded, gripping her chin. "Remember that. Never drop your head in shame." The words came out harsh and insistent. He'd thought they were past that.

"Open your eyes."

Cali shuddered, then slowly obeyed.

Jake let go of her chin and moved away. "Keep them open and tell us what you want."

His breath caught in his chest as he waited. Would she comply? He knew she had it in her, if she only let go of that last vestige of fear. Her eyes seemed to slowly come into focus and scan over the crowed. Did she see the awe? The envy and lust that mingled on the faces of the watching?

"Last chance," Jake said. "Tell us what you want."

She inhaled, her muscles going lax as she opened her mouth to speak. Relief and an overwhelming flush of pride swelled within him.

Then he caught it. The sudden stiffening of muscles, the catch of her breath, the clench of her hands on the chain, the widening of her eyes. All indications that something was wrong.

Very, very wrong.

Jake was already moving, the paddle clattering to the stage before the word was out of her mouth.

"Red."

TWENTY-TWO

No. The word screamed in her head, her gaze locked on the man in the front row of the audience. The man who wasn't there earlier. He couldn't have been.

But he was now.

Peter.

"*Red.*" The word tumbled out of her mouth before she'd consciously thought to say it. "Red." The demand was louder this time as she yanked on the chain holding her hands.

Panic clutched at her, making her heart race and breath stop. *God. No.*

"Red. Red. *Red.*" The single word repeated with increasing volume, riding the wave of horror flooding her mind and body. She thrashed against the bonds holding her captive and flinched away from the hands suddenly gripping her.

Rational thought left as the impact of her ex-husband's presence swamped her. The shock and disgust covering his face was more than she could take. What was he doing here? In this place? Her place?

The blood roared in her ears, blocking out all other sound.

She shook now, her whole body a quivering mass as she fought the hands restraining her, the bonds trapping her. "Red. Red. Red." The word continued from her lips in a litany of pleading.

"Cali."

Her name registered through the blind fog in her brain, but she jerked away. From him. Jake. This was his fault. This shame she felt, the mortification slinking through her was all because of him.

Through the haze she watched Peter turn and push his way through the crowd, his retreating back showing exactly what would happen when the rest of her friends and family found out about this. About her and her deviant desires.

"No," she panted, sagging against the chains, the word sounding like a hollow echo in her ears. This couldn't be happening. Would Peter tell their children? Would they all hate her? Despise her? *No. God, no.*

Suddenly her wrists were free, revitalizing her fight. She pushed blindly at the arms that held her. "No," she screamed, tears streaking down her cheeks. "Let me go."

But the arms held strong. Then her feet were free, and she was being lifted into Jake's arms.

"No." She thrashed against his hold, fighting unsuccessfully to free herself from him.

From his betrayal.

"Cali," Jake said, his arms tightening as he tried to move over the stage. "Cali, stop."

"Fuck you," she cursed at him, her mind beyond conscious thought. She had only one goal right then. To get away. From him. From the shame. From the horror and disgust she felt. "Let me go. Red. I said *Red*."

"Listen to me," Jake ordered.

Right. That's what got her into this mess in the first place.

Cali increased her struggle until she felt her feet hit the ground. Immediately she pushed away and stumbled when he let her go. Another set of arms caught her before she hit the ground, but they didn't trap her, only held her steady while she trembled.

It was then that she felt the chain rub against her neck.

The collar.

Panic returned anew, rushing up to choke her in the need to remove it. She gripped the metal pulling on the unforgiving links.

"Get it off," she pleaded. Her fingernails scratched her tender flesh and the chain dug into the back of her neck in her desperate need to remove his mark of possession. An entity she'd accepted with pride only moments ago.

Now it felt like a noose. One that was choking the last bit of pride and breath she had left.

Somehow the collar was suddenly freed from her neck, the chain dangling from her hand like a serpent of evil. A representation of just how far she'd fallen.

She threw the collar at Jake, a sob leaving her throat. Jake didn't even flinch when the chain hit his chest and dropped to the floor with a soft clinking of metal. Vaguely she heard the harsh wave of gasps and shock roll through the audience, but Jake's face was impassive now, his body stiff and frozen.

"Why?" she screamed at him, the betrayal tumbling out. "I trusted you. I gave you everything you asked. Why would you do this to me?" The arms were holding her again, keeping her from attacking Jake the way she wanted. She wanted to punch him, kick him, hurt him the way he'd hurt her.

She was dragged off stage, away from Jake, into the back room where'd she'd begun the evening. There were other people there, but she didn't register any of them. Jake stopped at the bottom of the stairs and stared at her, his jaw clenched, his eyes dark and guarded.

"Cali, please," he said. "Tell me what happened. Tell me what's wrong." He ran a hand through his hair, leaving a trail of spiked ends sticking up behind it.

He stepped forward and she retreated into the arms surrounding her, seeking safety in the strength behind her. Jake stopped, devastation tumbling over his features. She turned her head, hiding her face in the arm holding her.

"What?" he said quietly. "What did I do?"

"Was this another test? Another cleansing you thought I needed?" The energy drained from her, the despair sinking in. She sagged against the support behind her, thankful someone was there to hold her up. She inhaled a ragged breath and tried to pull herself together. She needed to get home.

"I don't know what you're talking about," Jake answered her. "This wasn't a test. It was me claiming you as my sub, Cali. As mine. Something I thought you wanted." Dejection was audible in his voice, but it didn't affect her. She was too numb, too cold to feel anything.

"Peter," she croaked out, a shiver raking her body from the cold within her. Her damp skin filled with goose bumps as the perspiration dried. "Why did you bring him here? To humiliate me?"

Jake's eyes widened, the denial flashing in the silver pools before the words left his mouth. "I didn't. I would never do that. What are you talking about?" He stepped toward her again, but Seth stepped in to stop his advance.

"Then why was he here? In the front row, watching my shame?"

"What shame?" Jake wrenched on the arm holding him before he gave up and growled, "There's no shame in wanting this. In what we have."

"Then why do I feel it? Huh, Jake? Tell me why I feel that now?"

Jake looked down, eyes squeezing shut as if he felt her pain. Cali tried to calm her breathing once again, more of the fight draining away. A woman stepped up and offered her a robe. Somehow it found its way around her shoulders and she numbly slipped her arms into it, clenching the edges together, shivering beneath the soft cotton.

"I love you, Cali. I would never hurt you like this."

Cali jerked her head up at the hoarse words. Her gaze locked on Jake's, the declaration hovering between them. If she trusted what she saw, the pain and misery that was on his face, she'd almost believe him.

But this wasn't love. She'd fooled herself into believing in a fantasy.

"No, Jake. You don't love me." Cali turned away needing to leave. To get away from him and the pain knifing in her chest. But she stopped and gave him one last look. "You only want to possess me. Own me. Control me. That's domination, not love."

And love was what she'd really, truly wanted all along.

How absolutely stupid she'd been to think she might have found it here. With Jake.

TWENTY-THREE

Cali pushed her way past the person holding her and forced her feet to move toward the door. Her mind was numb now, along with her body. Nothing mattered anymore. Nothing but getting out of there.

She faltered when she opened the door. Her fists clenched on the knob, the black haze of fear closing around her. She'd have to walk through the entire club to get out. All those people would see her, the ones who'd watched her. Saw the collaring, the paddling, her breakdown.

A true walk of shame. Could she do it?

The gentle touch on her shoulder got her attention. "I'll take you home, Ms. Reynolds."

She looked up and finally put a face with the arms that had supported her. Deklan. The man from her condo complex. Jake's business partner.

"This way. We'll go out the back."

For that reason alone, she followed him. She didn't want to trust him, to trust anyone from this place, but his offer would save her last bit of dignity. She ducked her head and blindly let herself be led through the building before she finally balked as she was being assisted into an SUV.

"Your car will be at your condo in the morning," he said. He kept his distance, seeming to understand she needed the space. "Please, let me take you home. You're in no condition to drive."

He was right. She was exhausted, both emotionally and physically. Instead of answering, she simply got in. That was easier than accepting.

The ride home passed in a blur and it seemed like only minutes later the car was parked before her condo. Her sanctuary. Without saying a word she got out when he opened the door for her. She tried to hide the reflexive wince caused by her tender ass rubbing against the seat.

"Will you be okay?" He sounded like he really cared.

She nodded automatically; she didn't want his concern. She'd be fine, just as soon as she was away from everything associated with The Den.

Cali stared at the ground and tugged the robe tighter to ward off the chilly December air, even though the cold invaded every pore of her body. Would she ever be warm again? Then her coat was around her and her purse was being placed into her hands. The man had thought of everything.

The trembling in her hands made her fumble as she tried to find her keys. But he was there again, taking the bag from her as he led her to the door. He found the house key, opened the door and stepped aside to allow her to enter.

Finally, she was home. Back to her normal life—not that it would ever be truly normal again. The shaking in her hands traveled through her entire body as she let the safety of her surroundings soak into her. She inhaled and absorbed the clean scent of the cinnamon air freshener, the smell of normalcy almost wiping out the lingering wisps of leather and arousal that clung to her.

She was turning to shut the door when Deklan spoke. "Jake had nothing to do with that man being there tonight."

She searched his face and swallowed, willing herself to hold back the well of tears threatening to drown her. "How could he not?" she asked, her voice quivering. "He owns the place."

"He would never hurt anyone like this. None of us would," Deklan said. "It's not what The Den is about. Whoever was there who hurt you was a coincidence. Not something planned or targeted."

Cali looked away and started to close the door. It didn't really matter anymore. The damage was done and it was her life left in tatters.

"He cares about you, Cali." Deklan's words stopped her once again. There was only a crack of space left in the door opening. His face was in shadows, the porch light reflecting behind him. "You are the only one he's ever collared. That means something to him. It's not a game or something done lightly. In our world, it's everything."

In their world.

But what about *her* world?

Cali finished closing the door. There was nothing left to say. No answer she could give. She clicked the lock, letting the deadbolt slip into place. If only it was that simple to lock down her heart too. She walked to the kitchen and grabbed the roll of trash bags from under the sink. She shifted into auto-pilot, focusing on her task, because doing something, anything, was better than thinking.

Than feeling.

Upstairs, she sat on the edge of her bed and slipped off the boots she still wore, stuffing them into a plastic bag. In her closet she pushed back her normal clothes and dug out her stash of 'gifts' from Jake. Mechanically she pulled out every item and stuffed it into a bag. The clothes, the shoes, the sexy underwear, the toys—everything.

Last, she stripped off the robe, along with the bra and thong, and shoved them into the bags with the rest of the items. Naked, she stared at the two bags full of her shame. Had it been worth it? Would she live to regret this brief lapse of judgment for the rest of her life? More importantly, would she ever get past the pain ripping at her heart?

Choking back a sob, Cali grabbed her own robe off a hook, tugged it on, then snatched up the bags and hauled them downstairs. She paused to slip on her boots then stepped outside. Ignoring the cold penetrating her robe, she carried the bags through the quiet of the night to the large dumpster hidden around the corner of the building.

The lid squeaked in protest as she lifted it, the sound raking against her frayed nerves. The final witness to her actions, it was almost like the inanimate object raised one last condemnation. She tossed both bags into the bin, grunting with the effort, and gently set the lid down, not wanting to hear another accusation from the dented, rusty metal.

Light flakes of snow had started to fall and Cali shivered in the darkness as she hurried back to her condo. Maybe if she just stayed out there, the cold would freeze out the pain. Numb her until she didn't have to deal with tomorrow.

With Peter.

With Jake.

With the mess she'd made of her life.

But she knew that wouldn't happen. Short of death, tomorrow would still come. And she wasn't pathetic enough to wish for death. Whatever the fallout, she would deal with it. Just like she always did.

She lifted her face to the falling flakes of snow, closed her eyes and inhaled. Icy shapes drifted onto her cheeks, her fore-head and her eyelids, where they settled and slowly melted into the heat of her skin, the water blending with the tears slipping from her eyes.

Tomorrow she would have consequences to deal with.

But tonight, tonight she would cry.

Jake stuffed a final pair of socks into his bag and yanked the zipper closed. He didn't take much, didn't need much. He slammed the drawer and stalked to the closet, stripping as he went. He blindly grabbed clothes but was aware enough to put on his thermals before pulling on jeans and a fleece.

"Where you going?"

The voice should have startled him, but it didn't. Of course he couldn't escape without an interrogation.

"Does it matter?" Jake snapped. He dug through the closet until he found his snow pants and slipped them on over his jeans.

"What about the club?" Seth asked, his deceptively placid tone hiding none of the tension rippling from his stiff posture.

"I don't care."

Jake grabbed his riding boots and wool socks and tugged them on. He didn't give a fuck what happened to the place. The sharp pain of rejection stabbed through him and he squeezed his eyes shut, keeping his back to Seth until he'd forced the emotion down. Unclenching his hands, he stood, picked up his bag and pushed past the other man.

Seth trailed after him into the living area. "I don't believe that."

Jake rounded on him. "You think I give a fuck what you believe?"

"Yeah, I do."

"Well, I don't," he denied before heading to the door. He had to get out of there. Away from them, the club, this life. *Fuck.*

"You bailing on Cali too?"

The question slammed Jake on the back like a physical force. He spun back to Seth, the rage boiling over. "Fuck you, Mathews. *Fuck you.* She *rejected* me. She humiliated *me.* So fuck if I care about her."

Seth's only reaction was a smile, which ratcheted up Jake's anger.

"You think this is funny? Enjoying my demise, are you?"

"No, Jake," Seth said. "I'm not enjoying this at all. But your reaction is telling."

Jake didn't want to hear it. He didn't need psychoanalysis or judgments. "Whatever." He turned his back on Seth and stomped to the entry closet.

"You're running from your dream," he continued. "When you were so close to having everything."

"The Den was not my dream," Jake growled, slamming the closet door with all the force of his rage. "It's a business. I'm done with it. It's yours." He thrust his arms into the lined leather jacket and tucked his helmet under his arm. *Fuck dreams. Fuck all of it.*

"I was talking about Cali."

Cali. The pain stabbed him. The torn look of betrayal and hatred that marred her face flashed in his mind and dug like bullets into his gut.

"Can I have her too?"

Like that, Jake was in Seth's face, his hand curled around the front of the man's shirt. "No one touches her but me."

Seth appraised him, his brown eyes nailing Jake with challenge. "You're leaving. She's a free agent if you're not here."

"The hell she is. She belongs to me."

"Not if you run."

Jake shook with the effort to control the impulse to pummel Seth. To punch and rail against the man who'd been his friend forever. He shoved away, pushing Seth back before he acted on his rage. What did it matter anyway?

There was nothing left for him here.

He grabbed his things off the floor, tossed his phone on the end-table and stormed out of the loft. He didn't care what Seth thought. What anyone thought.

There was no point in caring.

Impatience dug at him as the elevator descended to the garage. He jerked on his gloves, the thick lining encasing his fingers in warmth. The ping of arrival echoed in the small space, signaling escape to Jake. He was out the doors and at his bike seconds later.

With quick, precise movements he strapped his bag to the back of the motorcycle and pulled the helmet over his head, the face shield blocking out the cold and the world. The zipper on his jacket rippled hard and protested in the cold as he tugged it up to his chin.

Gear in place, Jake mounted the bike, pushed the start and cranked on the throttle. The rumble of the engine ricocheted off the concrete walls to roar around him. He hunched low over the gas tank and took off.

Away.

From the pain. The humiliation. The loss.

Her.

TWENTY-FOUR

Jake was numb—physically, mentally, emotionally. Frozen stiff from the long, exposed ride through the night. He straightened, his back protesting as he shifted on the seat and shook out his arms in an attempt to bring feeling into his numb appendages. He flexed his hands, the sensation rushing back to his fingers in a flash of burning pinpricks.

It'd been stupid to ride his bike through the night. But then, he had nothing to lose. No reason to be smart.

The sky was still dark, the city silent. Pre-dawn noises were just starting to creak through the sharp morning air. The low rumble of a garbage truck starting its morning route. The clank and groan of a delivery truck making its early drop-off.

Jake lifted his face shield, crisp air biting at his cheeks. The freshness welcomed after the hours of confined, stale air trapped under his helmet. He inhaled, the mixed stench of garbage blending with the distinctive perfume of the Missouri river instantly bringing him home. A menagerie of feelings and memories from his youth crashed through him, despite the fact that he didn't need or want the reminders of his past.

Yet here he was. Sitting outside of the first BDSM club he'd ever ventured into.

Hell, he hadn't even thought about where he was going when he'd left Minneapolis. He'd just need to get the hell out. Somehow he'd wound up back where he'd started.

Sioux City, Iowa, wasn't the hotspot of the Midwest by any definition. Trapped in the middle of the country, the city founded on the mighty Missouri was in many ways a blend of quintessential small town and gritty city living. Jake had been born into the small-town gloss and lived in oblivious splendor until it'd been cruelly yanked away when he was ten years old. He'd been tossed and doused in the dark underside of the city by his twelfth birthday and well on his way to juvenile hall before he was a teen.

He shook off the black thoughts and dismounted from the bike. His legs protested at first, but he ignored their complaints, shoving the cramping pain back with the rest of his issues. Behind the wall of caring. He should probably find a hotel to crash in, but he didn't want the quiet. Didn't want the silence that would allow those damn feelings to take hold and torture him some more.

No. He would control that, just like he controlled all things in his life.

All things until Cali.

Fuck. Jake stalked to the club and pounded on the back door, knowing someone would be there despite the time. It'd been years since he'd been back, but he still kept in touch with the owner, Doug Smith. The man Jake viewed as his benefactor and the only father figure he'd had after his own father was killed.

"What the fuck do you want?" The burly growl preceded the groan of the door as it swung open with a sharp thrust. A big-chested, stocky man with a bushy mustache and an angry snarl on his leathered face greeted Jake. A snarl that instantly changed to shock upon seeing him. "Well, I'll be damned. What the fuck brings you here?"

"Visit," Jake said. He took in the changes in the man before him. He'd aged, the years showing in the lines around his eyes, the liberal gray covering his long hair and the slight bulge under his tight black shirt—all things that had not been there when Jake left fifteen years earlier.

"Visit, my ass," the proprietor scoffed. "It's fucking freezing out here. You coming in or what?" He didn't wait for a response. Just turned and strolled back into the dark recesses of the interior.

Jake grabbed the door before it closed and followed Doug inside. The warmth immediately surrounded him, highlighting just how frozen he was. He shivered as he pulled off his helmet and followed the familiar path down the hallway to Doug's office. The man was already at the coffee pot perched atop the file cabinet in the corner, pouring the dark brew into two waiting cups.

Jake tugged off his gloves and accepted the steaming mug when it was shoved at him. "Thanks," he mumbled before he took a sip of the scalding liquid, letting the ambient warmth flow through him from the inside out.

Doug grunted his reply before he took his own mug to his desk and dropped into the worn chair behind it. The springs creaked in protest at the sudden weight and the man sighed. He eyed Jake, his gaze scanning from head to toe before he spoke. "Out for a casual night ride in thirty-degree weather?"

Jake sniffed and took another drink of his coffee. "Yup." He scanned the messy office. "I see nothing's changed since I left."

"Oh, a lot's changed, Jake." Doug leaned back in the chair, testing its stability. "You gonna tell me why you're here?"

"Nope." Jake absorbed Doug's scrutiny, keeping his face blank. "Just need a place to hang for a bit. You open to that?"

"You know there's always a place for you here."

Jake glanced down, his gratitude surfacing in a surprising flush. "Yeah. I know." He raised his head to look at the man who'd essentially saved him from a life of jailbait, crime and drugs. "Don't know if I've ever thanked you for that."

The older man waved his hand in dismissal. "You're not in jail. That's thanks enough." He set his mug down and stood. "Now, I'm tired as shit. You need a bed or do you have a pop-up stuffed in the trunk of that bike you rolled in on?"

Jake smiled, his first since the disaster with Cali. "A bed would be great."

He followed Doug up the back stairs to the small living quarters. The same ones he'd crashed in many a night during his youth. Often on the floor, depending on if Deklan and Seth had been there as well. But the floor was a welcomed exchange from the rancid foster home or back-alley dumpster that had been his alternative.

The scent of tobacco and grease welcomed Jake as he stepped into the cramped living room. This was good. What he needed.

Here he could forget. Go back to the basics and start again. Like he'd done before. Find his pleasure in the simplicity of Dominance without all the other trappings. He'd call that club back and see if the job was still there. He could spend a few weeks with Doug then go where he could submerse himself in the world and forget his mistakes along with all he'd lost.

Forget Cali—her soft smile, impossible courage, gentle touches—and move on.

Even if it killed him to do so.

Cali stared at the moving images on the screen, willing her mind to follow along, to forget about everything and get lost in the movie. But it wasn't working. She snuggled deeper into the cocoon of the blanket and blinked back the tears that threatened once again. She wouldn't cry.

No matter how much she hurt.

She'd been in an almost constant state of dread, fear and worry since she woke up. What little sleep she'd gotten had done nothing to relieve the ache encompassing her body and mind. The hot shower had only washed off the surface discomfort, leaving her internal dishevel blatantly exposed.

And the exposure made her feel the ache of loss simmering under the other emotions. She didn't want to admit it, didn't want to feel it, but it was there anyway. Maybe it had all been a game to Jake, part of his job. But to her, everything that happened over the last two months had been very real. She'd stupidly come to trust him more than she'd ever trusted anyone, and he'd betrayed her by bringing Peter to the club. Hurt her and potentially inflicted irreparable damage to her life.

She hated him for that.

But she still missed him. And a part of her still wanted everything he'd given to her. That was the kicker that almost broke her. How depraved was she that her life could be falling apart around her and she was sitting there mourning the loss of being spanked and whipped? Of being tied down and ordered to take whatever her Dom gave to her?

She really was sick.

A sharp knock on the glass of her patio door jolted Cali out of her internal berating. She looked up to see Allie and Kendra standing at the door, smiles lighting their faces as Kendra gave a short wave. *Damn*. It was Saturday afternoon.

Cali had forgotten to cancel their weekly coffee chat.

Pushing herself up, she shuffled to the door, thankful she'd at least managed to throw on some sweats even if she'd neglected every other aspect of her grooming. She brushed her hands over her hair, tucking the sides behind her ears before she opened the door, ready to make her excuses.

"Sorry, guys," Cali said through the door crack. "I'm not feeling well today. I should have called." She watched Allie's face shift from open and friendly to concerned and calculating.

Allie's eyes narrowed, her brows coming together as her lips tightened.

"Are you okay?" Kendra asked, the worry reaching through the door.

Before Cali could react, Allie's hand snapped out and pushed the door open. Cali jumped, startled by the abrupt action, and stepped back in order to avoid being run over by her friend as Allie stepped into the room. She turned on Cali, grilling her with attorney eyes.

"Spill it," she demanded. "What happened?"

Cali took another step back, her hand going to her throat. "What do you mean?" Her voice shook and she tried to clear it. "Nothing's wrong. I just got a touch of the flu or something."

"Bullshit. Your eyes are red and puffy, your nose pink from wiping. No makeup, wild hair, chapped lips and an outfit that screams of comfort. Those, my dear, are all signs of a woman who's been hurt and crying for way too long." Allie reached out and gave Cali's arm a caressing stroke. Her voice softened along with her eyes. "What happened?"

Cali turned away, unable to take the kindness. She walked into the kitchen and busied herself making the coffee. It was obvious Allie wasn't leaving.

"Cali." Allie was behind her, her voice gentle. "Is everything okay with the kids? With your family?"

Cali spun around and reassured her friends. "They're fine. Everything is fine with them. I didn't mean to worry you…" She exhaled, running a hand through her hair, and stared at the floor. "It's nothing. Really. I'll be fine tomorrow." Right. Maybe if she said it enough, she'd believe it too.

Not used to feeling so vulnerable, Cali turned back to the sink and filled the coffee pot with water. She sensed her friends watching her, taking in her shaking hands, her stiff shoulders. The room felt suddenly warm, her body flushing with embarrassment under their scrutiny. Then Kendra was there, taking the pot from Cali and shutting off the water.

"I'll get this," Kendra said. "Go. Sit down before you crumble and we get stuck consoling you on the kitchen floor." Her friend's attempt at lightness worked enough to make Cali chuckle.

"Okay," she agreed. Allie led her to the kitchen table and Cali plopped down in a chair. What in the world was she going to tell these women, these friends who were only trying to help her?

Allie waited patiently until Kendra finished with the coffee pot and joined them at the table. The gurgle of the coffee vibrated through the air as it slowly began to infuse the room with the smell of brewing grounds.

Allie leaned forward, resting her arms on the table, and stared at Cali. "What's wrong? Is there anything we can do?"

The honest concern and openness tore at Cali. How could she stand to lose these friends if they found out the truth about her? She'd already lost so many of her so-called friends with the divorce. All those people who didn't understand why she'd leave Peter and had slowly distanced themselves from her, like divorce was a disease they could catch.

Would Peter reveal everything and turn these friends against her too?

Cali swallowed and tried to work some moisture into her throat. She clenched her hands in her lap and gathered her strength to pull off the best acting job of her life. She forced a smile onto her face and met Allie's gaze. "I'm fine. Really. Just one of those days, I guess. Probably just PMS."

Allie wasn't buying it. She raised an eyebrow in smooth doubt. "And I'm your fairy Godmother here to wish away your sorrow." She sat back, crossing her arms over her chest. "Now, really. What's wrong?"

The coffee pot gave one last gasping snort and sputter as it emptied the remaining water into the grounds. Cali stared at her hands and willed herself to relax.

"Is it your ex, your kids or something else?" Allie persisted as Kendra rose to get the coffee.

Cali looked up and smiled. "We're not in a courtroom. I don't need to be grilled into a confession."

"Okay, then spill. What's got you so upset?"

Cali sighed. Maybe giving them a little would get Allie off her back. "What's the most common reason for woman trouble?"

Allie straightened, her eyes going wide. "You mean, this is about a man? Hold on." Then she was out of her chair and out the patio door before Cali could blink.

Kendra returned to the table with two steaming cups of coffee. "Where'd she go?"

"I don't know," Cali answered, taking the mug from her friend. "But it can't be good."

Kendra laughed and went back to the kitchen to bring the last one, along with the creamer and sugar Cali had gotten out.

Kendra took a seat and cupped her hands around her mug. Her blond hair was pulled into a ponytail, her clothing simple and plain. Much like the woman herself. No makeup, no jewelry, nothing flashy that would draw attention to her.

"You don't have to talk to us if you don't want to, Cali." Kendra watched Cali with guarded eyes. "Your privacy is your right. Just know we're here if you do want to talk." She tucked her head, staring blankly into the steaming liquid.

Cali cocked her head and looked closely at the other woman. There was something there, something she was hiding. But then, who was Cali to judge anyone about secrets? "Thank you, Kendra. That means a lot to me."

Kendra lifted her gaze and smiled, her features softening with the act. She opened her mouth to speak but was halted by Allie barging back into the condo.

"Got it," she declared, holding a bottle high. She moved to the table and set her prize down, a devious smile plastered across her face. "Our good friend Jack here is always in for a solid man-bashing session."

Cali stared at the bottle of Jack Daniels sitting in the middle of her table and burst into laughter. Deep, releasing laughter that caught in her gut and rolled out of her in waves of almost hysterical intensity. When she finally collected herself enough to focus back on her friends, she caught them staring at her with mixed expressions of concern and amusement.

"What?" she asked, wiping at the tears that had escaped from her eyes. "I haven't drunk Jack since college."

"Oh, we're not drinking," Allie said mischievously as she drew her hand out from behind her back, showing the three short glasses in her hand. "We're doing shots."

"Oh, God," Kendra groaned before she dropped her head to the table.

Allie laughed, setting the glasses down and opening the bottle. She poured three liberal shots and passed one to each of them. "Here's to it, ladies." She lifted her glass high. "Drink up." She tossed back the liquid, screwing up her face as she swallowed.

Cali met Kendra's gaze before she gave a shrug and reached for her shot. She sniffed at the amber liquid and flinched from the harsh, tangy scent. Closing her eyes, she chugged down the shot. She braced her arms on the table and swallowed, the whiskey burning a path down her throat to land like a rock in her empty gut.

Allie chuckled and motioned at Kendra to finish hers. With a dramatic sigh, Kendra picked up her glass and downed the whiskey with a practiced ease that startled Cali. Kendra licked her lips and set the glass back on the table with a shallow click. She met Allie's open-mouth stare and cocked an uncharacteristic grin.

"What?" Kendra questioned. "I happen to have a great deal of experience with man troubles." The blandness of her tone offset the lightness sparking in her blue eyes.

Cali burst out laughing, unable to hold it in any longer.

From there, the three women managed to get shit-stinking drunk. Three-quarters of a bottle and one delivery pizza later, they were spread across her living room, giggling like school girls.

"I haven't been this drunk in…" Cali paused to think, trying to focus. "Forever, maybe," she finished behind a snort. She collapsed on the arm of the couch, hiding her giggles behind her hand.

Allie twisted her head to watch Cali from her spread-eagle sprawl on the floor. "You mean you never got drunk like this before?" Her eyes were wide with disbelief.

Cali shook her head. "Nope. Way too conservative. Then, once I got married and had the kids, I was way too responsible."

Allie pushed herself into a semi-sitting position and regarded Cali like she was a bizarre aberration. "Seriously? Well, shit, girl. It's about time."

Cali rested her head on the padding of the couch. Why did it suddenly feel so heavy? Kendra snickered and Cali looked to her. She was curled in the recliner, her long limbs somehow contorted into a seemingly comfortable position.

"What?" Cali asked.

Kendra lifted her water, smiling around the glass. "Nothing."

"Ha," Cali countered. "You lie like shit."

Kendra looked away, the glass lowering to her lap. *Crap. What'd she say?*

"You going to tell us what started all of this?" Allie interjected, pulling Cali's attention back to her. "Why we're all three sheets to the wind in the first place?"

Cali stared at the ceiling, letting the world spin around her. Her head was fuzzy, her lips strangely numb and the world seemed to be spinning in her peripheral vision. She'd thought this topic had been successfully dropped, but evidently Allie had just been plotting her attack. Cali licked her lips and tried to remember what she was going to say.

"Man trouble," Kendra mumbled. "Isn't that reason enough?"

Right. Man trouble. If only it were that simple.

"But what man?" Allie persisted.

What would it hurt? Maybe they could help. The fuzzy logic made sense to Cali in her altered state.

"Jake," she finally admitted, keeping her gaze on the ceiling, which was now spinning counterclockwise to her peripheral world.

"Jake?" Allie asked. "Not the same Jake whom Edith dragged to the engagement party with our hunky neighbor, Mr. Winters?"

Leave it to Allie to remember a detail like that. Cali had no idea how she could even focus at the moment, let alone put together that lame trail of information. Cali closed her eyes, giving up on tracking the ceiling movement. "Yes. The same."

"What? You've been dating that man and not telling us?"

A pillow smacked Cali in the face, but it didn't faze her. The soft material bounced off to land on her lap before it even registered that Allie had thrown something at her.

"For how long?" Allie demanded.

How long? Was it dating? No. Definitely not dating. But they didn't need to know that. "Two months."

"Two months?" Cali felt the couch cushions dip. Then Allie punched her arm. Not hard, and Cali was only assuming it was Allie since her eyes were still closed. "You've been seeing him since the party and never said a word. Bitch." The last was said with more jealousy than heat and Cali smiled.

"So, what happened?" Kendra asked.

Oh yeah. That. "He betrayed my trust."

"What? How?" Allie demanded.

Cali shrugged. How could she explain that part? She was still coherent enough to know the complete truth wouldn't work. "He told me to trust him. And I did. I really did. Then, *bam*..." She let the words trail off, unsure how to finish.

"Then what?" Allie shook Cali's arm, apparently in an attempt to see if Cali was still awake. "What'd he do? Don't tell me you caught him cheating?"

Yeah, that wouldn't have hurt nearly as bad. Especially after only two months. "No. Wish it was."

"What? How could you wish that?" Allie's head settled against her shoulder. "He must have really fucked up if cheating is considered a better thing."

"Yeah," Cali mumbled. "Somebody fucked up."

"There are a lot worse things a man can do than cheat on you," Kendra said quietly. "Did he hurt you? I mean, physically?"

Now that question was a landmine. Was it considered hurting her when she wanted it? Cali shook her head, the movement causing her stomach to rock in time with the motion. Bad idea.

"No. He didn't abuse me." There, an honest answer while avoiding the direct question. Cali felt pretty proud of herself.

"That's not what I asked," Kendra said. "Did he hit you?"

Shit. So much for evasion. Cali fished around in her brain for a good answer, the obvious one of flat-out lying seemed to sprint from her consciousness. Maybe Jack Daniels was a secret truth serum because Cali found herself answering honestly. "Only when I wanted him to."

The silence hung in the room, the low background music suddenly seeming to rise in volume. Cali kept her eyes closed and waited for the outrage that was sure to come.

"Really?" Allie said sounding more interested than repulsed. "Did he tie you up too?"

Cali was pretty certain the last question was said in jest, but she answered anyway. "Only when I wanted him to."

Allie's head jerked from its resting spot on Cali's shoulder. "You're not joking. Oh my God."

Here it comes, Cali thought. *Here come all of the horrible accusations and condemnations.* Her muscles tensed as she waited. Her mouth was dry and the alcohol rolled in her gut, contemplating a return trip.

"Well, shit, Cali. You've been holding out on us more than we knew." Allie gave her shoulder a shove before returning her head to the same spot. "I don't suppose you're going to give us any details, are you?"

Cali snorted. "No." That was it? Really?

"So was this at that club those men own?"

Cali almost bolted upright in shock. Kendra's question was jarring enough to finally jolt her eyes open. Her heart thundered as she tried to feign a casualness she didn't feel. "You know about that?"

"What club? What are you guys talking about?" Allie asked, sitting up once again to glance between the two other women.

"The Den," Kendra said. "The most exclusive BDSM club in the Twin Cities."

Allie gaped at them. "How do you know this?"

"Googled their names." Kendra lifted her shoulder. "You can find anything on the internet, and it's not like they're trying to hide it."

Allie swore. "I really need to up my investigative skills." She shifted her attention back to Cali. "So? Was it? Did you go to that club?"

In for a…crap. Cali couldn't even remember the saying at the moment. Well, she was pretty much in it now, so she might as well see what happened. She was just too tired to dodge and evade or come up with believable lies. "Yes."

"Holy shit."

Allie stared at her. Cali shifted to see Kendra watching her, a definite smirk on her face. "What?"

"Nothing," Kendra said. "You just never know what goes on behind closed doors, do you? I never would have pegged you as being into BDSM, but here you are, admitting just that."

"And?" Cali asked defensively, letting the question hang, hoping Kendra would fill in the rest yet afraid of what she would hear. But she needed to hear it. Was desperate to find out what her friend thought now that she knew the truth about Cali's deviant activities.

"And…to each her own, I say." Kendra took a drink of her water. "I don't care what you do. The only thing that matters to me is how you treat *me*, and you've been nothing but kind and generous since I've moved in. Your sex life isn't my business. And frankly, that's something that should only matter to you and your partner. Period."

Cali could hardly believe her ears. Really? Kendra wasn't going to judge and reject her now that she knew Cali enjoyed being a submissive?

"Ditto. What she said." Allie agreed with a sharp nod and a point to Kendra. "Any chance I can come with you one night?"

"What?" Cali asked, dumbfounded.

When both women broke out in deep fits of laughter, she realized it was probably at the shocked expression that had to be on her face. Who were these women, and how in the world did they become her friends? She smiled and relaxed into the couch once again.

"If I was ever going back, maybe. But my days there are over," Cali said once the women had stopped laughing enough to hear her. "There is no way I'm ever setting foot in that club again."

Allie squinted, looking Cali over. "What happened? I'm assuming it has something to do with why we're all drunk."

Cali sighed and closed her eyes once again. She was getting really tired, the whiskey and lack of sleep pulling her into a lulling zone. There was no real way to explain the rest, so she short-cutted to the end. "My ex showed up at a rather inappropriate time."

Silence followed her declaration for so long that Cali almost willed her eyes open to see what her friends were thinking.

"I take it your ex didn't know about your other desires, or was that something you used to do with him too?" Kendra's question was gentle, not accusing.

Cali snorted again. "No. God. Peter didn't even like sex, let alone engage in anything remotely deviant from straight mission style." Shit. Had she really just admitted that too? She made a note to her drunk self to never drink Jack Daniels again. The stuff was definitely laced with truth serum.

"What do you mean, he didn't like sex?"

Cali tilted her head and squinted at Allie, who had a slightly shocked and dazed look on her face. "Well, I assume he didn't because he certainly never engaged in it with me. And no," she interrupted Allie's open mouth and obvious next question, "he wasn't having an affair. And he isn't gay. I'm certain of that. We were together for twenty-five years and I know he never cheated on me—with a man or a woman—nor me on him. For whatever reason, sex just never worked for us."

"So why was he at the club?" Kendra asked. "Was he checking up on you, or was he there for himself?"

Cali tried to focus on Kendra across the room. Her friend had a very good question, one she hadn't really asked herself. Until that moment, she'd just assumed Jake had brought him there. But then, how would Jake know who Peter was? How would he have found her ex-husband and made him come to the club? Peter being there of his own free will was something she'd never considered.

"I don't know," Cali finally answered. "Why *would* he be at the club? I thought Jake did it for some reason."

Kendra unfolded her legs and set her feet on the floor. She leaned forward in the chair, resting her forearms on her thighs. A feat Cali found completely amazing, as she didn't think she could balance like that right now.

"Cali," Kendra said softly. "I'm no expert, but I will say I have some experience in the Dom/sub world." Kendra stared at the carpet, her cheeks turning pink, her lips pursed. She exhaled and continued, "And it's my experience that only a sadistic, sick asshole would ever do something like that on purpose. I don't know Jake at all. But you do. And only you can answer what kind of person he is. Outside of being a Dom, is he the kind of man who would revel in hurting you like that?"

"Am I the only person who's never gotten kinky?" Allie

sputtered then flopped against the couch. "I'm obviously miss-ing out on something. And you, Miss Kendra, have some sto-ries to tell us."

Kendra immediately stood. "Nothing to tell. I've gotta get going." She gave each of them a salute then set her glass on the counter. She paused at the door, her coordination seem-ing remarkably good, given that Cali could barely sit without tipping over. "I hope everything works out for you, Cali. Let me know if there's anything I can do." Then she slipped out the door and disappeared into the dark.

"Well, shit," Allie mumbled. "I feel like I just chased her away. What'd I do?"

"Don't know," Cali managed to answer, her eyes too heavy to keep open. "Do you really want to go to that club?"

"Why not?" Allie said, keeping up with the conversation jump. "A girl can always expand her horizons."

"So you don't think I'm sadistic or a deviant or…some-thing?" Cali held her breath and waited.

"Ha! You? Cali, dear, you're an anal retentive angel with a kinky inside. Nothing wrong with that."

Cali released her breath and relaxed into the darkness pull-ing at her. So her friends knew about her kink and didn't think she was horrible. Didn't run away in disgust. What about that? Maybe she'd had the wrong friends before.

Her mind skipped over to the other topic that kept rub-bing at her. Why *was* Peter at the club? She didn't think Jake was deliberately mean. No, she'd seen too much of his tender, caring side for her to believe that. So *if* it was true that Jake didn't orchestrate the whole thing, why would Peter be there?

Why would her ex-husband, who barely engaged in basic sex, be at a club that excelled in way-out-of-the-box sex? It was a subject worth investigating and one she'd have to dig into when she could actually think clearly.

She pushed back the little glimmer of hope springing up
at the thought that maybe, just maybe, this wasn't Jake's fault.
But it still danced in her heart. So if Jake wasn't to blame, was
she? Did she just make a horrible assumption and throw away
everything she'd dared to hope for? She'd been so afraid of
people passing judgment on her that she hadn't even thought
about the verdict she'd thrown at him.

Her stomach churned, twisting the contents around the
sinking sense of dread that settled there. Jake had offered his
heart and she'd thrown it back in his face. Both the collar and
his words. Was she wrong?

Would he ever forgive her if she was?

Moaning, she rolled to her side and looked at Allie, sleeping on the other end of the couch. She needed to do that.
Sleep. She'd figure out the rest tomorrow. With luck, there'd
be something to salvage with her life and Jake.

TWENTY-FIVE

The soap splashed against the sides of the sink, the water cascading up the edges in a rushed attempt to crest the rim and strike the cheery reindeer apron Cali wore. She didn't care. Determined, she continued her attack on the pan and the remnants of the roast clinging stubbornly to the bottom.

Sighing, she tossed the scouring pad into the dishwater and rested her tired arms. Staring out the window over the sink, she glared at the colored lights framing the windows of the neighboring condos. She gave a puff in an attempt to blow the annoying strand of hair out of her eyes. It didn't work.

"Are you okay, Mom?"

Cali jumped at the sound of her daughter's voice. She'd been surprised when Stephanie had shown up unexpectedly that morning, searching for another reference book. Or at least, that's what she'd told Cali, who'd quickly downed Ibuprofen and three cups of coffee to cover the raging hangover she'd had the glory of waking up with. Allie had been too sick herself to stick around and ease the awkward silence that had fallen when her daughter had observed the mess in the living room and almost-empty bottle of liquor.

Stephanie had surprised her further by hanging around for Sunday dinner. As a family, that had always been their nice dinner. One they all counted on, especially when the kids got older and schedules had gone crazy during the week. But things had been stilted between them all day. Not intolerable, but not comfortable either.

"Of course," she answered with practiced superficial calm. "Just battling the last of the dishes." She kept her back to her daughter and retackled the project in the sink, the pan clanking loudly against the porcelain as she shifted it around to get a better angle on the offending grime.

"Mom." The soft word was barely audible over the noise Cali was making, but the light touch on her shoulder felt like a brick had landed there.

Cali froze, her body stiff as she waited. Was this where Stephanie finally told her she knew about her mother's sick desires? Where she told Cali how disgusted she was? But she didn't seem angry or repulsed.

No, Stephanie sounded concerned.

The fingers skimmed down Cali's arm, the touch scorching her skin through the silk of her blouse. Cali wanted to haul Stephanie in and hold her tight. A hug and kiss that would cure all. But those days were gone, and Cali doubted she'd ever get them back.

"Really." Her daughter leaned forward, trying to see her face. "Are you okay? You seem so...distant. Sad today. I'm worried about you."

Cali couldn't help the scoff that puffed out. Okay? That was a very relative term. Okay compared to what? "I'm fine. You're not supposed to worry about me. It's my job to worry about you." She dried her hands on the towel next to the sink, tucked the annoying piece of hair behind her ear and turned away from her daughter to finish packing up the dinner leftovers.

"I'm sorry."

Cali whirled back to face her daughter. "For what?"

Stephanie was leaning against the counter, arms crossed, lip tucked between her teeth. She sighed then looked up. "For getting so bent out of shape about you dating. It wasn't my place to judge you."

Judge her? Oh, her daughter could judge her, all right. "No worries. It's been an adjustment for all of us."

"But it was wrong of me," she insisted. "And now...you're so sad. I'm afraid I made you do something you didn't want to do." She fidgeted with the strings of her hoodie and shifted against the counter. "You didn't stop dating Jake because of me, did you?"

Dating Jake? Maybe if they'd been dating, things could have worked between them. But they hadn't and she couldn't change the past. Nor could she erase the memories of everything they'd shared. Things she had to force herself to stop thinking about because they weren't possible in her life.

Cali stepped in front of her daughter and tentatively set her hands on Stephanie's shoulders, not sure how she would react. "It had nothing to do with you. I'm so sorry any of this has affected you."

Her daughter studied her searching for the truth, and Cali hoped beyond hope Stephanie found it. "Then what happened? You were so happy at Thanksgiving."

Cali stepped back, not liking where the conversation was going, but Stephanie grabbed her hand and wouldn't let her retreat. Her grip was tight and insistent as her daughter suddenly morphed into the adult she was bordering on becoming.

"It was then," she continued, "when I watched you at Gramma and Grampa's house that for the first time in my memory, you seemed truly happy. Lighter, laughing, smiling openly at everyone. Almost free, in a way I'd never seen before. That's when I realized how much you pretend."

Cali tugged on her hand, wanting to run, but Stephanie held firm.

"How you hide behind the jobs of taking care of everyone, getting everything done while everyone else enjoys themselves. It's not that you're unhappy, exactly. But at Thanksgiving, for once, you were truly happy."

Cali backed up, blinking hard. How did her daughter see so much? She pulled her hand away and turned, moving to leave. Unable to answer her daughter for fear of all that would tumble out. Of having to admit to herself it wasn't just Jake, but it was everything she'd *done* with him that had given her that happiness. That freedom.

"So, I'm sorry, Mom," Stephanie said loudly, making Cali stop. "For not seeing this before. For taking you for granted and forgetting you're more than just my mom. I'm sorry for making you feel bad about dating Jake. And I'm sorry for all the grief I caused you over the divorce. It wasn't my place to judge you and I'm going to try hard in the future not to do that anymore."

My God. When had her daughter become so mature?

"You have nothing to apologize for," Cali managed to choke out. "I'm the one who's sorry. For disappointing you. For hurting you. For—"

"You didn't disappoint me," Stephanie interjected. "I just needed to grow up a little. I'm working on that now." Then her daughter's arms were wrapping around her, hugging her from behind. "Promise me you'll keep working on being happy. Okay?" She rested her chin on Cali's shoulder and Cali reached up to clasp the arms circling her.

"Thank you," Cali whispered. "I'll do that." The words

were said more to pacify her daughter than as commitment. She really didn't know if true happiness existed in the world of adulthood or if she would ever find it.

Stephanie eased away. "I need to head back to school. Thanks for dinner."

Cali watched her daughter bound up the stairs to gather her stuff, catching the shift of Steph's arm as she raised it to wipe her sleeve across her cheeks.

Cali quickly wiped at her own tears, grateful for her daughter. Grateful Stephanie didn't know about her mother's sexual desires. She rubbed a hand absently over her churning stomach. She'd waited all weekend for Peter to drop his bomb and destroy her precisely constructed life.

But he hadn't.

She'd heard nothing from him. At all. Or from Jake either. Not a peep since Friday night, which made her even more nervous. But then, would he really seek her out after she'd rejected him so publicly?

Casting a quick glance upstairs, she grabbed her cell phone and called him. She owed Jake the chance to explain and she was ready to hear what he had to say. The call clicked over to voicemail and she disconnected, unsure of what to say. Maybe he didn't want to talk to her after the way she'd humiliated him on stage. Just like she'd accused him of doing to her.

She'd reflected all day on the events of that night, and the clarity that distance and time provided gave her the chance to see the holes in the story that needed filling.

Stephanie bounced down the stairs, her backpack stuffed, keys in her hand. "I'll see you in two weeks for Christmas." She gave her mom a quick hug and was out the door with the speedy efficiency of youth.

Shoving the leftovers into the fridge, Cali removed her apron and gave up on the pan, leaving it to soak in the sink.

She grabbed her purse, slipped on her coat and headed out the door. It was time to face her mistakes, find some answers and see what the fallout would be.

Cali sat outside Peter's house—her old house—in the quiet residential neighborhood and thought about all that had changed. It wasn't long ago that she'd been the one to put up the outdoor decorations, hang the wreath on the door and attend the yearly neighborhood cookie exchange. They'd made a good life here. Raised good kids. Had a good family.

It was hard to see the house now, dark except for the interior lights indicating Peter was at least home. Every other house in the neighborhood was lit up with bright lights or some fanciful yard decoration reflecting off the snow. It was still a good family area, one Cali both missed with a passion and was happy as hell to escape.

Opening the car door, she stepped into the cold and watched her breath form white, puffy clouds before her. The car door creaked in resistance to the frigid temperatures and she quickly shoved her hands in her pockets to keep them warm. Trudging up the shoveled walkway, she contemplated one last time what she was going to say.

Oh, hell. She really didn't know what she was going to say; she just needed to see what Peter was going to say.

If felt strange, standing on the doorstep that had been her own for almost fifteen years. It was even more surreal to knock on the door instead of walking right in. It didn't matter that she'd moved out over two years before. The house still felt like hers.

The outside light flicked on. Then the door opened and Peter was there. He was still handsome. Tall, dark hair cut short and neat, deep blue eyes that crinkled at the corners now.

He was still decently fit, but his waist was noticeably thicker since the divorce.

"Cali?"

"Hi, Peter," she managed to say without her voice shaking. "Can I come in?"

She searched his face, looking for some sign of what he was thinking, feeling, but nothing showed. He stepped aside and motioned for her to enter. She wiped her boots on the door rug before following him down the hallway to the kitchen.

"Drink?"

She shook her head then watched as he poured himself two fingers of scotch. The silence suspended between them, and Cali held still, resisting the urge to fidget. She kept her hands firmly in her pockets and stood stiffly at the edge of the kitchen, waiting for him to start.

He didn't.

Jerk. He'd always done that. Refused to fight or engage in any kind of confrontation. It'd always been her who either started the discussion or let it ride.

"What are you going to do, Peter?"

He took a drink of his scotch before setting the glass down on the marble countertop. The marble she'd selected to match the dark oak cabinets and offset the high-end appliances and rich gold-toned paint she'd chosen when they'd remodeled the kitchen seven years ago. It'd been her dream kitchen. Just one more thing she'd given up when she'd left.

"What do you mean?" He didn't look at her but stared into the amber liquid in his glass.

She sighed and shifted her weight. She glanced to her left and took in the sparseness of the family room that opened off the kitchen. Peter hadn't replaced any of the furniture or decorations Cali had taken with her. There was a stack of newspapers piled on the end table, a couple of empty plates along with some soda cans—not beer, at least. Lights sparkled on the tiny, fake Christmas tree in the corner that was covered with a minimal amount of store-bought bulbs. Stephanie must have forced him into it. And being a good dad, Peter had let her.

Cali returned her gaze to Peter. She caught him studying her, hesitation in his eyes. "You know about what," she said, the exhaustion showing in her voice. "I've been waiting all weekend to find out what you're going to do, and now I just want to know. Are you going to tell the kids? Our families? Friends?"

Varying degrees of shock, repulsion and then shame crossed his features before he looked down. He took another drink of scotch and she was surprised to see the slight shake of his hand he couldn't hide. He licked the liquid off his lips and exhaled. "No, Cali. I'm not going to tell anyone." His voice hitched and he took a second to clear it. "Are you?"

Was *she?* "God, no. Why in the world would I?"

"To embarrass me," he said so quietly she had to strain to hear him. At that moment, under the glare of the recessed lights, Peter appeared more vulnerable than she ever remembered seeing him. Even when she'd told him she wanted a divorce.

"How would *I* embarrass you? I'm the one who was caught bound and half-naked on stage."

The glass clinked against the marble once more, followed by the soft glug of liquid as he poured himself another drink.

"But I'm the one who could never give you what you wanted." He cleared his throat again. "I was married to you for twenty-two years and I never once saw that look on your face. Never came close to giving you the pleasure that..." he inhaled then continued, "...that Dom did."

She narrowed her eyes, analyzing him, looking for a catch. Something, anything to make his words appear less sincere.

Less pained. But there was nothing except disappointment, an emotion that echoed in his voice.

"Why were you there, Peter? Why were you at the club?"

His face flushed and he turned away from her. She took a step forward but stopped at the far side of the island, keeping the object between them.

"Does it matter?"

"Yes," she insisted. "Did Jake make you come?"

His gaze snapped to hers. "Who's Jake?"

Her insides froze. The confusion on Peter's face was a silent confirmation of her rising suspicion. "Jake. The Dom."

"The one on stage with you?"

She refused to answer him.

He took in her silence before he finally said, "No."

"No?" Jake was innocent. She'd been wrong. Unable to deal with that, she tackled the issue she could. "Then why'd you follow me there?" She pressed her hands onto the hard marble, leaning forward as she pushed for an answer. "To gather dirt? To collect information to use against me?"

His face paled, his mouth gaping wide. "Is that really what you think of me? After all we've shared? That I would sink so low and have nothing better to do with my life than to follow you around, collecting dirt to…what? Shame you? Embarrass you? God, Cali. Listen to yourself." He shook his head in disgust—the first she'd seen since she'd arrived—before he tossed back the rest of his scotch.

"Then *why* were you there?"

"Why were *you* there?" His voice rose and he glared at her in challenge. His hands flexed on the counter, his jaw tight and stiff.

"You saw why I was there," she fired back before she could give into the urge to flee. "Every embarrassing inch of why."

"So, *think*. Think about why I might have been there."

Cali stepped back, her eyes going wide. Could it be? Peter's lips were thinned, his nostrils flaring with each breath he took. But he held her gaze, almost daring her to make the connection. One she didn't want to stumble over.

"Say it," she whispered, the softness almost eerie after the volume of their voices just seconds ago. "I need you to say it."

He held his anger for a moment longer before it deflated. His shoulders sagged, his gaze dropped and he pushed the air from his lungs in one long, extended breath. "Why? So you can wallow in your victory and my shame?"

"This is too important for guesses. It has nothing to do with shame or victory, Peter. This is about us. About all the things you would never tell me."

"Well, we're done now. So it really doesn't matter anymore."

She sighed and took a fortifying breath. "Because maybe, if we finally talk about it, we can get past this elephant that has plagued our entire relationship. Maybe, just once, I'd like you to speak to me honestly."

He squeezed his eyes shut, his fists clenching tightly on the counter. "I was there…at the club…to get what you had." He dropped his head into his hands and leaned on the counter. "It was my first night there. I'd finally found the courage to seek out what I'd always been too afraid to admit I wanted. And there you were, displayed on stage, getting everything I'd only fantasized about. And you looked so…beautiful." His voice cracked. "So fucking beautiful, and I was jealous. Mad and jealous because, once again, you got what you wanted while I was stuck watching and wishing it was me."

Stunned, Cali couldn't move. It explained so much. She swallowed back the slightly hysterical laughter threatening to bubble out—completely inappropriate for the moment, but so appropriate for the jumbled emotions of disbelief, confusion and amazement churning within her. Peter hadn't moved; his confession seemed to take the life from him.

"So that was it all along," she ventured, tiptoeing cautiously into the muck between them. "You're a submissive and wanted me to be the Dominant?"

Peter groaned, his hands scouring his face. "Hell. It sounds so pathetic when you say it like that." He dropped his hands and straightened but refused to face her, instead choosing to stare at the marble counter. "It's embarrassing for a forty-five-year-old man to admit he has no fucking idea what to do in the bedroom. The man is supposed to be the Dominant. Supposed to be in control and know what to do when it comes to sex. Not be some pansy-ass who wants the woman to control it all. For her to dominate and take away the stress so he can just enjoy it for once."

Cali stared at him, trying to process what he was saying. It took a moment for her mind to catch up to his words. "Sex with me stressed you out?"

"Yes, Cali. It always stressed me out. Knowing I never did enough or satisfied you or knew what to do to make you happy stressed the hell out of me. How manly is it to admit you suck at sex? That the one thing all men are supposed to excel at is the one thing I fucking suck at?"

"Why didn't you ever tell me this?" Her voice rose with her frustration. "Why, in all the times I tried to talk to you about our sex life, did you never, ever say anything even close to this? You always blamed it on me. On something I did or didn't do, until I finally gave up."

"Because I was the man," he yelled at her. "I was the man and if *I* sucked at sex, then I'm really not much of a man." His body was stiff and defiant and he glared at her, almost daring her to contradict him.

Cali took a chance and moved around the island to stand

next to him. For as much as his shunning of her had hurt, overall he was still a good person. "I hope you realize that's not true. Being a man has way more to do with who you are as a person than how you perform in bed."

He looked away. "Tell that to society."

"No, tell that to yourself."

He flinched, almost as if she'd hit him.

"I had no idea you felt this way," Cali continued gently, amazed at the revelation. "I wished I'd known. I wish you'd trusted me enough to tell me when we were married. I wish we could go back and take away all the hurt and pain this has caused. But I can't. We can't."

"It's not like you shared either." He shook his head—an act of dismissal or remorse, she wasn't sure. "I never had a clue what you wanted, least of all what I saw the other night."

Cali hung her head, conceding to his point. She couldn't hold it against Peter when she'd been just as chicken as him at voicing her sexual desires. "If you think about it," she ventured, "this explains a lot. Here we are, two submissives wanting the other to be the Dominant but both of us incapable of being that for each other."

A short bark of irony left his mouth. "Right. Pathetic, huh? I should have been able to be your Dom."

"No, Peter. That's not what I'm saying." She leaned down, trying to meet his gaze but failed. "We can't change who we are or what we want. I'm trying to accept that about myself. I have no bad feelings or thoughts about who and what you want. For as compatible as we were in life, we were never going to be compatible in bed."

He exhaled and finally faced her. "You make it sound so practical. So easy to accept. I can't say I'm quite there yet."

There was fear in his eyes. Fear and hesitation. She understood those feelings. It hadn't been easy for her to admit her needs. Hell, it still wasn't, which was why she continued to hide from them. But somehow, seeing Peter struggle with the same emotions made it easier for her to accept her own.

"Well, neither am I," Cali admitted. "I was so ashamed and embarrassed when you saw me like that...at the club. I've been a ball of nerves since then, wondering what you thought of me. Wondering what you were going to do with what you saw. Who you'd tell." Cali closed her eyes and bit her lip to keep the feelings tucked inside. It was hard to confess those things to him. The man she'd spent over half of her life with but no longer trusted with her emotions.

"And here I was, worried you were telling everyone about your pathetic ex-husband who could never give you what you needed."

He poured himself another glass of scotch then offered it to her. She accepted the glass and took a drink, feeling the liquid burn the entire way down her throat. She handed the glass back to him and he took a large swallow.

"So where does this leave us now?"

He laughed. "Two embarrassed, bumbling, mid-aged conservatives who are more repressed than a couple of virgins. Hell if I know." He ran a hand through his hair, exposing some of the gray. "Did that man mean something to you? The Dom who gave you the collar?"

Cali glanced away. "I can't have this conversation with you."

"Why?" he demanded, forcing her to look at him again. "We're finally talking to each other. For once in our goddamn lives, we're talking to each other. Why stop now?"

"Because this won't fix us. It won't bring us back together."

He lifted the glass to take a drink then paused halfway before setting it down. "It would be nice to have someone to talk to about this stuff."

"I can't be that person for you, Peter. It's too awkward."

He sighed. "Yeah, I guess you're right." He scanned her face, a half smile curving his lips. "Are you going back? To the club?"

It was Cali's turn to fidget. "I don't think so."

"Why?"

Oh, to explain all of the reasons behind that. "Too much has happened."

"Because of me? Of my being there?"

She debated on what to say then finally said, "Yes. Your appearance kind of shocked me back to reality."

"I wish it hadn't," he said, his eyes conveying the truth of his words. "I wish I hadn't ruined it for you."

The honesty in his voice struck at her. "Why?"

"Because I want to see you happy. Is that so hard to believe? And if that's what makes you happy, then don't let me stop you." He swore. "I've fucked up your happiness enough. I don't want to be the cause of it once again."

"There's a lot more involved for me than simply going back."

"So the collaring was significant."

She closed her eyes, trying to block the emotions, to keep them from her voice and not think about all that she'd thrown away so brashly. "Yes." Then she quickly deferred the subject to him. "What about you? You going back?"

"No," he said emphatically. "Barely got myself there once and after what happened with you, I wasn't sure I'd be allowed back in."

"You should go. Or at least find another club or something. You deserve to be happy too. And like you, I don't want to be the cause of your unhappiness any longer."

"We'll see."

They stared around the room for a moment, studiously avoiding each other's gaze. Finally, Cali shifted. "I should go."

He studied her. "Are we good? No secret-sharing with the world?"

She smiled, a stiff but honest gesture. "Yeah. We're good."

"Thank you," he said quietly. "For understanding."

"Same to you."

She walked to the front door and he followed, both of them silent. She opened the door and stepped into the cold.

"Cali."

She paused and turned back to him.

"I hope you get what you want."

She smiled, nodded, then moved down the walkway to her car. When she drove away, Peter stood in the open doorway, watching her leave. The bizarre nature of the entire conversation finally sunk in. It was hard to believe she'd just had an honest conversation about sex with her ex-husband. Something they hadn't managed while they were married.

But there was an understanding within her now. A peace she'd never felt before. There was no one to blame for their failures. Well, maybe it was equal blame, but it wasn't something she'd done. It wasn't her fault, just like Jake had tried to get her to accept.

Just like she'd tried to tell herself and never quite believed.

But finally, she felt it. She got it.

Which left the other truth she couldn't hide from. The one she'd pushed away and was now terribly afraid she'd never get back.

She turned the corner and pulled over as soon as she was out of Peter's sight. Her grip tightened on the steering wheel and she leaned forward until her forehead rested on it, the cool leather biting into her skin. Only then did she let the tears fall. A quiet mix of relief, exhaustion and fear.

She'd been so wrong about everything. Jake, Peter…her life. Was it possible to fix it all? Things with Peter seemed to be okay, but would Jake be as understanding? He hadn't betrayed her like she'd thought. If she'd only trusted him. Believed him when he said he loved her then showed her that love by giving her the collar. She'd been so afraid and acted so stupid.

Sitting back, she wiped away the tears chilling on her cheeks. She found her phone and once again dialed Jake's number. Her hands shook and her pulse increased as she waited for him to answer. He didn't. Voicemail picked up and she released the breath she'd been holding before disconnecting from the call. She couldn't apologize via voicemail. Not if she wanted him to listen.

And she did. Desperately.

She wanted *him* back. Not just what he did to her, but him. The man who knew she organized her closet by color and season and was ticklish behind her knees. Who held her all night and laughed at stories about her children. The man who demanded she give him everything and treasured everything he received.

She loved Jake and wanted him back.

TWENTY-SIX

His gaze cruised over the dark corners of the club, the scent of sex and leather lingering in the air to blend with the background din of the music. The sharp slap of a paddle hitting skin, followed by the cry of a sub, rocked through the air. In the center of the room, a female stood bent at the waist, naked and exposed, her head and arms locked in a stockade, her ass and pussy bared to all. Her Dom wheeled a whip with a precision that left a striped pattern of red across her back and legs.

Doug's club, Bound and Determined—also known as the B & D—was on the hard edge of the BDSM scene. Everyone was welcomed as long as you didn't abuse the unwritten rules within the community. Even then, if you could find someone who wanted to play, the door was opened to you.

"You gonna play tonight?"

The deep voice caught him from behind, but Jake didn't flinch. He shrugged in reply, not willing to commit to an action. He'd spent the previous night watching with no desire to partake in the activities. He'd received plenty of inquiries from both men and women, but he'd declined them all.

"Never known you to watch when you could play," Doug said as he stepped up next to Jake. The man's eyes were on the club floor, his acute scrutiny catching everything. After more than twenty-five years in the business, there wasn't much that got by the respected owner. One of the reasons his club was still around after so many years.

Jake's attention strayed to the line of available subs kneeling in submission along the side wall, waiting for a Dom. Some were naked, others barely clothed, all with their heads bowed in respect. All of them perfectly posed. And none of them interested him.

"Maybe later," Jake said, even though he knew it wasn't likely.

Doug grunted, a deep rumble that conveyed his understanding of exactly how unlikely that was. "You gonna tell me why you're here then?"

The other man hadn't pried since Jake had arrived unexpectedly on his doorstep. Then again, Doug had never pried, which was why Jake had grown to trust him when he was younger. Doug had offered the lost youth a safe place to work and be without intrusion or expectations of confessions.

Jake had started out cleaning the club after hours, mopping the floors and sanitizing the equipment. Over time, Doug taught him how to maintain the various pieces on the floor, making sure everything was safe and operational for the next night. The simple tasks had given him a purpose. When he'd brought Deklan and Seth around, Doug had nodded and handed over another mop and broom without question.

He owed the man an answer.

"Need a place to start again," he finally said, keeping his focus on the Scene playing out in the center of the room. A crowd had gathered around the couple, but Doug and he had an unobstructed view from their elevated balcony position.

Doug lifted his chin, face remaining neutral. "What happened to The Den?"

"Still there. Left it to Winters and Mathews."

"Looking to start another one?"

"No," Jake said too quickly. He paused, swallowed then tried to sound casual. "Need a break."

"But here you are." Doug nodded toward the open room. "Smack in the middle of the world. So what do you need a break from?"

Fuck. Jake looked away, his hands clenching as he grappled for an answer. He obviously didn't want this. He had no desire to find a random sub and run a Scene that would end up leaving him feeling empty and wanting. Which was how he'd felt before Cali, even though he'd continued to play his role and see to the needs of his clients. The ache for more had been there.

Despite his reluctance to admit it.

So what did he want to admit to now?

The silence stretched between them, the sounds of their world filling in when words didn't. Doug didn't push and Jake knew he wouldn't. Giving up, he turned away and strode out of the club area, finding his way to the back storage room. He shut the door behind him and absorbed the calming scents of oil, leather, lemon and wood.

He flicked on the light and looked around the cramped room. His gaze settled on a St. Andrew's Cross lying on its side against the wall and stuffed behind a broken spanking bench. Moving the equipment around, he pulled the cross into the open space in the middle. He let his hands run over the smooth wood, his mind already working with it. Eying the broken chains, the splintered wood on the top, the lack of arm supports.

This would work. He could lose himself in this project.

Without questions. Without intrusions.

Jake dug through the room, collecting the items he'd need. With luck, his mind would blank as he fell into the familiarity of the task and put a halt to the non-stop replay of the last Scene with Cali. The cross would be spectacular when he finished and until then, he didn't want to think about anything but the job before him.

He didn't want to think about her or all the mistakes he'd made. He'd pushed her but he'd thought she was ready. That she was right there with him. Obviously, she hadn't been. Cursing, he tightened his hand around a hammer before tossing it aside. He'd already caused enough damage; he didn't need to make more.

Picking up a rag, he attacked the cross, scrubbing off the dirt and dust in an ineffective attempt to rub away his thoughts. How could Cali think he'd hurt her like that? He'd given her more than he'd ever given anyone. Hadn't he proven she could trust him? Not if she could jump to the instant conclusion that he'd brought her ex to the club.

Hell, he'd asked her to spend the fucking holiday with him. Not in the club, but with him. She's missed the significance of that. He didn't *ask* people to be with him—it only gave them the opportunity to say no. But he'd asked her and she'd rejected him. Twice now.

He hissed, his knuckle scraping over a jagged piece of wood, taking off a chunk of skin. *Damn it*. He cursed again and wrapped the rag around the cut, absorbing the sting as punishment deserved. So much for not thinking about Cali. How far would he have to run before he stopped seeing her soft smile or imagining the smooth silk of her skin under his palms? But it was more than the physical things. That was the problem.

What he found under the embarrassment of being publicly rejected and the anger at having his declaration of love tossed in his face was the fucking fact that he missed her. That he still wanted everything about her. From the prim sweater sets to the wild leather-clad wanton, he loved all of her.

He paced to the tool chest and dug out a set of pliers and a chisel, refusing to debate it anymore. It was getting him nowhere but deeper into shit that was already done. She'd left him. Told him in no uncertain terms to get the hell out of her life, and he was giving her what she wanted. Like always. End of story.

It didn't matter how much he still ached for her. She was another part of his past he'd learn to forget. Eventually.

Cali stood in the small room, her hands clasped tight before her, heart racing. Ironically it was the same room she'd waited in the first night she'd come to The Den. The night Jake had walked through the door and changed her life. She couldn't sit this time. Was too nervous, too scared.

So she paced, the heels of her boots sinking into the carpet. The silence annoying instead of comforting. She tugged her jacket tighter around her and tried to hold back the shiver that raked down her spine, despite the sweat collecting on her skin.

The door clicked and Cali's gaze shot to the entrance, heart stalling, her breath held. All of the tension and expectation slipped from her when two men stepped into the room.

Neither of them Jake.

"Ms. Reynolds," Deklan said. She didn't want to speak to him, but obviously Jake had sent the other men down instead of seeing her himself.

"Deklan, right?" Cali said politely.

"Yes." He gestured to the other man, the one who'd interviewed her for her membership into the club. "I believe you know Seth Mathews, our third business partner. What can we do for you?"

She cleared her throat and let her palms rub over the soothing velvet of her pants. "I wanted to speak to Jake. Is he here?" She'd come to the club during the afternoon, hoping to catch him before things got busy that night.

Seth stepped forward. His long hair was tied back in a neat queue, his jeans and shirt clean and respectable. His Dom persona was packed away, but the authority that went with it was still present. "I'm sorry, but Jake is gone."

"What do you mean, 'gone'?"

"He left that night, after you rejected him." The man held her gaze as he let the words sink in.

She stiffened, her gut clenching in pain.

"We haven't seen or heard from him since."

Oh, God. She'd made him run. Her voice shook when she spoke. "Do you know where he went?"

"No," Deklan said from behind Seth. "I told you the collaring meant something to him. As did your rejection."

"B-but," she stammered, confused and suddenly very afraid of what she'd done. "I wasn't thinking rationally. I was stunned by my ex-husband's appearance in the crowd and just reacted. I want to explain…to him and he won't answer my calls."

"He left his phone in his loft. We don't know if he's coming back," Deklan said.

"Oh, God." Cali groaned, sinking into the chair behind her. "What have I done?"

He was gone. She'd pushed him away and he'd left. Her heart ached, the pain even greater than when she'd thought he'd betrayed her. Now it was her fault. She'd caused this pain. She didn't want to lose him. Didn't want him gone.

She felt a hand on her leg and opened her eyes, not realizing she'd had them squeezed closed. It was Seth who kneeled before her, his eyes gentle as he looked at her.

"What do you want, Ms. Reynolds?"

"Cali," she said softly. "Call me Cali. And I want Jake back. I want what he offered and more. I want…" She couldn't finish because it would kill her to say it and never get it.

"Were you and your ex into Dominance and submission?"

The question caught her off-guard. She recoiled as if he'd slapped her. "No. That's why I was so appalled and shocked to see him here. I was embarrassed and ashamed and acted without thinking."

Seth nodded. "And now? Are you still ashamed?"

She searched the man's eyes, seeking his intent but finding only questions. "I'm ashamed of a lot of things. The least of which is how I reacted four nights ago. But if you're asking me if I'm ashamed of being a sub, to Jake, then the answer is no."

"Why'd you come here today?"

"To talk to him," she answered impatiently. The third-degree grilling was getting annoying. She didn't owe these men an explanation, but they were her only connection to Jake. "To explain what happened and to apologize. To ask for another chance."

"How do you feel about him, Cali?"

The urge to answer his subtle command flashed through her so swiftly she cringed. It was how he'd said her name. Just like Jake, the inflection almost identical to the other Dom. She bit her tongue and withheld the impulse to answer honestly.

"I'm sorry, but that's something I need to discuss with Jake first." She didn't care how the other man took her response. She owed it to Jake to tell him she loved him, all of him, before she shared it with anyone else.

Seth inclined his head and stood. "If he contacts us, we'll let him know you were here." He extended his hand, a not-so-subtle indication that she should leave.

She accepted his hand and forced her legs to hold her weight as she rose. She licked her lips and withdrew her fingers from his grasp. "Thank you," she said before moving to the door, ensuring her spine was straight and her shoulders back the whole way.

"Cali."

She paused, turning to the two men who assessed her with serious faces.

"Jake is a brother to us," Seth said. "The little brother we've both fought to protect since he first bound us together. He's never given himself to anyone. Doesn't let anyone in." He lifted his hand, a silver chain falling to dangle from his fingers. Her collar. "This was a huge step for him. A leap we thought he'd never take. He wouldn't have done it if he didn't love you."

Cali blinked back the moisture in her eyes. "I know that now. I knew that then, but I wasn't thinking properly. I want that collar. I want what he offered. All that he offered…if he ever comes back."

Seth approached once again. "Then you should hang on to this until he returns." He pulled her hand up then gently pushed up the sleeve of her jacket to expose her wrist. He met her eyes, silently conveying the importance of his actions as he wrapped the chain around her wrist, making three loops before latching the clasp. The silver infinity links sparkled against her pale skin, causing the flesh around her neck to tingle with longing.

"Thank you," she whispered, her gaze blurring as she stared at the beautiful collar. She resolved right then that it would make it to her neck. That she would come back every weekend until Jake returned.

She wasn't giving up on him.

On them.

On what they had and all they could still have.

He was her Dom and damn it, she belonged to him.

TWENTY-SEVEN

"That's fuckin' amazing," Doug grumbled from behind Jake. He moved into the cramped storage space and made his way around the newly refinished St. Andrew's Cross Jake had been working on non-stop for the last two days. Doug gave the freestanding cross a strong shake; the object barely budged.

Jake clamped his arms over his chest and waited for Doug to finish his inspection. Damn. He hadn't needed this level of approval and reassurance since he'd wandered into this club over twenty years ago. But right then, Doug's praise was like a flimsy lifeline he desperately needed to cling to.

Doug's fingers stroked over the smooth finish then gave a sharp tug on the cuffs dangling from the chains at the top. He glanced at Jake, a slow smile curving his lips. "Your skills have only improved with time. I like the addition of the arm rests." He pointed to the small padded ledges that would support the occupant's arms, enabling the person to stay on the cross longer. "The detailing makes it stand out as a work of art. Every sub who walks through our door will want to be strapped into this."

"Thanks," Jake mumbled, wiping his hands on his now filthy jeans. The material, like his hands, was stained with grease, wood varnish and paint. He'd taken extra care with the intricate design he'd painted on the cross, differentiating it from just another piece of BDSM equipment. The polish he'd applied gleamed under the dull lights and would absolutely shimmer under the bright lights of a stage.

"Did it work?" Doug asked.

"Did what work?"

"Your forty-eight-hour marathon of labor. Did it get rid of the shit eating at you?"

Jake exhaled and stared at the ground. Did it? Not even close. "Shit's still there," he admitted.

"Running never did solve things."

"Been talking to Deklan?" Jake shot the other man a wry smile. "He said the same thing."

"Always did think that kid was smart." Doug chuckled. He moved from behind the cross, pushed some rags off a chair and took a seat with a low groan. "Damn, these bones are getting older than I want them to be." He rubbed a hand over his knee before he looked at Jake. "I'll listen to whatever you want to say."

Jake found another chair and spun it around to straddle it, resting his arms on the back. The ache in his chest had eased over the last few days. Not the part missing Cali, but the part that was devastated and humiliated at her rejection. Distance had given him perspective. During the long hours of manual labor, he had plenty of time to replay the incident over and over until he'd come to some understanding.

"I found the one," Jake admitted, lifting his gaze to meet Doug's. "And she rejected me. Publicly. Threw my collar at me in front of the entire club."

Doug winced. "Ouch. Fuck. What happened?"

"I collared her. Big show, on stage." He sighed, clamped his hands in his hair and thought back to that moment. How perfect it'd felt, slipping the chain around her neck. "I wanted the declaration to be grand. To show how important it was. I was so proud of her. I wanted to show everyone in the club just how exceptional she was. How lucky I was to have her. It was perfect. Right up to the point where she saw her ex-husband in the audience and freaked out in the middle of the Scene."

Doug's brows shot up. "Her ex-husband? I take it he wasn't supposed to be there."

"No," Jake scoffed, anger tinting the word. He shook his head. "He wasn't supposed to be there. Dumb-ass me didn't think about it being First Friday. Evidently, her ex decided to join our club as well. Somehow, the detail of his link to Cali was missed. But it doesn't matter, because she blames me for it. Thinks I arranged for him to be there."

"What kind of fucked-up thinking is that?"

"A logical one from her perspective," he admitted. "Complicated back-story, but I get where she's coming from. Why she'd think that." After the soul-purging Scene he'd put her through the time before, it was a very logical jump for her to make.

"Do you? Really?" Doug looked at him skeptically. "Because if you do, then what the fuck are you doing here?"

"Running. Obvious." But running from what? Himself? Her? Rejection?

Doug puffed out a breath and stood. He dropped his meaty hand onto Jake's shoulder, giving it a short squeeze before he walked to the door. "I get to keep that, right?" He pointed to the Jake's refurbished cross.

Jake chuckled, letting his hands fall to his thighs. "Yeah. The bike trailer's full. Consider it due payment for the many hours of therapy services."

"Well, shit, boy. Didn't know you needed therapy." Doug opened the door and glanced back. "You should really think about selling your equipment. There's a lot of people who'd pay good money for quality BDSM shit like yours."

Jake lifted his chin in acknowledgement and went to mentally dismiss the statement. But then, maybe the other man's idea was worth thinking about. Seth had said something before about Jake doing that as another revenue stream for the club. He'd shrugged it off then. After all, this was just a hobby. Something he'd grown into, not trained for.

He jerked up, the need to see the cross in use suddenly pressing and demanding. Calling down the hall, he got another employee to help him carry the cross out to the floor. Doug saw them coming and quickly got some tables rearranged, making space for the new piece of equipment near the center of the open room.

The response was almost immediate, the club members admiring the stunning St. Andrew's Cross with ripples of appreciation. Jake pulled a rag from his back pocket and polished away the fingerprints left from moving the large structure. He stepped back and looked the piece over with a critical eye. It was just as he'd envisioned it. His cock hardened as he imagined Cali strapped to it, open and waiting. Her eyes begging him for more.

"Will you, sir?"

Startled out of his thoughts, Jake looked down at the submissive kneeling at his feet. Where'd she come from? She was kneeling in the perfect obedient pose as she waited for his reply. What did she want?

"Please, sir," she said. "Will you use it on me? Will you let me be the first?" The sub's voice and body shook with repressed desire.

The dominant in him surged to the forefront. The woman

had blond hair—straight and long, past her shoulders—but he could make do. "Stand," he ordered.

She complied immediately, keeping her eyes down. She was shorter, her hips fuller than Cali's. But it didn't matter. Did it? He was a Dom, for fuck's sake. This was what he did, had done since he was legal to do so.

"Safe word?" he asked, tossing the rag still clenched in his fist to the side.

"Popsicle."

Jake logged the answer, his brain latching on to the unusual stop word with practiced ease. Every sub was different, and keeping track of the words was part of his job.

Jake circled around the sub, taking stock of what he had to play with. "Tools of choice?"

She inhaled. "Cane, please."

Jake's gut tightened. A pain whore. Canes were hard-core and stung like a bitch. She was a very trusting sub to ask for that when she didn't know him. He called her on it. "Trusting, aren't you?"

"I trust Doug, sir," the sub said. "You're a friend of his, so I trust you by extension. And if you made a cross that looks like that—" she paused, her gaze caressing the cross, "—then I trust you know what you're doing."

He met Doug's eyes over the crowd that had gathered. The man nodded, his mouth set in a thin line. So she could take what she was asking for. Jake nodded to the Dungeon Master on the floor and the man moved forward to assist in strapping the sub to the cross.

"Strip her. I want her back," he ordered. He didn't want to see her face. Jake felt the Dom persona dropping over him as he stepped up and removed her flimsy blouse. Her breasts were large, but they didn't interest him.

The Dungeon Master took care of her bottoms. Then Jake

grabbed a wrist and strapped it into a cuff. A wrist that was bigger than the one he wanted. The one he was used to.

Shit. He couldn't do that. He owed it to this woman to focus on her. That was his job. She trusted him and he couldn't fail her. Too.

Pain stabbed at him, twisting with the truth of his thoughts. He'd failed Cali when she'd trusted him. Failed his parents when they'd trusted him. Failed Seth and Deklan. And now, now, he wouldn't fail again. Damn it. He'd never failed as a Dom.

Not 'til Cali.

Cursing himself, Jake stalked to the equipment wall and ran his fingers over the line of canes in the cabinet. Each one varied in length, stiffness and texture, which would define the level of pain inflicted with each strike. He selected one on the lower-level of pain infliction, since he didn't know the sub.

The crowd parted as he returned to the woman. She was completely strapped to the cross now, her back heaving with deep gust of breaths as she inhaled. Anticipation rippled like a viable energy over the bystanders. Everyone waiting in expectation for the Scene to start.

Jake twirled the cane in his hands, the familiarity of the tool rubbing against his palm. But instead of the usual rise of adrenaline that came with a Scene, he was suddenly filled with repulsion. Not at the act, but himself. What was he doing?

Growling, Jake forced himself to stand behind the sub. She had followed every rule of a perfect submissive. She was a woman who had been in the lifestyle for a while. Who knew what she wanted. Before, this would have excited Jake. Before, he anticipated Scenes such as this, where both parties went into it knowing what they wanted and how to get it. Before, he would have been hard just looking at the strapped and bound woman.

Before Cali.

He raised his arm, the cane held high in preparation to strike. Silence descended upon the club as everyone waited for that first hit, the high hiss of the cane as it moved through the air until it stopped with a crack against skin. Jake's muscles tensed, his arm shaking with the strain of denial.

All he had to do was follow through. Finish the motion. Be the Dom he was supposed to be. Had always been.

But he wasn't that man. Not anymore.

Not since Cali.

Guilt swam through him in a rippling wave of accusation. He dropped the cane, the stiff reed clattering to the floor in a soft tapping of wood on wood that seemed far louder than it should. Surprise echoed through the room, but Jake didn't care. He couldn't do it. He couldn't go through with the Scene.

Cali was the only sub he wanted.

To finish this Scene would be equal to cheating on her. Not a true statement for all Doms, but for him—with Cali—that was exactly how he felt.

What the fuck was he doing?

Jake pushed through the sea of people. He needed air. Needed out of there. He stormed down the hall, thrusting open the back door and stepping into the freezing air of the night. His sweat-covered skin instantly chilled. He hunched over, hands clamping his knees as he tried to find his breath.

Shit. Shit. *Shit*. He couldn't even be a Dom without her? Couldn't do what he'd always done?

"You should wait 'til morning to drive back."

Doug. Of course he'd followed. "How do you know I'm going back?"

"How dumb do you think I am, boy?" Doug stepped outside, letting the door slam behind him. "I've never seen you drop a Scene. You've spent your entire adult life as a Dom submerged in this world, running from your demons. This is the first time I've seen them catch you."

Jake rounded on him, ready to fight. Ready to deny, just like he'd done with Seth. Like he always did. Anger fueled him, the only emotion he'd let in. But Doug didn't move. The big man widened his stance, bracing for whatever Jake would do, his face grim and stern.

"What do you know?" Jake challenged, his fist clenched and ready to strike.

"I know you've been running from commitment since the day your parents died."

Jake winced. Why did everyone keep talking about his parents?

"I know you blame yourself for their death and have done everything in your power to control every aspect of your life since that day."

Jake backed away, suddenly afraid to hear the rest. Unwilling to go back. "You don't know anything."

Doug stepped forward, not letting Jake retreat. To run, as he'd always done. "Who dragged you in off the street? Who gave you a chance when everyone else had forgotten you? Who saw the man beneath the scared, defensive boy? Don't tell me I don't know, because we both know that's a lie."

The older man was in Jake's face now, his breath hot and sharp against the chill surrounding them. Jake started to shake. He wanted to run, but his feet wouldn't move.

"You didn't cause your parents' death." Doug's voice softened, but the hard core of belief was still there. "There are things in life that just happen. Things you have no control over. Things you can't stop or change. You were ten when they died. There was nothing you could've done. It's past time you accepted that."

Jake twisted away, unable to hear any more. He dug his palms into his eyes, willing back the unaccustomed moisture that was suddenly there. It was as if Doug's words had opened the steel door he'd locked all those old feeling behind. The ones he'd refused to acknowledge since he was turned over to the care of the state and began his penance in the foster care system.

"They trusted me," he said. "They trusted me when I told them I was going to a friend's. I broke that trust and they were killed coming to spring me from the police station. It was my fault."

He'd been in fifth grade, having a sleepover at his best friend Cameron's house. It was Cam's older brother who'd urged them to come along. They'd felt so cool hanging with the older boys, to be included in their numbers. But it was Cam and Jake who'd gotten caught vandalizing the school, who hadn't run fast enough.

"It was the drunk driver who killed them, not you," Doug said.

"And they wouldn't have been on the road if it wasn't for me."

The guilt burst forth in a large dose of anguish. There'd been no family members to take him in after his parents died and they'd left no will or stipulations on his care. So Jake ended up a ward of the state. A position that had been a daily reinforcement of what happened when you failed the ones you loved.

Doug's hand came to rest on his shoulder. "You can't control everything. The only thing you can ever truly control is how you *react* to the shit in your life. You couldn't control the events with your parents, just like you couldn't control them at the club. You couldn't control how she reacted, but you do control your actions." He released his shoulder and stepped toward the door. "The question is, are you going back to get her, or are you going to keep running?"

Fuck if the man wasn't right. He'd been acting like a wounded child, running from what scared him instead of fighting for what he wanted.

Could he do it, though?

More importantly, did he even dare to try?

TWENTY-EIGHT

The snow was falling again, making the children excited and setting the Christmas spirit for everyone. After all, who could resist the pretty decorations, the sparkling lights, the uplifting sounds of seasonal music when it was all topped with a fresh layer of white stuff?

Cali waited for traffic then turned her car into the condo complex, thankful to be out of the chaos that always went with the insanity of holiday shopping. A trip she would have avoided if it wasn't for the one package she had to have for that evening.

She made a quick glance at the black and red bag sitting so innocently on the passenger seat. Her stomach twisted at the sight. She hadn't heard from Jake. But she was going to the club tonight, would keep going to the club until he came back. And that had meant buying an outfit that was right for the club. For him.

The first she'd actually bought specifically for him to replace the ones she'd so hastily thrown out last week.

She made her way through the maze of roads and parking

spaces, one of the cons of owning a unit at the back of the large complex. But the privacy and distance from the main road was worth it. She made the last turn to her building and slammed on the brakes.

Parked in her driveway was a flashy black and blue motor-cycle. Not a Harley, but one of those racing-style bikes. Her heart began an erratic beat, her eyes frantically scanning for the owner of the motorcycle.

Could it really be him? Did she dare hope?

Then she saw him. Jake. Sitting on her front steps, hands clasped as they draped over his knees. He focused on her.

She parked her car at the curb, quickly turning it off with shaking fingers. He'd come back. He was there. Waiting for her. At her house.

What did it mean?

Taking a deep, courage-boosting breath, Cali grabbed her package and purse then exited the safety of her vehicle. The snow fluttered around her face, the cold gripping her exposed skin. She looked at the ground, watching her footing as she walked over the slippery sidewalk, past his motorcycle and up the path to stop before him. Finally she lifted her head and met the deep silver gaze that held hers.

"Hi, Cali." His voice rippled over her, warming her with the sound alone. A sound she'd been afraid she'd never hear again. His hair and jacket were covered in a layer of snow, in-dicating he'd been waiting a while.

"Hi, Jake," she managed to answer, keeping her voice even. "I didn't expect to see you here." That was lame, but she couldn't get out all of the things she'd been hoping to say.

He looked away, his hands clenching. "I'm sorry."

"For what?"

He glanced back to her then slowly stood. His gaze held hers, his hands tentatively reaching out to brush her cheeks.

His fingers were cold from the exposure, but the touch burned against her skin. "For what happened last Friday. For running. For not being here for you when I should have been." He swallowed. "I never wanted to hurt you. I don't know what to do, but I'll do whatever it takes to get you back."

Her hold tightened on the thin cord of her bag, her last grip on stability. A snowflake drifted down to land on the edge of his eyelashes. He blinked rapidly, breaking the hold on the moment. She smiled and dared to hope for all that was forbidden in her life.

"I'm sorry too." She bit her lip then forged on. "I'm so sorry for humiliating you like I did."

"You didn't—"

"I did," she interjected, cutting him off. "Not on purpose. Not intentionally. But I realize now my actions on stage, throwing your collar back at you, was an awful thing to do." Tears formed in her eyes, but she didn't care. When she thought of the pain she'd caused him from her own stupidity, she wondered if he'd ever take her back. "I wasn't thinking and I regret it so much."

He stepped closer, his hands tightening around the back of her head. His eyes were dark and pained. "If I'd been thinking, I would have held on to you. I wouldn't have let you go. I would have been there for you. I regret running."

She closed her eyes, held back the tears and absorbed his words. Wanting, more than anything, to collapse into his arms and let it all be over. He was so close now; only a thin wisp of air separated them. His scent circled her, pulling her in with the enticing hint of the cold and him. But there were still things they needed to discuss. She opened her eyes and reached up to grip one of his wrists, holding tight to his strength and the hope that they would work things out.

"I know you didn't do it. I know you didn't make Peter be there."

His head tipped forward. "But I shouldn't have let him be there. It was my oversight that caused the mess."

"How could you have known?" she pushed. "I took my maiden name back when we divorced. It was an ungodly co-incidence no one was prepared for."

He puffed out a breath then looked at her again. "How are you so understanding? What happened to change your mind?" There was a flash of hope on his face, but he still seemed re-sistant. Like he was holding something back or ready to bolt again.

She dropped her bag, the item forgotten in her need to claim Jake. To convince him to stay there with her. She rubbed up his chest, over his coat, the memory of his muscled chest singe-ing her mind. "I talked to Peter. We finally had an honest conversation about the lack of sex in our marriage and about why we were both at the club. We both wanted the other to be the sexual dominant but were too damn afraid to ever admit it." She stepped closer, closing that final gap so they touched. Every nerve in her body was coiled and bound, waiting for him to respond.

"What do you want now?" His voice was hoarse, his hands fisting on the back of her head.

"You, Jake. I want you."

"Why?" His voice was as doubting as the look in his eyes. "I can't change who I am. I can give up the club, give up that life. But I will always be a Dom. Do you want that? Do you want that part of me too?" And there was the hope she was searching for. The one that let the butterflies loose to flutter from her stomach to her heart.

"Yes. More than anything. I want all of you. I want your world. What you give me. How you make me feel. I want to laugh with you. Be held by you. Cherished as I've only ever felt with you."

His hands slid down her back to pull her tight against him. "And I want you. Not as a possession, but as my lover. My friend. My other half. I want you in my life. What do I have to do to get that?"

Her breath caught. Here was her big, demanding Dom asking her what she wanted. Almost begging her to take him back. After she'd shunned him. How was this possible? He probably could have ordered her to kneel and demanded she obeyed him. And she would, in a heartbeat. But instead, he was giving her the power. Giving her the choice.

Her heart burst open, letting all of the caged hope free to rush through her.

She reached up and stroked her fingertips over his soft, warm lips. She'd missed those lips, missed all of him so much. "I love you. You're here. That's all I need. I don't need you to change. Don't want you to change. I just want you."

His lips were crushed to hers before she could think. Before she could even take a breath. And they felt so good. Hot and strong. Assertive as he claimed her mouth, her body and her heart. She opened to him and met the thrust of his tongue with all the need she'd been banking for the last week. All the desperation she'd contained when she thought she'd never see him again or taste that light hint of spice that was so him.

But he was there. Back. With her.

He leaned back just enough to breathe. "I love you, Cali. I thought I'd lost you. *God.*"

He kissed her again, his arms binding her to him, hands rubbing over her back, her hair, her arms like he couldn't stop touching her. She reveled in the tangy scent of gas fumes that clung to him and the feel of him against her.

A brief second of sanity merged its way through the fog of

her passion and she pulled back. "Let's go inside before we give my neighbors a show."

He backed up, chuckling. "You have Deklan as a neighbor. They might not be so surprised by us kissing."

She dug in her purse for her keys, a smile plastered across her face. "It's not the kissing I'm worried about." She found the keys and moved around Jake to the door. "It's what I want you to do to me after the kiss that I'm worried about."

The keys were yanked out of her hand and shoved into the door a second later. He pushed the door open and guided her inside, slamming it shut behind him. Her back was against the wall, his lips hovering over her a breath later. "If what you want me to do has anything to do with what's in the contents of this bag, then my dear submissive, I'm on it."

Her bag. She'd left it outside, but obviously Jake had grabbed it. She bit her lip and looked at him from under her lashes. "I got it for you. But maybe it's a Dominatrix outfit."

He gave a low laugh. "Babe, you don't have a dominant bone in you. But I'm willing to play along if that's what you want."

Just the thought of that turned her to mush. There was no way she'd ever want to be the Dominant, but the fact that he would let her meant everything. She closed the distance, peppering him with soft kisses that let her savor the slight roughness of his chapped lips and the harsher brush of his beard-roughened jaw. His skin was cold against the heat of her lips, chilling but alive. She wanted to give him everything. Show him how much she wanted him.

Loved him.

Her purse clunked to the floor right before her coat was slipped off her arms. The need to touch him was almost over-whelming. She grabbed for his jacket but a large drop of icy water splashed on her face, shocking her into stopping. She jerked back, laughing.

"You need a towel." She rubbed her hands through the melting snow clinging to his thick black hair.

He shook his head, spraying her like a shaking dog, making her duck and laugh some more.

She slipped off her boots then headed for the stairs, stopping on the bottom step to turn back to Jake. "Coming?" Then she took off, knowing he'd follow.

That he was with her.

Jake leaned against the wall and watched Cali disappear around the corner of the stairs. Her light laughter lingered behind as she raced away from him. But she wasn't running from him, he knew that. His chest ached, unable to believe he had her back.

Shaking himself out of his stupor, Jake shucked his outerwear, leaving his damp and snow-covered clothing in a messy heap in the entrance way. He pulled off his fleece and rubbed it over his hair as he ascended the stairs, anxious to feel her. His cock was hard and throbbing, his need for her barely contained.

His hands stilled on the fly of his jeans as he entered her bedroom. She stood across the room at the entrance to the master bath, her eyes uncertain, hands fidgeting with the buttons on her cardigan sweater set. Her beauty stopped him as much as her sudden hesitation.

"How do you want me?"

He almost dropped to his knees at her question. He tossed the fleece aside and stalked across the room to draw her into a crushing embrace. "I want you beneath me. On top of me. Around me. I want to fuck you until we both collapse from exhaustion. And then—" he skimmed his knuckles over her cheek, "—I want you beside me forever."

Her mouth dropped open, a gasp leaving her lips. Her fingers raked through his wet hair. "So do I," she whispered.

He claimed her pouty mouth in a kiss that poured out his soul. She tasted like coffee and peppermint. Like heaven and a drug more addictive than heroin.

And he'd almost lost her.

Never again.

He pulled her with him to the bed, his need to be in her overpowering everything else. He worked at the tiny buttons on her cardigan before he gave up and simply tugged it and the matching undersweater over her head. Her hands were under his thermal top, the heat of her palms stroking over his chest. He moaned and leaned into her touch.

Craving more, he got rid of his shirt before he paused to take her in. Her lips were swollen and red from kissing him, her hair slightly messed, her lacy red bra pushing the mounds of her breasts high with each breath she took. She moved her hands to the button of her jeans and his gaze followed their path.

That's when he saw it.

He snapped his hand out, yanking her wrist up to hold it between them. He stared, his eyes transfixed on the sight of the infinity chain looped around her wrists. His heart snagged, the beat pausing before it jumped to a racing pace. "Where'd you get this?"

She seemed uncertain, her fist clenching as she tried to pull her arm from his grip. After a moment, she raised her chin and answered. "Seth gave it to me."

"When?" he demanded. The last time he'd seen that chain, it was lying discarded on the stage.

"This week, when I went to the club looking for you."

He whipped his head up and met her determined eyes.

"You wouldn't answer your phone, so I went there to apologize, but you were gone. Instead, I got drilled by Seth and Deklan. Evidently I said something right, because Seth placed the chain on my wrist before I left." She looked at the object in question, her voice dropping. "He said it was mine. That I should keep it until you returned."

He flicked his thumb over the warm links of the chain. The infinity loops connected end to end in an elegant and simple design. It looked perfect against her skin. Perfect on her. "And you did. Why?" Did he dare hope she would want that? She'd said she wanted all of him, but did she really want the collar too? "After the stage incident, I thought you'd be done with that world and everything that went with it."

She stepped closer, trapping their arms between them. "I want it all. I need you. And I've accepted I need that side of you too. Not outside of your world, but in it. I don't know if I'll ever be comfortable with a big public Scene again. But I won't ask you to leave what is so much a part of you. I love being controlled by you. Being your submissive. I won't deny that anymore. I kept the chain, hoping someday you'd come back and put it on my neck. Where it belongs."

Too amazed to think, to respond, Jake simply reacted. It was like a caged animal had been set loose in him. He plundered her mouth, his arms crushing her to him. She was hot, open and accepting. His cock throbbed beneath his jeans as it rubbed against her stomach. Then her hand was there, stroking him over the material.

It wasn't enough.

He removed her bra and attacked her breasts, sucking each nipple into his mouth, squeezing the tender flesh and nibbling the hardened tips until she cried out in pleasure. Kneeling, he trailed hot kisses down her stomach, halting when he reached the waistband of her jeans. In two seconds he had the zipper down, the restricting material gone. He grabbed her hips and inhaled, rubbing his nose against the silk of her panties as the musky scent of her arousal invaded his senses.

"Jake," she breathed. "Please."

Fuck. He needed her so badly.

In one motion he stood, scooped her up and tossed her on the bed. She gave a small squeal of surprise but went silent as he got rid of his jeans and shorts then climbed onto the bed.

"You're beautiful, Cali." He bent and kissed her stomach. "I'll never stop telling you that." He pulled off her panties, the last barrier between them. Her legs spread as he kneeled between them. Gorgeous. "You're so responsive to me. So open and trusting."

"I need you, Jake." She squirmed on the bed, her hands reaching to tug on her nipples.

He almost came at the sight. He knew what he wanted. What she needed. He gave her sweet, waiting pussy one long lick then grabbed her and flipped onto his back, bringing Cali with him until she was lying on top of him, her eyes wide.

"Suck me, Cali." He rubbed his hands through her silky hair. "I want to feel your hot mouth on me. Sucking me until I can't take it. Then I want you to ride me."

Her eyes dilated, the green depths turning almost black, her lids lowering in a sultry look of longing. "Yes, Jake," she said before she dropped her head to take his nipple in her mouth. His back arched, her teeth biting down on the tender tip until he grunted at the enticing blend of pain and pleasure.

Her body was soft and hot against his as she slid down, leaving a trail of wet kisses in her wake, the light touches almost worshipful in their tenderness. The first stroke of her tongue over the length of his aching cock had him panting in pleasure. Another lick, a circle around the crown, then her mouth consumed him. He bucked his hips, unable to stop the reflex to be closer, to be surrounded by the heat.

"Cali." Her name came out as a mix between a plea and a command. One hand fisted in her hair, the other clenched a handful of sheets.

She sucked, her mouth moving up his shaft until her tongue swirled and prodded at the opening on the tip. *Fuck.* She was going to kill him.

She moaned, the vibration running down his cock and into his balls. He stared down, amazed at the sight of her mouth wrapped around his dick, her eyes closed in a look of ecstasy. One hand grasped the base of his cock, holding and rubbing it as she sucked him. But her other hand was between her legs, rubbing her clit. Her hips ground an erotic dance against her hand and he couldn't take it anymore. She seemed so wanton, so free and accepting of her sexuality and needs. So very different from when he'd first met her.

"Ride me."

She looked up, her mouth coming off his cock with a low pop that made him clench his teeth and suck in his breath to keep from coming. He flailed his hand around the edge of the bed until it landed on the condom he'd left there. He ripped it open and she took it from his hand to slowly roll the protection down his rigid, aching shaft.

"Come here, love," Jake said, reaching for her hips and settling her over him.

She grabbed his cock, positioning it at her entrance, then slowly lowered herself onto him.

"Fuck. You're perfect. So hot. So good."

She tucked her lip between her teeth and tilted her head back as she took him into her hot, wet channel. She felt so incredible. Looked so incredible. He yanked her down for a brutal, assaulting kiss, holding nothing back and giving her everything.

He thrust his hips up, forcing him deep, and they both

groaned. Then she was lifting and plunging, her hips matching his as the passion built. She drew her lips away from his and sat up, her hands pushing on his chest as she rode his cock.

"You feel so good." She swiveled, the motion rubbing the sensitive tip of his cock. "I've missed you. I don't want to lose you again."

He found her clit and rubbed the swollen nub, making her buck and moan, her pace increasing. "You won't lose me. Never again." The promise pulled from the depths of his heart. He'd never lose her again. "Come for me, Cali."

And she did, her cry echoing against the walls of the room, her muscles clamping hard around his dick until he came with her. He arched and pumped into her until he couldn't breathe, couldn't think, couldn't see anything but her.

She collapsed onto him, her chest heaving in deep breaths. He hugged her to him, her sweat-slicked skin sticking to his as they both recovered.

Like he could ever recover from her.

She kissed his neck and ear before slowly lifting to slide to the side, his softening cock slipping from her warmth. He almost groaned aloud at the loss but restrained himself enough to get up and make the quick trip to the bathroom to dispense with the condom. She watched him as he returned, her gaze caressing him before she shifted to push the bedding down. She crawled under the covers, holding the side open for him.

Her skin was still flushed from arousal, her eyelids heavy with sated bliss. He snuggled in next to her, drawing her close until her head rested on his chest, her fingers tracing lazy patterns across his torso.

"Thank you, Cali," he whispered into her hair, nuzzling the silky strands.

She turned her head and lifted up a little to look at him. "For what?"

"For understanding. For wanting me. All of me."

She smiled, her swollen lips curling in a tempting pull. "Ditto."

His heart swelled. It felt like it was going to burst out of his chest. He grabbed her wrist—the one with his chain on it—lifting it until they could both see it, the silver links gleaming in the paling light of the late afternoon.

Jake let his fingers run over the links. "This doesn't belong here."

She inhaled sharply, her body tensing on his, but she didn't say anything. Only watched him, caution and worry etched on her face.

He shifted until he could undo the clasp and unwind the chain from her wrists. She bit her lip, tracking the chain as he removed it and let it dangle between them. He could feel her heart racing where her chest pressed against his. A beat that matched his own.

"I love you, Cali. More than I ever thought I could."

She searched his gaze, hunting out the truth he hoped she'd see. She licked her lips, swallowed then whispered, "I love you."

He pushed up, pulling her with him until they were both sitting, facing each other. She shoved her hair away from her face, tucking strands behind her ears. It was styled straight today, not the curly, freer way she wore to the club. The ends brushed against her shoulders, drawing his attention.

Leaning forward, he pressed a kiss to her bare neck. To the place where his chain belonged. He drew back to trace a path over the front of her neck, pausing on the racing beat of her heart near her throat.

"Will you wear it, Cali?" He moved his fingers back and forth over her heated skin. "Here, where it belongs?"

She blinked, her eyes shimmering. "Yes. Please."

His breath rushed out, his relief exiting with the air. He'd barely dared to hope she'd say yes. That she'd want to wear his collar after all that had happened. He had to make sure.

"As a collar or a necklace?"

She straightened, her eyes searching his. She reached over and fisted her hand around his. The one that held the chain. "You bought it as a collar. You placed it on my neck as a collar." She studied their clasped hands then slowly pried his fingers open to reveal the chain. "It's a beautiful chain. An exquisite necklace." She looked back to him. "But it will always be your collar to me."

He kissed her. He had no choice. Her words busted through the last of his doubt. His fears. Finally, the itch was gone. In its place was a sense of contentment. Of belonging and being home.

He broke the kiss and lifted the chain, the links seemingly heavier in his hands. He slipped them around her neck, tipping to the side as she raised her hair so he could clasp it. His hands shook, something they hadn't done since he was a teenager.

Finally, it was closed.

Jake inhaled and stared at his collar hugging Cali's neck. Her fingers traced over the links, her bare chest lifting and falling rapidly.

"It looks perfect on you." His voice was gravelly, almost foreign to him.

"It feels perfect on me." She reached out to touch his cheek, her fingers soft against the scruff of his whiskers.

God, what she did to him. He growled. That was the only way he could describe the sound that came from his chest. He grabbed her tight and flipped until she was trapped beneath him. Every inch of her pressed tightly against his length. Heat seared his body, his cock once again hard and wanting.

He'd never get tired of her. His Cali.

"Hands over your head."

Her eyes flashed in response as she immediately moved to comply with his command. "Yes, Jake. Whatever you want."

Whatever he wanted. His voice softened, his heart leaking into his words. "I already have that. I have you."

She smiled. "Yes, you do."

EPILOGUE

"Are you sure you're ready for this?" Cali asked, squeezing Jake's hand. A nervous smile fluttered over her face in a hesitant dance his stomach mimicked.

"More than." His smile was assured, kiss encouraging. He'd learned the art of faking long ago and had no problem giving her the confidence he was far from feeling. She needed it from him, and he sure as hell wasn't going to fail her on something that should be simple.

Should be. But what the hell did he know about meeting parents? On Christmas, no less? A holiday he'd abandoned in the traditional sense before he'd reached his teens.

However, his gaze was unwavering when he stared down at her. "But if you're not, it's okay." He shot a quick glance to the wooden door, green wreath decorating the front with its festive cheer. "I think we can still sneak away." And damn, that would be such a relief.

Her chuckle was light as it drifted through the chilly air. "I doubt it. My mom probably knew the second we pulled into the driveway." Yet she still didn't move to knock or open the door. The oversize shopping bag stuffed with gifts crinkled against her leg where she clutched it tighter, her bravado faltering.

She was nervous, too. Maybe more than him, if that was possible. This was a big step for both of them. One he wanted to take, even if every old instinct told him to run.

But he was done running. From her. Life. Relationships.

In many ways, this meeting was more defining for their relationship than her collar. This had nothing to do with the club and everything to do with navigating life together. A life he wanted with her.

He wrapped his free hand around her shoulders and urged her into a hug. Her breath warmed his neck and he inhaled her scent, gaining as much strength from her as she took from him. "It'll be fine," he reassured, confidence flooding him now. They'd talked about this meeting, had worked through some of the unknowns over the past week. Long discussions on comfort, wants and needs that went beyond the bedroom and Dungeon.

"I know," she said, lips grazing the skin of his exposed neck. "Intellectually. Emotionally, I'm not as confident. I'm a grown woman with adult kids of my own and I'm still worried about what my parents will think of me and you. Of my new…boyfriend? Man-friend?"

Boyfriend. Man-friend. Partner. Dom—which one would she go with when he was all of them?

"Oh my God." The misery of her tone was mitigated by another low chuckle. "I'm acting like a teenager."

"Not even close." His insistence was immediate, firm. He ran his hand down her back, beneath the hem of her leather coat to rub her bottom. His touch was deliberate and rough over her wool slacks. Her hiss pierced the air through clenched teeth, the sound a sweet pained-pleasure intake. "It wasn't a teenager who took my spanking last night," he murmured near her ear. "Or begged me to let her come."

The memory rushed in, of her splayed across his lap, receiving the burning sting of his hand before he bound her to the bed and took her in a slow, drawn-out crest and retreat of her orgasm. His cock twitched and he sucked in a controlled breath. He'd give her whatever she needed, would do just about anything for her.

Including meeting her family.

"You're not helping," she admonished before pressing a kiss to his jaw, softening her words. "Are you still okay with going in?"

He cocked a brow. "Would I be standing here if I wasn't?"

"Maybe." She let a slow smile curl over her lips, green eyes dancing. Her honesty had him chuckling. A month ago he might not have. With any other woman he never had. "You did go shopping with me this week, and I *know* that wasn't because you wanted to wade through the throng of holiday shoppers."

His smile split with his love for her. "True. But you rewarded me later, didn't you?" Another reminder of how much she reveled in his subtle dominance in all parts of her life. They were still navigating that part. Would be for a long time. It was a give-and-take that wasn't without bumps or hitches, but the end result of having her in his life was worth every stumble.

She traced the collar with her fingertips, the delicate links a permanent reminder of what they'd found together. Pride filled his chest. The chain fit her perfectly. Elegant without being obtrusive. Symbolic to those who understood.

"I did." Her lids lowered, a shy yet sultry look that fired his blood and had his mind racing with thoughts of later.

Well, damn. He squeezed her bottom then forced himself to step back while he still could. "I'm in this with you." He tilted her chin up. Dropped one more kiss on lips he'd never get enough of before clasping her hand in his. His own bag rattled in his other hand when he lifted it to rap on the solid door.

"Thank you," she said before letting go of his hand to shove the door open. The homey scent of cooking food merged with the holiday songs and decor to welcome them. "Merry Christmas," she yelled down the hall, shuffling her boots on the entrance rug.

"I told you they'd eventually come in," a female voice said, loud enough to reach them.

Jake choked on a brief laugh, which had Cali rolling her eyes. "See?" she said to him.

He shook his head and helped her with her coat without a word. There was a smile on her lips, though. One that helped to settle more of his nerves. They'd be okay today.

Her palm warmed his as she led him down the hall to the kitchen, where her family was gathered. Small though the group was, with just her parents and kids, it was hers. And now he was here, too. Someone new and hopefully welcomed.

It was terrifying and warming all at once to realize how much he wanted to be a part of her family. For her, definitely. But for himself, too.

"Mom. Dad. Kids," she said, love flowing around the words to mask the flush that tainted her cheeks. "This is my—" she cocked her head, brow lifting with her grin "—man-friend, Jake."

That was perfect for here and all this group ever needed to know.

"I need to grab more liquor before heading up to Seth's," Jake said when the elevator opened on the first floor of the club.

The silence was startling to Cali, as was the darkness. Safety lights glowed periodically from the ceiling to light their way down the hallway to the bar area. The vast emptiness of the place had her stalling to stare as Jake made his way past the bar to unlock a door a few feet beyond.

It was a bit jarring to see the club so bare now. Just standard tables and chairs over industrial carpeting on this level. Nothing to identify the primary purpose of The Den.

She inhaled out of instinct, searching for anything that would give it away. All she got was the lemon-scented cleaner and a vague hint of stale beer. No heavier weight of leather or pungent wafts of sweat or sex. It was just a space, one that'd changed her life.

Her gaze landed on the big red doors, pulse kicking up a beat at the mere thought of where they led to. Of how much had changed since she'd first stepped through them with Jake.

"Did you want anything in particular to drink?" Jake called out, jerking her out of her musings.

She laughed at herself. It wasn't the place or anything in it that had brought the changes to her life. No, what she'd found and embraced with Jake was their doing. Most of which she wouldn't alter one bit. Even the embarrassing parts, because it all brought them to where they were now.

The storage room where Jake had ducked into was lined with boxes of wine, shelves of liquor and beer kegs. "I'll stick to a glass of wine," she answered.

She'd had two at her parents and was already close to her alcohol limit. A harsh shudder rushed through her at the memory of her hangover a few weeks ago. No need to repeat that anytime soon—if ever. He eyed the bottles on the shelf before adding two to the box at his feet. Her brows lifted at the sight of the eight bottles now in the box. "How much do you need for this party?"

He shrugged and picked up a clipboard, marking off columns. "There's usually twenty to thirty people. It varies every year, depending on who's available or alone."

"That many?" She swallowed and glanced down, gesturing to her outfit beneath her coat. "Are you sure I don't need to change?" The festive red sweater set and black slacks had been perfect for afternoon Christmas dinner at her parents, an event that had thankfully been relaxed and went remarkably well. But she wasn't so sure her outfit was appropriate for an evening party filled with club employees and Jake's friends.

He set the clipboard down and came over to cup her cheek in his palm, studying her. His intense gaze had her stomach twisting with a version of the same nerves that'd stalked her on her parents' doorstep. He was steady, though, and she absorbed his strength like she had all day. Let it ease through her until it became hers, too.

"You don't have to change. But if you'll be more comfortable in something else, then you should." The stroke of his thumb over her skin was reassuring and calmed her, like always. "There'll be a mix of leather and normal clothes. Some will be in full Dom/sub roles, but that's because they want to and can be here. There's no right or wrong, though."

She blew out a breath and told herself this was still new. That having Jake in her life all the time was familiar and foreign at once. "And you're not going to change?" His black jeans and sweater had been fine at her parents, but could easily transition to this scene, too.

He shook his head. "No. I don't need the clothes to be your Dom." He grazed his fingers over the links of her collar in a subtle reminder of what she already knew. She shivered, sighed and tried to let most of her worries go.

She didn't need the clothes to be his submissive either. Not now or in the Dungeon.

His phone buzzed, loud and stunning in the silence, but

he didn't budge to retrieve it, even though her gaze shot to his coat pocket where it was hidden. He was still focused on her when she looked back up to find true concern that erased the last of her nerves.

They'd figure it out. Navigate this next social hurdle together just like they'd done at her parents' house.

"Are you okay?" he asked, hand sliding down to cup the side of her neck. The links of her collar nudged into her skin, his palm warm in contrast to the chill of his fingertips. He could tell her to change or not. Define her actions for her by removing the choice.

And that wouldn't fly outside the bedroom. Not on a daily basis. Not for her. Yes, she loved knowing he was here for her in every way. But she was still her own person who could make decisions for herself.

"I'm good." Better than. She reached up to kiss him. Took his concern and let it flood her, along with his love. He opened to her, tilting her head so he could claim everything she was offering him. Hot and slow with a touch of forceful, he swept his tongue into her mouth to tangle with hers until his rich chocolaty taste filled her.

He was hard, solid muscle against her front as he snaked a hand around to grip her bottom in a firm hold. A sharp sting spread over her butt cheek to rip a moan from her chest. The lingering effects of last night's play heated her blood and was another reminder of the deeper connection they shared. She relaxed into him then, gave herself over for him to lead with the trust he'd earned.

Her lips were tender and throbbing by the time he pulled back. She blinked, focused and smiled. She'd never grow tired of the protective glint in his eyes. One tempered by love.

Another buzz had him reaching for his phone. "Seth wants

another bottle of vodka." He stuffed the clear alcohol into the box with the others and flicked the light off. "That's it."

The elevator ride to the top floor was mercifully short. There was no time for her worries to reclaim their hold. They made a quick stop at Jake's loft to leave their coats and her purse before crossing the hall to Seth's.

She clasped her empty hands at her sides. "I feel like I should've brought something." Drilled-in manners demanded a hostess gift of some sort should be filling them.

"I have the liquor." Jake lifted the box a bit. "Plus I'm one of the hosts. It was just Seth's turn to offer up his place." He entered the loft without bothering to knock, a jumbled mix of laughter, music and enticing scents flowing out to greet them. "Ho. Ho. Ho," Jake called into the fray. "And a merry fucking Christmas to you all." He hoisted the box high, a round of cheers going up.

"It's about time you got here," Marcus said, snatching the box away and heading to the kitchen.

Jack managed a slug to the man's arm before he was out of reach. "Pour me a rum and Coke while you're in there."

Marcus paused at the kitchen, brow raised when he turned back. "I thought you had a sub for that?"

Cali balked, blood draining from her face as she quickly glanced around. There were a few people watching the exchange, gazes assessing—including Seth's and Deklan's. What should she do? Was she really expected to wait on Jake, maybe everyone? Would she mind? It was what she tended to do naturally. But now...

Bitter anger rose hot and sour at the assumption she'd be willing to serve them all. Bring them drinks, pick up the trash, keep the food stocked—that was her default hiding role. The one she'd perfected during her marriage to disguise her loneliness. That was *not* the kind of relationship she wanted or would live with now. Never again.

Jake tucked her into his side, eyes never leaving Marcus. "*Cali* is my worry, not yours." The emphasis on her name had her heart pounding. "She's here to have fun, like the rest of us." His voice held an iron edge that sent a rush of love through her. In a different situation, it would've had her on her knees waiting for his command. Here, though, it almost melted her. He wouldn't let her default into her old role, nor would he allow anyone else to put her there.

Marcus raised a hand, chuckling. "Chill, man. It was a joke." He shook his head and disappeared around the corner into the kitchen.

Cali released her held breath and sagged into Jake's side. They'd only been at the party for a minute and she was already sweating with her returned nerves. Could they do this? Could she be his girlfriend and submissive among these people without being on her knees for him?

Jake lifted her chin, kissed her lips and whispered against them, "Trust me." Right. She did, too. "I have a something special for you when the night's done."

Her brows winged up, curiosity changing to speculation in a heartbeat. "You do?"

He nodded, one slow dip. "But only if you relax and have fun."

She puffed out a soft laugh. "All right." The flexing emotional ups and downs were exhausting, and she was beyond trying to manage them. "I can do that. If you can."

"Deal." He sealed it with a last kiss before leading her into the room.

Introductions were done all around, and like he'd said, the dress code varied among the attendees with no right or wrong. A few subs were kneeling at their Dom's feet and somehow it all blended without issue. This really was a casual gathering of friends, which she was now a part of.

As Jake's girlfriend. Submissive. Partner. Lover.

She was all of those things to him.

The dawning understanding meandered in to settle another piece of their forming relationship. She didn't have to be just one of them, like he wasn't to her. The situation would dictate which was in the forefront, but that didn't mean they weren't all in play at any given time.

They could be more than one thing to each other. Should be and were.

She squeezed Jake's hand, her love for him flooding her with another dose of happiness. She studied his profile, easily picturing a life with him. It wouldn't necessarily be smooth, but she'd lived for years in a one-note relationship and understood the value of one that was dynamic and real.

Alive, shifting, enduring—they had that.

Her heart constricted at the small epiphany. It didn't matter how improbable others thought they were. Not when everything was so right when they were together.

It was an hour or two later when Deklan stood on a chair, smacking a flogger against the marble bar to get everyone's attention. It was so much more appropriate and effective in that group than a clinking wineglass.

Cali rested her head on Jake's shoulder. Her sigh was one of contentment and pure happiness when he hugged her to his side.

"Well," Deklan started, voice raised over the hushed crowd. "I drew the short straw this year, so I'm stuck doing this damn toast." A wave of laughter rolled through the room as he lifted his glass. "Here's to good friends. Acceptance of personal choices. And five more years of the same." A hardy round of "hear, hear" went up, and Deklan raised his hand to quiet them back down. "Seriously, though. Thank you. I speak for all three of us—" he nodded at Jake and Seth "—when I say your support and friendship is appreciated." He lifted his beer bottle high, a rare smile spreading across his hard features. "Now drink up and don't fuck up."

Another boisterous round of agreement went up before Deklan took a swig from his bottle and hopped down. The music started back up, a rock version of Christmas songs that went with the BDSM Christmas tree in the corner. With red silk scarves as garland and anal beads and nipple clamps with chains as tinsel, it'd definitely caught her attention. Or maybe it was the lighted vibrators and what Jake had confirmed was a *really* huge butt plug in place of the star on top.

"Are you ready to go?" Jake asked.

"Yes." Her emphatic answer came out stronger than she'd intended, but he just laughed. "I'm tired," she quickly added. "It's been a long day." Emotionally draining. Good, though. Very good.

Her family had welcomed Jake with only a bit of hesitation from Logan, which she didn't begrudge him for. And she'd had fun meeting everyone tonight as friends, not just a sub. No one had treated her differently, even though she was certain most—if not all—of them had seen her submitting to Jake at the club at some point.

They said their goodbyes and made the short trip across the hall. Her shoulders dropped the second his door clicked closed behind them. He wrapped his arms around her waist, nuzzled the side of her neck. Her exhale was a release that went clear to her toes.

He was with her. Had her.

They'd survived the day.

"Is that it for our obligations today?" he asked, voice muffled against her skin.

"Yes." Her breathy answer was a languid mix of rising desire and drained energy.

His hum vibrated across her collarbone and down her chest to peak her nipples with its subtle promise. He skimmed his hands under her sweater, her breath hitching as his palms grazed her abdomen in slow strokes that heated her blood to a low simmer.

Her moan was heavy with the passion that bloomed to life with each press of his lips up her neck to the sensitive spot beneath her ear. He sucked the lobe into his mouth, warm breath sending goose bumps down her neck when he traced the shell. "Are you ready for your surprise?"

Her brain had shorted out and she struggled to focus on his question. "I thought we exchanged gifts this morning." At her place, dressed in pajamas by her Christmas tree, since her kids had stayed with their dad.

He tugged on her nipples, twirled the nubs between his fingers until she arched into his touch, wanting more. Needing to give him more.

"Who said it was a present?"

True. She was even more intrigued now.

He urged her arms up, and her sweater set slid over her head in one smooth swoop to be discarded on the table by the door. The cool air was a refreshing rush over her heated flesh.

He undid her pants next, lowered them to the ground and slipped each leg off over her black heeled boots. The matching lingerie had been an early gift with orders to wear the red-and-black lace today. Did they have something to do with his surprise?

Still behind her, he took small nips from each butt cheek, just hard enough to tease a slight sting out of her still tender flesh. She sucked in a breath, held it as he nuzzled the cleft between. She was liquid under his hands. Pliable only for him.

Always for him.

He placed kisses along her spine as he rose, the last one hitting her nape in a hard press and slow lick. Her sigh was hummed in a low note of pleasure. Whatever tension she'd carried all day was gone now. Wiped away by his knowledgeable touch and knowing hands.

"Wait here," he murmured by her ear before slipping past her to head to his bedroom.

Curiosity had her itching to follow, but it wasn't strong enough to override his gentle command. She'd stay put until he came back, certain it'd be worth the wait. A shiver took her by surprise and she hugged herself to ward off the chill coming from the large warehouse windows.

"Come here, Cali."

His call was hollow through the open loft, and she was moving before he'd finished her name. Her stomach clenched around the anticipation that was fed by the quiet excitement spinning through her.

What would it be? A new toy? Outfit? Bondage gear?

She turned the corner into his room, lit only by his bedside lamp, and almost stumbled. She froze, breath stuck in her lungs at the sight of Jake spread naked on his turned-down bed. Muscled thighs, toned abs, sculpted chest. Holy…gorgeous.

Unadorned by a bow or anything so foolish on him, she still assumed he was her surprise. Arms curled behind his head, legs open, erection laying prominent against his abdomen. Open, unrestricted and vulnerable to her. For her.

He was the perfect gift. One she was still amazed by.

She wet her lips, needing the moisture to speak. "What's this?" The rasp in her voice gave away her uncertainty. Any chance of pretending complete confidence or sultry control was gone now. Not that she could've pulled it off anyway.

He undid her.

"For you." His smile was almost devious below lowered lids before it shifted to open honesty. "You joked about being in charge last week. If you want to try it, then I'm willing." He blew out a slow breath. "Every aspect of our relationship is negotiable, including this. Whatever you want that I can give you is yours."

Whatever she wanted was hers.

"But what if…" She paused, moving toward the bed. She stopped by its side to slip her boots off, eyes glued to his. She crawled onto the bed until she was over him, looking down at the man she loved with all her heart and more. "What if I already have everything I want?"

His lips curled in a half smile that had her heart hitching as her sex tightened. "Then I'd say you're one lucky woman."

"I am," she whispered before taking his mouth in a kiss that left no doubt to her belief. His moan was rugged, deep with matched need and desire. His fingers dug through her hair before he jerked her down onto him.

In a flash, he rolled, tucking her beneath him without releasing her mouth. The weight of him on her, his presence above her, surrounding her, was like coming home. She wrapped her arms and legs around him, held on until he finally eased back.

Much-needed air reached her lungs in deep gulps, her chest panting along with his as she smiled up at him. "I thought I was leading tonight?" she teased.

"Oh, hell." He dropped his head to her shoulder, chuckles tickling her neck. "Damn. I suck so bad at following."

He did. And she loved him for it. Loved that he'd offered and tried. She ran her nails up his back, reveled as he arched into the scraping and groaned. He lifted, head shaking. She caught his face in her hands, pressed a firm kiss to his lips.

"I love you." She swiped her thumb over his lower lip, letting her words sink in. "On top. In control. Beside me. Under me. All of it."

His eyes dropped closed for a long moment before they re-opened, love spilling from the darkened depths. "I'm so damn happy you walked into the club that night."

"Me, too." She refused to even think about where she'd be right now if she'd never dared to take that first step toward what she wanted without knowing exactly what "it" was. Thank God Jake had been there to show her.

"I love you, Cali." He shifted to brush her hair away from her face. "We're going to make this work. You and I."

Today had proven that they could. That what had started in the Dungeon was strong enough to survive outside of it. Be even more than she'd ever dared to dream.

"Yeah," she agreed, heart filling impossibly more. "We will." Of that, she was a hundred percent confident.

★ ★ ★ ★ ★

ABOUT THE AUTHOR

Lynda Aicher has always loved to read. It's a simple fact that has been true since she discovered the words of Judy Blume at the age of ten. After years of weekly travel as a consultant implementing computer software for global companies, she ended her nomadic lifestyle to raise her two children.

Now, her imagination is her only limitation on where she can go and her writing lets her escape from the daily duties of being a mom, wife, chauffeur, scheduler, cook, teacher, volunteer, cleaner and mediator. If writing wasn't a priority, it wouldn't get done.

To learn more about Lynda, you can find her at:

www.lyndaaicher.com
www.facebook.com/lyndaaicherauthor
www.twitter.com/lyndaaicher

BONDS OF NEED

ONE

The bag taunted her. All glossy and black, with blood red letters embossed in an elegant script proclaiming the store name. It was a simple bag, really. A standard rectangle with rope handles in the style used by most clothing stores. Yet Kendra Morgan couldn't stop staring at it.

She moved to the right, edging around the end of her bed as if a different angle would change the effect. The shift in position caused the overhead light to glare against the shiny coating blurring the lettering, but the name was already imprinted in her mind.

If she was honest, and she was trying to be that now, it wasn't the bag itself that mocked her. No, it was the items inside that beckoned her in a silent whisper of repressed longing.

Kendra hugged herself as she struggled against her continuous inner battle. The one that waged between the desire to wear the garments and the repulsion that came with the thought of putting them on. But there was no denying the residual excitement building within her at the thought of the night to come. Of once again being in that environment surrounded by the sounds, smells and sights of forbidden acts and deviant desires played out.

Despite all reason and arguments against it, her body still responded. Her nipples ached for the pinch of a clamp and even now tingled with longing. It was a hunger that burned in her core and begged for release. Kendra inhaled, squeezing her eyes tight against the visions that dropped into her mind.

Spinning away from the damning bag and its seductive contents, she strode into the bathroom and turned on the shower. Letting the water warm, she dug through the drawers in the walk-in closet, hunting for the accessories she wanted.

Tonight was an opportunity to prove once and for all that she didn't want that—couldn't want that in her life. Returning to a BDSM club was another step in her own contrived rehabilitation program. She hoped it was the right one. The thought of living with her unfulfilled desires for the rest of her life was too discouraging to contemplate.

When she'd fled Eric eight months ago, she'd left with two bags, a prayer and a conviction that she'd never go back. It was all she'd dared to take. In truth, it was all she'd wanted. There'd been nothing in Eric's penthouse that had meant anything to her. He'd stripped everything of importance from her long before then.

Finding the box at the bottom of the last drawer, Kendra pulled it out and took it to the bathroom. The simple white cardboard was a standard discount jewelry box, nothing special to denote the significance of the contents. Setting it on the counter, she turned away, clenching her shaking hands in frustration.

She could do this. She needed to do this.

She left the room, her determination firmly in place, to make a quick check through her rented condo. First the sliding glass door at the back, showcasing the serene picture of the courtyard filled with clean, white snow in the waning light of early evening. The frosted chill reached in through the glass to brush over her cheeks and toes. She gave a tug on the handle before letting the curtain drop back and moved to the large picture window in the living room, then on to the kitchen. The front door was last. All were still locked, just like they'd been an hour ago.

The ball of tension in her stomach eased a touch at the confirmation, the reassurance that she was still safe. The ritualistic routine had decreased in frequency since she'd moved in, but she couldn't let it go. Not yet.

The smooth coldness of the wood floors soaked into her bare feet, making her shiver. She wrapped her robe tighter across her chest and hurried back to the waiting shower, a quick glance passing over the broom handle in the track of the slider. It was one last validation of safety as she mounted the stairs.

The one-bedroom unit was sparsely furnished, the owner's leftovers making the space echo with an almost hollow feeling. As depressing as that may seem to some, it was her safe haven.

Kendra stepped into the shower and let the hot water ease the soreness from her muscles. She twisted her head until the hard spikes of liquid kneaded every inch of her neck and back and forced an exhausted sigh from her lungs. She was so tired of looking over her shoulder. Of the constant worry that never completely left, never let her rest or relax.

Shrugging off the lethargy, she grabbed the shampoo and began the process of preparing. The faint aroma of lilacs filled the steamy stall before it flowed away with the bubbles. A sense of calm drifted over her, and she let the scent soothe her as she grabbed the soap and razor. She lathered and shaved her skin clean of hair, a habit she'd neglected since arriving in Minneapolis. It'd been a subtle act of rebellion, even if she'd been the only one to know.

Her palms slicked down the now-smooth skin, searching for missed spots. The patter of water hitting the floor was as lulling to her senses as the stroke of her hand over the newly exposed flesh. She trailed her fingers between her legs, touching the folds in search of stubble.

In the past she'd always waxed, preferring a professional see to the details. She shouldn't have even bothered with the full-body shave and had mentally fought against it for days. But she couldn't walk into a leather club without being clean and prepared. It was too ingrained.

She found nothing but smooth, soft skin and let her fingers roam, exploring the sensitive area with gentle grazes edged with the hard line of her nails. Desire flamed to life, igniting from the inside out, but she knew from experience it wasn't enough.

The frustrated moan caught in her throat and she shut off the water, cutting the shower short. The cold air attacked her wet skin, goose bumps shooting over her flesh and bringing a hard stop to her arousal. The lime green towel was small and abrasive as she dried off, but she didn't mind. The clearance item had been purchased with her own money, which was enough to let her overlook any inadequacies it might have.

The sudden chime of her cell phone pierced through the quiet room. Kendra jolted back, stumbling over the rug to crash into the shower door. Someday, she vowed not to do that every time her phone rang. She hurried into her bedroom, wrapping the towel around her as she snatched the ringing object off the bed. A glance at the caller ID had her breath easing from its locked space in her chest.

She cleared her throat. "Hi, Allie." She held the phone to

her ear as the wet ends of her hair dripped cold drops of water down her chest and back. "Change your mind?"

"Hell, no." The sharp retort snapped through the airwaves, her friend's voice holding the crisp conviction that flowed like the confidence she exuded. "I'm just making sure *you're* still in. You seemed a little nervous on our shopping trip this morning."

Kendra's gaze shot to the taunting, shiny bag on her bed. She gave a chuckle, feeling none of the reassurance she was trying to project. "I'm fine. And, yes, I'm still going. For Cali," she clarified.

Cali and Allie both owned condos across the courtyard in the same building unit as Kendra. All single at the time, the three women had formed a friendship over the summer that had offered her the inklings of normalcy and comfort she'd so desperately needed.

"Yeah, right," Allie scoffed. "And none of it's your own curiosity. Tell yourself that if it gets you there. Me, I'm dying to see what it's all about." There was a brief pause. "But then, you've been to one before, right?"

Kendra sank to perch on the edge of the bed, her legs suddenly unable to hold her weight. She tightened her hold on the thin phone before she answered. "Yeah, I have."

"I feel so naïve compared to the two of you." Allie laughed then halted abruptly. "Crap. I've gotta finish getting ready. We'll pick you up in an hour. Cali wants to be at the club before it gets too crowded." The line went dead before Kendra could respond.

Clicking the end button, she dropped the phone on the bed, watching it bounce once before going still. Yeah, she'd been to a BDSM club. Many times. A secret she'd only exposed as a means to comfort Cali.

Two months ago her friend had been tormenting herself

over her desires. Afraid of what others would think if they discovered she was into dominance and submission. Kendra had reassured Cali that as long as the acts were consensual, there was nothing wrong with her defined kink. It most certainly didn't alter Kendra's perception of her.

Safe, sane and consensual—three words that were the slogan of the leather world. Words that had been stripped from Kendra once before but never again.

Right. She held the power. A fact she was still rebuilding in her mind.

She grabbed the bag off the bed, the slick coating crinkling as it banged against her leg, and returned to the bathroom.

She quickly dried her hair. The sleek, platinum highlights had faded long ago, leaving behind the natural soft blond-brown shade that she'd forgotten existed. It didn't look nearly as sophisticated—something her mother would cringe over. But it felt good to her. Honest. With practiced movements she twisted her straight, shoulder-length hair into a sleek knot at her nape, pulling the hair tight to her skull.

Next was a heavy coat of eye makeup. The dark liner, thick mascara and deep blue shadow looked out of place on her face but brought out the blue of her eyes and provided a layer of distance. The splash of pale, pink gloss over her lips finished the process.

She grabbed the lotion, dropped her towel and quickly rubbed the cream into her skin. The ingrained habit of using unscented products was something she only overrode for her shampoo. Not that she planned on doing a Scene tonight. No, she was going to prove that she *didn't* need that anymore. But even still, the thought of a cloying scent clinging to her skin was unwanted.

Finally, she slowly took the items out of the damning bag. She systematically removed each tag from the sexy lingerie before slipping her leg into the silk of a royal-blue stocking. With each piece that went on, she slid one step further into her submissive headspace. The act of prepping herself—dressing to please another—was like a seductive mistress calling to her. Luring her back to something she couldn't possibly want.

She set the last two pieces on the counter and stared at herself in the mirror. The past eight months had taken a toll on her body. She was thinner than ever, her ribs showing under her bra and her hips bones cutting hard arcs toward her midriff. Eric would have been pleased.

Choking on the thought, she made a promise to start eating better and defiantly reached for the little white box. She popped off the lid and dumped the contents into her palm. The two charms clinked together as the gentle weight hit her hand.

Eric had insisted she only wear the jewelry he bought for her, but she'd kept these hidden. Her small rebellious side had held strong, despite his best effort to squash it.

The shelf bra pushed her breasts up but was scooped low, leaving her nipples exposed. She reached for her nipple ring and threaded one of the weighted sun charms onto the loop. Unaccustomed to the pull and attention, the bud puckered and ached in a teasing rush of awareness. She bit her lip against the sensation that tingled and spread through her.

She'd kept the piercings because they were hers. Something she'd done before she'd met Eric. And damn it, she wouldn't let him take everything from her.

Sucking in a breath, she finished the task, the second charm slipped on to the other loop as quick and efficiently as possible. The two gold and silver charms dangled enticingly from the silver rings. They hung just below the material line of her bra, popping against the stunning blue and drawing the eye to the display.

Of course, no one but her would see them. They would

be her little secret and a reminder that her body belonged to her and no one else.

The dress was last, a cotton and lace sleeveless number in the same royal blue of her lingerie. Naughty, but demure, it hugged her form and skimmed over the stocking line, allowing for glimpses of the garters when she moved.

The knee-high, black leather boots were the finishing touch on the outfit. The purr of the zipper as she pulled the leather closed around her calves was like a siren's song. Her breathing deepened, her mind settling lower into that quiet space.

She stared at herself in the mirror, her pulse increasing to shatter the nugget of peace that had started to form. It wasn't hard-core BDSM attire, but it was the closest she'd come to it in a very long time. Her stomach flipped and twisted, the acid churning on emptiness. Dinner had been a skipped event from fear of it making an embarrassing return later.

The sharp chime of her doorbell made her flinch before she forced out a long breath in an attempt to relax. She grabbed the last item off the counter, the final touch, and slipped it over her head. The Mardi Gras mask covered the entire top half of her face from nose to hairline and fit firmly to her cheeks. It was the same royal blue as her dress with gold and silver sparkles that swirled into a fringe of small, white feathers.

Her eyes looked dark and sultry behind the confinement, the makeup blending with the colors of the mask to give her the mysterious look she'd been going for.

Camouflaged in plain sight. That was the only reason she'd finally agreed to go to the club. Behind the mask, she could hide.

Even from herself.

TWO

The sea of bodies spread out from the already cramped dance floor to the more open bar and lounge area of The Den. Brightly colored sequins and feathers added an unusual slash of color to the normally predominant black that their clientele tended to wear. Even the normal bump and grind of the music was edged with a trace of jazz for the occasion.

Deklan Winters stood on the small balcony overlooking the ground floor of The Den, his arms crossed over his chest, the muscles down his back feeling as tightly pulled as the material of the black cotton T-shirt that covered them. Nights like this put him on edge. And not in a good way.

Seth insisted it was good for business, but it was a royal pain in the ass for security. Allowing a large number of guests into the private BDSM club always resulted in problems. No matter how careful they were.

Their annual Mardi Gras bash was only one of two times each year that they opened the doors to a larger than usual number of guests. Otherwise, they limited the number of guests members were allowed to bring into the club each night. The Den's security was more detailed and extensive than the Pentagon, guaranteeing the privacy of their members.

He sensed more than heard the click of the door closing at the bottom of the stairs behind him. The music booming over the crowded room below covered the minor sound, but Deklan's military training had tuned his senses to pick up on even the smallest changes in the environment around him.

The tread on the steps was doubled, indicating both Seth and Jake were encroaching on his coveted spot. The two men were like brothers and Deklan was closer to them than the family he'd been born into. He'd give his life for either man, which was one of the reasons he'd agreed to go into business with them.

The slap of a hand on his shoulder wasn't a surprise, and Deklan didn't react. He kept his eyes glued to the activity below, scanning back and forth, looking for anything that would indicate trouble.

"Loosen up, Dek." Seth's voice was raised to be heard over the grinding thump of the music. "You've taken every security precaution possible. It'll be fine."

"Not your ass over the fire, Mathews."

Seth squeezed his shoulder before letting his hand drop. "Just as much my ass as yours."

"As long as you keep my ass out of it." Jake's retort came from Deklan's other side, the two men having flanked him on the narrow ledge.

Deklan grunted. "Nothing new about that." He felt Jake's hard glare on his side but didn't acknowledge it.

"Who's Cali bringing tonight?" Seth asked Jake in his patented way of changing the subject to defuse tension. The pattern of banter between the three of them established long ago.

"Allie and Kendra."

"Allison English. Thirty-seven. Lawyer at Wilson, Pakish

and Marrow," Deklan recited. "Kendra Morgan. Thirty-one. Shelf-stocker at Target. Former middle school counselor."

"Christ. Don't tell me you know the stats of every guest."

Deklan didn't answer. Seth knew he did. There was very little about every person in the club that he didn't know about. Details had kept him alive for many years. Let one slip, and it could cost your life. Or worse, someone else's.

"When are they arriving?" Deklan directed his question to Jake, the man only recently having claimed Cali Reynolds as his sub. A move the other men thought he'd never make. As the oldest of the three men, Deklan looked out for the other two. It was as ingrained in him as eating. And that responsibility now included Cali.

"They'll be here at nine."

"You'll take care of the other women?"

Another glare. "Do I look that incompetent?"

"No," Deklan conceded. "Just preoccupied with your sub."

"How many guests will be here tonight?" Seth interceded once again, even though they'd gone over the information earlier.

Letting the subject change, Deklan unfolded his arms to rest his hands on the metal balcony rail. He tightened his grip and leaned forward to take in the already packed space. "We maxed at the one hundred limit."

The club had over five hundred active members, only a quarter of which showed up on any given evening. But this night always drew a crowd. The attraction of new faces, combined with the anonymity the masks provided, was too enticing for most to skip. That also accounted for the large crowd at such an early hour. The doors closed when they hit capacity.

Seth's shoulders lifted, his chest expanding with his inhale. Yeah, the tension was heightened in all of them that night. "It'll be fine."

Easy for him to say. "I'll confirm that when the night's over."

Jake shifted to pull his phone from his pocket, a smile curving his lips. "Cali's here."

In unison, their focus shifted to the lobby entrance. A few seconds later, the door opened, and three women filed through. Deklan scanned the first one, appreciation settling in his chest. "Did you select Cali's outfit?"

"Of course."

"Nicely done." The praise was edged with admiration. Cali was dressed in a leather corset. The dark green color looked stunning against the pale skin of her breasts, pushed up and rounded on display. The black leather skirt hugged her hips to calves and restricted her stride to a half-step. She turned to speak to the woman behind her, revealing the ties that ran up the back of both garments. "Did you lace her in?"

Jake stepped back to leave. "Before I left," he answered with a smirk. A flash of possessiveness sparked in his eyes before he gave a quick salute and bounded down the stairs. Jake had arrived at the club at three that afternoon, which meant his sub had been bound tight for the last six hours. Every restricted movement reminding her of whom she belonged to.

Deklan ignored the flare of longing that flashed within him. He had more than enough responsibility at the moment. Caring for the needs of a permanent sub wasn't on his radar. But it didn't stop him from being happy for Jake.

"She's stunning."

The longing in Seth's voice pulled Deklan's attention back to the room. "Cali? Yes, she is."

Seth shook his head. "No. The one behind her."

Deklan glanced to the next woman dressed in deep red silk. The halter-style top clung to her breasts before draping down to cinch at her waist. The full skirt was made of teasing strips of gold and ruby that brushed her knees and allowed for tantalizing glimpses of her legs as she walked. Her dark brown curls tumbled in ringlets to her shoulders, hiding the string of the sparkling gold Mardi Gras mask that covered the top half of her face.

"How can you tell?"

The other man laughed. "There are some things you just know."

"And you know that?"

Deklan had met Cali's guests before at the condo complex where they all lived and knew that her friends were both attractive. The fact that he owned a condo in the same unit was a stretch of coincidence that still bothered him.

"Without a doubt," Seth affirmed, a smile lingering on his lips. "Too bad she doesn't have the first clue about what she's walking into."

His observation finally pulled a grin out of Deklan. The three women had moved to a spot along the wall next to the bar. Led there by a bouncer, their location was secured by Jake. The regulars all knew Cali by now and, more importantly, to whom she belonged. The only one of the three not wearing a mask, there was no hiding Cali's features or the collar around her neck.

Standing between the other two women, the one in red maintained a constant swivel of her head, her body leaning back and forth as she moved to take it all in. The experienced eye pegged her immediately as a novice. Every Dom or sub in the place would see her for the BDSM virgin that she was.

"Jake needs to keep an eye on them," Deklan said. "Allie's too fresh to be let loose on her own."

Seth stiffened before he nodded. "The wristband will keep her safe." All guests wore a thick black band around their wrists while at the club. It marked them for who they were and let everyone know their visitor status at a glance. A light on the band indicated their boundaries within the club. A red light restricted them from participating in any of the more explicit activities behind the red doors without the consent of one of the three owners. They could watch, but playing was prohibited. A green light gave them full access to participate in every aspect of the club.

The middle one wasn't who Deklan was concerned about though. His gaze consumed Cali's other guest, the one he'd expected not to show. He paused to admire the silver three-inch heels on the black boots before continuing to the hem of her royal blue dress, the peek of garters teasing and tempting with every movement of her long legs.

She drew attention, not because she stood taller than the other women. Or because her dress hugged every willowy curve of her figure and scooped low enough to pool in layers over the swells of her breasts. It wasn't even the mystery of who she was behind the blue and gold mask she wore. No, she drew the eye of every Dom in the club. Just as obvious as the other woman's newness were the subtle movements of her knowledge.

It was a curveball in his assessment of her that made Deklan's jaw clench in irritation. How had he missed that? Or had he?

"I'm not so sure about the other one, though," Seth said, as if reading Deklan's mind. "But then, she doesn't look like she needs protecting."

Hell. Everyone needed protecting in some way. Life had taught him that. And that one down there needed more than most. "How do you figure?"

Seth tilted his head, his lips thinning in concentration. They both watched as Jake approached the trio. Cali smiled, her focus holding on her Dom as he bent to kiss and claim her. Jake's hand smoothed around to hold the back of her neck, his mouth driving hard until she melted into him, her body going lax against his.

Deklan straightened and cleared his throat against the sudden dryness.

"There," Seth said, tilting his chin up in indication. "The one in red is staring openly. The one in blue has her eyes diverted, her head tilted down in respect, even if it's only incrementally. Her spine is straight, her hands clasped behind her back, but the pose isn't forced. It's natural enough to be ingrained. A habit I doubt she even recognizes, but every Dom here does." Seth gave another hard shake of his head. "Nope. That one knows exactly what to expect. The hard nipples say she's ready for whatever happens tonight."

Deklan's focus shot directly to her breasts. Of course he'd noticed that detail earlier, but hearing the other man state it so bluntly fired something protective and possessive within him. "She's not a piece of meat to manhandle." His voice held the sharp edge of reprimand.

"What the heck?" Seth jerked back, his angry glare landing on Deklan. "Get the stick out of your ass and stop being such a dick, Winters." Seth turned and pounded down the stairs, the loud slam of the door at the bottom punctuating his exit.

The guilt hit fast. Seth hadn't deserved that. In fact, of the three men, Seth was the least harsh, preferring straight Dominance over the harder forms of sadism and masochism. Most people outside of the BDSM world assumed they all went together, when in truth there were varying degrees and levels for everyone, just like most things in life.

Deklan was drawn back to the cause of their quarrel. Kendra Morgan. Jake was leading the women through the crowd to a reserved table located in an alcove under the balcony. Kendra brought up the rear, her hips swaying with each step, her head held straight ahead with her eyes downcast. She'd dropped her resting pose to let her arms move naturally at her side, but her shoulders were back, her hands loose in a posture defining obedience.

Christ. Jake looked like he was leading a small harem to his private lair. The parting sea of people seemed to recognize the same thing, making the procession even more noticeable and drawing the attention of half the room. Deklan's jaw tensed as he caught more than one Dom assessing the women with clear appreciation. Their eyes traveling over the three the same way he'd done earlier. The way they all paused and held on Kendra, a few leaning together, heads nodding in indication, left no question that they were drawing the same conclusion as Seth. The lady in blue was a very experienced sub who knew exactly what she was doing in this world. It smacked of trouble for reasons he couldn't define but had learned long ago to trust.

She projected a smooth image of confidence. But he caught the quick fist of her hand, the slight shift of her chin as her gaze shot to the side before jerking back to the ground. The facade of assurance was underscored by little signals of doubt and nerves.

She jerked her head around to stare directly at him, as if she'd known he was watching her. His breath stilled as he was consumed by the challenge he saw in her eyes, throwing away every submissive indication she'd been projecting just seconds before.

Kendra didn't smile. No taunting curl of her lips in flirtation or request. It was like she was daring him to stop her.

Or claim her.

THREE

Kendra's heart raced in a beat that flushed her with heat, the liquid warmth rushing through her, making her hands clammy and her nape damp. The slow, forced breaths did nothing to calm the tight fist of nerves that balled in her stomach.

She couldn't let him get to her. Deklan Winters—club co-owner, condo neighbor, Dom. The man had been watching her for months, something he probably assumed she didn't know about. She almost laughed out loud at that thought. Maybe she wouldn't have if she weren't so aware of him.

What the hell was she thinking to challenge him like that on his turf? She knew better than to look a Dom in the eyes, and wasn't that exactly why she'd done it? Damn it. She shouldn't be here.

She cut off her thoughts and gripped her hands in her lap to keep them still. She sat at the edge of the booth, the concave circle of seats providing a clear view of the dance floor and bar area. The privilege of being in the VIP seating area also meant they were on display. She realized it was Jake McCallister's way of establishing his territory over the women.

Not in dominance but as protection. The added attention increased her unease, yet she welcomed the safety of being attached to one of the club owners.

The room was full of distractions, and Kendra attempted to find one. She'd been surprised at how standard the main area looked. Expectations and past experience had her envisioning a large room full of blatant displays of submission, dominance and everything that went with it. The dance bar atmosphere they'd walked into was calming and spoke to the sophistication of the place. It was just one more reason why people were willing to pay so much for a membership.

The dance floor was large enough to encourage the activity without overtaking the space. The bass of the music vibrated through the vinyl seat, enticing with a rhythm that inspired the sultry grind playing out between couples, but the volume didn't prohibit the conversations taking place around the room.

Despite the elements of normalcy and the brightly colored sequined outfits and masks that stood out among the black leather, there was no question what The Den's main attraction was. She looked over at two submissives dressed in skimpy spandex, kneeling with their heads bowed as their Masters talked. Another couple passed them, the man being led by a chain that snaked out from his tight leather briefs and pulled taut over his chest before threading through the loop on the collar around his neck. Each tug on the chain made the sub's eyes glaze over with that heady blend of pleasure and pain.

Kendra licked her dry lips, forcing her attention from the intoxicating sight and back to her table. Cali and Allie were engaged in a spirited question and answer session on what went on behind the big red doors.

"They do what?"

The startled gasp made Kendra smile. If Allie was shocked

over a ménage voyeur Scene, then she would probably pass out cold at seeing the Dungeon.

Dungeon. Just the thought of it had Kendra inhaling against the wave of longing that tingled through her, tightening her nipples and making her pussy clench. She shifted on the seat and crossed her legs to hold back the rising flush. She couldn't go there.

But her body so desperately wanted to.

After so many months, she'd hoped that maybe she'd outgrown it. Forgotten even, though she'd known that wasn't so. Her nipples were aching, hard nubs sliding against the teasing fabric of her dress, pulled gently by the weights. The crotch of the tiny thong was wet, her clit ripe and needy for stimulation. She squeezed her thighs together in a failed attempt to ease the almost painful desire.

She sensed the heat of Jake's gaze assessing her with an intensity that missed none of her movements. She let her attention trail back to the crowd, pretending ignorance or obliviousness. She didn't care which one the Dom bought.

It wasn't hard to keep her eyes averted. She'd been raised to keep her chin up. To look away was to show weakness. But here, around all the Doms, her instincts deferred from her upbringing to her training.

"Do you want to go back, Kendra?"

She turned back and met Allie's smile. "Where?"

Allie leaned closer, peering over Kendra's shoulder in the direction of the red doors in discussion. "In the back. To the *other* areas of the club."

It was impossible not to be amused at the blatant curiosity in Allie's eyes. The lure of the forbidden was both enticing and scary. "Why not?" she answered, keeping her voice light. "That's why we're here, right?"

"Right." The word was reinforced with a sharp nod, an act

of confirmation for herself. Allie looked back to Cali. "How'd you ever find the courage to come here by yourself?"

Cali laughed. "Call it desperation, maybe." She leaned into Jake, his arm tightening around her shoulders. "I was just lucky that it was Jake who welcomed me into the club on my first night." She looked at her Dom. "It was him I came back for."

The complete devotion that passed over Jake's face as he stroked a finger down her cheek made Kendra's heart ache. She'd wanted that once. That connection that was only made stronger because of what they shared sexually.

Kendra had no idea to what degree they were into the scene, but it was obvious to anyone that they were more than just Dom and sub to each other. Jake traced his finger over the intricate silver choker that circled Cali's neck. He was lean muscle under his dark shirt that understated the power he projected. His black hair bordered on too long and his silver-gray eyes seemed to instantly assess each person he met. He had a commanding strength made stronger by his bad-boy allure. Cali shivered under his gentle touch, an action Kendra mimicked as she imagined that touch over the empty expanse of her own neck.

Was it in longing or revulsion?

When she'd left Eric, she swore she'd never wear a collar again. But watching Jake and Cali reminded Kendra of how it was supposed to be.

"Welcome to The Den, ladies."

Kendra jumped at the unexpected male voice at her side. She looked up to take in the tall man standing by the edge of the table. His long, brown hair was pulled back into a queue, showing off his strong features. Muscled arms and chest were on display from under the black leather vest and the matching leather pants accented his trim hips, leaving one to speculate on the treasures beneath.

He was a Dom, without question. Identification registered, she immediately diverted her eyes to stare at the brown table top. Her breathing deepened, but she kept it controlled.

"Seth," Jake said. "Joining us?"

The man held up a hand before anyone could move. "No, but thanks. I just wanted to introduce myself to your guests."

Jake took the lead. "Seth, this is Allie and Kendra, friends of Cali's. Ladies, this is Seth Mathews, friend and co-owner of The Den."

Kendra managed a low response and was grateful that Allie jumped in to cover her lapse. The other four chatted for a few minutes before Seth made his excuses and moved away, allowing Kendra to breathe once again.

"So, how many owners are there?" Allie asked Jake. "I thought Deklan owned the club with you."

Jake nodded. "He does. The three of us own equal shares."

"Is he here tonight, too?" Allie scanned the crowd, her back straightening to allow for a better view as she leaned to see around the room.

Kendra looked at the ceiling of the little alcove, knowing exactly where the other man was.

"Yeah, but he's busy with security," Jake answered. "He doesn't socialize much on these nights."

"Too bad," Allie said, her spine curling into the seat in a deflated motion. "He's damn fine to look at." Kendra stiffened at her friend's comment then cursed herself for the reaction. "But then, Seth is too," Allie continued. "No wonder you've been hiding this place from us, Cali. Keeping all these gorgeous men to yourself."

Cali laughed, but Jake leaned over the table to nail Allie with a hard glare. "Cali knows better than to notice other men." He turned to his sub. "Don't you?"

She quieted, her face softening as she looked to her Dom. "Yes, Jake."

Allie stared openly at the exchange, obviously trying to process what happened. For Kendra, it was beautiful. It shouldn't be, not in this generation and time. But the subtle show of power and exchange given and taken freely hit her in the chest. What she saw so clearly was love and trust. Commitment and understanding of what they both needed and wanted in the relationship.

"Shall we continue?" Jake asked, looking to Allie and Kendra for an answer.

"I'm game," Allie replied after a second of hesitation. "You?"

Everyone turned to Kendra, the expectation on the collective faces making her flush. Concentrating on Allie, Kendra forced a smile. "Yeah. I'm game." The deep, throaty timbre of the words surprised her and had Allie's eyes narrowing behind her mask. Kendra cleared her throat and ignored the unasked question, refusing to acknowledge the desire mixed with anxiety that bloomed with her agreement.

She was going deeper, closer to what she knew she shouldn't.

Jake stood holding his hand out to Cali, who took the offering and scooted out of the booth to stand beside him, eyes down, a smile on her lips. Kendra swallowed then stood when Jake gave an almost imperceptible nod her way. Her pulse accelerated as she kept her focus on the floor and stepped past him to stand beside Cali.

Jake knew. It didn't surprise her that he figured it out. That the Dominant in him recognized the submissive in her. It was like a built-in instinct that forced one to hone in on the other. She just wished she'd been able to cover it better.

Maybe I wanted him to know, the devil in her whispered.

A quick glance to her friend, and she saw that Cali had

caught it too. Cali's eyes were wide, a series of questions and understanding flowing over her face before she looked away, a knowing smile on her lips.

"I'm so nervous," Allie chatted through the strain that had descended between the other three, completely oblivious to the revelation that had just passed between them. "I don't want to embarrass myself by doing something stupid."

"Just watch," Jake said, inflicting calm in his voice. "You don't have to do or say anything. If you get uncomfortable for any reason, let me know and we'll leave."

Allie inhaled deeply, her hand pressed against her stomach. Exhaling, she nodded. "Okay. I can do this."

Kendra was last again as Jake led them to the set of red dou-ble-doors at the back of the main room. Even with her eyes cast down, her skin prickled with the awareness of every gaze that moved over her. Especially the one that bore into her back from its elevated position over the room. It made her insides flash hot and cold at once. Logic fighting desire—a war that couldn't be won by either side.

Despite all reason and arguments against it, her body still responded with a longing that burned in her core and begged for a release she could no longer find without the inclusion of pain. She inhaled against the visions of whips and bonds that dropped into her mind. A shudder raced up her spine to twist with the fear and nerves sitting heavy in the pit of her stomach.

She shouldn't go back there. Through those doors that would only lead her closer to everything she'd run away from. Recriminations tumbled on her, making her falter if only for a second.

Eric couldn't win. She wouldn't let him. This was just one more step in taking back her life. She could do this. Her stride restarted; the continued momentum pushed her forward. What was back there wasn't inherently bad. It was only perceived that way by those who didn't know better, or made that way by those who chose to twist it for their own desires.

As long as she stayed within the circle of Jake's protection, she wouldn't be touched. No Dom would encroach on his territory, even if it was by extension only. The risk was too high. Add the wrist band to that, and she was untouchable.

It was up to her to decide if she wanted to remain that way.

He tracked the slow sway of Kendra's hips that drew his eyes to her ass. The fabric hugged it but was loose enough to tease over her skin and make a man's hands ache to smooth it down and discover the firm mounds beneath. The gentle glide of her legs with the almost deliberate step of each heeled boot only emphasized the swivel. Unconscious or not, she knew how to entice.

Deklan's mind called up her image. Her guest application picture had been plain, non-attention-getting in its simplicity, the same as what he'd observed at the condo. Her hair pulled back into a tight ponytail, her eyes covered in only a hint of makeup, but there'd been nothing she could do to dull the bright shine of her big, blue eyes. Her lips were lipstick free and full, but not fake, just pouty enough to make a man long to feel them under his.

Fuck. He pulled his concentration away from her retreating form and deliberately scanned the rest of the club. He rolled his head on his shoulders, the muscles and tendons stretching, only to snap back to their clenching hold the instant he stopped. There was one thing that eased him when he was wound this tight. Unfortunately he wouldn't be indulging in that tonight. He had too much responsibility to the club to worry about his own needs. It didn't matter that the object of his lingering interest was present within his domain.

He'd first spotted Kendra last summer around the condo

complex. Although he didn't attend the social gatherings in the courtyard, he often watched from his own unit. It was habit to know who and what was around him. Keeping tabs on his environment was second nature.

So he'd noticed the way she stood to the side at any given event, her gaze constantly scanning the exterior, her body held slightly tense, shoulders stiff under the laugh or polite smile she'd give to someone else. Just like he'd noted Cali's warm, but reserved interactions and her need to stay busy, which also kept her detached. Or Allie's brash forwardness and strong personality that didn't let anyone run away, but also kept her protected from the inquiry of those she accosted.

Kendra was a woman who had secrets, and that interested him. Everyone had secrets, but hers ran deep. A fact his observations had verified over the last six months. She didn't keep to a consistent routine, her shades were rarely opened and she moved with a sure stride that covered the ingrained hesitation—a look over her shoulder, a moving away from touch or contact with others—that spoke of abuse.

All were subtle actions that would only be recognized by someone who had personal knowledge of that life.

The instant flash of anger made his jaw clench in restraint. It was his push button, one others would laugh at, given his sexual proclivities. But what he did with a willing submissive was always consensual. He gave the sub what he or she needed within the boundaries they defined. It never crossed into abuse, something he reinforced and ensured within the club as well.

Seeing Kendra here, her submissive nature and knowledge flashing like a red cape to the circling bulls, made him see red, a bright ruby and scarlet glare that dimmed his focus and set off his personal warning signals. Within these walls, she'd be safe. But where did that leave her once she left? It shouldn't be his concern, but by extension of Jake, she now fell under his protection. Or so he told himself.

Once again, his attention targeted back to her. They were clustered by the red doors, waiting for the bouncer to grant them access to the restricted areas of the club. To where the real fun played out in all its deviant forms.

Kendra turned her head until she caught sight of him out of the corner of her eye. This look was more circumspect than the direct challenge earlier, but it was no less impactful. The message was clear—she knew he was watching.

Like last time, he returned her stare until she turned away to walk through the doors. Would she enjoy the voyeur rooms? Or did she like to be the one on stage, playing out the Scene for all to watch? What if Jake took them upstairs to the Dungeon? Did she like the harder aspects of bondage? Would she moan as the tender, pink flesh on her ass was blistered to a deep rose?

The fact that he wanted to know those answers, was drawn to her with a strength he was almost powerless to resist, had him running. With a hard shove on the rail, Deklan turned away from the room below, a scowl on his brow.

His boots thumped loud on the stairs before he paused at the door, his forearms resting against the metal as he leaned in to listen. He heard the group pass down the hallway, Jake's deep voice describing the Scenes that were playing out behind the doors. His nose twitched like he could smell her, his body reacting to her unseen proximity with a force that had him biting back a groan, grateful that no one could see him.

He waited until their voices quieted and the normal sounds of the club reclaimed his concentration. He jerked the door open, a quick check down the hall confirming Jake's entourage was in a voyeur room. Setting his shoulders, he turned from the temptation and exited into the crush of the main room.

There were other customers to worry about. Things he should be doing besides obsessing over a confused sub. And it wasn't even ten o'clock yet. Which only confirmed one thing—it was going to be a very long night.

FOUR

The woman on the stage let out a long, guttural moan that snaked across the open room to wrap around Kendra, drifting into her senses until she clenched her teeth to hold back her own verbal response. Moisture settled on her skin, her body flushed with arousal from the Scene before her.

She shifted in her seat, uncrossing and recrossing her legs in an attempt to ease the growing ache at her core. Her cheeks and forehead were clammy and sticky under the confines of the mask, but she didn't dare remove it. She was safer behind it, no matter how uncomfortable it became.

"Does this turn you on?" The low question was asked against her ear.

Kendra inhaled at the tingles that shuddered down her neck to her nipples. That it was Jake asking only made her more attuned to her reaction.

She glanced at Cali, sitting on his other side. Her focus was on the stage, but her body hugged and molded with her Dom. Kendra wasn't worried about Jake coming on to her; he was clearly a one-sub Dom. However, it was disconcerting that he was attuned enough to her to know to ask.

"Yes." There was no point in lying, since he already knew the truth. She wasn't going to think about the fact that it was almost impossible for her to lie to a Dom.

"The Dungeon is upstairs if you want to go."

Kendra inhaled against the information, her stomach contracting with the loaded piece of intel. Of course she assumed a Dungeon was on the premises, but to know its exact location was another thing.

"Thank you, sir," she managed to mumble, her gaze dropping to stare at the polished surface of his boots. Her hands fisted tighter where they rested in her lap, a reflexive spasm that shimmered through her.

The woman on stage chose that moment to release another cry, this one a high-pitched squeal that chased the goose bumps down Kendra's arms.

Allie released a startled gasp beside her, and Kendra's attention launched back to the Scene on stage. The man circled the female, who was bound to a large, inclined bed. The back elevated to allow the viewers a better angle to see all that was going on. Her ankles were spread wide, giving everyone an unobstructed view of her naked pussy and the large vibrator inserted within it, the strap around her waist keeping it in place.

The woman's chest heaved up and down, her large, fake breasts shoving into the air with each breath. Kendra had no qualms labeling the breasts fake, since real ones that size did not stay so rounded and pert when reclined. A grin slipped over her lips at the thought. The Dom on stage didn't seem to care if they were fake or real.

He pulled the woman's head back with a firm fist of her hair until she strained against his hold. "Was that a complaint?" the Dom asked.

"No, sir," the submissive replied, her voice hoarse and thick.

"Do I need to gag you?"

The woman's throat worked, the deep swallow visible to Kendra from her chair three rows in. "No, sir," the woman finally answered before she jerked, her hips arching off the mattress as the muffled vibrating sound increased.

Kendra bit her lip, her body on edge. One touch, she was certain. Just one touch over her throbbing clit combined with a sharp slap on her ass from a Dom right then, and she would come. It would be a gut-wrenching spiral into oblivion that had eluded her since she'd left this world. But no, she didn't need that. She was here to prove just that, right?

The woman on stage was close to coming, but she held it back, waiting for her Dom's permission. She shook with the tension, squirming within her restraints. The distinctive scent of arousal permeated the air. It was impossible to tell exactly where it came from because it was clear everyone in the room was turned on to some level.

There were little whispers among the crowd of thirty or so, murmurs of approval, desire or longing. There was a couple standing along the wall, the man's hand under the woman's skirt, blatantly rubbing between her legs as she undulated against him. Her mouth was open in unspoken pleasure, her eyes heavy lidded as she stared at the stage as ordered.

To distract herself, Kendra looked at Allie on her other side. Her eyes were open wide, accentuated by the framing of her gold mask. Her cheeks were tinged pink under the rim of the covering, her lips parted in a small gap of disbelief or amazement. It was hard to tell, but her friend wasn't running away. She leaned forward, sat back then crossed her legs, squeezing her thighs tight in time with a small, abrupt inhale.

Kendra gave a knowing grin. Allie liked what she saw, whether she would admit it or not. Cali had taken a risk, bringing them to this private world of hers. They both could've easily condemned and scorned her. Many would. Thankfully it appeared that Allie wasn't going to do so. But then, Kendra hadn't really thought Allie would, no matter what she personally felt.

Kendra certainly couldn't condemn what she herself craved.

The intensity had increased on stage, with the Dom pinching, sucking and pulling on the sub's nipples until the woman was in a state of wound-up oblivion. Her toes were curled tight to match the strain of her leg muscles against the ankle cuffs and chains that held her captive.

Unable to take any more without combusting herself, Kendra made a quick excuse to Allie, who barely acknowledged her, and stood to leave. Jake caught her wrist as she moved to pass him, his grip strong as he looked into her heart in a brief instant. He nodded then tilted his head, indicating the far end of the hallway. His eyes transferred his meaning, even if he remained silent.

Her pussy clenched, a ripple of longing flashing to her nipples that was chased by disgust at her own weakness. She cast her eyes down in acknowledgement, and Jake let go. She mouthed the word "bathroom" to Cali's inquisitive look and eased out of the aisle. A quick glance back showed Jake tapping on his phone. She didn't have to be a genius to know what he was sending. Permission.

God. Did she dare? Could she not?

A gulp of fresh air filled her lungs the second she entered the hallway. She stalled there, shaking as she slumped against the wall. She locked her knees to keep herself upright, an act that brought a smirk to her lips. Eric always punished her for locking her knees. One of the first lessons she was taught as a sub was to keep her knees loose to limit the chance of fainting.

She took a moment to people-watch. Some gave her notice. Most were too focused on their partner to care. In general, the clothing choices behind the red doors were more revealing, most aligning to the leather and latex that dominated the BDSM scene. Although a number of people still wore the colorful masks like herself, maintaining the role-playing theme of the evening, the aura only adding to the excitement.

She turned her head and stared down the long hallway to the stairway at the end. The faint sounds of the Dungeon drifted down to her like a lure, pulling her in, closer to temptation, to the forbidden acts taking place just beyond her reach.

Closing her eyes, she centered in on the distant crack of a whip, the smack of a paddle against flesh, the wail of a sub timed with the clinking of chains. Her lips compressed as she struggled against the desire to join. The need that tugged at her to walk up the stairs and take what her body so desperately wanted.

She twisted the black band on her wrist, her mark as a visitor to The Den. But her status had been elevated, the red light having changed to green. She could play if she wanted. Her safety catch had been released, and now there was nothing stopping her but free will.

Her decision to make.

She opened her eyes and stared at the beckoning stairs. The choice was hers. One made of her own desire. Not out of obligation or forced complacency. That made it different. Right? Her mind said yes, but was it the answer she wanted to hear in the moment? One she would regret come morning?

She turned her head in the other direction, the back of the red doors beckoning. That was the way she should go. The smart choice. But was it braver to run or to succumb?

Straightening, she squared her shoulders and pushed away from the wall. Her call. Her choice.

Kendra lifted her chin and walked down the hall, the stairway coming closer with each committed step. Tonight, for one night, she would play once again.

Deklan shot out of the chair, the object wheeling back to crash into the table behind him. He didn't care. He was absorbed by the lethal movements of the woman as she moved down the hallway toward the stairway that led to the Dungeon. The screen didn't do her justice, but it adequately captured her determination, the set of her shoulders, the tilt of her chin, the long strides that surely clicked on the hard flooring beneath the boot heels.

Fuck. His hands fisted against the counter he leaned on, pulling his arm muscles taut with the tension. She was going up alone. What did Jake do?

Deklan hadn't responded when he'd received Jake's text authorizing Kendra to play. Overriding the other man wasn't in his protocol, but he hadn't anticipated Kendra following through on the opportunity.

His focus was glued to the security screen as she ascended the stairs and entered the Dungeon. His gaze jumped to another screen and found her instantly. She paused for a moment, her head moving as she took in the large room, scanning over the equipment and Scenes taking place.

Tapping a button, he forced a camera to zoom in on her face. Behind the mask her eyes were intent, heavy with smoldering desire. Her lips were parted and forming small O shapes with each deep exhale. Another click and tap, and he pulled up the wide-angle view on a second screen, his attention flicking between the two.

He stiffened and went completely still as he watched Lucas

swoop in on the new prey. She'd moved to the wall and assumed the submissive pose in an open invitation to all Doms that she was willing to play.

Lucas was an employee, on the newer side, but he'd been a member for a number of years before they'd hired him. He was a hard but fair Dom who held an edge of the little-man syndrome that he carried around. With her heels, she stood a couple of inches taller than the blond Dom, which Lucas would only take as an added challenge.

Deklan couldn't hear their conversation, but damn, he wanted to. Why hadn't he installed audio on the Dungeon cameras? Because this was the first instance in over five years that he'd ever had a desire to hear what was going on in the public room. Generally there was no need, with the Dungeon Masters on the floor.

She gave a short nod, her eyes still downcast. A smile painted over Lucas's face, a gleam of anticipation lighting his eyes. He reached out to caress the black cuff, his finger touching the green light, indicating a point of their discussion.

Deklan spun away from the security monitors and stalked to the door of the small room. His movements were tracked by his second in command of security, Rock. A man he trusted from their years of shared service in the military.

"Problem, boss?" The man glanced to the screens Deklan had just left.

"No." Deklan paused, his hand on the door. "Buzz me if I'm needed."

"Right." The brief reply didn't withhold the skepticism, but the man was wise enough to keep any thoughts to himself.

Making his way down the back hallways and employee-only areas, Deklan struggled to rein in the raging beast that slithered under his skin. It made no sense, this predatory, protective instinct that was digging into his gut and pushing him toward her.

She was an adult with the right to do as she wished. She could take care of herself.

The logic didn't stop his progress.

He entered the Dungeon through a side door and paused until he found her. The negotiations had finished, and the two had moved to an area that contained a spanking bench and stockade. He eased along the wall to stake out a corner near the couple, keeping to the fringes. The sounds of the Dungeon—the slap of paddles, hiss of whips, moans of pleasure—faded to background noise as Deklan zeroed in on Kendra.

"Dress off, on the bench."

He was close enough to hear the commands as the other Dom pointed to the spanking bench.

She slipped an arm into her dress, hesitating for a second before she grabbed the cotton and pulled it over her head, ensuring her mask stayed in place. Deklan responded almost instantly to the sight she revealed.

His gaze traveled up her long legs, encased in royal blue silk to her thighs. The matching undergarments made her skin glow like pearls against the bright color. The low-rise garter belt contained a lace ruffle that teased with the illusion of coverage without concealing the tiny attached thong visible behind the layer of fluff.

His scrutiny continued over her toned stomach and held on her round breasts, pushed up and on display. The shelf bra cupped the underside of the mounds, leaving her nipples exposed, the deep rose-colored buds puckered tight in arousal. But it was the unexpected bonus of the weighted gold and silver suns hanging from her nipple piercings that made him groan.

She was a vision of innocence and mischief. Naughty, but nice.

Something Lucas honed in on immediately. "Wait." He stopped her before she could finish his command and lie on the bench. The Dom stepped forward to stand before Kendra.

Her eyes closed behind the mask, her nostrils flaring slightly when Lucas lifted his hand to tug on the nipple jewelry. Her fist tightened around the material of the dress she still clenched, but other than that she didn't move.

"Lovely," Lucas praised. "So much to play with." The off-handed murmur applied to more than the jewelry he held. It was clear that he was referring to the entire package Kendra presented.

She was new, fresh to the club, but experienced. Already there were a number of members edging closer to see what would happen. What would Lucas do and how would she respond? The fresh reaction was always so alluring.

Every sub responded differently when under the control of a Dom. Would she comply with meek acceptance, or would she hold a hint of defiance just under the layer of submission? What was her pain tolerance, her triggers, her unspoken desires that she hoped the Dom would find?

Cursing silently, Deklan pulled in the feral urge to shove the other Dom aside so he could discover those answers himself. But she wasn't his. He had no right and wouldn't overstep his bounds just because he was the owner. He'd never abused his power in that manner.

Lucas gave the nipples a sharp tug, which forced Kendra to arch her back against the sudden pain that would've shot through her sensitive nubs. She withheld a gasp, and the clean line of her throat undulated as she swallowed.

She was beautiful.

Stepping back, Lucas took her dress from the clutch of her hand. "Safe word."

The curt demand pried her eyes open, her gaze landing directly on Deklan. Her eyes widened in an instant of recognition, the artful application of makeup making them appear larger than normal behind the mask before they zoomed downward to stare at the floor.

"Lilac," she answered, the low word drifting over the sex-laden air to sink into Deklan like the scent of the fragrant flower.

He inhaled automatically in a fool's attempt to catch a wisp of the nonexistent aroma.

She shivered, the action rippling down her body, making the suns charms shimmy and bob and the ruffle on her low garter-belt flutter. The movement made all the more enchanting because it was natural. There was no pretense or forced reactions coming from her. A grunt of appreciation sounded from a Dom standing behind her, his focus clearly on her ass cheeks, which Deklan assumed were on display. But the other man's face stilled and hardened as his eyes lifted to her back. An unheard curse left his lips, the definition clear on the defined movements of his lips.

Lucas turned from hanging her dress on the wall hook and paused to admire his sub, his erection outlined in the tight leather pants he wore. "Bench, my dear."

She nodded and moved to the designated piece of equipment. It was one of Jake's designs, the back elevated with the bench sloping down at an angle that would fully expose a sub's bottom while adding to his or her vulnerability in a forced pose of submission. The bench seat was wider at the base to support the hips and then narrowed near the front. It was broad enough to hold the frame of a sub but allowed for a woman's breasts to hang off the sides, granting easy access to the Dom.

Lucas let her keep her lingerie on instead of making her strip, and Deklan wondered if that was part of the negotiations. Now more than ever he wished for the audio that would've allowed him to hear their exchange, know the rules they both established before playing.

Her chest rose and fell with each breath in a rhythm that seemed to match her steps. There was a predatory grace to her stride, the same one he'd noticed in the main room. Another shiver rattled through her, her fist clenching at her sides as she grimaced.

Deklan straightened but he remained rooted in the corner. The warning hairs on the back of his neck rose to tingle over his flesh. Something was off. Exactly what he'd sensed since she'd entered the club. She was here willing, but there was more to the Scene than what was playing out.

Lucas's eyes narrowed, the intent Dom having caught the same vibe as Deklan. "Kneel, sub. Your disobedience is begging for punishment." Lucas's command was presented as a challenge. A demand to see if she would comply or run, the tension holding her body indicating the latter was a viable option.

One last inhale, and she dropped, her knees hitting the soft pad of the knee ledge with a thud. Her breasts jiggled with the impact, her eyes closing again as she leaned forward and braced her hands on the floor, the definition of her ribs and the stark outline of her hipbone showing as she sank to the bench.

She was model thin, but the muscles defined in her arms and legs gave proof of her dedication to the long runs he'd seen her take religiously, no matter the weather. Her stomach displayed the contours of each muscle in a way that only the truly fit achieved.

She was thin, but she wasn't weak.

The curve of her back compressed in a sigh as she laid her

cheek against the bench, her face turned toward the wall, depriving the spectators of the view. Deklan gritted his teeth against the infraction. He wanted to see her every reaction. But what he wanted even more desperately was to be the only one to see them.

Cursing himself for the unattainable desire, he forced his face to remain emotionless, a tactic he'd mastered years ago.

Lucas moved to Kendra, his boots clumping forcibly on the wood floor. Her muscles twitched and tensed with each step he took. He stopped beside her, knees in her line of sight, eyes scanning from her head down the length of her back. The Dom stilled, his mouth thinning before his gaze shot up, seeking, until he met Deklan's. His eyes did a quick flick down and up in an unspoken message that had Deklan stepping out of the shadows.

Lucas stroked his fingers down the sub's spine in a light caress that was gentle in its barely there touch. Kendra shook, a full-body reaction to the soothing touch that was in direct contrast to the desired response. Lucas removed his hand, but she continued to shake in an apparent uncontrollable manner.

The Dom eased back, his eyes holding on the sub's face before he looked to Deklan. Lucas tipped his head down in indication of Kendra before he took another step away and moved out of the Scene area. A movement that was choreographed to match Deklan's entrance.

A Dom who was an employee of the club only stepped aside in an instance when a sub was in danger. No safe word had been said, but there was something wrong. One of the Dungeon Masters was already at Lucas's side, his head bent in muted conversation over the situation.

Deklan tuned out the others as he neared Kendra. She trembled almost convulsively now. Her legs were still spread on the kneeling pad, the globes of her ass cheeks on high display. He swallowed a curse, not wanting to frighten her when his eyes landed on the long expanse of her back and saw what had angered the other Doms.

Criss-crossed over the smooth, pearly skin of Kendra's back were stripes of white. The unmistakable scars layered in the imprecise pattern of someone inexperienced with a whip. His hands instantly tightened into fists, wanting to deck the sadist who had done that to her.

A choking sob jerked Deklan's attention from Kendra's scarred back. He stepped around the bench, his chest squeezing at what he saw.

She still trembled, small vibrations that shivered over her back. Her hands gripped the bench handles, making her knuckles white and the tendons on her wrists bulge. But it was her face that had him dropping to his knee. The anguish displayed behind the hidden features hit him like a kick to his balls.

Her eyes were squeezed shut in the clamped denial of a child, her lips compressed to a slit between her teeth to hold back the quiver. It was the tears that broke it all. The large drops of liquid rolled from her eyes, despite her effort to hold them in. They ran down the side of her face and over the bridge of her nose in a trail of blue and black makeup until they disappeared under the edge of the mask.

Compassion and an unwavering need to protect, to hold her until the pain eased and her body stilled, had him lifting his hand to rest his palm against the back of her neck. The move deliberate in its authority but soft in its touch.

"Kendra," he said just as gently as his palm settled against her skin.

Her eyes flew open to stare at him. The anxiety, mixed with fear, almost cut him down.

He sucked in his breath and said, "Lilac."

There was a brief flash of panic, much like a cornered animal, that had him soothing her with soft sounds and murmurs of comfort. She swiveled her head in denial, her mouth working before she cleared her throat.

Her gaze held his, the pleading look in her eyes kicking him as hard as the anguish that edged her raspy words. "Please, sir. I need this."

FIVE

No. He couldn't stop her now. Not after she'd made it this far. Kendra shook, and she stiffened her muscles in an effort to halt the fear that had overtaken her. The warmth of his palm baked into her nape in a press of dominance that made her ache for more, regardless of her reaction.

Despite her every resolve never to beg again, she licked her lips and did it anyway. "Sir, please. Don't stop it. Not now. Please." Every ounce of urgency she felt went into the low plea that made her voice quiver almost as much as her body.

Another tear fell, but she refused to let go of the bench handles to wipe it away. Her hands weren't buckled down. They were held there by the lack of permission to let go.

Deklan studied her, his face still. His lips were pulled thin, forcing his jawline to cut in hard-edged definition. But his deep blue eyes were filled with a mix of compassion that confused her. "No."

The single word stabbed her, his decision final.

There was no denying the authority that radiated from

every fiber of him. The word held little room for negotiation. How could he deny her?

He pushed to rise, and desperation had her reacting. She clenched his wrist, halting the powerful man in midaction. She pleaded with her eyes, despite every instinct that told her to run. That taunting the beast bordered on insanity and would only result in harm. Punishment. His pulse accelerated beneath her fingertips, giving her the push of courage to go with her daring.

"Please." She squeezed his wrist, the whispered appeal her last hope. She blinked rapidly, trying in vain to hold back more tears. To show him the strength she thought he was looking for. She bit her lip to keep it still but continued to watch him, hoping he understood.

Long moments later, he finally rested his knee back on the floor. His chest expanded with his deep inhale as his free hand folded over hers—holding, not removing. Leaning forward, he spoke softly in her ear, his words for her alone. "Not here."

She shook her head, his lips brushing over the sensitive shell of her ear with the caress of his breath.

"I won't hurt you. I won't touch you without your permission." He paused to blow a breath of air over her ear. "But I won't do it here."

Her entire body shook once again. The trembling moved from the heat of his mouth on her ear, down her spine, over her clenching pussy and out her toes. This time it was in longing and barely suppressed need as his unspoken promise flowed through her.

"You can trust me, Kendra," he continued once she'd stilled, her breaths increasing to pants as the offer sank in. "You'll be completely safe with me. I promise."

The last two words were spoken as a pledge. She whimpered, the needy sound startling her. His cheek grazed the top of her head in a tender brush that was intimate in its gentleness.

"I need the words." His breath was the only contact on her ear as he hovered above it. His hand tightened over her forgotten hold, reminding her that she still gripped his wrist. The solid beat of his pulse holding her to him. "Will you trust me?"

Trust a Dom, alone. Could she?

"Not in private," she managed to answer, her voice catching on the parched lining of her throat, knowing she'd just thrown away her chance at finding release. She waited for his reaction, for the anger and disappointment that would come. The next words were automatic, the ones that always followed when she'd done something wrong. "Sorry, sir."

Sometimes the plea lessened the punishment. Sometimes it had no effect. She squeezed her eyes closed in expectation of the cutting remark. The reprimand and shunning that would come for such disobedience. For embarrassing the Dom in public.

She could take that. It was nothing new. But she couldn't take the risk of doing anything with a Dom in private. That's where the real danger stalked. In public he could only go so far with witnesses around. In private there was no one to stop him. No one to call a halt or hear her safe word. Her muscles contracted, her fingers flexing tight on their hold as she flinched away from her memories.

He exhaled a long, slow breath that skirted her neck and sent another shot of heat rippling over her skin before he leaned back. She tracked him, trepidation building as he eased his fingers under hers to transfer her grip from his wrist to his hand.

"Thank you for your honesty." His voice was filled with patience, the words bordering on a caress. He studied her for a moment. "What do you need, Kendra?"

"Release." The answer came out almost immediately, as desperate as she was to get it. "Sir."

He narrowed his eyes, scanning her back before looking to her again. "And you need that for release?" It wasn't censure in his voice as much as question.

She swallowed and dug up the courage that had gotten her to this moment. "Not the blood. Never that. Or the humiliation and degradation." She blinked rapidly to hold back the threat of new tears that stung in her eyes. He squeezed her hand but kept silent, waiting for her to finish. His patience was a new experience, something she wasn't used to. "Just the pain, sir," she finally finished. "I can't come without the pain."

She let her eyes close, hiding behind the darkness to hold herself together. Admitting the truth out loud brought a new level of shame to her already battered confidence. She couldn't focus on that though, so she searched for something else.

The hiss of a whip reached her ears and the image formed in her mind as the cry of a sub followed. She heard others too. The low, throaty moan from a male close to her bench. The pleading whine from another sub begging for release. She conjured pictures of their pain. The male strapped in a swing, a cock ring preventing him from coming as the Dom stroked a large dildo up his ass. There were nipple clamps too. And his ass cheeks were bright red and hot from the recent paddling.

The other begging sub was covered with little square crop marks patterned over her bottom and the tender flesh at the back of her thighs. She was strapped in a stockade, unable to move away as the Dom teased her clit then retreated, leaving her begging.

A low moan of need vibrated in Kendra's throat at the visual images she'd created. The scent of sex, sweat and desire made her pussy contract where it was still raised high and open in the air, aching to be filled.

Deklan rubbed his hand up her arm, his palm rough with calluses. The light hint of sandalwood pushed out the other aromas and she inhaled, letting it linger in her senses. Was it his soap, aftershave, shampoo? It fit him. Strong, yet secretive and filled with hidden qualities.

He traced the edge of her mask, his finger light over her cheek, and she opened her eyes. "You would trust me here?" he asked. His head was angled to match hers as he searched her eyes for the answer.

"Yes, sir." The immediacy of her answer made him smile. Just a hint, but it was more than she'd ever seen on him before.

"Why?"

It was her turn to search him for answers. Did he really want to know or was it some game he was playing? There was only one way to know for certain. "Because you have to listen to me here."

His fingers stilled on her hair, and she cringed away from the coming anger as his smile flattened. "I would always listen to you. You never have to doubt that."

Words. They were only words that could mean nothing later. She wouldn't risk it. Never again.

He straightened his spine, his shoulders pulling back to make his chest appear even broader as his hand fell away from her hair and he looked around the room. She was facing the wall filled with play tools and only now did she remember the circle of people who had been watching the Scene. Were they still there? God, she didn't want to know.

"No toys."

She blinked, and her attention shot back to see him studying her. "Okay."

"Safe word?"

"Lilac," she said, daring to hope.

"Are you positive?"

More than ever. "Yes, sir."

He stared at her for several moments longer before he released his grip on her hand and stood. "Keep your hold on the bars," he ordered. "I won't strap you in."

"Yes, sir," she breathed, too relieved to make her voice stronger. She took hold of the handles under the bench, following his order with a calmness that hadn't existed before. With Deklan, her nerves eased away to be replaced by a gentle quiet she hadn't experienced in years.

He stood but continued to stare down at her. "I'm going to spank you. Skin against skin, so you know it's me who's striking you."

She bit her lip to keep the moan from escaping. The image flushed her with heat and made her ache for his touch. "Yes, sir."

"You come for me, Kendra." He leaned down to speak in her ear. "I'm not him. Remember that."

She trembled again, a quick shake that passed through her limbs so fast she couldn't even process what it was from. Fear, anticipation, nerves? She didn't know. He pulled back, not even reprimanding her for not answering, and moved behind her.

"Any other limits?" His question made her pause. Of course he asked, but would he listen?

"No nudity," she said. She couldn't be that exposed. "No blood or intercourse. And no name-calling."

"Anything else?"

"No, sir." The silence that followed was unnerving, but she resisted the urge to seek him out. She would wait for him.

The touch of his warm, roughened palm on her back made her jump, her legs jerking closed only to stop when she remembered her orders. To keep her legs spread. Opened to him.

Chills followed the path of his fingers as he traced the lines that marked her back. She thought she heard him curse, a low, venomous bite, but couldn't be sure.

He settled his hand on the small of the back, pressing down to hold her to the bench, and she prepared for the strike that was to come. The smack was firm yet yielding against her ass. The sharp crack of skin hitting skin rang like a soothing melody in her ears. *Yes.*

The tears flowed again as Deklan kept up a steady pace, spanking each cheek in a pattern that let her fall into the rhythm. The tears weren't in pain or shame or any of the other condemnations that still hounded her. Under this Dom, they were cleansing. He understood what she needed and was giving it to her without judgment.

The sting now encompassed her entire bottom, heat spreading down her thighs and between her legs. She twisted on the thin bench, trying to rub her hard nipples over the edge; the light pull of the weights was not enough to relieve the ache. If anything, it only reminded her more of how neglected the nubs were. Eric had always clamped her nipples so tight that over time they seemed to have lost their sensitivity. Now she realized how wrong that perception was.

"Is this what you need?" The purr in her ear flared her desire. The biting pinch where she was just wishing for contact made her moan.

"Yes, sir. Please…more," she panted out between gulps of air.

And he did. Flicking the weights until the suns danced under his fingers, the little movements teasing her. She squirmed on the sweat-slicked bench and pushed her chest into the board, trying in vain to get closer to his touch.

She ground her forehead into the leather, the yelp leaving her lips unchecked when his mouth closed over one of her nipples, his teeth trapping it in their grip. Her eyes flew open to see him lying on his back beneath her so he could access her breasts. Deklan's mouth was warm and wet on her heated flesh as he suckled the nub. He twirled his tongue around the nipple jewelry, flipping the weight before threading the tip through the ring to give it a tug.

It was amazing, the lighter touch doing so much more to her system than Eric's cruel approach. The ends of his short hair brushed the underside of her arm every time he moved his head, another teasing caress that made her desperate for more. He gave one last nip then switched to the other nipple.

She tightened her grip on the bar, her arms trembling as she struggled to keep her hold. She wanted so bad to let go and hold his head to her breast. To run her fingers through his hair and feel the soft bristles against her palm. But he told her to hang on, and she would.

To please him.

But she watched. It was impossible not to. His eyes were closed, dark lashes long and soft against his cheek. Seeing his jaw and lips work as he played with her nipple made the dual sensation of seeing and feeling what he was doing even more erotic. His deep, woodsy scent surrounded her, almost forcing her to inhale long, slow breaths in an attempt to get more of the drugging aroma.

By the time he finished playing with her nipples and eased out from under the bench, she was almost begging to come.

"Do you want more?" He was asking? Eric never asked.

"Yes. Please, sir."

His palm returned to her back and a strike followed before she could take a breath in preparation. It landed on her upper thigh right at the tender crease between her ass and leg, the garter strap denting into her skin. The next smack hit right below it, the sting spreading even wider as the two blended to-

360 BONDS OF NEED

gether. Then another on her now-sensitive ass cheeks, quickly followed by a strike on her other thigh, then back to her ass.

She couldn't keep up, his rhythm intensifying until she stopped trying to anticipate. She let go and followed where he took her. Trusting he wouldn't hurt her.

Maybe that made her a fool, but for the first time in a long time she felt alive. For that she was willing to take the risk.

Deklan's hand was on fire, but he wasn't stopping. Not until Kendra was ready for him to do so. He absorbed every strike into his palm, measuring the intensity of the hit, the amount of skin he struck, the reaction of her body under him.

Only now was she letting go, the tightness easing from her back muscles, her grip on the bar loosening until her knuckles were no longer white. Her skin was smooth under his hands, even the marks on her back, the scar tissue having healed with a minimum of puckering.

He slowed his brutal pace to rest his burning palm against the flaming heat of her ass. She was all muscles, just like she looked. Even there, where she should be soft, the muscles were firm and hard from the hours she spent running. She didn't jiggle anywhere, and he appreciated the dedication it took to achieve that.

A low moan came from her throat and she pushed her bottom back to press into his resting palm. Sweat dripped from his forehead to fall on the black leather of her boots. She was a vision, bent over the bench like that, boots still clinging to her calves, her stockings and garters a bright blue against her now-red skin. Her pussy was hidden behind the thin strap of her thong. The ruffled garter top flipped up to bare her warm cheeks.

He bent low and inhaled; her scent flooded him. There was no perfume or other smell to hide the pure musky aroma of her arousal. He let his pleasure show in the low growl that rose from his throat.

There was a muffled rumble of approval from the people who still watched the Scene. His earlier scowl had chased away most of the people, yet a few stubborn Doms had remained. But then, an audience had never bothered him before.

Focusing back on Kendra, he eased a finger under the top of the thong and trailed a slow line, following the path of the material down her ass into her crack and forcing her cheeks apart until he rubbed over the little bud of her anus. She pushed back into his touch. Intentional or not, it let him know that she was receptive.

The whole Scene was about giving her only what she wanted and needed. Building her trust. He wanted to beat the shit out of the man who'd taken that from her.

He let his finger rub over the bud, pushing and teasing but going no further. They hadn't talked about that. Another press and circle, then he moved down to find the wet heat that was waiting for him.

He groaned and leaned forward, almost as if he was seeking the heat he'd found. His cock ached hard and ready, pressed uncomfortably against his leather pants. He rarely wore underwear, preferring the convenience, but now the leather was chafing. A reminder of what this wasn't about.

She squirmed and whimpered. Her hips undulated as she sought what he was withholding. Relenting, he inserted his finger into her channel and felt the almost instant contraction of the muscles clenching the intruder. Fuck. She obviously worked those muscles too. She pushed back, forcing him deeper, her hips wiggling seeking more. Another time, another sub, he wouldn't accept such actions.

But she wasn't someone else.

So he gave her what she was silently begging for. He started with slow thrusts, adding another finger to increase the sensation. He slid his hand from her back and let her move, her pelvis rotating and grinding against him.

She was lithe, wild and beautiful. There were no inhibitions, only reaction and feeling as she worked her body on his fingers. Her forehead was pressed into the bench, her spine arching and dipping in a supple erotic dance. The moisture on her skin shimmered under the lights, beckoning him to taste her, lick her, consume her.

A mixed desire to prolong the moment and to end it fast warred with his usual collected calm. Seeing her react to his touch was intoxicating, a drug that eased his tight muscles and diminished the worry that kept his senses on constant alert.

Right now there was just her. Nothing else.

He kept his fingers in her and leaned over, bracing his free hand on the ground until his chest pressed into her back, adding just enough weight to make her completely aware of him without trapping her. "How do you feel?" He murmured the question into the exposed juncture of her neck before trailing his tongue over her skin. Her breath hitched even as she stretched her chin to give him more room to play.

"Good, sir," she moaned. Her eyes were closed, and he wished he could remove the mask. More than her face was hidden behind the obstruction; he wanted to uncover all of her secrets.

Letting his fingers move within her once again, he tracked his lips up her neck, savoring the taste of her sweat and skin. Tangy, yet sweet. Just like he imagined her pussy would taste.

Bracing his legs on either side of hers to hold himself up, he deliberately ground his erection into the tender flesh of her ass. She hissed in a breath but pressed into him. In that second, that exact moment he'd been waiting for her to reach for the pain, he moved.

He lifted his other hand to twist a nipple while he yanked his fingers from her to pinch her swollen clit. She bucked beneath him, a yelp-mixed moan startled from her, and he ground his hips, knowing his leather pants would irritate and burn against her freshly spanked flesh.

"Come, Kendra," he commanded between gritted teeth.

She convulsed beneath him, arching and lifting him with the force of her orgasm. The sounds of her pleasure mixed with his own growl as he checked his desire and concentrated on extending hers. He stroked her clit, wanting nothing more than to sink into her. Doing the next best thing, he thrust his fingers in her, her vaginal muscle gripping him instantly. The spasms rippled over the digits and blew his mind with the power and the image of how that would feel around his cock.

Sensing her descent, he eased up, letting her drift to a slow finish. He removed his touch, using his arms to hold himself up and give his aching legs a break. But he kept his body around her, not touching but hovering just inches away.

Reminding her who had given her the release she'd needed.

"What's my name?" he asked her, telling himself that the rough grind of his voice was from his exertion alone. It had nothing to do with the tightness in his chest as he waited for her answer.

Her panting ceased and she went still for one long agonizing moment before she finally said, "Deklan."

His breath rushed from his lungs, head sagging until his forehead rested between her shoulder blades. "Yes," he mumbled against her skin, not completely sure what he was agreeing to. But that was the only thought he had. Yes.

SIX

Deklan eased to the side, the air rushing in to cool Kendra's back the second his warmth was removed. The moisture chilled almost instantly and felt good against her heated skin.

She kept her eyes closed and centered on her breathing, her mind floating for a bit. It'd been so long since she'd allowed herself to let go like that. Long before she'd left Eric. There'd been many times that she'd hidden within herself to get away from him. But this light, freeing, drifting sensation was something she'd forgotten about.

"Kendra."

He was still near her. Deklan hadn't left. Even with her eyes closed she knew he kneeled beside her. Waiting until she was ready to move. His voice rumbled close to her ear, his breath ruffling the damp hairs at her nape. He seemed to like doing that. Speaking close to her. Only to her.

Eric had always been loud, ensuring everyone could hear his commands. Know the control he had over her. She shuddered, the thought driving a chill through her flushed system. Damn him for invading her good space.

There was a thump of boots then something soft was placed over her back, covering her with warmth. More importantly, it shielded her exposed body, cloaking her from prying eyes. A courtesy so rarely extended to her that the tears threatened once again, but she wouldn't allow them to fall.

"Thank you." The low words slipped from her lips. Did he know what it was for?

"Of course," he said before his hand eased under hers to pry her fingers from their hold on the forgotten bar. "You can let go now." There was a lift to his voice, as if he was amused by her actions. "The Scene's over."

He rubbed each finger, easing the ache that had cramped them. So gentle, despite his obvious strength.

"Cali and Allie are probably wondering where I am." She should move. She knew that. But she didn't. It felt too good lying here, letting him care for her.

"Jake knows where you are," Deklan said, his massage extending up her arm to work at the muscles in her biceps. She prayed that Jake had kept her friends from the Dungeon. She didn't want them to see this side of her. Cali might know about Kendra, but seeing a friend morph into a sub can have a shattering effect on a relationship. Blending the two personas and accepting the new perception wasn't something everyone could manage. Even if they were into the scene.

And she couldn't lose her friends. That alone forced Kendra to open her eyes. She needed to move before they found her.

She blinked until her vision came into focus. Deklan was right there, smiling at her. It seemed strange. She was pretty certain it wasn't an action he did often. But it softened his features, making his jaw less pronounced, his lips seem softer and his blue eyes lighter. It also showed just a hint of a dimple on his left cheek under the shadow of his beard.

Kendra stared at the little indentation, fascinated that it

dared to mar the hardened presentation. She imagined it would completely ruin the impenetrable image he projected if he ever let a full smile show. She'd like to see that.

Clearing her throat, she propped her hands on the bench and started to push up. Immediately Deklan was there to lift her until she was standing. Her legs were weak and she leaned into him, even as she tried to keep her exhaustion from showing. He held her, tucking the blanket around her shoulders and taking the time to ensure that it offered the full privacy she now wanted.

With the Scene over, her body and mind sated far more than she'd hoped, the unease returned. Wrapped in his arms, his woodsy scent blended with the muskier smell of her release and reminded her that he hadn't come. Would he expect that now? She started to step away, but he tightened his arms, keeping her close. She tensed, that one restrictive action taking away any sense of calm she may have had.

"No second-guessing," Deklan said.

"You're a mind reader now too?" she tried to joke, unwilling to let him know how close he was to the truth. She swallowed. *He isn't Eric.*

Deklan rubbed his hands over her back in a soothing motion, and eventually she let herself relax into his chest. Her arms were crossed in front of her to hold the blanket and provided a small barrier, keeping her from fully collapsing into his offered strength.

"No. Perceptive."

Too perceptive. "I need to go," she said. But she still didn't move. It would be so easy to stay there within the circle of his arms. But it was only a temporary haven. She stepped back and that time he let her go.

Without saying anything, he grabbed her dress from the hook on the wall and extended his hand to her. She searched his face but found nothing of what he was thinking. Any hint of the lightness from seconds before was gone.

As much as she wanted to—her training told her she should—she couldn't follow him blindly. "Where're we going?"

"You need to dress, and I need to see that you're okay." He didn't seem angry at her question. It was more like a Dom finishing his responsibilities.

"I can go to the locker room."

His lips thinned but he kept his hand extend. "I'd like to see to your care," he said, confirming her suspicions. He was just finishing his job.

Shaking off the bit of closeness she'd let herself feel, she placed her hand in his and let him lead her from the room. She kept her eyes downcast, grateful for the mask that covered most of her face, but she wouldn't let her shoulders slump no matter how much she wanted to hide.

Deklan moved through the Dungeon, his pace slow as if he was aware that any fast movement would result in her fleeing, even if he did have her dress. She couldn't look at those she felt watching her, so she placed all of her concentration on keeping her feet from stumbling, moving one foot in front of the other.

She didn't look up until he released her hand to open a door then stood aside. She paused at the entry, seeing the empty room before her. It looked like an employee lounge with a small kitchen area along one wall. There was a large refrigerator and soda machine in the corner and a seating area with a couch and two chairs taking up the rest of the space.

He leaned in and pointed to a corner by the ceiling. "There's a camera there. Everything we do is monitored. You're safe."

Her hands flexed on their hold of the blanket and the nerves returned to ball in her stomach. This wasn't a Scene. He wasn't playing Dom now. But she still couldn't enter a room alone with a relative stranger and trust that he wouldn't harm her.

Damn Eric for stealing that from her too.

She couldn't do it. Shaking her head, she backed away. It was too much. "No. Sorry..." She couldn't look at him knowing the censure she'd see. "I can't."

Why had she followed him this far? She twisted her head around, taking quick stock of her surroundings. They were alone. *How'd I let this happen*? Her pulse started thumping loud and insistent, beating a tune for her rising panic.

"You're okay, Kendra," Deklan said. His voice sounded distant, barely penetrating the drumming beat of her heart.

She shook her head, denial her first response. She wasn't okay. God, she was so pathetically far from okay. She backed away, cautious steps of retreat from the threat before her. She never should have come here. Back to this world.

"Kendra."

No. She had to breathe. Her chest constricted. Take a breath. Just one. Then another. She had to go. Get out of there and away from the danger.

"*Kendra*." The sharp command snapped her out of her daze, her eyes shooting to stare at the Dom.

He stood in the open doorway, but she was halfway down the hallway. His face was hard, impassive as he watched her. He was so big. Taller than average, with muscled arms and chest that took up most of the door space. The urge to run was so strong that she turned to do just that.

"You need your dress."

She stopped. Right. She squeezed her eyes shut, attempting to get a grip. She couldn't leave the club wrapped in a blanket. He wasn't threatening her. She could process that logically, but it didn't change her emotional reaction. Breathe. She had to get air.

"Should I get Cali?"

She shook her head. "No," she croaked, her throat too constricted to speak. "They can't know."

His sigh reached her ears and sounded too much like a reprimand. She cringed. When he spoke however, his voice held only patience. "I can't leave you like this. I'll wait out here. You can change in the room by yourself."

"I…I can't," she managed to stammer, her voice shaking to her shame.

Kendra opened her eyes and edged farther down the hall, closer to the sounds of other voices. Witnesses. The heels on her boots clicked on the tile floor with each movement, each tap a measure of her failure.

He paced her keeping his distance, his steps matching hers. Not stalking, she reminded herself, her eyes on the plain black door in front of her. Her safety exit. But it seemed so far away. Was the hall that long? *Focus.*

Finally her hands clasped the cold metal bar on the door and she pushed it open, using every bit of strength that she had left. Warm air, heavy with the scents of the Dungeon, hit her face and she was able to take a shallow breath. She gasped, stumbling away from the door before she propped herself against the wall.

A couple of people turned to look at her and she could almost hear their unspoken questions. Their judgments. God, she must look so pathetic. Her chest tightened again, any ground gained at leaving the hallway retracted by the pressure of so many eyes. Her fists pressed against her breastbone, her lungs seeking air but finding none.

Deklan stepped into the room and crossed his arms over his chest as he leaned against the door after it closed. He didn't approach her, just quietly stood guard.

"Breathe, Kendra." His calm voice reached her in a hollow

echo, as if he was speaking through a long pipe. "Come on, do it with me. Deep breath in, hold one, two, and out one, two. Again. Deep breath in…"

She listened, anchored to his voice and repeating words, following his commands until she was able to take slow, deep breaths through her nose. Her heart rate slowly decreased as the tightness in her chest eased and the queasy sickness in her stomach subsided with the waning of her panic attack.

She hated them. Damn, how she hated them. They made her feel weak. And now, in the glaring light of the Dungeon, the reason for the attack seemed so trivial. Then again, the triggers usually were, which only made her feel guiltier. She looked at Deklan out of the corner of her eye, expecting to see anger or at least impatience. Instead she saw concern, which was almost worse. She didn't know how to deal with that.

"I'm sorry." Her voice was hoarse and she hoped he heard her. Again, she was grateful for the mask that now hid her discomfort.

"My fault," he answered, taking a small step closer but still giving her space. "You said not private. It was my mistake."

She looked to him, surprised by his admission and the genuine distress in his voice. His eyes were narrowed, causing frown lines to wrinkle his forehead. He was a study of concentration with her as his focus. It made her uneasy but not scared.

"I'm sorry," he continued, extending his hand to hold out her dress. "I didn't mean to cause you distress."

Was this for real? A Dom apologizing? She was at a loss, having never experienced such a thing. A Dom never showed a weakness even if he was wrong. But here was a very strong man doing just that.

A man. Not a Dom. Maybe that was the key.

She reached for her dress, another wave of embarrassment

flushing her skin at her inability to keep her hand from shaking. "Thank you." She didn't know what else to say.

The dress was silky and soft against her palm, reminding her of why she'd bought it. Thankfully the hysterical laughter stuck in her dry throat. The misguided beliefs she'd tried to convince herself were truth seemed so glaringly false now. Who'd she been kidding?

She hated this world and all it represented. It'd stolen her life and forced her to leave everyone and everything she'd known. Yet here she was, unable to leave behind the one thing that had brought her nothing but pain. The literal truth of that almost made the tears flow once again.

No. She wouldn't cry. Not again. Not over this. Not in front of him now.

Kendra straightened, pushing away from the support of the wall to stand on her own. She looked around the room, filled with all the things that both repulsed and attracted her. More than the equipment, it was the distinctive blend of scents and sounds that triggered an immediate reaction in her. A need she didn't want but couldn't seem to purge.

And she wondered for the thousandth time, would she ever be strong enough to shake this addiction? But this time a new truth emerged—did she really want to?

Deklan seethed. Within himself he battled an anger he hadn't felt since he'd slammed his stepfather against a wall and almost beat the man to death. That was over twenty years ago and in all the years since that event—fifteen years of military service, countless official and not-so-official wars, the unjust deaths of too many comrades—he hadn't experienced this kind of rage.

For the second time in his life he wanted to kill a man. Whoever the faceless bastard was who'd done this to Kendra deserved to die. But then, death would be too merciful for that asshole.

She was struggling to keep it together, and he couldn't help her outside of talking to her. In fact, talking was his only option. Every dominant male bone in his body was urging him to hold her, to offer comfort and take away her pain. But he'd blown any chance of doing that with his own stupid mistake.

He'd wanted to protect and comfort her. Instead, he'd screwed the fuck up. When had he ever forgotten such an important detail? Not private. One simple rule, and he'd blown it. Even if the Scene had ended, he should've known based on her actions that the rule still applied.

He'd been so proud of her when she'd gotten through the Scene. She'd obviously been seriously abused by someone in her BDSM past. Yet she'd trusted him. The connection between them had been so strong. He'd never felt that close to a new sub. To any sub.

Now she didn't trust him at all.

She clutched the blanket around her shoulders, pulling the material tight as if it would hold her together. She was trying hard to marshal her anxiety and hide her emotions. But behind the mask he could see her teeth working the inside of her tender cheek. And nothing could hide the mixture of fear, pain and that god-awful shame in her eyes.

Damn it. He wanted to take that all away. To show her there was nothing to be ashamed of. That BDSM was about much more than fear and pain. As far as he was concerned, fear should never be a part of any play. She was a masochist, and someone had twisted her need for sexual pain until it was now a dirty little secret she wanted to hide from.

He could change that. He *wanted* to change that for her.

She squeezed her eyes tight, a quick second of courage

boost, before turning back to him keeping her gaze lowered. "I'm gonna go. Thank you...sir. For the Scene."

So polite and correct. Actions so ingrained she probably didn't even recognize them for what they were. Deklan's jaw ached with the effort it took him to keep his expression neutral. Were her submissive behaviors natural, or drilled into her by the sadist who'd whipped her bloody?

Kendra turned then and fled before he could respond. Despite the rampant urge to follow, he remained motionless. To move a muscle—to even blink—would break his control. He was trained to hold his position, even when every instinct told him to do otherwise. Any movement would endanger and hurt others.

And he couldn't do that. He'd already harmed Kendra enough.

He watched her sandy blond head disappear down the stairs, her retreat from the Dungeon made with a precise dignity that spoke more to her character than any training could.

Even with her gone, he didn't move. The anger still raged too strong for him to give it motion. The shallow breaths he allowed were just enough to get the oxygen he needed, not that anyone would see his chest moving.

Another second, and Seth's brown hair appeared over the stair wall. He made his way straight to Deklan, no pretense provided. The other man gave him a once-over before matching his pose against the wall. "That was a fuck-up." Seth's straight shot was exactly what he expected. And needed.

Deklan grunted. "Saw it all?"

"Rock called as soon as you left the security room."

Of course his security guy would do that. Should fire his ass, but the man did the right thing. "She okay?"

Seth glanced over his shoulder toward the stairs, as if he

could see her now. "I sent Cali after her. Told her not to ask questions."

Like that worked with women. "Fuck." The curse was biting and low but did nothing to release his anger. "What was Jake thinking?" Deflection wasn't his normal reaction, but if the other man hadn't switched her wristband color, she never would have entered the Dungeon.

The prolonged silence from Seth said as much as the not-so-subtle arch of his brow. Deklan looked away. The muscle twitched along his jaw, sending little Morse code messages of indictment straight to the tension headache clamping down on the back of his skull.

"Anything else go wrong tonight?" Deklan changed the topic to something he could deal with at the moment.

"No," Seth answered before his lips curled in a smirk. "You're the only one causing trouble tonight."

"Fuck you."

"No, thanks." He glanced down. "I'm not the one who needs it right now."

So much for topic changes. Deklan's erection had only partially subsided, not that he cared. A hard dick he could handle. Hell, sometimes it felt like he'd lived in that state for the last five years. As a Dom, he found satisfaction in maintaining that control.

Seth shifted, leaning his back against the wall as he let his gaze roam over the room. There were three Dungeon Masters on duty that night, but the responsibility of being the club owners never left them. "What's her story?"

"Don't know it all." Deklan finally released the tension that had held his pose immobile. He stepped away from the wall and rubbed a hand over the back of his neck, even though experience told him meds would be needed to loosen those muscles. "You know the background checks on guests aren't as detailed."

"But you know more."

Was it Seth's business? It was doubtful Kendra would ever be back, so her past wasn't the club's concern. "The club's protected."

Seth's glare burned into his side. "I wasn't worried about the club."

The snort of self-disgust couldn't be held back. Deklan shook his head and rested his hands on his hips. "Is Jake taking them home?"

"Yeah," Seth answered, straightening away from the wall. For a long moment his attention was fixed on the deep red blush that covered the back, ass and thighs of a male sub strapped and spread on a St. Andrews Cross. The band on the sub's wrist tagged him as a visitor, but with his face hidden, Deklan couldn't identify the man. Not surprising, based on who the Dom was. A prominent politician who paraded in a variety of twinks to satisfy his closet desire for males, only this sub looked beefier than his normal taste.

"You need to let this go." Seth kept his eyes on the Scene before them, but his words were for Deklan. "She's not yours to protect. Or save."

Just like that, the anger returned. Pain stabbed at the back of his head as his jaw tightened against the rising resentment. "She needs help," he ground out.

"Maybe," Seth conceded, his calm tone only aggravating Deklan more. "But it doesn't have to be you."

"And maybe there's no one else to give it."

"Always the savior. That's you, Dek. Only sometimes, people don't want to be saved."

Like Deklan didn't fucking know that. He only had to look

at his mother to remember that lesson. "And sometimes people are just waiting to be saved."

Seth gave a thin smile. "Or just waiting to die."

There was nothing to say to that. Seth had his own demons that wouldn't influence Deklan. He turned around and yanked the door open. There was work to do and one security employee to cuss out.

"Watch your back," Seth warned.

Deklan paused to stare at his friend. The other man's focus remained on the male sub, his predatory stance saying far more than words. The night was getting to Seth too. Not that he'd ever admit it.

That's why Deklan hated these events. Trouble always happened, and there was always shit to clean up afterwards. The fact that it was his own shit he had to clean up only irritated him more.

SEVEN

Kendra worked mechanically, going about actions and movements without thinking. The trek down the stairs to the women's locker room had been executed in a dim haze of survival. Dropping the blanket, she shivered in the sudden cold and quickly slipped her blue dress on, smoothing her palms over the wrinkles and situating it over her chest.

She exhaled a shaky breath, still searching for that deep lungful of air that refused to come. Giving up, she moved to the long vanity mirror and removed her sticky mask. One glance at her reflection confirmed what she'd already known—she was mess. Her overdone makeup was now smudged and smeared from tears, her cheeks were flushed and damp from being confined under the plastic mask and long pieces of hair had escaped their bindings to hang limp around her face.

A small, mirthless laugh puffed from her lips at how she looked. Almost clownish if it wasn't for the sadness that marred her eyes and mouth. She jerked a paper towel out of the dispenser and quickly wet it down, the hollow echo of the locker

room making the rushing sound of the water seem more pronounced.

The clanking metal slamming of a locker door a few rows
over made her flinch, and her fist clamped around the wet
towel. The quiet was interrupted by the bubbling laughter and
conversation from a trio of women who entered the room.
Kendra ducked her head, patting the moist towel over her
cheeks before they could see her.

She paused and held the towel to her eyes, hiding behind the
cooling pad for a moment, searching for the calm that would
enable her to leave the room and find her friends. Pushing
out a long breath, she lowered the towel to find Cali staring
back at her, gentle concern covering her face and filling her
green eyes.

Kendra turned away, not wanting her friend to see her like
this. *Damn it. Damn it.*

"What happened?" Cali's soft question did little to quiet
Kendra's apprehension. "Can I do anything to help?"

Everyone was so patient with her here. Why?

"I'm fine, sorry," Kendra mumbled, forcing herself to turn
back to the mirror and use the wet towel to clean the smeared
makeup from her face. More forceful now, she tried to reassure her friend. "There's nothing to worry about. I'll be ready
to go in a moment."

Cali propped a hip against the corner and picked up Kendra's discarded mask to stroke the small feathers with her fingers. "Are you hurt?"

"No," Kendra quickly denied then added, "At least, not
more than I asked for."

The slight smile that curved over Cali's lips made her feel
better. There was an understanding there that was more help-
ful than Kendra had thought it would be.

"I won't pry," Cali started then sighed, setting the mask

back on the counter. She met Kendra's eyes in the mirror, touching her through the reflection if not in person. It was as if her friend knew Kendra couldn't handle being physically touched at the moment. "You never prodded into my business, so I won't in yours. But know that I'm here if you need me. For anything. I mean that."

Kendra forced a smile and gave Cali a nod. Words weren't possible without tears right then. Leaning into the counter, she flipped the towel over and used a corner to clean the black mascara smudges from under her eyes. "Where's Allie?" she asked, hoping to change the subject.

Cali laughed, the light sound filling Kendra with something normal. "She's out front with Jake, for once silent."

"What? Allie at a loss for words?"

"I know, right?" Cali nodded, her eyes flashing in agreement. "I think we shocked her speechless."

The laugh that left Kendra was full and healing. It reminded her that she wasn't the only one with issues and let her focus on something else for bit. "What'd you guys do after I left?"

Cali fixed her hair in the mirror, a smirk on her lips. "Jake took us to another room. This one had two men and a woman." She met Kendra's eyes. "Let's just say Allie did a lot of squirming, but no complaining."

Kendra tried to picture that and could only laugh at the image that formed. "She'd seemed rather, ah...entranced... with the Scene in the first room. I can only imagine her watching a ménage."

"In her defense, I blushed bright red the first time Jake took me to one of those rooms."

"Yeah. Thankfully the people I was with for my first voyeur experience were all too drunk to notice how much I enjoyed it." Kendra picked up her mask and grabbed a clean towel to wipe the perspiration off the inside of the plastic.

Cali tilted her head. "I wonder why it's so hard for women to be open and admit that sexual acts excite us. I mean, not all women have this hang-up, but God, it seems like a large majority of us are still taught that admitting to enjoying anything outside of 'vanilla' sex makes you a slut."

Kendra assessed her friend, wondering at the sudden spilling of personal information that she usually kept so tightly bound. "Is that what happened to you?"

Cali looked down, her fingers absently running over the silver links around her neck. "Yes and no," she admitted. "Part of my fear came from my upbringing. The rest was all my own. After all, what would people think if they knew I longed to be dominated? That I enjoy being held down and spanked and…" She looked up. "I'm guessing you know what I'm talking about."

Yeah, Kendra did, and she'd never spoken about it to anyone. She still couldn't. Not here. Now.

Sliding the mask back on her face, she adjusted the plastic until it rested comfortably on her cheeks and nose. Her eyes were still a telltale red, but otherwise she was once again camouflaged behind the shield. Turning to her friend, she took the woman's hand, the one still caressing her collar, and squeezed her fingers. Cali froze, her eyes wide and vulnerable after exposing herself.

"Thank you, Cali," Kendra whispered, her voice strained with emotion. "I can't talk about it right now. But thank you for sharing. For letting me know I'm not alone."

The soft smile Cali gave her was warm with affection and understanding. She tugged Kendra into a hug, her words soft against Kendra's ear. "It'll be okay. I'm here when you're ready."

Kendra clung to her, taking the strength that was being offered, before she stepped back. Her attention strayed to Cali's collar. It was tastefully done. A delicate piece of jewelry that anyone outside the club would assume was just that. But within this world it stood for so much more.

"Your collar is beautiful," she said before she could think better of it.

Cali's hand went right back to the object in question, her brows rising in uncertainty and doubt.

"Yeah. I know what it is," Kendra answered. "And I don't judge you. In truth, there was a time when I thought it was all I would need to be happy. But it takes more than an inanimate object to make that happen."

Cali snorted, a choked laugh swallowed behind her tightly closed mouth.

Kendra gave her a puzzled look then laughed out loud and rolled her eyes when she realized what she'd said. "Fine. For long-term happiness, it takes more."

"And if the object is animated?" Cali left the question hanging and tried to look innocent as she struggled to hold back a grin.

Kendra dropped her head back and stared at the ceiling in mock affront. "Okay. Animated objects can get you a bit of happiness."

Cali finally let her laughter free, choking on the rolling giggles behind her hand, her cheeks turning pink.

Thank God for friends. Kendra joined in with her own open laughter. It was freeing and wonderful. Probably one of the best laughs she'd ever had over something so silly and dumb. But it lifted her as nothing else could've at that moment.

Not waiting for her friend to calm down, Kendra grabbed her shoulders, spun Cali around and started forcing her toward the exit. "Go," she commanded. "Your Master is waiting for you."

That brought Cali up short, the amusement dropping from

her face. She searched Kendra's face before asking, "You're okay with that? Knowing what Jake is to me?"

"Oh, Cali." Kendra wrapped her arms around the shorter woman and pulled her in for another hug. "Of course I am." She eased back so she could look at Cali, needing her to see the truth. "It's obvious how happy he makes you. And I'm willing to bet he's much more than your Master."

The shy smile that spread over Cali's face confirmed the question even without her words. "Yeah, he is."

Opening her heart just a bit, Kendra revealed one of her secrets. "I'm a little envious of you, you know that?" Cali's brows rose in a mix of shock and question, prompting Kendra to continue, her words a bit slow and tentative as she sought the right ones. "There's a closeness, a bond that comes with a relationship like yours. One that goes beyond the usual levels of love and commitment. It's beautiful to see when it's right. Why wouldn't others want that?"

"I had no idea you felt that way." The disbelief was clear in Cali's voice. "Honestly, I wasn't sure how you felt about this whole world. I mean, I know you didn't judge me, but I got the impression that this wasn't something you…well, that you enjoyed."

Kendra shook her head, staring at the tile floor, a gurgle of derision escaping her lips as she wrapped her arms protectively around her waist. "I don't know if I do either. I thought I didn't, but I don't know anymore." She looked up, searching for understanding, answers or maybe just acceptance from her friend. "I don't want to, but sometimes it feels like I don't have a choice on that." The words sounded empty to her own ears, like an excuse, as if she could blame her desires and needs on something besides her own free will.

"Hey," Cali said as she reached out to give Kendra's arm a reassuring rub. "I get it. I understand exactly what you mean."

"You do?"

"Yeah, I do. I struggled with that for years, thinking there was something wrong with me."

Kendra licked her lips and dared to ask, "And now?"

"And now I understand that something that feels so right and so good with Jake can't be wrong." Like a magnet, Cali's fingers returned to stroke the chain around her neck. "I know that others wouldn't accept it or understand. Well, you saw how messed up I was over it not too long ago."

A small laugh found its way out of Kendra's chest, surprising her. "I'm still not ready to meet another bottle of Jack Daniel's," she admitted as she recalled the night Allie had declared that alcohol was the best way to get over "man trouble." Cali had definitely grown and changed since that night over two months ago. She was happy, content now in a way that Kendra hadn't seen before. "How do you reconcile it with yourself?"

"I'm old, remember?" Cali chuckled before pausing. "Seriously? I don't know if I would have without Jake. With him, it's okay. I know it's not bad or wrong or shameful in any way because he won't let it be." Her gaze drifted down, her voice softening. "And I lived for way too many years feeling empty and alone before I finally found the courage to discover this side of myself. Now that it's free, I'm free, I don't think I could go back to the shell of who I was before. I *know* I don't want to. I like this me. A lot." She reinforced the last words with a snap of her head and an honest smile that lit up her face with conviction.

"Wow," Kendra whispered, again envious of her friend but amazed at the same time. "I don't know if I'll ever be that content." The words were out before she thought about them.

"I didn't either...until I was honest with myself," Cali said. "And who am I kidding? I was forty-four before that level of self-realization struck. Give yourself a break, Kendra. You're what, thirty?"

"Thirty-one." She'd celebrated that milestone by herself with a chocolate bar and a glass of wine two weeks ago.

Cali smiled. "See? You have years yet to figure it all out."

"I really hope it doesn't take me that long," Kendra mumbled around a sigh.

"Me too," Cali agreed, grabbing her arm as she turned one more time toward the exit. "But truthfully, I don't know if anyone is ever completely content. There's always something new we're discovering and exploring about ourselves, right? Otherwise we'd become very boring, and what fun is that?"

"With age brings wisdom, oh wise one?" Kendra's quip brought the laughter she was seeking.

"Watch it, punk," Cali chided as she opened the door and motioned Kendra through. "You're supposed to respect your elders."

"I thought it was Masters?"

"Only if they earn it."

"Too true." Way too true. And maybe that's what Kendra needed to remember. Respect was earned not forced. Not demanded or taken. Just like trust.

Just like love.

EIGHT

The consistent beat of her running shoes hitting the paved path was a rhythm Kendra lived for. If she focused enough, she could get her feet to match the pace of her heart. When she added the secondary tempo of her breathing, she found her zone. In those few moments, when her body was in sync, she finally felt a level of peace. This was something she could control.

The scent of newly freed grass blended with the lingering hint of the rain from the previous night to invigorate her with the anticipation of spring. The air was crisp and perfect for her morning run but had the undercurrent of warmer weather to come. With the sun peeking through the breaks in the clouds, Kendra imagined the afternoon would be beautiful.

Too bad she'd be stuck in a windowless stockroom counting inventory by then. Way to put her Human Development degree to work. Her parents would be so proud. But then, there wasn't much in her life that her parents had ever been proud of. Why it still mattered to her was a question better suited for therapy. There was no point in trying to analyze something that simply was.

Another jogger passed her on the path, her golden retriever panting at her side, a big happy doggy-grin on its face. Kendra swerved to the left and glided past a pair of moms pushing strollers, their laughter fading behind her as she held her pace and breathed into the burn that was building in her thighs.

The unexpected warm streak in early March was being enjoyed by many, including the ever-present squadron of ducks at the edge of the small lake. As if on cue, the small pack started to quack madly, scaring the little boy trying to feed them pieces of bread. He squealed, running for his mom, who swooped in to lift the frightened toddler into the shelter of her arms.

Kendra smiled. The distractions were nice, but more importantly they meant safety. She always did her runs during the day in areas full of people. Headphones were also out. She wanted to hear the footsteps that approached from behind, not be surprised by them.

She checked her watch then upped her pace, loving the way her heart rate increased with the extra push at the end of a run. It broke the rhythm, put her body into an erratic jumble that matched her emotions and oddly made her feel balanced, which was a rarity in her life.

Coming around a bend in the path, she saw him jogging toward her when it was already too late to turn around or dodge down another trail. He'd seen her too. Even though he was still a ways away, it was clear Deklan's focus was on her. It'd been over two weeks since she'd fled from him at The Den; maybe he would ignore her. A moment later he smiled and gave a wave, causing her to almost stumble over her own feet.

Not a fan of the whole damsel-in-distress scenario, Kendra slowed her stride before she did fall and make a complete fool of herself. She'd already done that in front of him once.

Etiquette kicked in, and she managed a short wave back. Maybe he'd just jog on by. It wasn't like they had a real reason to chat. Just because she'd let him spank her then freaked out in his club didn't give them grounds for a friendship. Hell, they barely qualified as acquaintances.

The fact that she wanted to talk to him had her running faster again. But there was nothing coordinated or soothing about her gait now.

When he reached her on the path, Deklan executed a simple U-turn and came up on her right, matching her stride. She was instantly aware of him, her entire side tingling with the undercurrent of electricity that seemed to flow unseen between them.

"Hi," she panted, glancing his way. She knew she had to say something and that was about all she could manage around her stuttering mind. What did he want?

He didn't answer. In fact, he didn't even look at her. He just stared straight ahead, keeping pace with her. His silence was more unsettling than the effects of breathing in his rich, woodsy scent. He smelled of sweat and man and reminded her way too much of their Scene in the Dungeon. She'd done her best to avoid him since that night. It hadn't been hard, given that he worked nights and she rarely left her condo after dark unless it was for work.

Now here he was, being normal and silent, acting as if they did this all the time. She gave him another side glance, trying to figure him out. His gray long-sleeved running shirt hugged his muscled torso and was darkened with sweat down his chest and under his arms, indicating he'd been out for a while. But he showed no other signs of exertion.

Her pulse quickened with appreciation for his well-toned

form. She was certain he was older than her by a good ten years, but he hadn't let his body deteriorate. Not even a bit. Instantly she flashed back to the feel of his hard chest pressed against her back, his muscled thighs supporting his weight as he made her writhe in ecstasy.

Clenching her lips, Kendra forced her attention back to the path, reminding herself that she couldn't be attracted to this man. To any man, for that matter. There was just too much risk involved.

Another five minutes, and she finally slowed to a cool-down pace, hoping the silent partner at her side would continue on without her. He didn't. Slowing, he stayed with her.

Once her breathing was regulated enough to carry a conversation, Kendra finally crumbled and asked, "Did you need something?"

"No." His voice was steady, not even a hint of breathlessness showing from his workout. "You okay?"

"Yeah. Never better," she lied. The words easily repeated after months of practice.

"I don't believe you."

"Why should I care?"

She felt his gaze on her as he finally looked her way. "I want to help you."

"I don't need any help." Another almost-lie. The truth was, she didn't know if she could accept any help.

"Yes. You do," Deklan said with conviction, not a hint of doubt or hesitation in the firm words.

He slowed then stopped, and she was tempted to keep on running, but something compelled her to follow his lead. Maybe she was just tired of running—both physically and mentally.

She rested her hands on her thighs and filled her lungs with slow, measured intakes of air before stepping onto the grass to start her cool-down routine. Ignoring his arrogant insistence, Kendra exhaled into a lunge, the burn of the stretch absorbing her focus.

"I can help you if you let me."

Focus snapped. "How? What can you help me with?" *Typical arrogant male*, she grumbled to herself. They always thought they knew what the weak little female needed. She switched legs, leaning heavily onto her thigh to increase the pull along her calf.

Deklan lifted his arms over his head, using one hand to pull on the elbow of the other to stretch his triceps. "I can help you accept what you need." His voice was low and intimate, despite his casual actions.

She studiously ignored the display of rippled abs that peeked out from under his shirt as he stretched. "What I need is for you to leave me alone."

"No," he countered before bending at the waist to stretch the backs of his legs. His fingers hit the grass and he walked his hands forward until his head was next to hers. His blue eyes held hers, preventing her from looking away. "What you need is pain."

Did he really just say that? She stared at him, searching for the joke or, worse, the snide dig that was bound to come next. Instead she found concern and an unwavering belief in what he'd said.

"No." The denial was automatic, the rising panic just as reflexive.

He kneeled before her. Immediately she was reminded of him posing just like that next to the spanking bench. The look on his face was almost identical to then, with all that patience and compassion showing in his eyes. "There's no shame in admitting it."

Oh-so simple for him to say. She wobbled, having forgotten her stretch, and let her knee bend to brace against the grass. Giving a quick look around to ensure their privacy, she straightened her back and faced Deklan with all of the challenge that she felt. "What do you know? One spanking session with me, and now you think you know what I need?"

He didn't flinch away, not that she thought he would. He wasn't that kind of man. His voice was hard and smooth as granite when he spoke. "You told me you need the pain to come."

Right. She closed her eyes, blocking his knowing look. Embarrassment flooded her face in a wave of heat that she hoped was camouflaged by the flush from her run. There was nothing to say to that. No way to counter the statement, and denial was pointless.

She pushed to a stand and started back to her condo, the clipped stride nothing more than a cool-down walk. But of course he didn't let her flee. Once again he was at her side, matching her pace and ruffling her composure.

"Who did this to you?"

His question seemed out of the blue, but she knew what he was talking about. After all, it was the giant effing elephant between them. But she couldn't answer. The words stuck in her throat, which was clogged with shame, guilt and mortification.

"Kendra." He grabbed her hand, and an instant jolt of awareness shot up her arm. He eased to a stop and again she followed his lead before he stepped in front of her, his broad chest blocking her view. "Look at me."

She didn't want to. God, she didn't want to. She bit her cheek and willed herself to ignore the command. But she couldn't. Every ingrained compulsion made her lift her chin until her eyes met his. The look of appreciation that covered his face was unexpected.

"There's nothing wrong with you." When she started to look away, he grabbed her chin to stop her. She winced, expecting the hard pinch of fingers at her error. When he simply caressed her jawline with long, slow stokes of his thumb, she tentatively returned her eyes to his. Only then did he continue speaking. "I want to help you see that."

"Why?" She didn't understand why he'd even be interested in helping her. "You don't even know me."

"Because I want to."

She froze. His simple, straightforward answer didn't appear to have any hidden meanings. No secret motives or ulterior goals that would trap her. Still she doubted. "But why?"

"Because I see you, Kendra." His tone was so certain. Strong without being commanding.

Her breath hitched and the air caught in her lungs, as if her subconscious was trying to hold on to the words and all they offered. In the distance a group of birds chirped and sang in tune with the crying of a baby, but it all came to her as a muffled backdrop.

"Really? And what do you see?" She tried to inflict doubt and cynicism into her voice, but it sounded weak even to her own ears.

His thumb continued to play on her jaw as his lips curled in that half-smile, his dimple showing. She couldn't look away even if she'd wanted to. "I see a courageous woman who is lost. Someone did you wrong. My guess is he used the guise of BDSM to abuse you until you felt ashamed of your need for sexual pain." He searched her face, brushing the loose strands of hair away from her temple. The touch so light, so… caring. A brief flash of uncertainty marred his brow before it smoothed away as quickly as it came. "I'm also betting this man encouraged your need for pain while condemning it at the same time. And worst of all, he turned around and blamed you for making him do it."

The knife turned in her chest, the invisible wound bleeding with fresh pain. How could he possibly know that? Was she that transparent? No, damn it. He wasn't going to manipulate her that easily.

She pulled away from Deklan's grasp, surprised when he let her go. "What do you know?" she snapped, pushing past him to get away.

The light pressure of his hand on her arm was all it took to stop her from passing him. She stilled, even though she was itching to flee from everything he represented. But she was stalled by that one lone touch that seemed to tremble ever so slightly.

"I've known both, Kendra," he said, his voice low, like he was remembering as well as telling. "The pain from an abuser and the pain received from a sadist. They're very different. One brings shame. The other pleasure. You know that. Otherwise you wouldn't have done the Scene at the club with me." He paused as another runner sprinted past, head bobbing in time with the beat of his headphones. "But you don't believe it."

Kendra stared straight ahead, concentrating on the man playing with his black lab in the grassy field fifty feet away. The simple game of fetch reminded her how cyclical life was. Out and back, retrieve and return, over and over until you dropped from exhaustion.

Deklan's answer was so close to the truth. He had half her story pieced together after only one Scene. How much would he figure out after another?

He stayed at her side, facing the other way, but his fingers continued to skim over the sensitive area of her inner arm through the thin material of her running shirt. Only a light pressure, a touch that was comforting. Not frightening in its aggression, but terrifying as hell in the temptation it stirred.

"I want to show you that until you believe it," Deklan continued, his voice hoarse. "We can sign a contract, lay down rules beforehand. I'll do whatever you want to make you feel safe. But you shouldn't fear what you need. You shouldn't be ashamed of something that brings you pleasure. Let me show you how it can be. How it *should* be."

"And how's that, Deklan?" The warring factions of denial and desire battled within her, making her bristle with indignation. "You gonna whip me a few times until I come? Tell me what a good girl I am before you slap me across the face? Maybe you'll go for the nipple torture, squeeze them until I cry and then release the pressure, making me come instantly? Is that what you want to show me? Well, I've done all that." Her crude answer was meant to make him leave. No Dom wanted a snotty sub. And damn it, she didn't want what he offered. She couldn't want that.

"And there's a part of you that doesn't want to admit that you liked it." He was staring at her now. She could feel his gaze drilling holes in the side of her head. But she refused to look at him, to let him see how incredibly close he was to the truth. "Not all of it," he continued. "But there was enough of it that you enjoyed. Enough that it brought you back to a sex club even though I bet you swore to yourself you'd never return to one."

"You think you know so much." Her throat ached, parched and filled with everything she'd been holding back. There were no tears, only the empty void of lost dreams and broken promises.

"No. With you, I don't know enough."

He didn't know enough… She stood there stalled in limbo, her world balancing on a moment of indecision. The raw hon-

esty behind his words made her wish—and dear God, did she
dare hope? Could Deklan truly help her, or would he be the
one to finally destroy her?

Her conversation with Cali replayed one more time. Did
Kendra have the courage to be true to herself? He was offering her exactly what she told herself she didn't need. Only, she
was lying to herself. Yet she wasn't sure if she had the strength
to take the risk. What if she was wrong about Deklan, like
she'd been with Eric? On the other hand, what if this was her
best chance of overcoming her past and she was too scared
to take it?

There were so many questions and no answers. And beside
her, Deklan was waiting.

"There's more to the story."

"I'm sure there is." Deklan stared at Kendra's profile, so
strong yet vulnerable. Right then all of her emotions were
held in check, not a glimmer of her inner struggle showing.
"And that story won't end unless you choose to change it."

Her chest rose and fell with each deep breath. Slow, measured inhales that told of the battle she was waging with herself. He wanted to push, to force her into accepting his offer.
But that wouldn't solve anything. And this was about her
needs, not what he wanted.

He'd held back the last two weeks, giving her time, waiting for the right moment to approach her. Even though he'd
wanted to chase her down almost immediately, he'd resisted.
It was a game of strategy, a sport he was trained to excel at.
Only the stakes had never been as great as they were right now.

Kendra kept her chin pointed high, exposing the long line
of her neck and the sharp edge of her jaw. Her hair was pulled
back in a ponytail, but small wisps curled in the damp moisture along her brow, enticing him to brush them away once

again. Instead he scanned down, appreciation filling him. The tight running pants and top that hugged her thighs and breasts seemed to emphasize the power behind her toned muscles. She was strength disguised in a lean form.

And damn how he ached to harness that strength…and then set it free.

"I'm trying," she said long moments later, only a hint of desperation showing in her soft tone. But it was just enough for Deklan to grasp.

"I can help you." Then he put it out there, that one last dare that said it all. "Trust me."

Slowly she turned her head, her bright blue eyes searching his face but giving away nothing. "How?" The doubt was clear, but this time it was edged with hope.

"A step at a time."

"And if I fall?"

"I'll be there to pick you up," he said, meaning every word. "Or let you go. Whichever you need."

The sun broke free to hit them with a blast of brightness that raced across the ground as it emerged from behind the clouds. The rays heated his face, putting hers in shadow, but it couldn't hide the turmoil etched so clearly on it now. Perspiration gathered to trail a slow path between his shoulder blades, each inch downward tracked by his senses, ticking off the seconds as he waited for her reply.

She looked away then down to stare at his fingers, which still skimmed over her inner arm. Physically she was so close, but the space between them felt like miles. "Okay."

Fuck, yes. The childish desire to whoop in victory hit him with a surprising punch. Not cool. Thank fuck none of that emotion was displayed. She wasn't a prize to be won, even if it felt like he'd been handed a precious gift nonetheless.

"Okay," he repeated, his relief exiting with the word. She

studied him, seeming to wait for his next move. And what was that? For once his strategy had been consumed by getting her to this point. Now he needed to move forward with caution or risk stepping on a landmine and watching it all blow up. "At the club then? In public?"

"Yes."

"I'll draw up the contract. Two months, once a week minimum." It was the Dom setting the terms now.

"Okay," she agreed without a hint of hesitation. "But I want rules."

"Of course. This is a partnership. Not a dictatorship."

She nodded, swallowed and took a step away before pausing. "I'll be at the club at nine. We'll sign the papers before we start." She was all business, and he suspected it was her way of holding back the fear. Fine for now, but she couldn't hide forever.

"Email your terms. My name at The Den. I'll be sure to include them in the contract. We can discuss the details when you arrive."

He trailed his fingers down her arm as she took off at a slow jog without answering. He forced himself to stay put as she retreated once again. Only this time, as he watched her blond ponytail bob and sway in time with her steps, he was filled with anticipation. The running pants hugged her firm ass, reminding him of how perfect it truly was. His palm tingled just remembering the sting from connecting with her flesh.

He couldn't mess this up. Somehow this had quickly become his most critical mission. He could help her. Heal her and make her see that she had nothing to be ashamed of. Focused on his task, he turned around and continued his run, his route taking him away from her. But that was only temporary.

Soon she'd be right there with him.

NINE

She stumbled up the two small steps leading to her door before letting herself stop. Bracing a hand on the wall, Kendra leaned over and forced her lungs to take the deep gulps of air they desperately needed. *Shit, shit, shit.*

She squeezed her eyes shut and focused on the hard grit of the brick beneath her hand, the cool gust of wind that chilled her damp skin, the faint scent of dirt from the flowerpot in the corner. All of the little details that kept her from thinking of the bigger, more terrifying things.

"Hey, Kendra."

She jerked around at Allie's voice, startled that her friend had snuck up on her like that. Forcing a smile, she responded as was expected. "Hi, Allie."

Allie walked up the short path from the drive, her heels snapping on the cement in a crisp rhythm that seemed to match her. She tilted her head, scrutinizing Kendra as she approached. "You okay? You don't look so good."

Kendra puffed out a snort. "Thanks."

With an exaggerated sigh, Allie pursed her lips. "You know

what I mean. You always look good." She waved a hand in Kendra's direction. "With a body like that, how could you not? What I meant was it looks like something's bothering you."

Kendra turned away, pulling the key out of her tight jogging bra. "I'm fine," she said, concentrating on unlocking the door. "Just tired from my run. What brings you over here?" Allie lived in a condo across the back courtyard from Kendra's and didn't usually have a reason to be on this side of the building.

Kendra pushed the door open but stopped frozen before she could enter. Her eyes were trained on the plain white envelope sticking out of the empty flowerpot. It hadn't been there before. She always checked the area when she left.

Instantly everything went dark except for that white piece of paper. Nausea rolled her stomach and she swallowed against the sickness. Feeling heated, her skin tingled with the flush of fear and she swayed before her hand shot out to grab the doorjamb.

"Kendra." Allie's voice drew her out of the void, a precious sound that kept her from tumbling into the blackness. Then Allie's hand was on her shoulder, holding her steady. "What's wrong? Kendra. Tell me what's going on."

"Nothing," she managed to mumble. She shook her head and yanked her attention away from the letter. "It's nothing. Really. I'm fine."

"You're not fine. Don't bullshit me."

That pulled a sardonic chuckle of agreement from Kendra's chest. "Can't bullshit the lawyer, can I?"

"No. You can't," her friend insisted, not even offended by the comment. Without missing a beat, Allie reached over, yanked the upsetting object from the flowerpot and knocked the clinging dirt from the paper before holding it up. "Shall we go inside and see why this has you so upset?"

"No." Kendra shook her head and held out her hand. "We won't. Just give it to me."

Allie's eyes narrowed as if she was debating her options before she handed the letter over. "I'll listen if you want to talk."

A tempting offer, but where would Kendra start? "Thanks. I'm sure it's nothing." She tried to brush it off, waving the letter like it didn't weigh a ton in her hand. "Probably just a note from my landlord."

She turned away and stepped into her condo, only to freeze a second time. She looked back to Allie and worked to keep her voice even. "Do you want to come in for a minute?" Even though the door had been locked, she was suddenly petrified to go inside by herself.

"Sure." Allie pushed up the sleeve of her gray suit and checked her watch. "I have an hour before I have to be back."

Able to move again, Kendra exhaled and continued inside. She couldn't stop from giving a quick check over everything. She scanned the sparse contents of the living room, just a faded blue couch and chair, a garage sale coffee table and an old TV on a do-it-yourself stand. The few magazines she'd collected appeared untouched in their neat stacks beneath the low table. Her inspection ended on the pole still wedged in the track of the sliding door and she breathed a little easier.

"Wow," Allie said from behind Kendra. "I take it you haven't finished unpacking yet."

She tried to laugh at Allie's joke, but she was all out of bluffs for the day. Instead she turned away from the living room content that everything seemed untouched and went to the fridge, tossing the letter on the counter as she went. "Can I get you anything? Water, soda?"

"Water's fine."

She grabbed two bottles and handed one to her very first houseguest. "I guess you can tell decorating's not my thing."

She cracked her bottle open and took a long, refreshing gulp of the icy liquid. It felt like heaven against her over-parched throat. After a couple more swallows, she lowered the bottle, only to be nailed by Allie's searching scrutiny.

"Do you at least want to open it while I'm here?" Allie crossed her arms over her chest and nodded toward the letter. Her long, curly hair was pulled back into a large clip at her nape giving her look a severity that matched the sleek, navy suit. Silk, if Kendra was guessing right. Her mother would be disappointed that she couldn't name the designer too.

Clearing her throat and the thought, Kendra set her bottle down and picked up the discarded letter. She flipped it in her hands before quickly sliding a finger under the seal. There was only her name written in block letters across the front. It could be anything.

But it wasn't.

Somehow she knew that. Just like she knew that her sought-after sense of security was going to be shattered and the quaint little life she'd built here would be ripped apart.

After so long, there were some things she just knew.

That still didn't stop the tremble of fear that clamped around her heart when she read Eric's words: *I know where you are.* That was it. Of course he would find her. She hadn't gone to extremes to stay hidden. She still used her real name and had been forced to draw from her trust fund to pay for the condo rent, even though she tried to use her Target income to pay for everything else. It'd been blind desperation that had her hoping he'd just let her go.

That thought almost seemed funny now. Just another thing in the long line of truths she'd been hiding from.

Folding the paper back up, she ripped it in half, then again until there was nothing left but a pile of tiny scrap pieces.

"Your landlord must be a real dick," Allie observed, her dry wit making Kendra smile. "Makes me glad I own my condo."

"He's the biggest," she agreed.

"Do you need my help?"

Here was another person offering to help her. It was like she'd fallen down the rabbit hole and ended up in an alternate world of unbelievable kindness. "Thanks. I'm fine."

"Right. And I'm the handsome prince coming to sweep you off your feet." Allie set down her unopened water and moved to the door. "My services are always free for you. Okay?"

"Services? What do you mean?"

"Legal. If you need them. I have a ton of pro-bono hours I need to rack up to maintain the firm's public image." Allie checked her lipstick in the small mirror next to the front door then tucked an escaped curl back into the clip. She turned around. "The *other* services I charge for." She wiggled her eyebrows in a lascivious manner.

Kendra laughed. "I'll remember that. Thanks."

A quick glance at the clock, and Allie was out the door. "Gotta run. Be careful, Kendra. Call if you need anything." And she was gone, a whirlwind of energy that had the force of a sledgehammer. And the tact too.

Feeling better than she had ten minutes ago, Kendra turned back to the pile of papers on her counter and swiped them into the garbage can. It wouldn't be that simple to get rid of Eric, but she wasn't going to let him stop her. She liked it here and she was done running.

That meant she was done running from herself too. For once she had to thank Eric. She wasn't going to be scared by him, and his little letter gave her the determination to do exactly what he'd hate for her to do.

A smile on her face, she locked the front door and wandered upstairs. She had an outfit to pick out for that evening.

★ ★ ★

"You sure you know what you're doing?"

Deklan shot a glare at Seth before he turned back to his task. Not a chance he was answering that question. Instead he ran the towel over the vinyl-covered table, all of his focus put on cleaning the piece of equipment he was going to use that night. His plans included something that would build Kendra's trust. He was preparing, even if he still doubted her appearance. She'd said she'd show, but her actions said something different.

Seth moved around the table until he stood in front of Deklan. "I assume you'll see to all of the paperwork. Just because you're being stupid doesn't mean you're an idiot."

"Fuck you." Deklan straightened, throwing down the rag he was using. "I train subs. That's part of my job."

"And I take care of the club." Seth leaned in, pressing his hands on the table. "That's *my* job. Did you do the full background check on her? Screen the medical? Sign the legal work? Or are you bypassing all of the rules in your quest to be the savior once again?"

"Watch it," Deklan warned. "You're pushing too far." He bent down and picked up the bottle of cleaner and jar of metal polish with slow, controlled movements.

He walked away, putting the cleaning supplies back before going to the long row of cabinets that held the Dungeon toys. The entire time he was aware of Seth silently stewing near the middle of the room.

"Is the club okay?" Deklan asked as he opened a cabinet, the door hinge squeaking. Even with all of the equipment filling the unoccupied Dungeon, the large space felt hollow. Every sound seemingly magnified in the quiet when the room was normally filled with a large variety of noise.

"What? Oh, yeah. It's fine."

He scanned the floggers and crops lined up in neat rows on the different shelves for a second before glancing over his shoulder at Seth. His hands were shoved deep into the front pockets of his jeans, his hair unbound and hanging around his face as he stared at the ground. Seth had been on edge for the last few months, little things ticking him off when they normally wouldn't. "The paperwork will be on your desk before the Scene starts."

"Right." Seth gave a tight nod, his lips pulled thin. "Of course it will."

Deklan turned his attention back to the floggers, contemplating which one to use that night.

"Do you trust yourself with her?"

Seth's question was so out of the norm that Deklan actually jerked around to stare at the man he'd known for over twenty years. The other man wouldn't look at him. Instead, Seth continued to stare at the ground, which was even more uncharacteristic of him.

"What's going on, Seth?" Deklan forgot his task for the moment and walked back over. He crossed his arms over his chest and waited.

The other man shook his head as if he was clearing away cobwebs then gave a shrug. "Nothing. Just taking care of the details." He glanced distractedly around the room before yanking his hands from his pockets to comb his fingers through his hair, pulling it away from his face. "Just be honest with yourself on this one. She's more than a trainee."

Yeah, she was. But was he going to admit that to anyone else? Fuck, no. Zero point in giving anyone that kind of leverage. "I'm fine."

Seth assessed him for a long moment, his face tight like he was holding something back.

Before he could say anything more, Deklan switched gears.

"Help me move this table." He stepped around and grabbed the end of the padded massage-style table. "I want it over by the wall." He nodded toward the space he'd already cleared in the far corner.

With a long sigh, Seth did as Deklan asked. Together they lifted and maneuvered the table around the other equipment until they could set it down in front of the mirror that covered a large portion of the wall.

Seth wiped his palms on his jeans and assessed the setup. "What are you planning?"

Nudging the table until it was aligned perpendicular to the mirror, Deklan tried to gauge Seth's question. Was it curiosity or judgment on the other man's face? Did it matter?

He returned to the toy cabinet before he answered. "Nothing extreme. She's still too skittish for me to give her what she really wants."

"And you already know what that is?"

What was up with him? Deklan turned to stare directly at Seth, meeting the waiting confrontation with his own irritation. "Yeah. I do. You gonna doubt that too, or are you done being a dick for the day?"

Cursing, Seth turned away and headed toward the stairs, his boots slamming hard and frustrated on the wood. His non-answer as clear as any words he could have said.

Deklan looked back to the crops but didn't really see them. Did he know what he was doing with Kendra? Of course he did. Fuck Seth for putting doubts in his head.

TEN

Kendra stepped into the dimly lit entry of The Den at exactly nine o'clock. The bouncer looked her over, his slow perusal assessing, not judging. She gave him a tight smile, willing her voice to work. "I'm expected." That was all she could get out. She was incapable of forming whole sentences at the moment. It was almost as if the sound of her own voice would change her mind. Make her run away instead of moving forward.

"Name?" the big, bald man asked as he picked up the clipboard sitting on the table next to him.

"Kendra Morgan," she answered, her voice only slightly raspy. She cleared her throat and swallowed but resisted the urge to close her eyes. She wasn't going to hide or run. It didn't matter how much her stomach ached or her palms sweated. This was an opportunity she had to take.

The man's head snapped up, a slow grin forming on his lips. "Ms. Morgan. It's a pleasure to meet you." He stepped aside, unblocking her view from the rest of the entry area. "Check-in's over there. I'll let Master Deklan know you've arrived."

Kendra nodded her thanks and managed to walk over to

the indicated area on mostly stable legs. Taking a breath, she gave her name to the buxom blonde dressed in red latex behind the counter. The body-hugging dress had a zipper up the front that looked stretched to breaking from the strain.

The blonde gave a full smile, easing some of Kendra's tension. "Do you want to check your items, or would you like a locker key?"

"Check," Kendra answered as she removed her trench coat and handed it over with her purse. She didn't plan on hanging around long enough after the Scene to need a locker. The cool air that lingered in the entry area hit her skin, and she shivered. The black mini-skirt and tank did little to keep her warm. The outfit wasn't exceedingly sexy, compared to what other subs would be wearing. But she also didn't plan on having it on for that long.

The muffled thump of the dance music hit full-blast into the area as the door to the main room opened. Kendra jerked around to see Deklan moving through the open doorway. Instantly, heat flared within her, chasing away the lingering chill. Dressed again in all black, the tight T-shirt stretched over his chest, showing his well-defined muscles and hugging the girth of his biceps.

He didn't smile, not here. Now, he was all business. Stubble covered his jaw, matching his short-cropped hair, lending a hint of darkness to his appearance. Everything in her warned that this was a dangerous game she was playing, but she couldn't make herself stop.

She didn't want to stop.

If there was any chance at all, even the slightest, that Deklan could help her accept her need, then she had to try. She had to do this because she didn't want to continue living in the pit of shame that trapped her now.

"Kendra." The low purr went straight through her, ramp-ing up the anticipation but also stirring her nerves. He stopped before her, his dark military boots coming into view. She sensed his presence, the energy reaching out to her in an almost tangible way.

Her skin prickled, the small hairs on her arms rising with the goose bumps. "Sir," she mumbled. Here, at the club, he wouldn't want to be Deklan anymore.

He reached down, separating her clasped hands before taking one in his. "This way."

She followed, all too aware of the number of people loitering around the area watching them. He led her into the main room of the club, the loud music and crowd of people putting her at ease. Here she was only one of many.

He kept a firm hold on her hand, weaving his way through the people until they reached the same VIP booth she'd sat in the last time she'd been there. She slid onto the bench seat and he followed, his large body edging her around until she was resting against the back curve, giving her a clear view of the room. But her eyes couldn't stray from the papers that lay on the table.

The contract.

"Do you want a drink?"

"No, sir."

A pause. "Kendra?"

"Yes, sir?"

He placed his hand over the contract, blocking her view of the print she wasn't reading anyway. "Eyes up."

Instantly she obeyed.

His deep blue eyes peered into hers and held her as captive as shackles. "The contract has everything in it that we agreed to over email. To confirm—no blood. No public nudity. No intercourse. Nothing in private until you tell me you're ready. The rest of your hard stops are also defined."

He lifted his hand and brushed her hair behind her ear, his gaze straying to track the action. "I like it down." His fingers threaded through the locks and followed the path until it reached the end just past her shoulders. "You'll wear it down when you're here unless I tell you otherwise."

His touch was so alluring. Once again, it was tender when she'd been so used to harsh. Was it fake, this softer side of him? This was what drew her to him, she knew that. This show of caring that pulled her in until she almost begged him to hold her. She swallowed, wishing she'd accepted that drink offer.

"I have one more demand," he said, her attention yanked back to the negotiations. "You'll call me Deklan. Not sir. Not master." He ran his finger over her lips, the pad rough over the softness, and her tongue immediately snuck out to chase it, seeking a taste of him. "Only Deklan. You'll remember you're with me. Not him."

She cringed, pulling back before she could stop the action. "No."

His command made her freeze, her pulse increasing as the memories threatened to invade and ruin the opportunity. She kept her focus on the table, her doubts resurfacing, making the print on the contract blur.

"Kendra," Deklan prodded, his voice calm. "I'm not him. Whoever he is. I'm not him. Remember that." He touched her chin and lifted it until her eyes met his. "Trust *me*. I will never abuse you. *Never*."

Never. God, how she wanted to believe that. She had to try. Releasing a long, slow breath, she forced herself to respond. "Yes, Deklan."

He smiled that crooked, half-lip curl of his, and she looked immediately for that hint of his dimple. The approval in his eyes was enough to make her almost return the gesture. "Look over the contract. Take as long as you need." He stood, and the bench felt big and empty without him next to her. "I'll be right over there. Signal me when you're ready or if you have questions."

"Yes, Deklan."

He frowned, his brows coming together in a dark line over his eyes. His hand fisted where it rested on the table. "You can talk. In fact, I want you to talk. Your words aren't something I ever want to control." He moved away then, his stride sure and long.

She stared at his back, too stunned to move.

She could talk.

A simple freedom. One she hadn't even realized she needed. It was so common for a Dom to demand silence from a sub or to exert control over when a sub could talk that Kendra hadn't even thought about having that option. But for him to give it to her…she didn't know how to process that.

Blinking rapidly, she looked down. The last of her doubts were removed by Deklan's command. She forced her shaking hands to pick up the papers before she realized that wasn't going to work and set them back on the table so she could read them.

The music faded into the background as she read every line and processed every word. She'd made mistakes in her past, and she wouldn't repeat them. Eric hadn't given her a choice or asked what she wanted. And he would never have considered agreeing to a contract or negotiating terms. He was an abuser, not a Dom.

She got that now.

And Deklan was showing her what a real Dom could be like. The kind of Dom she wanted. The kind she was slowly coming to admit she needed to keep herself sane.

Deklan stood about twenty feet away from the private booth where Kendra sat reading through the contract. He leaned against a support beam, his arms crossed over his chest, giving her space but keeping her close. Even though it wasn't official until she signed the contract, Deklan already thought of Kendra as his.

Her brow wrinkled in concentration at certain points as she'd tilt closer to the pages before smoothing out again as she leaned back. The edge of her lip slipped in and out between her teeth in an absent way he'd bet she wasn't even aware of.

Jake stepped up and leaned against the other side of the pole. "Cali's worried about her."

She wasn't the only one. Deklan doubted Kendra knew how many people were worried about her. "I won't harm her."

"I never thought you would."

"Yeah? You're one of the few."

Jake grunted. "I'm sure Seth's already raked you over the coals, so there's no need for me to do it."

Deklan's attention returned to Kendra as she leaned back against the booth and picked up the pen. She flicked the object back and forth between her fingers and stared down at the contract. Anticipation tightened his chest; he pushed away from the beam. This was it. She'd either sign or decline.

He explained away the urgency that pushed at him as his instincts telling him she needed help. That's why he was doing this. Right? *Christ.* Since when did he doubt himself? Yet the relief that hit when she leaned over and signed her name to the bottom of the contract was equal to any he'd felt walking safely out of a mission.

"Cali doesn't need to know about this," Deklan said to Jake.

"She's going to find out."

"Maybe," he conceded. "But it's Kendra's place to tell her. Not yours."

Jake ran a hand over the back of his neck before he nodded.

"You purposely making my life hell?" But there was a smirk on his face when Deklan turned to look at him.

"No more than usual," he answered back, grateful that the other man understood.

Deklan shot Jake a tight grin then moved toward his sub, eager to get the night started. She looked up, her gaze holding on him, and everything else faded into the background with each step he took closer to her.

His sub.

ELEVEN

Kendra vibrated with the tension that held her stiff as another moan and whimper wrapped around her, taunting her with its seductive lure. Or was it a warning? Her fingers ached in the tight grip she held before her, but she couldn't loosen the hold. She stared at the ground, unable to make herself look up. Not at the room or the man or whatever piece of equipment was waiting for her.

Deklan came up behind her, pressing his body to hers until his entire length heated and shielded her. "It's okay, Kendra." His breath ruffled close to her ear as he skimmed his hands up her bare arms. "You're safe with me. Remember that."

She shivered, but it wasn't from fear or cold. Deklan had led her straight to the Dungeon without any preamble. She was grateful for that. Her nerve might not have lasted if he'd prolonged the event after the paperwork was signed. And it was an event to her. A monumental one.

Thankfully, Deklan got that. But then, he seemed to get a lot about her. More than anyone else ever had. Squeezing her eyes shut, she swallowed down the hope that rested in her chest. This was an experiment—a test. That's all.

Forcing her eyes open, she took a deep breath and inhaled the unique musky, pungent Dungeon scent of sex, sweat and leather. Only this one had the slight underlining hint of lemon that she remembered from last time. She turned her head toward him and inhaled again, catching that faint hint of sandalwood that was him. The tightness drained from her shoulders, her body sinking into his as if his scent was a magical muscle relaxer.

"Safe word."

"Lilac," she answered automatically, her mind sinking incrementally into the low, floaty mentality that made everything else go away.

"Desires?"

She frowned, confused by his question. "Sorry?"

He nudged her hair aside to trail light kisses down the length of her neck. "Anything you'd specifically like for this Scene?"

Stunned, she couldn't answer. Again he'd hit her with the unexpected, giving her a freedom she didn't know what to do with. She looked up and froze at the sight before her. They were standing in front of a huge mirror that went from the floor to at least twelve feet high and ran down three-quarters of the wall, clearly reflecting everything that was happening behind them.

But the only thing she could focus on was them.

He was all muscle and girth behind her, his hard body providing a wall that supported her thinner frame. Their black clothing seemed to blend together, her pale skin and blond hair standing out in striking contrast while his olive skin-tone and dark hair made him appear even more intimidating. He could crush her if he wanted, yet his hold on her was gentle. Almost caring.

His lips continued their soft exploration against her skin, her blood heating under the distraction. It was incredibly erotic to see his tongue dart out to lick her skin at the same time that she felt the warm moisture brush the sensitive tissue.

She reached back to grab his thighs, her knees going weak. It seemed like she was seeking proof that the image before her was actually them—her. Her firm grip on the smooth leather over hard, corded muscles grounded her only a little.

In the next instant he nipped her, a sharp, hard bite at the juncture of her shoulder. Her muscles tensed and she moaned into the pain so unexpected but so welcomed. Her eyelids drooped, but she wouldn't let them close. She absolutely couldn't take her eyes off their reflection.

"Answer me, Kendra," he demanded before he bit down again, catching just the barest amount of skin in a series of small, trailing nips. The pain was acute, intense and quick to fade.

"No," she finally managed after scrambling to remember the question. Her voice was low and full of gravel. "No desires." She tilted her head, giving him more access to her neck. The persistent nibbles aroused her and made her hunger for more. The unspoken implication of her answer was that she trusted him. But then there was the safety of the contract too.

"I have plans for you," he murmured as his hands smoothed under her tank to stroke her abdomen. "Did you wear your nipple charms?"

She shook her head. "No. Just the hoops." His palms were warm and coarse against her belly and she arched into the touch, seeking the warmth. It felt so good, those caresses that were getting firmer, rougher, sensitizing her flesh with each broad pass.

"Next time, you'll wear the suns for me." He moved his hands up her sides, and she lifted her arms without being asked. Her top was pulled over her head and discarded in one swift move. She let her head fall back to rest on his shoulder, her hands returning to grip his strong leather-clad thighs. The desire built within her and she eased her hands up to grab his firm ass.

He looked up, meeting her gaze in the mirror. His eyes were dark with lust, his features appearing soft and flushed, much like hers. Together they watched him move his hands over her stomach until they cupped the underside of her breast, lifting and squeezing the mounds without touching her hard, aching nipples.

"These bras are the sexiest thing on you," he murmured. She was so focused on what he was doing that his compliment barely registered. His butt flexed under her hands, and she swayed her hips just enough to feel the outline of his hardening cock against her ass. In return, he slipped a finger under the top edge of the black shelf-bra to run it over her breast, teasing without satisfying.

The garment was a compromise—access without nudity. The silver nipple rings flashed in the light like they were signaling for attention. But he didn't comply, which only made her nipples harder.

"Who do you see?"

Startled by his question, she gave him the obvious answer. "Us."

"Who am I?"

A soft smile formed on her lips. "Deklan," she breathed. "My Dom."

Without warning he grabbed both nipples in his fingers to pinch and pull on the tips, sending sudden jolts of intense pain radiating from her breast. She cried out, her knees bending and hands clenching as she winced against the surprise of the attack.

"Yes," she panted, her pussy contracting at the force of the need that pulsed through her. "More."

"This is what you ache for?" His question was more of a challenge that he backed by looping his pinkies through the nipple rings and tugging on them until the nubs were stretched tight.

She arched her back, following the pain even while she begged, "Yes. Please." This was only the start of what she ached for. But at the same time it was so much more than she expected. The contact with him, the touches and closeness—just like last time. He wasn't detached and distant from this Scene, making her experience it. Instead he was right here with her, in the Scene.

He let go of the rings and stepped back, his hands on her hips to steady her. He studied her in the mirror, her chest rising and falling in large, swelling breaths. "Skirt and shoes off. Then I want you on the table, on your back."

She licked her lips, needing the moisture. "Yes, Deklan."

The flash of approval that crossed his face warmed her to her toes. She wanted to please him as much as she wanted him to please her. With a small nod, he moved away to a metal cart along the wall next to the table. He lifted the cloth from the top, his broad back blocking her view of what she assumed were the toys he'd selected for the Scene.

It was only then that the rest of the sounds of the Dungeon penetrated her consciousness. The cries and wails, coupled with the smacks and slaps, reminded her exactly where she was and why. Motivating herself, she removed her skirt and heels then picked them up with her top and set them in a neat pile by the mirror, even though Deklan hadn't said to do that. Old habits were still ingrained within her.

She avoided looking at her reflection as she turned toward the table. Somehow, seeing herself undressed and alone would have left her too exposed. The table Deklan had indicated could best be described as a modified massage table. It was about waist high, padded vinyl, only it was half the normal length. She'd never seen anything quite like it, but its design elements were pretty obvious.

Stepping up, she sat on the edge and lay back like Deklan had instructed. It was only natural that she spread her arms out on the two pieces that extended horizontal from the sides. The table wasn't long enough for her legs, but she easily found and rested her heels in the cups that were added to the table legs so her legs were bent and spread, exposing her lower half.

Kendra stared at the ceiling, taking long slow breaths to control the rising panic that constricted her chest and threatened to take the moment away from her. She concentrated on the little things, like the material that was cool and sticky against her back, the exposed black beams overhead, the sharp edge of the table where it hit the back of her calves.

Anything to keep her thoughts from the open, vulnerable position she'd willingly placed herself in.

Heat flushed down her in a wave of prickling insecurity that had her breath hitching, her pulse increasing. Her hands fisted, and the stab of her nails in her palms gave her another focus. She squeezed her fingers tighter, her nails digging into her flesh, until her fingertips hurt from the force and she could ground herself in that slow throb of centered pain.

Sinking into the self-inflicted pain, her muscles contracted, tensing her entire body from her arms to her abdomen to her legs. She clenched her teeth and simply felt the strength it took to maintain the strain.

"Kendra."

Her head jerked toward Deklan's voice, her eyes wide as she

was startled from her internal struggle. He was at her side, his large presence instantly soothing. He smoothed his hand down her arm and her muscles relaxed, her control gone.

"Who am I?" he asked her, pulling her away from the gulf that threatened to swallow her. "Say my name."

"Deklan," she answered, her voice hushed and weak from anxiety.

"Again."

She cleared her throat, gaining confidence in the small action as if she was clearing away the residual apprehension that lingered. "Deklan."

"Remember that," he ordered, all firm Dominant now. But he wasn't rough. There was no censure or blatant meanness in his voice or on his face. And she searched it hard, hunting for the warning sign—the sneer or the dropped brows or the narrowed eyes—only to find none.

At his urging, she let him uncurl her fingers, the joints aching from the prolonged stress of her hold. He rubbed her palm where her nails had dented her skin, and she waited for his reprimand. His lips thinned briefly, but that was it.

He grabbed the bands attached to the arm board. "I'm going to strap you down now," he explained as he tightened the buckle, pulling it snug to hold her wrist firm before he did another strap around her upper arm next to her torso. He moved around the table, adding restraints to her other arm, a thick one across her lower ribcage just under her breasts, and around each ankle.

With each strap that was cinched against her skin she struggled against the dual rise of excitement and fear. But he kept touching her, the heat from his hands giving her purchase as he warned her about each belt before he put it on.

When he finished with the last restraint, Kendra took a moment to just feel the restriction. Instinctively, she tested them and found she had little room to wiggle or struggle. She closed her eyes and dug through the series of emotions that rolled within her until she centered on the most prominent one.

Contentment.

How?

It wasn't rational, but it was there and growing stronger with each second that she recognized and accepted it for what it was. A foreign sense of quiet surrounded her as she let herself settle into the stillness.

There was no fear here. No worries or anxieties. Just a peacefulness she'd almost forgotten existed.

"That's it," Deklan said, his hands rubbing up her legs. "Trust me. I'll take care of you. I promise."

She clung to that. "Yes, Deklan."

Kendra opened her eyes and lifted her head, searching for him. He stood between her legs, a hand braced on each of her knees. Maintaining eye contact, he dipped and exhaled, forcing his hot breath over the thin strip of fabric covering her pussy. It felt so good. Yet another tease, and she pushed against the restraints, trying to get closer.

He grinned at her as he straightened, a hint of mischief lighting his eyes. "We're almost ready. Just a few more things." He bent down and picked up a spreader bar, which he placed between her legs, the large cuffs attached right above her knees. The bar was adjustable; he extended it until the stretch pulled on her inner thigh and hip muscles.

Finished, he gave her pussy a parting caress with the barest brush of his fingers before he stepped to the side. She bit her lip against the whimper that almost escaped.

Then she was distracted from everything as the table started to lift. The low grind and whirl of a motor came from the mechanism that tilted her torso up until the table was just past a forty-five-degree angle. The bindings dug into her skin, holding her in place, and her quads adjusted to the added strain in their bent position as more of her weight pressed down on them.

"What is this?" she questioned, looking to Deklan. She'd never seen or experienced anything like this table before.

Deklan chuckled, a deep sound that rose from his chest. "It's one of Jake's creations." He grabbed her chin and turned her head until she was forced to stare straight ahead. The visual stole her breath.

It was her—spread, bound and open—at Deklan's mercy. Her cheeks were flushed, her red lips parted as she gaped at her reflection. His gaze traveled over her body, followed by his fingertips as they trailed down her chest to the edge of her thong, leaving a line of goose bumps in their wake.

"Beautiful," he murmured, his face reflecting the truth of his word.

She stared, transfixed, as he threaded a long, silver chain through the hoops on her nipples before connecting the ends of the chain and letting the links drape over her abdomen. Her breath was coming faster now, the slow building anticipation working to excite her, making her forget the doubts.

He grabbed a small clip off the edge of his shirt sleeve and efficiently pulled her hair back from her temple to clasp the strands away from her face.

"I want you to watch it all," he told her. "To remind you where you are. Who you're with." He turned and met her eyes in the mirror. "Who do you see?"

"You," she breathed. "Deklan." And he was magnificent, but she wanted to see more. She asked something she'd have never dared to do with Eric. "Will you remove your shirt?" She wanted to see his chest and watch his muscles move as he worked.

He snapped his head around to stare directly at her face. She followed the move, searching his eyes for a reaction. Slowly he nodded and gave her that half-grin, his dimple flashing to melt her more. "For you, yes."

Pleasure shuddered through her when the simple request was granted. Right then she itched to touch that little dent just visible in his cheek. She wanted to feel the beard stubble under her fingertips or better, against her tongue.

Reaching behind his neck, he pulled his T-shirt over his head, fisting it in his hand. Her heart beat faster as she scanned every inch of bared, smooth flesh. He was as strong as he appeared, each muscle in his chest and abdomen etched and defined to a toned perfection. But there were imperfections too. Hints of his past that made her ache to touch him.

A long, jagged scar ran from his right pectoral down his side. Another puckered scar stretched just above the low line of his pants, stopping almost exactly below his belly button, the actual end hidden within the line of hair that disappeared into his waistband.

There were other smaller nicks spread across his torso too. Little marks that made him somehow seem both threatening and vulnerable. Her appraisal stopped on the large tribal sun tattoo decorating his pectoral muscle right over his heart, the long rays cutting out in a jagged angle like the sharp edges of a throwing star. It was a distinctive mark, one that intrigued her more than it should.

"You done?" he asked, the question holding a hint of amusement, not scorn.

Unbelievably, she found herself smiling. "Yes, Deklan. I'm done." When was the last time she smiled during a Scene? *Never* was the answer that came to her.

He tossed his shirt into the corner, picked up something from his table of supplies just out of her line of sight then moved between her legs. The flogger landed on her inner thigh with no preamble or warning. One quick flick of his wrists and the leather strands smacked against her flesh, leaving the desired sting and needles behind. The spreader bar between her knees stopped her automatic response to shield herself, even though she wanted the pain.

Deklan didn't give her a chance to respond. He hit her other thigh almost immediately then continued in a brutal pace, working his way up and down her inner thighs. The rapid strikes cut sharp streaks of fire that spread and merged until the insides of her legs were engulfed by the fresh burn.

Kendra reveled in it. Her eyelids grew heavy, but she kept them open, mesmerized by the man before her. He was all focus, his concentration completely on his task. His muscles flexed and bunched as he wielded the flogger with a controlled precision that made her sigh.

As if sensing her shift, he reached with his free hand to grab the chain he'd threaded through her nipple rings. The hard tug made her wince as the nubs were stretched tight.

"Yes," she cried. The centered jabs of pain were so good, the sensation flowing down her breasts to heat her chest.

She felt alive. Her body was awake, responding to just this. Just now.

The leather tails of the flogger struck the tops of her feet, making the pain surge through her entire legs, the heat trail racing up to the juncture of her thighs. To her pussy. Her vaginal muscles clenched, seeking more.

Her tiny thong didn't cover much, but it still shielded her from full exposure. Only now, she didn't want it blocking anything.

"Take it off," she begged. "My thong. I want it gone."

He dropped the chain to rip the flimsy material from her hips in what seemed like one continuous motion. The air brushed over her pussy, teasing in its own light way that had her twisting what little she could in search for something stronger.

Deklan answered her unspoken request with two sharp slaps of the flogger directly to her most sensitive flesh. She cried out and gritted her teeth against the intense fiery pain that covered her crotch from top to bottom.

He paused for a moment, and Kendra's breath hissed between her teeth as she absorbed the ache that radiated through her lower body.

"More, please," she found herself begging when he didn't start again. "Don't stop."

"Patience, Kendra," Deklan answered, smoothing a finger through the heated lips of her pussy. He stopped to circle her opening before pushing against her clit with a slow, continuous pressure that made her moan.

He swirled the ends of the flogger over her sensitized skin, the leather nipping and stroking at the same time. They hit her calves, her legs then finally her pussy. The little stings like tiny love bites that spit back pain. God, how she loved it.

Deklan stepped away and came back to kneel between her legs. She panted, fascinated by the reflection before her. His head blocked the view of her lower half and his back gleamed under the lights, the shimmer of sweat making his muscles appear even more distinct. It was only when she looked at her position that she noticed the pinch on her arms and ribs from the straps holding her up, or the discomfort that was growing in her thighs and hips from the crouched, spread position.

Yet it was so good, each little ache welcomed.

Behind them, the Dungeon carried on and she briefly skimmed over the other deviant acts being carried out, but none of them registered. She could see a few people watching their Scene and it didn't bother her because when she looked down she saw him. Deklan.

He glanced at her then, his blue eyes dark and filled with the power he got from controlling her. The cool touch of plastic at her opening was her first warning of his plans before he slid the long, hard object into her channel. The dildo went easily into her wet passage and he pressed it in and out several times before bending closer to slide his tongue over her aching clit.

She gasped and jolted at the slick warmth. It was amazing and caused her orgasm to build deep within her core. The pleasure mingled and blended with the soreness that remained from the flogger.

"Do you want more?" His low question was spoken directly against her pussy, each movement of his lips blending with the light vibration from his voice.

"Yes…please." Her answer came out as more of a plea than a flat response. She didn't care.

He chuckled. "Perfect." He flicked her clit with his tongue one more time before moving back, withdrawing the dildo as he did so. He pressed the object against her anus, rubbing in circles against the small opening. "Okay?"

A small whimper escaped as she tried unsuccessfully to push down on the taunting object. He continued to circle, applying enough force to tease but not enter. The pressure felt so wrong yet good. She was already envisioning the burn that would come with the entry.

"Yes," she panted, her breaths now fast and choppy.

She bore down, experience helping her once again, and the object slipped past her tighter outer muscles to enter her anus. She gulped against the initial burn that came with the stretching of the muscles and squirmed what little she could on the vinyl, slippery from her sweat. Deklan braced his other hand on her lower abdomen, ceasing her movements.

"Oh God," she moaned, twisting her head to the side as he

slowly pressed the object into her. It seemed so much bigger in her ass than it had in her vagina. He eased it out then back in, the little increments getting easier as her muscles slowly relaxed. The burn was intense but it was underscored by the odd pleasure that came with the sensitive tissues being stroked in such an unaccustomed way.

The last larger ring on the object popped inside her then Deklan stopped pushing. "There. It's in." He twisted it, the sensation against her tender inner walls making her suck in a sharp breath against the blended fire and bliss. "Still good?"

She nodded and managed a weak, "Yes."

"Still watching?"

Her gaze shot back to meet his, a devious gleam shining in his eyes. He grabbed the chain and pulled it down, stretching her nipples and setting them back in flames. She couldn't tear her eyes away from his. She was transfixed.

He gave her that half-smile. "Remember, no coming."

"Yes, Deklan."

She should have known there was a reason for the warning. The sudden hum buzzed through the air at the same time the vibration shot through her ass and down her nipples. Kendra flinched, jerked and cursed at the shock of sensation. Her butt muscles clenched around the vibrator in protest even as she squirmed into the rising pleasure. The tremors chased up the chain that hugged each side of her pussy until her sore nipples tingled in a teasing torture. Deklan still blocked her view so she could only assume that he'd looped the chain around the end of the vibrator.

She bit her lip and rode the bliss that eased into her until she thought of nothing but the feeling. Deklan slapped her lower butt cheeks, the slice of pain dancing with the pleasure. He gave one more smack directly to her oversensitive pussy and she gulped down the groan that rose from her chest.

Giving her no time to regroup, Deklan grabbed the flogger and started on her thighs once again. He moved down her legs quickly, each strike reawakening the pain receptors that had just started to quiet. The hard tips clipped her flesh, leaving their sharp bites of stinging fire over the larger spreading warmth.

It was so right even when she knew it was so wrong. She was so bad to want this. It was proof that she was a dirty little whore, just like Eric said. How could she possibly want the pain after all that he had done to her?

Then she was back there, Eric looming over her, flaying the whip against her back while she begged him to stop and her body yearned for more. The flash of fear blindsided her. Her muscles tensed and she struggled against the bindings, gulping for air. What was she doing? She shouldn't want this. How could she want this? No. This wasn't right.

"Kendra. Don't."

Don't what? Don't run? Don't be a slut? Don't shame yourself like this? Too late. She was clammy and hot, feverish and cold. And she couldn't breathe. Oh God, she needed air. She gasped, trying desperately to suck air into her lungs but couldn't. *No. No. No.*

"Kendra. Open your eyes." The sharp command broke through the fog and rambling words in her mind. "Now. Open your eyes and tell me what you see."

No. No. No. She couldn't look. Didn't want to see.

Warm hands cupped her face and she tried to twist away from the touch, but they held her firm. A choked sob left her mouth then warm lips were there, brushing hers with soft, tender touches that broke through her barrier with their gentleness. She stilled, a shallow breath hitching into her chest.

This was different. Affectionate. Kind.

The lips returned, warm and moist, to brush over her bottom lip before it was nibbled on. Again, the action was so soft, so *not* Eric, that it stirred a longing deep within her. Roughened pads traced her cheekbones, abrading her skin with light caresses as another nibble on her lip was immediately soothed by the stroke of a tongue.

"Who do you see, Kendra?" His voice was low and filled with a grated command. But there was no anger. No force. "Tell me who you see."

The strokes on her cheeks continued, a repeated back and forth pattern that was calming in its gentleness. She was so hot, her flesh flushed with heat, but she shivered when a chill raced over her skin. Gasping, she sucked in a deep breath, catching a full whiff of sandalwood.

Not Eric.

Her eyes flew open to stare at the blue-eyed, dark-haired man treating her with such kindness. No, he was definitely not Eric.

TWELVE

"Deklan."

The throaty answer almost knocked the wind out of him. He was so relieved to hear his name and see the clarity in her eyes. He'd thought he'd lost her again—knew he almost had. His mind raced through the last few minutes, trying to identify the trigger that had pulled her away, but he couldn't nail it.

"That's right," he confirmed, his thumbs still brushing her cheeks. "It's Deklan. Not him. You're safe."

Her pupils were large and dilated from her panic, but her chest dipped and rose at a more normal rate with each slow breath that she took. Again, he wanted to kill the man who'd put this fear in her.

"Yes," she whispered. Her attention shot to his mouth and she slowly moistened her lips, as if she was remembering the kiss.

Invitations weren't needed, but he accepted hers. Something he never did. He didn't question the instinct had made him kiss her to get her back and he didn't regret it either. Her lips were soft and slightly chapped from where she'd chewed on them, giving them a roughened texture that reminded him why she'd been biting them in the first place. She looked so fucking hot strapped to the table, writhing in bliss and pain.

Trusting him.

He kissed her harder this time, pushing his tongue into her mouth to tangle with hers. She responded, meeting his aggression with a rising one of her own. She had a fight within her that pulled at him. Her mouth was hot and she tasted bitter like fear and sweet like passion. He gripped her face, tilting her head for a better angle to thrust his tongue in farther. His dick was already rock hard and aching in his pants, but it pulsed even more with the searing fire stoked from her kiss.

Deklan trailed his hand down her chest to pinch and twist one of her nipples, causing her to moan into his mouth. He eased back and she tried to follow him, lifting until she was forced to stop. Her head dropped back to the table, and he released the nipple to run his fingers over her chest and circle the other one. She lifted her eyelids to reveal blue eyes dark with desire and passion.

"Who am I?"

"Deklan." To his relief, there was no hesitation or fear in her throaty answer.

"We're still green?" He had to be sure.

She squirmed on the table, lifting what little she could of her chest toward his circling finger. "Yes."

Thank you, he silently answered, unable to speak the words aloud. He rewarded her by giving what she begged for. He gripped the nipple in a punishing hold that had her wincing against the ache. He scanned her body, the sight filling him. She truly was stunning when she gave in to the pain. He was amazed at the way she responded so quickly to his touch. Even more at the way he responded to her.

She was like no other. Her submission meant so much more,

knowing that this wasn't easy for her and that she was coming out of a situation that had destroyed her trust. For her to give it to him was humbling. It was what he'd wanted, but now that he had it, the responsibility was both daunting and heady. He wouldn't let her down.

Stepping away, he picked up the flogger and brought it down on her stomach. Not hard, just enough to sensitize her skin, waking her nerve endings so she was aware of every part of her body. He moved quickly now, over her abdomen, up her chest, now her arms until her skin was pink and flushed. She whimpered, a hoarse blend of need and angst that went straight to his groin. The adrenaline was running high in his system and he recognized it for what it was, letting the buzz take him.

Sweat eased down his back and over his brow and he wiped it away with the back of his hand. He swallowed back a groan and adjusted himself, accepting the dawning truth. For the first time in years, he ached to fuck a client.

But he couldn't.

He tossed the flogger aside, needing to touch her, to feel her under his hands, her every response sinking into him. Moving between her legs, he ran the blunt tips of his nails down her breasts, over her ribs and across her firm, muscled abdomen to the top of her pubic bone. Her hips bucked and she gave a silent cry against the harsh scratching over her sensitive skin.

"Yes," she whimpered, a deep pool of mixed misery and ecstasy in her voice. She looked to him, eyes blazing with emotion, and said one word. "More."

Jesus Christ. She was so fucking perfect.

He gave into his base need and dropped to his knees to suck her clit into his mouth. She let loose with a long, high wail and thrust her hips up what little she could. He pushed on the vibrator still in her ass and flicked her hard, swollen nub with his tongue. She tasted like lust and smelled of musk and arousal. It was pure heaven, and he had to reach down to adjust himself once again before his zipper left a permanent impression on his shaft.

"Please, Deklan."

Holy fuck. Her desperate plea shot straight to his throbbing dick. He was hard enough to pound nails and for once that sense of satisfaction he got from withholding his release was replaced by impatience and a flaming need to come.

He leaned back with a growl and smacked her ass right over the vibrator, knowing the area would be good and tender now. The stimulation would drive her crazy, but she wouldn't come from that alone. Teasing her more, he eased the vibrator out of her anus, stroking it over the ring of nerves that guarded the opening before plunging it back into its full depth.

Her whimpers were like sweet music that drove him higher. The ability to control someone's desires to this extent, to have the person submit to him completely and to allow him to see to those needs was what gave Deklan the rush. Knowing he was the one who could help.

He spanked her again, loving the sting that resounded in his palm each time his flesh met hers. She was so close. Fuck, *he* was close. Control was his refrain yet with her he was barely hanging on to it.

He looked up the length of her and let out a low groan. Her hair was damp with sweat, her lips full and red from his kiss. They blended with her cheeks and skin, which were flushed a deep pink. Her eyes were dark with need and leveled directly at him under heavy come-fuck-me lids.

"Deklan," she breathed.

Gone. That's the word that flashed in his mind. He was gone. "Come, Kendra."

He plunged three fingers deep into her vagina and bit down

on her clit while giving a hard tug on the nipple chain. She screamed, a shallow cry that was filled with the dark edge of pleasure that came with the rush of pain. Her eyes squeezed tight and her pelvis worked in small thrusts that matched the clenching of her vaginal muscles. Then her whole body tensed in a spasm that reached clear to her curled toes and fingers.

Drill routines, gun assembly, fucking sandpits full of fleas— he dragged his thoughts through every damn one to keep from coming in his pants like a goddamn sixteen-year-old. Yet he kept himself centered on Kendra. He sucked on her clit and worked his fingers in her until the crest ended and she started to slide back down, her muscles unclenching in a slow wave of satisfaction.

Releasing her, he turned off the vibrator and eased it from her body, going slow to lessen the ache. He stood, making a harsh swipe at the sweat that stung his eyes. Taking measured breaths through his nose, he savored the moment, simply enjoying the view. Kendra's eyes were closed, her head resting limp to the side, her chest heaving in gulps of air that pushed her ruby nipples high as she continued to float in the afterbliss of the orgasm.

Before he thought about his actions, Deklan undid the spreader bar at her knees and fell forward, grabbing her chin to plunder her mouth in a hot, desperate kiss. The groan that filled their joined mouths came from deep in his chest. He wasn't soft or gentle. Now he was all raw need as he took over her mouth, tongue-fucking her in time with his hips as he ground his erection against her open, sensitive sex. The leather of his pants slid and rubbed over her primed and ready clit, the moisture from her orgasm easing the action.

Her nipples brushed his chest, two hard points of overstimulated nerves that he knew hurt. Yet she reveled in it. Arched into him while opening her mouth to accept all he gave her.

"Who am I?" he growled against her lips.

She opened her eyes and exhaled, "Deklan."

Her second orgasm shot through her with a suddenness that shocked them both. She tensed and moaned into his mouth and he pulled back so he could hear it. See her. Her eyes were clenched tight, her chin thrust up, making the cords on her neck tighten in strain. The low, keening sound that came from her open mouth was as beautiful as her expression.

She crashed just as quickly, every muscle seeming to go lax once the euphoria passed. She sagged into the table, her breath coming in short pants that passed over his jaw in little wisps of thanks.

His sweat dripped onto her chest and his breath came in the same accelerated pace that matched hers. His pulse raced and he clenched the edge of the table, searching for direction. The throb in his dick was almost unbearable, yet he couldn't come. Wouldn't come.

The Scene was for Kendra, and she didn't need that.

He shoved away, cursing himself for his loss of control. God, what had happened? He thrust his hands through his damp hair and ground his teeth against the desire that burned within him. He was seconds away from ignoring the contract and going against everything he believed in just to plunge himself deep within her. What the fuck?

Two steps, and he was out of her line of sight. Keeping his back to the mirror, he slammed his hand down his pants, squeezing the shit out of the base of his cock. A slick string of pre-come clung to his wrist, taunting him with the soon-to-be-glue that would rip out every hair it dried to when he was finally able to remove his fucking pants.

It was no better than he deserved.

The air hissed through his teeth, the long draw of breath chasing back his pending failure. Another breath and he released his vise grip on his betraying prick, confident that he was back in control.

He had to be.

Turning around, he was back in his Dom role. He lowered the table until Kendra was lying flat and started to undo the straps that held her arms.

Fortunately for him she was still pretty much out of it, floating in the aftermath and exhaustion that usually came after an intense Scene. Deklan diverted his focus from his own wants to his duty of caring for her. He gently massaged each arm after removing the straps, helping to speed up the blood circulation and ease the ache that would have set in from the unaccustomed position.

He took his time, enjoying the feel of her skin under his palms, admiring the outline of muscle that was so defined for a female. It was almost a selfish act, his care for her, because of the enjoyment he was receiving. He finished her arms and grabbed a towel to remove the moisture from her brow and neck. Small tendrils had curled once again at her temples and nape and he looped his finger through one, the softness teasing over his skin. She was starting to stir when he took off the waist belt and smoothed away the dampness that had gathered on her ribs under the tight binding.

He took extra care removing the chain from her nipple rings, keeping the touch to a minimum. Her nipples were a deep red and looked tender as hell. There was cream that would help them. He'd make sure she left with some.

Deklan was standing between her legs removing the ankle bindings when he looked up to see her watching him from under heavy, sultry lids.

She wet her lips, her voice hoarse and raw sounding. "You can come on me."

His chest constricted as his dick jumped at her offer. It was

a sucker-punch to his gut that spoke to every possessive dominant gene in him. The instant urge to come was right there,
teetering on the edge at her offer. *Fuck.* The curse was harsh
and feral-sounding in his mind. The visual of him standing
over her, his ejaculation over her stomach and breast marking
her as his, was almost too much to resist.

"No," he bit out, yanking his attention to the leg cuffs. His
fingers fumbled on the buckle before he finally got the first
one off and he moved to the other.

"Why?"

The simple question barely reached his ears over the noise
of the Dungeon, the sounds that were just coming back into
his consciousness and a solid reminder of why he couldn't.
Not here.

Not with her.

He straightened to lean over her, bracing his arms on the
table until his nose was just inches from hers. He stared into
eyes that had gone wide and told her the truth. "Because you
deserve better."

Her shallow inhale was her only response as her eyes
searched his—hunting for the lie, he was certain. He brushed
a soft kiss over her lips and finally she blinked, a flutter of
lashes that foretold the emotions churning and building behind her bright blue eyes.

He backed off to retrieve the blanket from the chair he'd
positioned in the corner earlier that day. "Come on," he said,
easing an arm around her to help her up. "The Scene's over."

She let him move her, scooting her back on the table so
she could sit as he wrapped the blanket around her shoulders.
She was starting to shake, the endorphin and adrenaline crash
beginning to hit her.

Before she could object, he scooped her off the table and
carried her to the chair, positioning her across his lap so she

was cradled against his chest, facing the wall. She started to struggle, pushing away, but he held firm.

"No, Kendra," he said into her hair as he maneuvered her head to rest on his shoulder. "Just relax. I got you. It's okay. It's safe."

Incrementally she did, listening to him even now.

He picked up the water bottle once he was certain she wasn't going to bolt and offered it to her. "Here, take a drink."

This time she didn't resist, just opened her mouth and let him hold it for her, accepting the water as he poured some into her mouth.

She curled into him then, almost as if that last little act of submission was the one that finally broke her. He'd expected this, had planned for it even with the chair, blanket and water. But it still ripped at his heart when the tears came.

They were soft, quiet sobs that vibrated through her back and puffed against his skin. He wanted more than anything to take her pain away. Simply annihilate the internal torment that was causing her so much grief.

He understood that for many it was the need to quiet that inner pain that inflamed the craving for the external pain. It was cleansing for some, a focus for others and still something altogether different for another.

There was no one reason why anyone was called into needing pain or submission or dominance or any of the fetishes The Den catered to. It was the simple acceptance that they existed and needed a safe outlet that had been one of the driving forces behind opening the club in the first place. Helping others get what they need without shame or judgment.

Yet even with all his experience, understanding and acceptance, the whisper of doubt hovered on his conscience. He wasn't one hundred percent certain if this was truly helping Kendra or only harming her more.

THIRTEEN

Kendra hid in the cocoon of the blanket, surrounded by Deklan's strength, and let the tears fall. She shivered, the chills racing under her skin, leaving tingling pinpricks of sensation that seemed to shimmer without sinking deep.

She was still floating, slowly coming out of her submissive head space. It was quiet there. No worries or stress. No recriminations or shame. Just the strong arms of her Dom… yeah, her Dom keeping her safe. Deklan might not want her to call him Master or Sir, but after that Scene, there was little question that he was her Dom.

How in the hell had she let that happen? He was supposed to be just a Dom, not *her* Dom.

Kendra knew enough to go with the tears. To let them fall and release the ache that had burdened her soul for so long. She'd given her trust to Deklan and he hadn't abused it.

No, he'd cherished it.

Even after her panic attack he'd pulled her back, calmed her down and then gave her exactly what she'd wanted. The incredible mixture of pain and pleasure had been beyond anything she'd imagined.

Eric had been mostly about the pain, with her pleasure being an afterthought. Deklan had been the other way around, just like last time. It was clear that her enjoyment was his first priority. It was both a comforting and unsettling realization.

She wasn't certain how long she sat like that, bundled in Deklan's arms, but eventually the tears stopped and the fog around her mind started to clear, bringing her into the moment. The consistent slap of a paddle worked into her consciousness and she smiled when she found she was automatically counting the number of hits. She was up to fourteen before she made herself stop.

She blinked then wiped her nose and face on the edge of the blanket, the scent of powdery laundry softener seeming completely out of place but decidedly normal. Without asking, the bottle of water was back at her lips and she took the offered drink almost on reflex. The liquid was cool and welcomed on her raw throat. She took another swallow before finally shaking her head to indicate she'd had enough.

"Doing better?" Deklan's voice was low and intimate and matched the light brush of his lips as they pressed a kiss to her temple.

She swallowed, blinked back the new tears. "Yeah." She cleared the roughness out of her voice before continuing. "Thank you," she said, staring straight ahead at the black wall. Deklan had kept his public promise but still managed to offer her some semblance of privacy.

"Are you telling me the truth, Kendra?" The light teasing that was blended with the question made her smile.

"Yes, Deklan," she said, emphasizing his name with a hint of sarcasm. "The Scene was good. More than I expected actually."

"How so?"

Maybe it was the lull of coming out of her sub space or the security she felt within his embrace, but she found herself answering openly without fear. "You gave me pleasure too."

He shifted to the side and tilted her chin up until she could see his face. His brows were drawn together, his eyes intent. "It hasn't been like that for you before?"

"No…well, maybe. But if it was, it's too far back for me to clearly remember."

"Then why?" He looked truly baffled. "What drew you to this lifestyle?"

She tried to turn away, uncomfortable with his questioning, but he gripped her chin, keeping her still. Angered, she scowled and pulled away, ducking her head back against his shoulder. Her brain suddenly caught up with her actions and she held her breath. *Damn it.* It was that exact defiance that had always gotten her in trouble with Eric.

Deklan only chuckled. Instead of punishing or reprimanding her, he removed the clip he'd put in her hair and gently combed his fingers through the strands, tugging lightly to get the tangles out.

There it was again. A simple act of kindness that reminded her he wasn't Eric. Not even close.

Exhaling, she relaxed once more. She debated for a moment on if she should respond when he didn't seem to be demanding an answer. Yet maybe that's what made her want to answer him.

"It was curiosity at first," she started, tucking her hands under her chin to draw the blanket closer. "Rebelliousness too. The first time I went to a club was with a group of college friends pumped up on liquid courage and all daring each other to see what it was about. Only I really liked what I saw.

Of course, I couldn't say anything, but I didn't forget it. Or how it had made me feel."

"And how was that?"

"Excited, turned-on, envious...of the submissives. I was watching a woman being flogged and then whipped by her Master and instead of horrified like some of my friends, all I could think was I wanted to be her." She remembered back to the first sight and the light bulb of recognition that had gone off within her. "To me, it was beautiful."

"When did that change?"

The warmth that had been creeping back within her at the good memories was suddenly frozen as her mind switched over to her recent past. "Eric," she whispered, the chills returning to race under her skin.

Deklan tightened his arms around her, hugging her to him. "Do you want to tell me what happened?"

Did she? Yes, no, maybe. Another tear slipped from her eye to run down her cheek and she let it fall, concentrating on the slow path it made down the side of her face. Before she could fully understand why, she found herself admitting weakly, "I don't know where to start."

He brushed her hair from her temple then tilted her chin up to kiss her softly before he spoke. "Start wherever you want. I'll listen." That was all he said, but his eyes communicated so much more. In their deep blue depths she saw compassion and understanding.

The impulse took her and she leaned in to kiss him, absorbing as much of his strength as she could take from his soft lips and tender touch. She pulled back and searched his face again. "You're not acting like much of a Dom right now," she said before she could think to halt her thoughts.

He flashed his half-grin, a short chuckle escaping with it. "And how's a Dom supposed to act?"

"You order me to talk and don't give me a choice or allow me to hide."

His eyes narrowed. "In a Scene, maybe, if it's right. But this isn't a Scene." His thumb caressed her jawline. "We're two people talking now. You share what you want."

She swallowed. "Would you force me to talk about this during a Scene?"

"Only if you wanted me to, but that kind of trust is built over time. And I haven't earned it." He sighed and pulled her close until his lips grazed her forehead in the gentlest of touches that made her heart ache in wonder and longing. "A Dom isn't any one stereotype. It's my job to give each sub what they need, but there's no single way to do that. The last thing *you* need is to be forced into doing anything. I don't work like that. Submission that is forced holds little attraction compared to submission that's given freely."

She curled into him, his words replaying in her mind. Submission given freely. The black wall before her melded until it became a screen flashing back the mistakes of her past, highlighting with 20/20 hindsight exactly how naïve she'd been. But then, she already knew that.

She thought of all the times her safe word had been ignored until she was told she had no safe word, that her Master knew when she'd reached her limit. Or the very first time Eric forced her to cancel her plans with her friends then punished her for questioning him. The slow evolution from mutual consent to abuse that she let happen.

"Can I ask you a question?"

Deklan's voice jerked her back to the present. She closed her eyes to block her mental slideshow and nodded.

"During our Scene, what triggered your panic attack?"

His hand was back, combing her hair, the strands threading through his fingers until they reached the end and fell back to ruffle against the side of her face or down her back. The lethargy of the action calmed her with its slow, repeated consistency.

She wanted to hide from the question and avoid the shame that came with it; however, that wouldn't help. So she dug her nails into her palm and forced the answer out. "I was enjoying it too much."

"What?" The confusion was evident in his voice.

She cleared her throat and took the second to get her words right. "You were whipping my legs and it hurt, but I was thinking about how good it felt. How much I loved it all. The vibrator, the chain, the flogging...I shouldn't like that. It's so wrong." She gasped out the end, her voice cracking on the last word.

"No!"

"What's wrong with me?" She begged for an answer, barely hearing his adamant denial.

"Kendra." His sharp commanding tone had her jerking back to look at him. His jaw was held tight, but his eyes fired a conviction at her. "There is *nothing* wrong with you. Or with what you want."

"But why do I want this? Why in the hell would I find pleasure in being beaten?"

"That's where you've got it wrong," he insisted. "There is no pleasure in being beaten. That's an act of violence. And I would never be violent toward you. No real Dom would. The pleasure comes in submitting and trusting. In finding release in the freedom you get from letting go. The pain only heightens the feelings, releases the endorphins and reaffirms the trust you've given away."

"But I like the pain."

"And there is nothing wrong with that. We all like different things. Some people hate chocolate or bacon. Can you believe that?"

She smiled at the look of complete disbelief on his face and swerve in conversation. "No," she answered around a small laugh. "I can't believe that."

"Do you think they're weird?"

She laughed again. "Yes."

"Do you think they care what you think?"

"No."

"And will your opinion of them make them suddenly start liking chocolate?"

"No."

"Exactly," he said with triumph. "So just because someone finds your enjoyment of pain to be weird doesn't mean it's something you can change. It's simply who you are. It's part of your make-up. And, Kendra..." He paused to lean in. "It's okay." He pulled back, a grin of pure conviction displaying his dimple and matching the belief in his eyes.

"Wow," she breathed as she tried to process his logic. "Just... wow."

As if to underscore his point, a loud wail pierced the room to echo above the other sounds as a submissive found release. The cry was edged with that heightened mix of pain and pleasure that only an ear trained to catch it could hear. Or one familiar with the sensations being experienced.

His dimple showed when he touched under her chin to close her gaping mouth. "It's not that hard to grasp when you think of it like that."

"No," she managed to agree. It felt like a leaden weight had been lifted from her chest. "I guess it's not."

"You are who you are. It's as simple as that." He tapped her on the nose, causing her to blink and pull back, shooting him a glare. "The hard part is accepting who you are.

But once you do, life becomes easier." With that, he slid her legs around until her feet landed on the smooth surface of the hardwood floor. "You ready to get changed?" He rubbed her arms through the blanket and planted a kiss just below her ear.

"Yeah," she agreed as she stood, his hands remaining on her hips until he was sure she was steady. She stepped away and went to pick up her clothing and shoes. To say she was reeling from the events of that night would be an understatement.

She was completely muddled on the inside, so many emotions and thoughts being processed after all that had happened and been said. But under it all was a dawning sense of clarity.

She straightened, stopping to stare into the mirror. Around her the world revolved just like it had when she'd entered the Dungeon. Acts of Dominance and submission played out all over the room, interspersed with sadism and masochism. There were those who enjoyed giving the pain, and matched with them were the ones who enjoyed receiving the pain. Those who needed to dominate and those who needed to submit.

She scanned from one Scene to the next and realized she saw nothing wrong. The sight of a submissive bent in half, hands bound to ankles, her ass bright red from her Master's paddling, was still beautiful to her.

Deklan stepped up behind her and followed her focus to the Scene displayed in the mirror. "You looked better than that," he murmured into her ear.

That made her smile. "You're just biased."

"True," he chuckled. "But I don't lie."

She leaned back, liking the feel of him holding her. Her clothes were bundled in a pile against her chest under the blanket and she paused a moment to just take him in. His short hair was still damp, his face rugged, hard and so uniquely handsome.

"Why didn't you come on me?"

He met her odd question with complete seriousness. "I told you, you deserve better than that."

Her brows drew together. "I don't get it."

He started a gentle massage on her shoulders, her muscles almost groaning under his kneading fingers. "From your perception, why do Masters usually do that?"

"It's a show of dominance and ownership. The Master marking his property."

"And how would that make you feel right now, in front of all these people?"

Her gaze shot to the people behind them and her stomach clenched into a hard knot as understanding dawned. *Oh my God. How had he known*? She looked back to him and whispered, "Used."

"That's why."

His blue eyes held hers, and she had to look away from the intensity before the tears started. He was getting to her, but not in a bad way. He was making her wish and hope for dreams she'd abandoned years ago.

"Thank you." The session was ending much the same as it had started, with the two of them standing before the mirror, him big and solid behind her. Supporting her. He was strong, full of muscle and strength that could easily harm her if he chose to.

And that was the key. If he chose to.

Yet another thing that distinguished him from Eric.

"You're bigger than he was," she said out of the blue, catching Deklan's attention. She smiled at his hesitant look, as if he wasn't sure how to respond. That he was okay showing that said a lot. "But I'm not afraid of you. I should be, but I'm not."

"Good," he said, refocusing on massaging her shoulders and upper arms. "I don't want you to ever be afraid of me."

Deklan was bigger than her ex in both size and build. Eric

had been just a touch taller than her, a fact he'd always resented. She'd never been allowed to wear heels with him because he didn't like being shorter than her.

Again with the hindsight, she could see Eric's insecurities that festered behind his over-confident front. The fine gloss of refined Harvard graduate with Daddy's money and family prestige was only a cover for the angry, cold man that was his true self. A man she'd foolishly thought she could help or change or…heal. But then, a person had to want to change, and Eric would never admit that he had problems let alone need to change.

No, he blamed all of the problems on Kendra.

Even with her counseling experience—maybe because of it—she'd believed she could make a difference and had subsequently created excuses for all of his failings. Hers too.

With more confidence than she'd had since fleeing Eric, Kendra stepped into her new commitment with an open mind and a lighter heart. This was okay. She was okay.

Or at least she was working on it. Eric couldn't scare her anymore. Damn him and his letter and his threats.

"I know our contract says once a week, but…" She had to pause and wet her lips, her arms tightening around her bundle of clothes to draw the blanket closer. "Can we meet again on Tuesday? I think…I think I'd like another session."

He turned her then so she was held in the circle of his arms, his eyes both warm and commanding. "I'll see you at nine."

FOURTEEN

A chilled wind smacked against Deklan's back, rushing around his neck in a failed attempt to force him back indoors. Not gonna happen. The air was so cold that morning that each exhale left puffs of clouds in front of his face. He'd take the cold any day over the sweltering, life-sucking heat of the desert.

Deklan braced his leg on the lower rung of the wood fence that bordered the condo complex and leaned forward, letting the motion stretch the back of his leg. The pull was good, reminding of times he would have killed to have the luxury of stretching his cramped muscles. His knee popped, and he grimaced at the bite of pain and the sharp reminder of how lucky he was to be out of active duty with only minimal injuries. He knew too many good soldiers who hadn't been so lucky.

He jogged in place for a moment, his muscles warming up, and swung his arms, searching for that tug across his shoulder blades and chest. Doing a few more stretches, he wondered how long he could drag out the tasks. It was hit or miss if he'd catch Kendra. But given the day, the odds were pretty good that she'd be out around this time. Even though she probably thought her schedule wasn't consistent.

A few moments later he spotted Kendra making her way through the condo parking lot toward the entrance of the path where he waited. The tightness across his shoulder blades that hadn't eased with his stretches now loosened as he appreciated her sleek form. The colder weather had forced her to put the warmer gear on, like he had. The blue spandex running pants hugged her legs, showing off their slim form and making them appear a mile long. The matching jacket zipped up the front and molded over her breasts and arms.

She smiled when she saw him, a short wave that matched the sway of her ponytail. Slowing as she reached him, she didn't question his presence. "Hi," she said before starting into her own pre-run stretches.

"Hey," he responded, working to keep his voice casual. She didn't need to know that he'd planned this meeting. "Just heading out?"

"Yeah." She leaned forward, and he caught the wince that she wasn't able to hide.

He sobered. "How you feeling today?" They'd had a pretty intense session two days ago and it appeared that Kendra was still tender from the caning she'd requested. He hadn't gone easy, having learned over the last three weeks that her pain tolerance was fairly high. A fact that pleased the sadist in him while oddly disturbing the man in him.

She shot him a tight smile. "Good. Just a little sore."

"Was it too rough last time?" Damn. He'd been careful. Had he missed one of her signs? Seeing her wince like that didn't bring the usual rush of pleasure that came with knowing he'd been the one to give a sub that lingering pain.

She made a quick glance around before straightening to pull an arm across her body to stretch her triceps and shoulder blades. "No. It was fine." She kept her eyes diverted, staring down the running path. "I'd have told you if it wasn't."

He stepped closer, forcing her to meet his eyes. "Would you, Kendra? Honestly?" He wanted to believe her. There was no way they could continue their sessions if he couldn't trust her to halt a Scene for any reason.

"Yes, Deklan. I would." She didn't back down. But how she addressed him took him back to the Dungeon, pleasing him in a way that shouldn't be appropriate outside of that space.

"Good." He turned to the fence and leaned on the rail and repeated his leg stretches, yanking his head out of his ass while he did it. He'd been tempted right then to cup her face and kiss her senseless, but he couldn't do that. She was only a contract sub, not someone he could kiss at will anywhere. Even if he wanted to. "Do you mind if I run with you?"

Her head snapped around at his question, her eyes boring into him, searching for something. He kept his attention on his task and pretended not to notice her hesitation. He hoped she'd say yes but would respect her answer if she said no.

When her consent finally came, it was low and quiet. "Sure."

They started off at a steady pace that was slower than Deklan usually ran, but he didn't mind. He matched her stride and let the rhythm of their shoes hitting the pavement beat out a tune that was solid and soothing. He inhaled, the cool air hitting his lungs with a punch, and let her lead, taking the paths and trail system that she wanted, oddly content for the moment to follow her lead.

They completed their run in silence, the quiet of the morning broken only by their measured breaths and the occasional other jogger. Based on the consistency and frequency of Kendra's run, he suspected she needed them just like he did. Running was like an addicting drug to him. His body and mind started to go through their own version of withdrawals when he didn't get his fix.

His jogs had become a solitary event since he'd left the service and he was surprised to find that he'd missed the sound of another's rhythm matching his own. She'd been coming to the club two to three times a week since their contract started and in that short time he'd begun to anticipate their sessions with a growing desire until it felt like he needed their Scenes as much as she did.

There was no denying the connection they'd had since the beginning. One that grew stronger each time they were together. For the first time ever he was seeking the company of a sub outside of the club in the bizarre desire of learning more about her. He wasn't probing that feeling any deeper than the skimming pass he'd given it as he'd set his alarm last night to ensure he'd be up in time to "bump into" Kendra this morning.

She started to ease up on the pace, indicating she'd reached her cool-down phase. "You can keep going," she panted, gesturing to the path ahead of them. She'd taken the park loop, a good six-mile route, at a decent clip. Normally he'd go a little farther, but today he was content to stay with her.

"I'm good."

Her lips thinned at his response, but she didn't say anything more. Gradually she slowed to a fast walk as they circled back to where they'd started. The path had been fairly empty that morning, even though it was nearing ten o'clock. He was guessing that the sudden dip in the temperature after their two-week warm spell had kept most people back indoors.

"How long you been running?" he asked, pulling on his arms to stretch them as they continued to walk.

She shrugged, her hands resting on her hips. "Since I was a teen. Maybe earlier. I joined the track team in junior high as something to do besides going home and fell in love with the distance running. Then I found cross country and haven't stopped since." She looked to him. "You?"

He gave a little laugh. "I didn't start until the army made me. Hated it at first. Hated everything about the military in the beginning, but once I finally stopped resisting and started experiencing I learned to enjoy both."

"What made you join then?"

An innocent question, and he debated his answer briefly before giving her the truth. "I didn't have a choice. It was either the service or jail. The army sounded like the better option."

When she didn't ask for more details, his respect for her went up another level. Most people would instinctually dig for more dirt, but then he suspected she had a healthy appreciation for secrets. There weren't a lot of people who knew his past simply because there weren't that many who needed to know.

"When did you leave the military?"

"About six years ago."

"Miss it?"

He gave it some honest thought before answering. "Some parts, yeah. Most parts, no." Their pace had slowed to a walk, their breathing returning to normal by now. He took a deep breath, welcoming the way his lungs expanded and ached with that pleasant twinge that came at the end of a good workout. He let the crisp scent of the cold fill him before exhaling. "I miss the camaraderie, but not the war and death."

She shot him a glance. "I can understand that." She waited until another jogger passed, then asked, "So why the club? I mean, other than you like being a Dom?"

He puffed out a short laugh. "That was one reason. But the main one is that Seth and Jake were involved." Revealing details of his life to Kendra, even little ones, was hard. The more someone knew, the more ammo they had. Information equaled vulnerability, and being vulnerable wasn't his thing.

"You're not brothers, are you?"

He shook his head. "Not biologically. But I'm closer to them than my real family. The three of us survived a lot together when we were kids. And you? Any family?"

Her back straightened at his question, the relaxed posture immediately gone. "Don't you know that?" The tightness in her voice told him she didn't like that he might.

"No," he told her. "The background checks done by the club don't dig into family history. I know you have a good credit history. Have never been arrested but have a penchant of speeding, with three tickets in the past five years. You're from Chicago and have a degree in Human Development and used to work as a middle school counselor before leaving that job two years ago. In Chicago, you were a member of the fetish club Scarlet Letter for four years. You moved here last June, have worked at Target since July and rent the condo unit you live in using money from your trust fund."

She'd stopped at some point during his admission to stare at him, her mouth slightly ajar.

He faced her and held back the smile that wanted to form, knowing she wouldn't appreciate it. "The security at the club is staffed with ex-military. There isn't much we can't find out, but a lot we don't need to know. Every member signs off on the background checks."

She gave her head a shake as if clearing her thoughts then sputtered, "I…I know that. I just didn't realize it was quite that extensive." She scanned him head to toe, her hands still propped on her hips. "Is there anything else I should know?"

"No. I only thought it was fair that you know exactly what I did know about you. Anything more than that, it's up to you to tell me."

"Right." She studied him again as if seeing him in a different light. Only he couldn't tell if it was a good one or not. "That's really kind of scary."

He shrugged. "It's not that much more than can be found by anyone on the internet anymore. Most people just don't know how to find it."

"Like I said, scary." Her eyes look wary, but not frightened or mad. The relief let him breathe again as she turned and resumed walking. "Big Brother really is watching us, huh?"

Laughing, he rolled his shoulders, loosening the remaining tension. "More than we want to know."

She gave an exaggerated shudder. "I don't need anyone else watching me."

The tightness across his shoulders returned instantly. "Who else is watching you?" His voice sounded sharper than he'd intended, and she leveled him with the same narrow-eyed stare that he gave her.

"No one…besides you," she said, the challenge laid down for him to deny.

He couldn't. The fact that he'd been caught picked at his pride. "Not in the way you meant. I've watched you because you interest me. Who *else* is watching you that's put you so on edge?"

"No one," she gritted out.

"Now you're lying."

She whipped around like he'd hit her with his harsh statement.

He winced at his error, taking a breath before explaining. "Only people who've had their privacy invaded know what it feels like to be spied on like that. It's like an unknown survival instinct that hones in quick and precise when it senses danger."

"Is that why all kinds of warning lights go off whenever you're around?"

He stopped now and waited until she turned back to look at him with wary eyes. "Do they, really? The warning lights?"

Every emotion drained from her face to reveal nothing but blankness, making him uncertain if she would answer. Christ, he wanted to know what caused her to be so guarded. Would she ever trust him enough to tell the details?

"You have to know by now that I would never harm you, Kendra." She didn't back away as he took the three steps, bringing them chest to chest. "So what are those warnings really about?" Taking a chance, he reached out and stroked the back of his fingers over her rosy cheek. Her skin was chilled despite her flush.

Her breath stuttered when she inhaled and her eyelids drifted down in a sensual half close even as her hands fisted at her sides. "I'm not afraid of you physically hurting me more than I want," she said quietly. "In or out of a Scene. You've proven that to me. It's all of the other ways you can hurt me that make the lights go off."

There it was. The first indication from her that maybe what they had, what they were doing, was more than just Scenes in the Dungeon.

He tilted her chin up to see her face. "How can I make them stop?"

She swallowed, hesitating. "I don't know."

He admired her honesty. He couldn't ask for more than that right now. Leaning down, he brushed his lips over hers, wanting to reassure her. Wanting more than anything just to hold her. It was a chaste kiss by club standards, a light touching of warm lips that slowly nibbled and nipped at each other before he pulled away.

Her eyes were wide with wonder and confusion, so many things flashing in their depths that he couldn't catch them all. "I'm sorry," she whispered, her breath fanning his cheek.

He wrapped her in his arms, tugging her in for a hug as he'd ached to do. "There's nothing to be sorry about," he reassured, his lips grazing her temple, the tiny curl there tickling.

He closed his eyes, savoring the moment when her arms went around his waist and she let her weight sink into his. For once in his life, everything else faded away. He was aware of only her. Her warm breath against his neck, the wisp of lilac, her breasts where they pressed to his chest. This was a trust that went outside of the club, outside of a Scene. And God, he hadn't realized how much he'd wanted it until she'd given it to him just now.

They stood like that until she started to shiver. "You're getting chilled," he said as he loosened his hold, and she did the same.

They finished the walk in comfortable silence. When they got back to the corner of their condo building where they'd split to their own units, he paused. "Would you mind if I joined you again?" Another chance meeting on the trail wouldn't get past her as coincidence.

She thought about it for a moment. "I don't have a set time that I run each day."

He caught himself right before he responded with *I know.* The grin she gave him said she knew that too. He chuckled. "Right. How about you text me when you're heading out, and I'll meet you if I can?" They'd exchanged cell numbers right after signing the contract, making it easier to schedule sessions.

She assessed him for a second before turning toward her condo. She glanced over her shoulder as she left. "I'll think about it." Taking off in a light jog, she didn't look back again as he watched her until she went up the path to her unit, waving and chatting briefly with her neighbor, Edith Jennings, before heading inside.

This meeting hadn't been an out-of-the-park success, but it

wasn't a strikeout either. Baby steps. That's what he was taking with her. Lots and lots of baby steps. He had no clue if his patience would be rewarded. But with her, he had to try.

Once again she had evaded anything personal about herself. He could find out more on his own, but he wouldn't break her trust like that. She'd tell when she was ready.

When she could trust him.

He just had figure out what he needed to do to fully earn it. If he ever could.

FIFTEEN

"You cold?" Cali asked, noticing the shiver Kendra couldn't suppress.

She tucked her hands under her legs, the snug spot a warm place for her icy fingers. The room wasn't cold, not really. With the fire burning across the room in the gas fireplace and the aroma of coffee filling the space, it was actually quite cozy. But she couldn't seem to shake the chill that had settled under her skin.

Coffee time with Cali and Allie was one of the things Kendra looked forward to each week. Yet she couldn't get into the light chatter today.

She moved her hands to cradle the coffee cup, looking for some residual warmth, and made an effort. "I'm fine. How's the new client going?" Cali's bookkeeping business had been the topic of many conversations since the three women had started meeting for Saturday coffee last summer.

"They're fine." She brushed off the subject with a wave of her hand. "Disorganized as heck, but I'll get them figured out. Or their books, at least. I can't do much for the rest of the place." She shook her head, a look of disbelief mixed with disgust on her face.

"I hear you," Allie piped in. "I don't know how people can manage to work in total chaos. There are lawyers in our firm who can barely find their desks. It would drive me nuts."

"I agree." Cali leaned on the table tucking her hair behind her ear, the shoulder-length blond strands smooth and silky as always. Even on a Saturday afternoon, she was neatly put together in black slacks and a burgundy turtleneck sweater. Cashmere, if Kendra guessed right. "I can't stand to work with piles of random papers stacked around me. Of course, that usually presents a problem when I go into customer sites."

The other women laughed in their mutual agreement, and Kendra pushed back her chair heading to the kitchen for more coffee. She couldn't sit still. It'd been five days since she'd been to The Den. Only five pitiful days since her last session with Deklan, and her body was acting like it was deep in withdrawals. It was insane.

She rubbed her palms on the jeans, tried to generate some circulation in her fingers before picking up the coffee pot. The stress of wondering when Eric would strike next, of when he'd drop in and ruin this nice little world she'd made for herself, was getting to her. The letter was a taunt that was working exactly as he'd wanted it to.

On top of that, she'd finally admitted to herself that Deklan was getting to her too. Their schedules had been off that week so she hadn't even seen him for their runs, which she'd somehow allowed herself to get used to. This was the longest she'd gone without seeing him since they'd signed the contract, and it really pissed her off that she missed him. Not just the sessions, but him. Damn it. She didn't want these feelings.

"Do either of you want more?" She held up the pot, trying to focus back on the conversation in the room. At their consent, she took it with her back to the small breakfast table. By some unspoken agreement, the three of them always met at Cali's house for coffee. It was comfortable here, homey in a way that Kendra's place wasn't even close to being.

"Did you work today?" Allie asked.

Kendra returned the now-empty pot to the coffee machine and switched it off as she answered. "I did the early morning shift." Her shelf stocker job at Target wasn't her life goal. Hell, it wasn't even close to what she'd envisioned for her life. But it paid her bills and kept her hidden for now.

Allie watched her as she rejoined them at the table, steaming cup of coffee in her hands. "Why do you work there anyway?"

Allie's directness, although jarring, was not surprising. "Because they pay me." She kept her face passive. It was the truth, after all.

Allie shoved her curly hair away from her face and leaned in, her posture forceful like she was gearing up to grill a defendant. Her brown eyes narrowed as she assessed Kendra, her intensity undiminished by her casual attire. Even in jeans and a sweater, Allie could pull off the lawyer inquisition with ease. "But it's obvious that you can do better than that. You're intelligent, educated, well-spoken…so what gives? What are you hiding from?"

"Allie," Cali snapped, shooting an annoyed glare at her. "Let it go. It's not our business."

"What?" Allie raised her brows. "Am I wrong?"

"It's okay," Kendra found herself saying, laying a hand over Cali's arm before she could respond to their pushy friend. She gave Cali a smile of reassurance at her concerned expression. "Maybe it's time I talk about it." She needed to do something before she combusted.

Cali covered Kendra's hand with her own, her warmth easing into Kendra's frozen fingers as she searched Kendra's face.

"You sure? It's up to you, of course. Don't let us pressure you into talking about anything."

Kendra pulled her hand away and stared at her coffee. Was she sure? She didn't know for certain but it felt right. Finally. She couldn't run forever. Maybe it was time to face this part of her past as well. Her many sessions with Deklan over the last six weeks were helping her overcome her pain issues. Or more truthfully, come to accept her pain desires. A part of her healing process meant accepting who she was, and that included all of her past as well. Talking about it with friends was another step in establishing trust and moving forward.

"Hey," Allie said, breaking into Kendra's thoughts. "We only want to help. We've been worried about you for a while."

Kendra gave them a weak smile and hid her nerves behind a sip of coffee. Fortunately her hands weren't shaking enough for anyone to notice. Her stomach churned and did a small flip as the warm liquid hit it, and she took a deep breath to keep the coffee down. "Thanks," she finally managed to say as she set her cup down. "That means a lot."

"You know we're here for you no matter what, right?" Cali looked at Kendra until she nodded. Cali gave a small laugh. "Heck, if you guys can accept my admission about being a submissive, then I doubt there's much that would stop us from accepting whatever's haunting you."

"Hey." Allie straightened, hands propped on the table, ready to push to a stand. "Do I need to get the Jack back out?"

"No!" the other two said in unison as Cali grabbed Allie's arm to keep her from rising.

They all laughed at the memory of the last time she'd brought over a bottle of Jack Daniel's and they'd ended up wasted and babbling like school girls. Of course, that was when Cali had found the courage to admit her secret. Only Kendra knew she needed to find her own courage to talk about the skeletons in her closet.

Allie slumped back in her chair and gave Kendra a reassuring smile. "Okay, no booze. But we'll still listen."

Again she was at a loss. She fidgeted with the mug, traced the path of the handle up and down the long curve as she gathered her thoughts. Exhaling, she cut a quick glance at Cali, who gave an encouraging nod. Okay, she could do this. No, she *needed* to do this.

"I like pain," she blurted out then cringed. That was the wrong place to start, but it was out there now. She rushed on, hoping to clarify the statement before the other women thought she was completely mad. "What I mean is…I enjoy…" She swallowed and drilled a hole in the table with her stare. "I'm a masochist," she finally whispered. Saying it out loud left her chilled and flustered at once.

She squeezed her eyes closed, her shoulders hunched as she waited for her friends to call her crazy or sick or demented. A soft "oh" came from Allie, but there was nothing from Cali.

The low hiss of the gas fireplace pierced through the air, seeming loud in the too-quiet room. Kendra's leg bounced in a nervous jitter under the table as the silence grew, lengthening to an unbearable span that almost had her bolting from her seat. Had she just push the tolerance of her friends too far? They had to think she was a complete loser to like pain.

The soft touch on her arm made her jump, but she couldn't look up. "Kendra," Cali said quietly, her voice matching her touch. "What does that have to do with why you're hiding?"

"How do you know I'm hiding?"

"We don't exactly," answered Allie. "But we're not blind. There're a whole lot of signs that say you're running or hiding from something or someone or both."

Kendra should have expected they'd figure that out. It was

part of the risk of making friends, but she'd needed their friendship and now she had to trust in it. "My ex. He called himself my...Master." It was hard to say. But after blurting out that she was a masochist, this shouldn't be so bad. She concentrated on the faint lines in the wood grain of the table and forced herself to continue. "It took me too long to figure out he was really just an abuser. By the time it sank in, I was so stuck in the relationship I didn't know how to get out."

"Oh, Kendra." Cali squeezed her arm, the sympathy flowing from her in waves that threatened to drown Kendra.

She sniffed and wiped at the moisture that accumulated at the corner of her eye. She wasn't going to cry over this again. "I tried to leave a couple of times, but he wouldn't let me. I know—" she rushed on, "—that sounds as pathetic as it is. But he'd taken control of everything in my life. I'm not weak, I swear. And I never thought that would be me. It was just so gradual, and he was so manipulative. Plus, my family thinks he's perfect." She exhaled, gathering the strength to finish now that she'd started. "It wasn't until he whipped me bloody one night in a fit of rage that I knew I had to get out or risk being permanently injured or killed."

"Oh my God." The whispered exclamation came from Cali, and Kendra had to pull away from her gentle touch. She felt too dirty. Her skin practically crawled with the need to clean the scum from her body every time she thought about that horrible night. Even now she could still feel the blood as it ran off her back and down her sides as she huddled on the floor.

"What'd you do?"

Allie's voice held that practical edge that allowed Kendra to answer. "I waited until my back had healed. Then one day while he was at work I got on the bus and didn't look back. I told my family I needed to breathe so they wouldn't worry about me, but that was it. It's kind of sad that I'd rather my family think I'm flighty and inconsiderate than to know the truth."

"I can understand that," Cali offered. "I don't want my family finding out about the other side of my relationship with Jake. If they knew he was my Dom as well as my boyfriend, I'd probably die of mortification."

"But this is different," Allie objected. "He was abusing you. Controlling you until you had no power at all. That's not the same as having a Master hiding in your closet."

"Maybe. But would they have believed me? Eric always threatened to tell my parents about my deviant desires if I ever said anything. I couldn't risk that. I'd be too humiliated."

"And it was better to get beaten every day?"

Kendra cringed at Allie's challenging slice. She hadn't really expected her to understand. Not someone so strong and independent. "It was my fault," she admitted in a low voice, her chin tucked in tight as she let the shame flood her.

"What?" The indignation and disbelief radiated stronger than the palm slap on table. "How was it your fault?" Allie demanded. "Did you make him hit you?"

"No...but I was the one who..." Kendra swallowed, digging for the strength to finish. "Who asked him to the first time."

Silence met her declaration, just as she'd expected it to. Guilty. The verdict rang through the quiet, making her shake. Why did she start this? They wouldn't understand. She was going to lose the only friends she had all because of Eric once again. *Damn him, damn him, damn him.*

"You were into submission before you met Eric?" Cali asked, her words wading into the tension-filled room with the non-judgmental tone of someone who understood.

Kendra dared to raise her head just enough to take a quick look at Cali. Her expression was one of concern, the worry marring her brow, her lips pressed into a thin line. "Yes. Some."

"What do you mean, some?"

It was only because she detected true curiosity, not doubt in Allie's voice, that Kendra responded. "I had…played a little at a club. Nothing major. Just enough to know that I…that I liked it." The heat crawled up her neck to cover her cheeks and face in a slow flush of embarrassment. "The first time I asked Eric to spank me, I thought he was going to throw me out of the bed. But then he smiled and did as I asked without any further questions. I never had to ask him again."

Another lengthy silence passed before Cali probed further. "How long were you with him?"

Kendra blew out a breath, preparing for the next round. At least they hadn't abandoned her yet. "Over three years."

"Were they all bad?"

"No… Like I said, it was gradual." She tightened her hands around the coffee mug, searching out the last bit of fading heat. "At first the play remained in the bedroom. I should have seen the first warning sign when he jumped into the Dom role without question. Within a week of me first saying something, he was fully stocked with an arsenal of tools. He really got off on ordering me around, and I…well, I enjoyed being sexually submissive."

"I take it the play didn't stay in the bedroom for long."

"Yeah." Kendra nodded in absent agreement to Cali's statement, her mind half in the past. "Before I knew it, I was his submissive whenever we were alone or went to a fetish club. The really stupid thing is that I didn't mind it at first. I was a little uncomfortable, but he'd put on the charm and persuade me to do it." She looked up, catching the eye of both women. "You have to understand another thing. Eric works for my father. He went to Harvard with my older brother. He has all of the family credentials required to impress my parents and the connections to get whatever he wants. On paper, he's the perfect guy."

Allie made a sound of disgust. "Anyone can sound good on paper. Trust me, in my line of work I've met more than my fair share of men who look good on paper but are really the scumbags of the earth."

"When did it start getting bad?" Cali's question was asked with the gentleness that good mothers seemed to culture.

Kendra pushed away from the table and stood, taking her coffee cup to the sink. Staying seated was impossible. She poured the almost full cup down the drain and watched the brown liquid splash over the white porcelain, marring the pristine surface. She braced her hands on the edge of the counter, pressed the sharp edge into her palms and stared, unseeing, out the small window over the sink.

"I agreed to move into his penthouse about a year after we started dating. Our parents were certain the next step would be marriage. 'A perfect match,' my mother said. I realized my mistake almost immediately. I became his full-time slave the very first night. He chained me to the bed, laid down the rules, set the punishments and never looked back. Only I didn't get a say in any of it."

"I don't want to sound harsh," Allie said. "But why didn't you leave?"

"How?" Kendra cleared her throat, hating the way her voice shook. "I'd just given up everything to move in with him. For once in my life, my parents were proud of me. According to my dad, I'd finally done something right in my life. And Eric wasn't a monster all the time. So I justified his actions. Took the blame for starting it all and felt the shame even more for actually liking the pain."

"How?" The confusion was blatant in Allie's voice. "I just

don't understand that part at all. What can you possibly like about pain?"

"I get it," Cali said so softly, Kendra almost didn't hear her across the kitchen. She looked at her friend, aware that the admission was hard for Cali. Her hands were clasped in her lap, but her spine was straight as she challenged Allie with a cool stare. "At least, part of it. When the pain and pleasure blend it becomes something different. Then it's not about being harmed. It's about…" She paused, her hand motioning as she searched for the right words.

"Letting go," Kendra finished for her. She moved to lean her forearms on the island that separated the kitchen from the breakfast area. "About trusting someone to give you an ecstasy you can't get anywhere else. When it's done right, you can ride the high for hours." At least, she could after her Scenes with Deklan.

Allie's perplexed glance swiveled between the other two women. "You guys make it sound like a drug."

"Sometimes it feels like one."

Kendra nodded her consent to Cali's statement and added, "But for me, it goes even further. It gives me focus and makes everything else go away. Eric caught on to that quickly and used it." She looked at her hands, picking at the cuticles, the small bites of pain grounding. "The degradation and humiliation didn't start until after I moved in. The name-calling, the list of rules, the looks of disgust that eventually surpassed all the others. That became my life. He forced me to quit my job, drop my friends, and took away everything until he *was* my life. By then, pain was my only out."

Cali's soft sound of sympathy was meant to be soothing, Kendra was certain, but it rubbed against her like sandpaper, exposing all of the areas of her soul left raw from Eric's abuse.

"But, Kendra…" Allie leaned on the table, her eyes earnest. "That's not good for you."

"I know," Kendra scoffed, the self-disgust coating her words. "By the second year he had me hooked on the pain-pleasure mix until I couldn't…I couldn't come without the pain. By the third year it had digressed to mostly just beatings without the pleasure. Of course, he blamed me for 'making him that way.'" She mimed the finger quotes around the last words. God, she hated him. Hated everything he'd done to her. Everything he'd made her feel.

"Asshole," Allie mumbled under her breath.

Kendra smiled in agreement.

"Didn't your family notice anything?"

She shook her head, her stomach cramping at even the thought of her family knowing. She dug at her cuticles, absorbing the sting until she could continue. "They saw what Eric wanted them to see. What I let them see, which was anything but the truth. The pressure was mounting for our engagement and I knew I couldn't do that. I tried to leave, and he cuffed me to our bed for three days." She couldn't acknowledge the gasp that came from Cali. "So then I got smarter and I planned. The night he whipped my back to shreds was when he found the packed bag I'd stashed in the closet. After that I hid it in my gym locker. My gym membership was one of the few things I was allowed to keep. After all, he couldn't have me getting fat." Running had truly saved her then.

"Did you ever think of pressing charges against him?" This came from the lawyer of course.

Kendra actually laughed at that question. "Right. The scandal alone would've had both of our families pointing accusations at me. There's no reason for them to believe me."

"I'd say a bloody, whipped back would have been reason enough to believe you."

"But he always had the trump card," Kendra admitted, her voice low with the weight of her confession. "He kept my membership to the leather club from before we dated. There were pictures too. Ones he took of me…" She couldn't finish and instead let the sentence dangle.

They were all quiet for a moment before Cali said, "We could always kill him." Kendra's head snapped up to see Cali looking completely serious. "I'm sure Deklan knows people who could take care of that."

Kendra tilted her head, trying to determine if her friend was bluffing or not. A quick check to Allie told her the other woman was as equally confused. The notion was so strange, coming from the normally straight-laced Cali, that it only took another second before Kendra burst out laughing.

"Yeah," she said around a chuckle. "I can just see me bringing up that topic."

"What?" Cali's brows arched, pulling off the innocent look. "You don't see yourself saying, 'Yes, sir, I'd like a spanking. Oh, and could you off my ex while you're at it?'"

"God, don't," Allie implored, reaching across the table. "The man would probably take her seriously. Then we'd all be charged with accessory to murder."

"Only if we're caught."

Allie shook her head and tapped her forehead on the table in fake affront, which caused them to laugh even more. She lifted her head and shot the others her best courtroom death glare before she straightened, pushing her hair away from her face. "We've digressed. And I'm going to assume that last bit was a joke." She pointed at Cali, whose only response was to hide a choked laugh behind her hand.

Kendra couldn't resist adding, "I'm sure Deklan wouldn't get caught."

"Right." Allie shook her head and stood, taking her cup to the sink.

Cali followed her, and the three of them all turned to lean against the counters, forming an intimate triangle in the open kitchen.

Allie crossed her arms over her chest and looked at Kendra. "Are you okay now?"

She braced her palms on the counter behind her and stared at the floor, giving the question some thought. Was she okay? She nodded and looked up, smiling. "I'm getting there."

"Is Deklan helping with that?"

Allie's gaze whipped to Cali. "What do you mean?"

Kendra cleared her throat, her attention back on the wood floor. She couldn't bear Allie's scrutiny. "I've been seeing him at the club for the last six weeks." The heat rose up her neck once again and she wished she'd left her hair down so it would hide some of the flush.

"And has it helped?" Cali asked again, gently nudging for an answer.

"Yes." The answer barely left her lips to hang softly between them.

Cali stepped up and engulfed Kendra in a tight hug. "Good. That's good. There's nothing wrong with that." She stepped back. "Deklan's a good man. He'd never harm you."

Kendra sniffed and nodded. "I know. He's proven that to me too." He really had. In more ways than Eric had the entire time they were together. But she wasn't a fool. She'd gone to great lengths to protect herself this time. But then, meeting outside the club on sometimes solitary jogging paths wasn't exactly safe and protected.

"Wait a minute," Allie said, finally catching up with the conversation. "You mean you're still doing that stuff after everything you went through?"

"Allie," Cali admonished. "Don't judge."

"I'm not judging. I swear. I'm just trying to understand."

"I know it sounds crazy," Kendra agreed. "I've told myself that over and over and over. It didn't matter though because as much as I tried to deny it, the need was still there." She finally met Allie's eyes, trying to get her friend to understand. "You said earlier it sounded like a drug. For me, the need for pain is. Not abusive pain, but the consensual pain that comes with pleasure. Going to the club, signing a contract with Deklan was better than sliding back into another abusive relationship."

She clenched her fist and blew out a long release of air. "When I left Eric, I swore I'd never go back to that. And I won't. Not the kind of relationship I had with him. But as much as I tried to deny it, as much as I told myself I was crazy to want it, I couldn't stop the cravings. Mardi Gras night I finally gave in to the need."

"So that's what happened to you," Allie cut in. "I never believed you'd been dancing that whole time."

Kendra lifted her shoulder and shot her an apologetic glance. "I told myself it was just once. To prove that I didn't need it. Only Deklan took over." She thought back to that first night, to how he'd made her feel. How safe she'd been with him in control. "And he showed me what I'd been looking for all along. I went back two weeks later and signed a contract with him."

"A contract? They have contracts for those kinds of things?"

Cali chuckled at Allie's disbelief. "I know. I had that reaction when I first found out too. But if you think about it, it's a really smart and safe thing to do."

Allie shook her head. "Who knew?" She focused in on Cali, her eyes narrowing. "Did you have a contract with Jake?"

"No. We just kind of evolved." She rubbed her fingers absently at her neck and Kendra smiled, knowing what was under the turtleneck sweater. "He actually dropped all of his client contracts to be with only me."

"But you and Deklan are in a contract?" Allie's brow was wrinkled as she tried to understand the dynamics.

"Yes," Kendra said, finding Allie's confusion funny when it probably shouldn't be. "I knew that if I was going to try that stuff again that I wanted the safety of a public setting and having the rules defined in writing before I played. And I only agreed to do it with Deklan because, well, I knew him outside of the club some. And—" she tipped her head toward Cali, "—because I trusted Cali's judgment."

"Mine? Really?"

"Yeah. I'd met Jake enough times and had seen you together to know that he's not an abuser. He makes you happy. Really happy, not gloss happy."

Cali's cheeks flushed and she smiled. "He does."

"But that's not a guarantee that Deklan isn't the same as your ex," Allie challenged, ever the doubter.

"You're right, it's not. But I have to trust myself and my instincts at some point." Kendra shifted, crossed her arms over her chest and met Allie's intense brown eyes. "I know exactly what I overlooked in Eric to gain my parents' approval. I'm not stupid and I refused to let that man control my life any longer." She blinked rapidly, holding the moisture back. "Deklan has helped. A lot. He's a decent man, which makes him an even better Dom. I won't live the rest of my life hiding from myself because I'm afraid of what I might find."

Kendra's voice had risen in intensity, and the sudden quiet seemed stark and heavy. Her chest heaved, the fire in her blood chasing away the chill and making her skin clammy under her sweatshirt. She processed her own words, let the truth of them sink in and ground her further. Six weeks ago she'd never have been able to say that.

"Wow," Cali said softly. "That is so courageous. I wish I'd had your strength when I was your age."

Allie stared at the floor, but she nodded in agreement. "Yeah." She looked at Kendra. "You got me there. Case closed." She gave Kendra a quick hug then stepped back, shoving her hands into her jean pockets. "I don't understand it all, but then, I don't need to. It's clear that you know what you're doing."

"Thanks," Kendra said, another weight lifting from her chest. "I finally feel like I do."

Allie tipped her head to the side and her eyes narrowed once again. Kendra tensed, knowing that look. "There's just one more thing though. You never answered why you're working at Target. Who are you hiding from?"

Kendra exhaled, her shoulders drooping with the reminder of her other problems. She gave her curly-haired friend a grim smile. "I'd hate to face you in a courtroom."

"I'd have to be in one first," Allie said under her breath before she waved it away. "Never mind. So spill."

"Fine," Kendra sighed, swiveling her head, trying to loosen the muscles that were gripping her neck in a vise lock. The rest of her confession seemed minor compared to what she'd already revealed. "Everyone. Eric, my parents, his family. I know Eric won't let me go. My parents will only pressure me to return and lecture me on commitments and image, and I can't deal with that. I needed time to find myself again. To get strong enough to face them all."

"Wait, go back." Allie rolled her hand mimicking a rewind. "What do you mean, Eric won't let you go? Is that what that letter was about last month?"

"What letter?" Cali looked between the two. "What'd I miss?"

Kendra rubbed her hands over her face, both exhausted

and agitated at once. "Yes," she admitted before dropping her hands to rest on her hips. "Eric tracked me down. The letter was a warning."

"Oh God, Kendra," Allie exclaimed. "You have to go to the police."

"And do what?" Kendra challenged back. "It won't solve anything. Nothing's changed, except I'm not letting him control me anymore. I didn't go back. I didn't run again. I'm still here, living my life as I want."

"What if he hurts you again?"

She shook her head. "He won't do anything that would reflect back on him. Right now he's just full of threats." Closing her eyes, she put out a silent prayer that she was right about that. But if she truly believed what she said, she wouldn't have taken all of the precautions over the last nine months to stay hidden. She wouldn't jump at every person who came up behind her and she wouldn't panic over a letter.

A hand-delivered letter. But she wasn't running scared again. She would deal with Eric when he finally manned up and showed his face.

"I hope you're right," Allie said, looking unconvinced. "You'll ask for help if you need it, right?"

Kendra nodded, not sure if she could answer verbally. She glanced at the clock. "I've gotta get going." Not that she had plans that night. She didn't go to the club on the nights Cali would be there. Deklan understood that and would text her when he knew Cali would be at the club, and Cali was almost always there on Saturdays. Kendra still had a strange hitch about letting her friend see her in a different light. Maybe someday she'd be brave enough for that, but not yet.

"Me too," agreed Allie.

In unison they moved to the sliding door that led to the back courtyard. Now that most of the snow had melted, Allie and Kendra could cut through the open area to get to their condos.

"Be careful, okay?" Cali said, pulling Kendra into a quick hug. "Thank you for trusting us and sharing so much. We're here for you. Got it?"

"Yeah, thanks."

"You know," Allie inserted, giving Kendra a one-armed squeeze, "I'm starting to feel like the old prude, hanging out with you two."

Cali laughed. "What are you talking about? You're younger than me."

"Maybe, but I can assure you my sex life is very vanilla when I do have one."

"You could always try the club," Cali hinted with a sly look.

"No, thank you." Allie gave a firm head shake of denial. "I tried it that one time. That was enough for me. To each their own, but that stuff is not for me."

"Oh, come on," Kendra chided. "It wasn't that bad. You seemed interested enough from what I saw."

Allie gaped at her, her big brown eyes opened wide in apparent shock. "Interested? Try stunned stupid. I mean, I knew places like that existed, but I was totally unprepared to actually see it."

A low rumble bounded out of the air, and all three women peered out the window in search of the source. Dark clouds were rolling across the sky at a fast clip, leaving an ominous feel to the early evening.

"That does not look good," Allie observed. "And here I thought we were done with snow."

"Ha!" Cali laughed. "How long have you lived in Minnesota?"

"Yeah, I know. We can all dream, right?"

Kendra pulled the slider open to a cold gust of wind that

had the evergreen bushes swaying in resistance. "Damn, the temperature's really dropped." The sky lit up in an odd glow, making the clouds look like dark puffs of cotton. Another low rumble echoed through the sky, and Allie pushed on Kendra's back to get her to move.

"Kendra, call us if you need anything, okay?" Allie turned back to Cali. "Thanks for the coffee. Next Saturday good for both of you?"

"Should be," Cali said. "I'll let you know if something changes."

"Me too," Kendra said. "And thanks again." She waved goodbye and took off across the dead lawn to get to her condo. The wind had really picked up in the last couple of hours and she hunched her shoulders, wrapping her arms around her middle against the bite of the cold. Her tennis shoes squished in the grass made soggy by melting snow and lack of sun as she made a beeline across the courtyard to her condo.

She peered through her glass on the sliding door, checking the interior for any signs that someone may have entered. Everything looked normal, but then, that didn't really mean anything. The addition of the external locking feature on the door had been one of the things she'd installed after renting the unit.

She gave one last quick look at the gathering storm before slipping inside. Securing the door behind her, she dropped the broom handle back in the track then sagged into the overstuffed chair, suddenly exhausted. Her head flopped against the back cushion and she closed her eyes, processing all that she'd revealed to her friends.

It felt good to talk about it, even better that they were still her friends. It was nice here. Nicer than she'd expected when she'd rented the condo online from a library computer. Staying here would be good. Her fresh start away from Chicago was turning out to be okay. Maybe there was a chance for new beginnings after all.

SIXTEEN

He pumped his cock, swift, firm strokes with his hand meant to find release fast. The water beat hard and hot on his back, and Deklan braced his free hand on the slick wall of the shower, angling forward for more leverage. He fucking needed to come.

Two more hard jerks with a twist right on the tip and he achieved his goal. His come splattered over the wall in time with his rough groan, visions of Kendra splayed and begging flashed front and center in his mind. Chest heaving, he leaned his forehead on his wrist and caught his breath for a second before resuming his shower.

Holy mother of God, he needed that.

The rest of the cleaning process was completed briskly. The addition of the daily hand-jobs added minutes to the whole routine that Deklan didn't exactly like but saw as necessary.

He was going out of his fucking mind *not* fucking Kendra. And these daily shower jobs were his only hope of maintaining his sanity.

The woman was killing his control. Over the last two

months, each Scene had become a test of his will and determination to keep his dick in his pants. She'd opened up and started to really let go. Giving him her trust and taking every sadistic thing he did to her. The last three Scenes had left him with a raging case of blue balls worse than when he'd been a teenager dry-humping Susie Bowman in the back of her dad's Chevy.

It didn't help that Kendra had offered more than once to relieve him—something he'd had to grit his teeth to decline. He wouldn't act on those urges until the contract terms were changed. Deklan would respect the rules she'd laid out in advance, respect her. That was his job. The fact that the contract only stated no intercourse didn't matter to him. Technically, blowjobs or hand jobs weren't off-limits. But it didn't feel right. He didn't want the rest of the club to watch. Doing that with her was private.

He'd admitted a while ago that this contract was more than a job. It had been since the beginning. That made it even more important that he restrain himself until she consented outside of a Scene. When—if—they became truly sexual it would be because she wanted it, not because she felt like she should or he ordered it.

That's what he really wanted. He wanted all of her given freely. Just for him. And fuck if he knew when that was going to happen.

Cursing, Deklan jerked the towel from the rack, scrubbing it over his skin in hard, abrasive swipes. He wrapped the damp towel around his waist before pulling out his shaving supplies and setting to work on scraping the day-old scruff from his face. He had to be at The Den later and for the first time since the club opened, the Scenes he had scheduled that night with other clients truly seemed like a job. One he didn't want to do.

The trump card in all of his frustration was his complete

disinterest in relieving himself with any of his other clients. He only wanted Kendra, and she was testing his hard-fought control like candy before a child. Not on purpose, but that irritated him as much as the perma-boner.

The knock at his door came as he was wiping the last of the shaving cream from his face. He grumbled at his reflection then glanced at the clock in his bedroom as he yanked on some shorts. He wasn't expecting company. And he sure as hell didn't need any Girl Scout cookies.

Stomping down the stairs, he jerked the door open to a blast of cold air and a grinning Jake. "What do you want?"

"Hey, great to see you too," Jake replied, his voice dripping in heavy sarcasm, unfazed by Deklan's abruptness.

Deklan turned and strode back into his condo, the door left wide open for the freezing air to draft in. Maybe he'd be fortunate and Jake would decide his visit wasn't needed. The click of the door closing followed by the scuff of boots on the rug told Deklan he wouldn't get that lucky today.

"So what's eating you?"

The problem was who wasn't eating him. Cursing at his crude thought, Deklan went to his bedroom, slipped on a sweatshirt and took a deep breath. Then another. Venting his frustrations on Jake wouldn't solve his problems.

Problems he created.

Forcing out a long, slow exhale, Deklan returned to the kitchen and grabbed a beer from the fridge. He held one up to Jake. "Want one?"

Jake took the bottle, opened it and chased it with a long drink. Releasing a pleased sigh, he started opening cupboards until he found a bag of chips and grabbed them with the comfortable ease that came with being family. He turned to Deklan. "You watching the Glaciers' game?"

Deklan grunted and moved to open the doors on the entertainment center as his answer. The hockey game would be in the first period and would hopefully keep Jake occupied. Deklan was in no mood to talk that afternoon.

"Cool," Jake said as he plopped down on the black leather sofa and reached down to release the foot rest before relaxing back with a contented sigh. Copying his friend, Deklan settled into the other end of the couch and flicked through the channels until he found the game.

Jake tipped his beer in Deklan's direction. "Thanks for letting me crash here for a bit. I forgot Cali did coffee with her neighbors at this time and since I was already over here, I didn't feel like driving back home." He flashed a grin, something he did a lot more now that Cali was in his life. "Besides, I thought you might be missing me."

"Yeah, right." Deklan took a drink of his beer. "It's just damn convenient that I live in the same complex as your girlfriend."

"Can't deny that." Jake held up the chip bag in a silent offer, which Deklan declined. "Did you hear about Hauke being traded from Carolina?"

"Winger, right? Last-minute deal before the midseason deadline."

"Yeah."

"What'd the Glaciers give up?"

"Not much. A defenseman and two draft picks."

"That's it?" Deklan shot a doubting look at Jake. "I thought Hauke was an up-and-coming hotshot. The kid tank under the pressure or something?"

Jake frowned. "Not that I heard."

They focused on the game for a while, the room filled with the sounds of cheering fans and sports announcers. In truth, Deklan couldn't care less about what they watched just as long as Jake stayed quiet.

"Have you talked to Seth lately?" Jake asked after the Glaciers scored a goal, taking them into the lead by one.

"No," Deklan grumbled, glancing at the other man. "Why? Something wrong?" Had his preoccupation with Kendra made him miss something with Seth?

"Don't know." Jake scowled and gave a shrug. "He's been buried behind his desk a lot."

Deklan had noticed that too. "He telling you anything he's not telling me?" All three men put in a lot of hours to keep the club in its top slot, but Seth's seemed excessive even by their standards. Deklan made a mental note to check in with Seth when he went in that night.

Jake shook his head. "Nope. Nothing outside of the normal business updates."

"Speaking of business, how's the equipment thing going?" At the beginning of the year, Jake had started a side revenue stream building custom BDSM equipment. He was a pro with that shit and it gave him more time to spend with Cali while still supporting the club.

"Good," Jake said. The smile that filled his face was open and content. After all the years of personal anguish, Jake had finally found some peace. "I haven't even branched outside of The Den's membership list and I can't keep up with the orders."

"I thought as much. Your shit's good, Jake."

The other man only grunted at the compliment before rising and heading to the kitchen, automatically bringing back a beer for Deklan too. The buzzer when off and they looked to the game; the Glaciers still led by one in the second period. It was a close game, but he couldn't stay focused on it. His damn mind kept straying back to Kendra. Pathetic, really.

"Is your wrist sore yet?"

Deklan snapped around at the strange question. "What the

fuck?" He glared at Jake, not liking where the question was leading.

Jake shrugged, his eyes on the TV screen, but his attention clearly wasn't. His false indifference was unsuccessful. "You haven't screwed a sub in almost two months."

"How the hell would you know that?"

Again with the shrug. Deklan was tempted to reach over and punch the shit out of that damn shoulder.

Jake finally turned his head to level him with a calculating look. "You're not the only one who's observant."

"Whatever." Deklan scowled and looked back to the game, intending to ignore Jake's unwanted probing. It was none of the man's business anyway. Jake's low chuckle was more annoying than the damn shrug. Deklan ground his teeth then forced his jaw to relax before he took a swallow of the tasteless beer.

"She's getting to you, huh?"

Not answering, he stared at the game in stony silence. If Jake was smart, he'd take the hint.

"Take my advice, don't fight it," Jake offered. Apparently, he wasn't smart.

"Who said I was fighting it?"

"Right," Jake agreed, the mockery rolling off the single word. "Of course you wouldn't."

Deklan's scowl deepened, his muscles zapping the back of his head with the spike of pain. "What are you getting at?"

"Look at you, man. You're the one who always charges into confrontation. Never backing down, taking on every challenge, trying over and over to prove that you can protect everyone around. Twenty years later and you're still making amends for your past."

His jaw clenched against the truth in Jake's words. It wasn't that he had to prove he could protect everyone because he knew he couldn't. But fuck, why was it so bad to want to protect those he cared about? He let his glare communicate his thoughts before he looked away. "And you're one to talk."

Jake jerked his chin around, imitating a punch to his face, then rubbed at the phantom punch. He tipped his beer toward Deklan in acknowledgement of the hit. "At least I got over my issue before I lost what was really important."

A half-smile of satisfaction curled over Deklan's lips. "I don't plan on losing anything."

"Ahhh," Jake said, as if the world's answers had just been revealed. "And that's the problem. You of all people know you can't win everything, just like you can't save them all."

Fuck all. Deklan's fist clenched around his now-warm beer bottle, but he loosened his jaw enough to grit out, "Been talking to Seth?"

"Seriously? I only need to look at your leg to know that much."

Automatically Deklan's hand reached to rub the back of his leg, his fingers stroking over the unseen names. His chest tightened and he swallowed back the angry retort as he battled against the rise of emotion that wanted to suck him under. "Fuck you, Jake." The small vent of venom was delivered between clenched teeth.

"What? You can throw my fucking past in my face, but you can't take it yourself?"

Deklan slammed his bottle down on the side table and thrust to his feet to keep from pummeling the younger man. He paced to the windows to stare at the empty courtyard. Small piles of snow still huddled in clumps under the shrubs and along the corners of the buildings where the sun couldn't find it. After four months of being compressed under the snow, the grass was matted, yellow and soggy-looking.

Every face that was memorialized on the back of his leg

flashed across his mind in a parade of failure. A cheer went up from the TV, the crowd celebrating a point scored. In a fractured corner of his brain it felt as if they were applauding his mistakes. *Go, Deklan. Look at all the people you let down.*

A low rumble of muffled thunder rolled through the sky, and Deklan's eyes jerked up in search of the source, thankful for the distraction. A dark bank of clouds tumbled across the sky, rolling over the dense layer of white clouds and chasing away any hope of sun for the day. Spring thunderstorms were expected in the Midwest, but this one held an odd edge to it. The sky suddenly brightened again as if someone had turned on a light switch in the clouds, followed by another clap of thunder about ten seconds later.

He glanced at the outside thermometer. The temperature hovered around the freezing mark, explaining the strangeness of the thunder. It'd been a weird spring weather-wise, with the temperatures going up and down in a pattern that was more extreme than normal.

"Looks like snow," he said to Jake.

The other man released a long groan. "I'm so done with snow."

Deklan chuckled, agreeing. "I hope Seth has the plowing contracts extended through April. By the looks of it, we're going to need them."

"Knowing Seth, he has them setup for year-round service." Jake laughed. "Boy Scout code—always be prepared."

Deklan looked at Jake, his chest constricting. The man might irritate the shit out of him sometimes, but fuck if he wasn't family.

"Some things never change, huh?" Jake said, shaking his head. "Damn. Remember that summer you and I were sleeping under that bridge and he showed up with a tent, sleeping bags, cooking stove, the works?"

Yeah, Deklan did. "Never did understand why he stuck with the two of us."

"Me either. Damn Boy Scout loyalty or something. He sure as shit could have done better than hanging with us."

"Still could."

"Ain't that the fucking truth."

The wind beat against the window in a sudden gust of force that shook the glass. Deklan looked back to the court-yard, his focus honing in on movement across the way. He went still as Cali's back door slid open and Kendra stepped out, followed by Allie.

"Coffee's done," he said to Jake, his eyes glued on Kendra.

The wind whipped the ends of her ponytail across the side of her face and she hunched her shoulders as she hurried over the grass to her condo. She was in the second unit from the end, flanked by Edith Jennings and the engaged couple, Lacey and Paul. Given his lack of socializing, it would probably surprise most that he knew the names of everyone in their building.

"Cool."

He heard Jake slam the footrest down and then move toward the kitchen, empty chip bag crinkling as he threw it in the trash. Outside, Kendra looked through her slider window before digging her key out and opening her door. Deklan had been impressed that she'd been smart enough to add a lock on that door. They weren't standard, and most people didn't seem to care that they were as easy as shit to break into.

Case in point, Allie pulled hers open and walked in. She'd obviously left it unlocked during their entire coffee time. Careless. It didn't matter how safe the area might be; there were assholes everywhere.

"I'm out of here," Jake said. "Thanks for the beer."

Deklan turned away from the window once he saw a light

flick on in Kendra's condo. Jake was slipping his coat back on and moving to the door. "Cali coming to the club tonight?"

"It's Saturday," Jake said with a devious smile. "Of course she'll be there." His gaze skidded past Deklan to look out the window. "As long as the snow doesn't stop us."

Sure enough, the white stuff had started to fall from the clouds, just like they'd threatened. "If it gets bad, don't bother," Deklan told him. "Seth and I can handle it. The club will be dead anyway."

"I'll call you later." Jake let himself out, leaving Deklan with a blast of cold air that drifted down the hallway and the sound of the hockey game.

He stared at the falling snow, the heavy flakes blurring his thoughts. In a matter of minutes, the snow intensified until the outside was a haze of white. Instincts and years of living in the north told Deklan the storm was going to be a bad one.

Great. If they were lucky, it would fuck up the roads *before* the club got busy. There was nothing like trying to clear out the club when the roads sucked. Maybe he could actually convince Seth to keep it closed for the night. They'd take a revenue hit, but it might be worth it.

Whatever. He still needed to get dressed and head on over. Glancing at the clock, he headed upstairs to change. Staying busy was way better than stewing on his screwed-up situation. Even if he didn't want to perform, he had a job to do.

SEVENTEEN

Kendra stared out her kitchen window, watching the snow come down in big, heavy flakes at a staggering pace. Winter definitely wasn't done with them. The weather didn't care if it was the second week of April and everyone was waiting for the showers that promised flowers.

She leaned on the edge of the sink, the weight of the day settling in, a deep sigh gushing into the silence. There were times when the loneliness really got to her. Most days she was okay being by herself. It'd actually felt wonderful when she'd first gotten here. Now, it often just seemed empty.

She spun around and sprinted upstairs. The change into her running clothes was quick and efficient. If she made it a short run, she could be back before the storm got really bad. She needed to burn off some energy or the night was going to drag on forever. The itch to go to The Den was almost undeniable. The desire to see Deklan, to simply be with him, was growing too intense.

The man had wormed his way into her life as more than just a Dom fulfilling her needs. She'd really enjoyed their runs together, his quiet presence by her side. He calmed her when he should have made her nervous. A fact she didn't understand but had stopped doubting.

Ready, she hustled back downstairs. She didn't question herself when she picked up her phone and sent a quick text, letting him know she was heading out for a run. He probably wouldn't join her with it being so late in the day, but it'd become habit to text him when she left for a run. Not because he ordered it, but because she liked it when he joined her. And it had become like another level of safety, having him know when she was out running. She smiled at the thought before bending to tie her shoes.

She did a few quick stretches then zipped up her running jacket, stuffed her phone in the zippered side pocket, and headed out. The cold hit her instantly and she inhaled the briskness into her lungs before turning to lock her door and stowing the key.

It felt good. *She* felt good.

The snow swirled around as she stepped off her porch and she couldn't resist doing a quick spin, arms extended, stopping just short of sticking her tongue out in an attempt to catch the heavy flakes. She grinned, feeling lighter than she had in possibly years. This was going to be fun.

A fresh set of footprints in the snow running down her path brought her up short. Had Deklan decided to meet her for the jog? He hadn't sent a message back, but then, he didn't always. She looked around, trying to spot him through the veil of white. Her gaze landed on a black Mercedes parked in a guest spot and she froze. Her stomach clenched against the sickening dread that crawled over her skin, flushing her in heat despite the outside chill.

No. Not now. She wasn't ready for him. Not yet. Not when her life was going so well.

She pressed her hand at the tightness in her chest and gasped for air. The door opened and when he stepped out of the car, her legs almost crumbled beneath her. Just the sight of him made her weak. She squeezed her eyes closed, blocking out his image, but it only brought the horrors of her past closer.

Damn him. She wasn't going back. Never with him.

Corralling her determination, Kendra straightened her shoulders, fisted her hands at her sides and prepared to fight. Eric stood about twenty feet away and was somewhat obscured by the falling snow, but every detail of his image was already etched into her memory. From the dark brows to his deep brown hair, cut and styled to the side, not a strand out of place. His aristocratic nose and jutting chin that gave the impression of looking down on others combined with his designer clothing to provide an air of sophistication that turned many heads.

She had a sudden crushing desire to run inside and put on her highest heels just to pick at his most sensitive peeve. His height was his one shortcoming that he was incredibly touchy about. The thought gave her strength and made her smile on the inside, even if her lips couldn't follow through on the action.

"Kendra," he said, his voice low and flat. The snow had already blanketed the ground in white and added that strange sense of padded softness to the air.

"Eric," she answered, keeping her voice just as void as his.

His hands were tucked in the pockets of his leather trench coat, but his face was as blank as his voice. "It's time to come home."

Her jaw dropped and she stared at him, searching for the punch line but finding none. "No." She shook her head, her teeth grinding. "I'm not going anywhere with you."

Eric's brows lifted, a look of challenge falling over his features. He took a step forward. "Yes. You are."

"No." She retreated a step even though she hated the way it made her appear cowardly. Darting a quick glance back at her door, she judged the distance, gauging if she'd have time to get inside. Not with the door locked. "I'm never going back with you. We're done, Eric."

"Really?" Although it was a question, she knew he didn't expect an answer. His lip curled in a mocking smile. "You aren't the boss. Or have you forgotten your place so quickly?"

"Screw you," she bit out, her anger rising at his overbearing attitude. Maybe it was the semi-public location or the relief that had come with telling her friends about her past. Or maybe she was finally strong enough to stand up to him. Kendra didn't know for sure, but she wasn't going to take his shit anymore. Not today. "You don't own me, and I'm not your fucking slave. I never was. You're an abuser. Plain and simple. And I'm done being your whipping post."

"Ah, but Kendra, my little pain slut. You love being that." He took another predatory step closer, his head tipping in an exaggerated scan of her body. "Remember how you used to beg for your Master to hit you more. Harder. 'Please, Master. Please, hit me hard.'" His voice went higher in an insulting imitation of her. "I'm sure your parents would like to see that video."

She blanched at the threat. It wasn't a new one, but it still held all the weight that it'd had since he'd first shown her the video. The one he'd secretly made and was conveniently absent from because he'd forced her to submit to another Dom at the club she'd belonged to. Just another one of his asshole moves.

Bluffing it off, she tried to keep the fear from her voice. "How long are you going to use that empty threat, Eric? If you ever intended to show it to them, you would've done it by now."

"Maybe." The mocking smile returned. "Or it could be I've been saving it for just the right time. Like, say…next weekend."

Kendra's brain did a quick shuffle, cataloging what next weekend was and why it was supposed to mean something to her. She was so disconnected from her old life that it took her a moment to put it together.

"No!" She advanced on him before she realized what she was doing. "You wouldn't do that." Her hands were shaking, her world dropping out from beneath her at the thought of what Eric was implying.

He laughed, a sound that was laced with menace, showing his true character. "It would be such a shame if the video clip got mixed in with the nice little montage your brother put together for the event."

"What? How?" She refused to believe him.

"Everyone can be bribed for the right price," he said without care. "Finding someone at the production company your brother hired wasn't that hard to do. The guy's just waiting for my call to make the switch."

She panted around the vise squeezing her lungs and pressing on her chest. He wouldn't do that, would he? Was he truly that cruel? "Do you really want to hurt me that badly? Hurt my family like that? It's my parents' wedding anniversary, for God's sake. Chris is your best friend. He's been planning that party for a year. You would do that to him?"

Her older brother had decided to celebrate their parents' fortieth wedding anniversary with a grand party at the country club. It was the event of the spring that would include all of their relations, friends and business associates. A video like

that would mortify her entire family. She'd be shunned forever. Humiliated and shamed beyond her deepest imagination.

Eric didn't even appear troubled by the thought. He lifted
his shoulder in dismissal. "I'd be there to support him. Of
course I'd be shattered too. You were almost my fiancée, Kendra. To think I didn't know about that pathetic side of your
life. The jilted lover shamed by your betrayal." He faked a
shocked expression, his hand pressing to his chest. "Everyone
will survive with sympathy garnered after the shock wears off.
Everyone but you."

She stumbled back, too stunned to respond. He meant it
this time. She could tell by his blank emotionless delivery and
deadly seriousness in his eyes. "And who would want to hurt
me that bad except you, my jilted lover?" she rallied back,
scrambling for holes in his plan.

"You've made that so easy for me, Kendra." He gave her a
pitying look. "It'll be simple to convince everyone that if the
outcast of the family enjoys shit like that then you must have
made enemies who'd want to hurt you."

And her family would believe him. They all thought he
was perfect. It didn't help that she was partially to blame for
that incorrect perception.

Her bitterness and anger came through in her voice. "You
bastard. You're nothing but a selfish, self-serving prick who
gets off on beating women. Why in the hell do you even want
me back? I won't submit to your abuse ever again."

"You say that now, but I know you." A cruel smile marred
his face, the same one she'd come to recognize as the precur-
sor to his anger. She'd come to think of it as the real him. All
the charm and polish he showed the world only hid his demented, hateful core. "Under your fake resistance and objections, you love what I do to you. I watched you writhe and
moan with the pain and I know you love it. I've seen you

come from it. You can't fool me, Kendra. I know exactly how perverted you are."

The snow continued to fall around them, making the entire ugly situation seem almost surreal. Clouded in white, the flakes sticking to his hair and shoulders, Eric still looked like perfection. Right up until she looked in his eyes and saw that he truly believed what he'd said.

She shook her head, amazed that she'd once found him attractive. That she'd been as fooled as the rest of world. "You need help, Eric. You're really sick."

"Me?" His voice rose in volume and triggered the hairs on the back of her neck to rise in warning. "I'm not the one who likes to be hit."

"No," she challenged back, ignoring the pressing threat, her words grounding out the absolute hatred she had for him. "You're the one who likes to hit the defenseless. You abused me under the guise of desire for years. You asshole." She yelled the last at him, the anger expelling in the harsh curse.

"Bitch," he snarled right before he pounced.

She turned, dashing for her condo, but Eric was on her before she could run. A scream tore from her lungs and she fought the hold he had on her arm before his other arm clamped around her chest.

"Shut up," he growled into her ear as he yanked her tight to him. "You don't get to call me that."

"No!" she shouted, continuing to struggle. She wouldn't go with him. Never. She clawed at his arm, twisted her hips to try and kick him. "Let me go."

He released her arm and grabbed her ponytail, the vicious yank whipping her chin up to expose her neck and increase her vulnerability. Big snowflakes landed on her cheeks, leaving cold, wet kisses.

"Are you going to beg?" he growled into her ear, his breath hot against her neck.

"No," she managed to grit out. She wouldn't give him the satisfaction.

"Kendra?" The soft voice of her elderly neighbor penetrated the surroundings with startling clarity.

"Hey!" another deeper voice yelled. "Let her go!"

Paul came out his door, Lacey right behind him. Panic, compounded by embarrassment, made Kendra whimper. The sound of her heart roared in her head, muffling everything else. She didn't want anyone to see her like this. At Eric's mercy.

"What the fuck!" Eric roared right before he was jerked away from her. She was pulled back with him before he let go and she stumbled forward, gasping for air.

The thud of a fist hitting skin had her spinning around to see what was happening. Deklan stood over Eric, who was sprawled in the snow-covered grass, a hand to his bleeding lip. Deklan's face was contorted in pure rage; his lips peeled back, showing his teeth as he seethed. His fists were clenched at his sides, his chest heaving as he looked ready to kill.

"Who the fuck are you?" Eric shuffled back on the ground before he pushed himself up to stand, his attention on his attacker.

Deklan took a step forward, his fist raised, and Kendra jumped between the two men. "Stop."

Behind Eric, Edith Jennings stood on her porch, a phone in her hand. Paul had taken up position a few feet away, ready to help if needed.

The support stunned and warmed her. Gave her strength. "You need to go, Eric."

"Is everything okay, Kendra?" Edith called over. "Should I call the police?"

Undecided, Kendra didn't answer right away. Eric dabbed at his lip, pulling his fingers back to see the blood on them before he licked at the small cut. His eyes cut to hers, flashing the warning she so clearly knew. His nostrils flared, the struggle to control his rage making him visibly shake.

"Kendra," Deklan growled from behind her. "Are you okay?"

"Yeah," she answered, taking an unconscious step closer to his voice. To the safety he offered. She spotted Deklan's truck idling in the middle of the condo lot, the driver's door wide open. She reached back for his hand, and he grabbed it immediately. "Let's get out of here."

The simple warmth of his hand around hers gave her the power to walk to his truck. She had to get away from Eric. She felt him watching as she retreated, but she didn't care.

"Should I kick his ass?" Deklan rumbled at her side.

That got a smile out of her. As tempting as the offer was, she declined with a shake of her head. It wouldn't solve anything and with Eric's money, it would probably only land Deklan in jail.

"Remember what I said, Kendra." Eric's threat carried through the crisp air to wrap around her chest and squeeze it tight. Her step faltered against her will. Eric laughed, and she turned back to him. He flashed a cocky smile, a look of knowing in his eyes. "You have a week."

The chill reached her then. She shuddered, but she didn't know if it was from the temperature or the ice that had filled her blood. He would do it. She knew without a doubt that Eric intended to follow through on his threat this time.

Deklan turned back, his fist ready as if he was going to beat the shit out of Eric anyway. She grabbed his arm to stop him. A slight shake of her head was all it took to halt the large man. He could've easily ignored her wishes, but he listened to her despite his obvious desire to do the opposite. His jaw was clenched tight and his neck muscles bulged over the line of his leather coat. His eyes were almost black with his need to retaliate, only he didn't.

He closed his eyes, inhaled and gave her a short, precise nod.

Letting both relief and defeat suck her under, she turned away. Deklan ushered her around his truck and helped her inside. The heater blasted the interior with warmth that did nothing to stop her hands from trembling. She took a deep breath, the new car smell hitting her senses as she vaguely registered the pristine, black cab complete with bucket leather seats and a dashboard full of gadgets.

She pulled on her seat belt out of pure habit then stared out the windshield to meet Eric's hard glare. He stood in the same spot. His face was like stone, his hair wet and messed from the snow, his lip red and bleeding slightly. And still he was handsome. Only it didn't affect her anymore. She knew the evil that lived within him.

The slam of Deklan's door jerked her out of her trance. Her attention shot to Deklan's hard profile as he shifted the truck into gear and drove away. He reached for her hand, shooting her a quick look as he weaved the truck out of the maze of the condo complex.

His grip was strong, warm and provided more comfort than she'd expected. She bit her lip and stared at their clasped hands resting on her leg. In many ways she felt disconnected from it all, as if she was viewing the events from a distant lens. Yet her body was wired. Her leg bounced and her free hand shook where it rested on her thigh.

The low sound of an alternative rock song filled the cab under the hum of the heater fan, and she was grateful for Deklan's silence. He didn't pressure her for answers or ask inane questions, like he knew she wasn't ready to talk. And she wasn't. She didn't know what to say.

She stared out her side window, not really seeing the businesses they passed. The snow was still falling heavily, covering everything in its pure coat of white. Already there was a good inch or more on the ground, enough to make the road slushy and encourage people to stay indoors. Twilight was close enough that the street lights had come on, providing beams of light for the snow to dance under as it fell.

It dawned on her slowly that she was alone with Deklan, trapped in his truck without escape. Just six weeks ago she'd have been deep in the throes of a panic attack at even the thought of the situation. She pondered that, searching for the fear that would send her heart racing and her chest constricting until she gasped for air, but found nothing.

Deklan rubbed small circles over her knuckle with his thumb, a soothing touch that reminded her of how gentle he could be. A cold drop of water slid down the side of her head and was followed by another to trail down her neck, making her shiver. The snow was melting off her hair and she used her free hand to knock the rest from her head, scattering wet droplets everywhere.

She studied the man beside her and waited for the shot of anxiety to set in. His short hair was damp like hers, making it appear glossy and jet black. His cheeks were cleanly shaven and in profile his nose displayed a slight bump, as if it'd been broken before. His lips were pulled thin in a grim line, his focus on the worsening roads. She knew he was older than her, but his hair showed no gray or his face any sign of age. There was a maturity there, one that came from experience, not time.

Deklan was about as opposite from Eric as she could get. Where Eric was cultured sophistication, Deklan was gritty reality. They were both handsome, but Eric was GQ cover model, where Deklan was all bad boy.

Yet she felt safe with this man. He glanced at her, sending her a tight smile before returning his attention to the road as they entered the highway. He let go of her hand then, needing his to help steer on the slickening pavement.

"Where're we going?" she finally asked. The fact that she should care was just taking hold.

He looked to her again, his eyes scanning her face in a quick assessment before darting back to the traffic. "The club."

She nodded in acceptance, even though he wasn't watching her. The thought of going there didn't scare her. The Den was now a place of comfort, oddly enough. Her time there had become one of healing to the point where she instantly relaxed when she entered the building, the distinctive smells and sounds triggering good feelings instead of bad. She hadn't expected that when she'd agreed to the contract with Deklan, but it was a pleasant byproduct.

Just one of many, if she was honest. After all, she'd never expected to find this easy comfort so quickly with a man. One who was her contract Dom first, but was now someone she thought of as a friend. Her lover? Not completely, but he was closer to that than Eric had ever been, even if they hadn't had sex.

Was that it? The fact that Deklan had followed everything she'd asked for, both written and verbal? He'd more than proven his trustworthiness to her. Yet she was still resisting that last connection, even though she really ached to feel him in her. She'd made multiple offers to service him during a Scene and he'd declined every time. She didn't truly understand why, yet each time her respect for him increased.

There was a part of her that knew if she had sex with him it would be more than a casual event, part of a Scene they both walked away from. And that scared the hell out of her. She didn't want a relationship with a man who was also her Dom. They were separate things, and her past proved to her that they couldn't mix. Maybe it worked for others. But she wasn't ready to fall down that path again.

Deklan was her Dom. She had to remember that.

EIGHTEEN

He opened the door to Jake's loft and went in, holding it open for Kendra to follow. Deklan wasn't surprised when Seth's door opened across the hall. The man came out of his loft to lean on the doorjamb. The questions were clear on his face.

Deklan stepped back into the hall, keeping the door partially ajar behind him. "Heard from Jake then?" He'd sent Jake a text after parking the truck to check on using his loft. Apparently the condo gossip line had already alerted Cali to the scene outside of Kendra's place.

"Yeah. Everything okay?"

"Think so." Deklan stared down the hallway to the large warehouse-style window at the end, showing the rapidly falling snow through the square blocks of glass. "Should we keep the club closed for the night?" The Den was scheduled to open within the next half hour.

Seth followed his gaze to stare out the window. "It'd be safer. Hell of a hit on our income, but last thing we want is people getting stuck here for the next two days. Most of the employees are already here, but I can send them home."

Deklan focused back on Seth. "Is it supposed to get that bad?"

"The weather reports are predicting the worst spring storm in over fifty years."

"Great." He swiped a hand through his hair, the dampness from the snow wetting his fingers. How would Kendra feel about being stuck here if that was true? Fuck. He'd deal with it if it happened. "What's your call?"

Seth groaned as if he was in real pain and hung his head, his long hair falling forward to brush past his face. "Fuck. I hate this." He straightened, swiping his hair out of his eyes as he did. "We're gonna piss people off no matter which way we go. But everything's shutting down and if the weatherman is even remotely right, we should probably close." He blew out a breath. "I'll take care of the club. You take care of Kendra."

"You're sure?"

"Yeah. I got it." He narrowed his eyes. "I'll be here if you need anything."

Deklan glanced over his shoulder to see Kendra pacing along the far wall, her thumbnail being whittled down between her teeth. He stepped back into the loft, preparing to close the door. "Thanks, Seth. Same to you."

All thoughts of the club dropped from his mind the second the door clicked closed. Jake's loft was open and spacious with only a minimal amount of furniture. There was a sitting area with a flat-screen setup to the left. Two large windows like the one in the hallway ran along the far wall, letting in a lot of natural light to make the space feel bright despite its starkness. The kitchen area was to the right along the back, with an eat-in island bar that served as Jake's table.

Kendra's shoes squeaked on the hardwood floor as she pivoted and walked toward the TV area in a path she seemed unaware of. Her agitation was clear and understood. His hand fisted, just remembering the hold the other man had had on her. He'd seen red the second he'd turned the corner and started toward her unit.

Coming back to the present, Deklan removed his coat and boots, calculating the best way to approach her. The car ride over had been mostly silent, partly because he hadn't trusted himself to say anything. The desire to explode in anger was so strong it'd seriously frightened him. At least his time in the service had taught him how to channel his rage. It was that same anger uncontrolled that had landed him in the military to begin with.

He sent a quick text to Rock in security telling him he wouldn't be down before crossing the room to grab two bottles of water from the fridge, taking them over to Kendra. He stood in her path and waited until she turned, heading toward him, only to pull up short when she realized he was there. Her head snapped up, her eyes big with unfocused worry.

"Water?" He held up the bottle and it took her a second before her gaze dropped to the beverage and still another before her mind seemed to catch up with what he said.

She nodded and took the water from him. "Thank you," she mumbled before twisting off the cap and taking a long drink. She exhaled slowly as she lowered the bottle, her eyes closing with the movement.

He ran his knuckles over her cheek, wanting to hold her so badly his arms ached. She turned her face into his touch and that was all it took for him to follow through on his inclination. He tossed his unopened water onto the couch and surrounded her in his embrace. Thankfully, she came willingly. Almost melting against his chest as her arms circled his waist.

A gust of wind beat against the window and the sound echoed through the open space. The low purr of the refrigerator could be heard if he strained, but otherwise the room was silent. He took a deep breath, the relief at knowing she was safe flushing through him. The crisp smell of the outdoors mixed with the light scent of lilac from her shampoo helped to calm him further. He waited for her to cry, to hear the sobs he expected after what she'd been through, only none came.

After a while she took a deep breath then pushed away to resume her pacing. "Thank you for that too," she said almost dispassionately. "You didn't have to help me."

The words alone had his temper rising once again. He understood she was being defensive and he reached for his patience before answering. "You're right that I didn't have to help you." That made her pause, her eyes searching him for the catch. "I wanted to. I told you I'd never harm you and I'll never let someone else either."

"Of course." She nodded, as if that was the only reason he'd want to help her. With that she changed her direction, her new path taking her in front of the TV then back toward the window.

"Kendra," he said after the silence stretched on. He needed to do something to help. But what? "I assume that was your ex. The one who abused you." She'd yet to tell him the whole story of her past. Maybe now would be a good time. He wouldn't force her, but it was killing him not knowing. He'd had Rock collect the information soon after they signed their contract. It was still unread. So many times over the last weeks he'd sat down to read it, only to leave the electronic folder unopened on his computer.

She stopped at the window, took another drink from the bottle then continued to stare outside. "Yeah. That was Eric." She spoke to the glass, and he took a step closer to hear her better. "He found me and wants me to come back."

Red. Flaming, crimson shades of red clouded his mind instantly. There was no way in hell he'd let her go back. Never.

Fortunately she wasn't looking at him to see the rage that must surely be showing. "And?" he managed to prompt with calm.

She looked to him them, her brow furrowed. "I won't go. I might be slow, but I'm not completely stupid."

"I never thought that."

Looking down, she closed her eyes and shook her head, puffing out a small breath of defeat. "I felt it," she said softly.

"Hey." He moved closer until he could tilt her chin up. Her eyes were rimmed with pending tears but she blinked rapidly, holding them back. His chest tightened and he wanted nothing more than to take away all of her pain. "Don't ever think that."

She searched his face for a long moment before pulling away to pace back to the sitting area. Wrapping one arm around her waist, she took a drink of the water, the shaking bottle showing how unsettled she really was.

"Kendra."

Her shoulders rose and fell before she turned to him.

"What was his threat about? One week?"

She closed her eyes again, her jaw tightening with her compressed lips. The water sloshed in the half-full bottle, where it trembled in her hand. In a sudden explosion she turned toward the wall and hurled the bottle. "Fuck him," she cried. The bottle smashed against the plaster, water splashing out of the open top to splatter across the wall before it dropped to the hardwood. "God, I hate him. Fucking hate him." She spun around, paced two steps before her knees buckled and she dropped to a crouch, breathing deep, her head grasped tight in her hands.

Her anguish was so strong that Deklan was actually lost at what to do. He felt helpless, an emotion he detested above all others. He was a fucking Green Beret; he'd faced enemy guns and shitholes most people never dreamed existed. Yet he was clueless on what to do right here. Right now.

She rocked on her heels, the lean muscles in her calves and thighs standing out under the tight navy running pants. "He's going to ruin my family." Her voice broke and she cleared her throat.

He dropped to his knee beside her, gathering her huddled form to his chest. She toppled into him without resistance. "You're safe," he soothed into her hair. "It's okay."

"But it's not okay," she insisted, her voice muffled. Two seconds later she exploded out of his arms, nearly nailing him in the chin.

He let her go, even though his instinct was to pull her back and hold her until she calmed. But Kendra couldn't seem to stay still. She was back at the window, staring at the almost darkness, her fist tapping against her lips, leg bouncing in a matching beat.

"He has a video," she said to the window, her breath forming a cloud on the glass. "One he took of me. Tied up. Begging…for more." She sniffed, eyes closed. She wet her lips behind the fist that still rested on the small space between her mouth and nose. "He's going to add it to my parents' anniversary montage at their party next weekend if I don't come back."

"Fuck," Deklan breathed before he could stop himself.

Her head whipped around to stare at him, her eyes wide. A puff of defeated laughter came out as she shook her head. "Yeah. Fuck is right."

He stood. "What can I do?"

"Nothing," she snapped. "There's nothing anyone can do."

"Can we get the video? Destroy it?" Deklan was already planning how to do that, details unknown. He knew plenty of men who could take care of it without getting caught.

"No." She shook her head. "He's too rich. Too much old money to get to. Plus, he probably has a ton of copies made by now."

"Money doesn't worry me. Everyone has a weakness that can be exploited."

"No!" she insisted, her hand cutting through the air as she glared at him. "This is my problem. One I made and I have to take care of."

Fuck. He ran a palm over his hair, his own frustration grinding away at his gut. "I can help," he ground out, fighting to keep his calm.

She stalked away, her hands clenching her hips. "You don't get it." She whirled around. "He's going to humiliate my whole family in front of everyone. Eric works for my father. He's my brother's best friend. I lived with the damn man for two years and it all means nothing to him. He's a heartless, cold bastard. If I don't go back now, I'll never be able to."

He advanced on her, his long strides bringing him close. "You can't seriously be thinking of going back to that asshole. I won't let you."

Her spine snapped straight. "You won't let me?" She gaped at him, her eyes blazing with fight. "You don't have a say in what I do, Deklan. Our contract ends at the door to your stinking club. My life will never be controlled by anyone but me ever again." She thumbed her chest, her face flushed with her passion.

Damn it. He hadn't meant that as it sounded. Or had he? Fuck. Backing down, he took a step back and raised his hands in retreat. It wasn't a move he was used to making, but for her he did. "You're right. I'm sorry." He moved away, taking his turn to stare out the window. Darkness had fallen, but the snow was still highlighted by the safety lights mounted along the building three stories down and the dim flare of the streetlights. "It just…" His jaw clenched as he struggled to hold back the anger. "It kills me to think of anyone harming or threatening you. That you would go back to him to save your family is noble, but there has to be another way. I don't know if…" He couldn't finish. She wouldn't want to hear that he couldn't let her go.

"I already told you I wasn't going back to him," she hurled at his back, the anger still heavy in her voice. He imagined if she still had the water bottle it'd be hitting his head right about then. "I'll handle it."

He spun around. "How?"

"I don't know, but I will."

"Is it so hard to accept that I want to help you?"

"Yes," she cried then jerked up short. Her hand flew up to cover her mouth as if she wanted to capture the words and slip them back inside. "Oh, God…that sounded so bad." She fumbled backwards until her hand rested on the back of the couch and she slumped against the support, her eyes dazed. "How did it get this bad? I don't trust anybody anymore. Not even myself."

"That's not true," he challenged, then he took a risk. "You trust me."

She didn't move or respond to his bold statement, but her eyes never left him. The faint glow of light from the kitchen cast her face in shadow, her features appearing soft and vulnerable. Exactly opposite of what she was.

"If there wasn't trust between us, you'd have never allowed me to do the things we've done together. Every Scene is a venture of trust. Every time you let me restrain you, you give me your trust." He moved closer once again. "I value and cherish what you give to me." He stopped directly in front of her and held her gaze, needing her to understand the importance of his next words. "I value and cherish you."

Her lip quivered behind her fingers. "I don't understand why."

"Why what? Why you trust me or why I cherish you?"

"Both," she whispered.

He folded her into his arms, pressing her long length to his body until her head rested on his chest. She was so brave. Strong. He wished she could see that. Get her to believe that. Only he didn't know what he could say to convince her of any of it.

He was just starting to relax, letting her presence so close to him ease his tight muscles, when she pushed against him, forcing him to step away. She swiped at her cheeks and sniffed away the rest of the tears. "I won't cry," she said, determined, the strength returning to her voice. "I'm done with that."

She pushed away from the couch and strode around the sitting area to the kitchen counter. Bracing her hands on the edge, she leaned against it, stretching her calves like she was preparing to go for a run. She stopped, straightened then fidgeted with the zipper on her jacket as she bounced lightly on her toes.

"Damn it," she cursed, squeezing her eyes shut. "I need to do something. I can't just sit here."

"Do you want me to take you home?" He was completely against that idea since they had no clue where the asshole might be. But he felt compelled to offer. He didn't want her to feel trapped here with him.

"No." She shook her head, rubbing at her arms. Her head snapped around to stare at him. She contemplated him long and hard before finally speaking. "Do a Scene with me."

Her voice was firm and controlled and she appeared completely serious. But every warning signal flashed within him that it was a bad idea. "No way. Not now."

She marched toward him, determined. "Why not? I trust you. You told me that. So let's go. I need it."

He stood his ground. "No. You're not in the right frame of mind for a Scene."

"Bullshit. I know I want this. I'm asking you for it. Do you want me to beg?"

"Stop it, Kendra. You know that's not it."

"Then what? Prove I can trust you, Deklan," she pushed. "I need the pain right now. I'm going nuts." Her hands gripped her neck as she paced back to the kitchen island. When he didn't answer she cursed under her breath then strode to the door and yanked it open before he realized her intent. She was out of the loft and in the hall when he finally reacted.

"Fuck," he vented, chasing her down. His socks slipped on the polished floor and he cursed again, feeling as coordinated as a hippo. At the door he saw that the elevator was already sliding closed and she smiled at him, the challenge clear as they finished closing. "Goddamn it!"

He slammed the door shut behind him and sprinted to the stairwell, jumping down the steps four at a time, hitting the third floor in a matter of seconds. She must have heard him coming because when he opened the stairwell door, she was already sprinting down the long hallway, heading for the stairs that ended at the Dungeon.

"Kendra," he growled, taking off after her. Damn woman. His pulse raced but he wasn't sure if it was from frustration or excitement. His hunter instincts kicked in and he stalked her down the hallway, letting her get safely down the stairs before he accelerated after her.

"Come on, Deklan," she called out as he entered the Dungeon. She stood in the center of the room already stripping her jacket off, pulling it down her arms and tossing the material aside. "Let's do this."

The room was strangely empty for the time of night and Deklan growled low in his chest when he remembered why. "We're all alone, Kendra. The club's closed for the night."

She froze in the middle of removing her shoe, one leg cocked up to rest on the opposite knee as she braced her hand on the edge of a freestanding St. Andrew's cross. She scanned the room as if the fact was just dawning on her. Taking a breath, she exhaled it slowly then continued to undo her shoelace, toeing it off before she began on the other shoe.

"I'm not doing this." He crossed his arms over his chest and hardened his resolve. It didn't matter that she looked absolutely outstanding, stripping down in the middle of the Dungeon. Her skin was flushed with her anger, her actions resolute. His cock hardened beneath his leathers despite his best efforts against it. "Our contract clearly states not in private. I won't break that."

She kicked her other shoe aside and faced him, chest heaving. Tilting her head, she pointed to the corner of the room. "Cameras. As you told me before, we're not alone." She flashed a victorious grin then yanked the tight running top over her head.

He sucked in his breath, absorbing the vision she presented. Nothing flashy or seductive. Just pure, muscled female. The jogging bra hugged her firm breasts, defining her hard nipples and showing the small outline of the teasing rings and charms she wore in them. Her stomach was lean and ridged with muscles that expanded and contracted with each quick breath she took. The skin-tight leggings hid nothing. Instead they showcased the long length of legs sculpted from the hours spent running.

He jerked his eyes away from her body and cursed at himself when he saw the knowing gleam in her eyes. It wasn't like he could hide his erection in his tight leather pants. With a slash of a smile, she pulled her bra over her head, exposing her perfect breasts, the nipple rings gleaming in the light, the sun charms dancing beneath. He groaned and forced himself to look away.

He couldn't do this. Damn it. He fucking trained his Doms to never do a Scene when feelings were too heavily involved. Control was the key, and there was never control when emotions were strung high.

The rustle of fabric told him she was removing her pants. "Stop it, Kendra," he growled, his voice hoarse with his barely held restraint. "We're not doing this." His fingers dug into his sides, where he gripped his hips.

"You might not be. But I am." Her running pants hit his chest and he flinched, not from the impact but the knowledge of how she would look if he turned to her. When skimpy white panties followed the path of her pants, Deklan almost choked on his own spit as it got stuck in his raw throat. She was naked.

"That's against our contract," he gritted out.

"Screw the contract. I'm saying it's okay. All of this is fine." Her breath gushed through the silence of the Dungeon. "Where do you want me, Deklan?"

His jaw ached with the familiar tension and he squeezed his eyes close, resisting his desires. He couldn't do this. No way. It was wrong. "No."

"I didn't say 'lilac,'" she spat back. "If you won't do this, I'll find someone else."

His eyes flew open, his head snapping up to glare at her. "Like hell you will."

When his brain logged the vision before him, he froze. She was stunning. Standing completely nude and waiting for him in the middle of a room filled with all means of BDSM torture and play equipment. Weak wasn't even close to being in the long list of descriptions that flashed in his mind for her. His cock hardened even more, his focus held on the strength displayed before him. She wasn't bodybuilder pumped up, but long, lean cords of physical beauty.

She was a woman who wouldn't break beneath him. She could match him, challenge him and turn him inside out. "Damn it, Kendra. Put your clothes on."

Instead of complying, she reach up and tugged her hair out of its holder, giving a small shake and fluffing her released hair until the long strands settled over her shoulders in a tempting length of silk.

Fucking shit. He was a breath away from breaking every self-imposed rule he had. Years of hard-learned discipline was the only thing holding his feet firm.

"Do you like what you see?" She held her arms out and slowly turned in a circle, giving him a view from all sides. *Fuck* was the only word his brain seemed capable of forming. He'd seen her many times close to naked, but the actual sight was leaving him struck stupid.

"Why?" he choked out.

Her head whipped around to peer at him over her shoulder, her eyes full of questions.

"Why are you doing this?"

"Because I trust you."

Sucker-punch. That was so not fair and she knew it.

She let the words linger before walking over to a spanking bench and dropping to the kneeling pad, her eyes on him the entire time. "Because I need this." She stretched out on the inclined bench until she was spread out, prone and waiting for him.

His submissive.

"I need you, Deklan."

Ah, fuck it all to hell. Now what was he supposed to do?

NINETEEN

Kendra's words rang like a gong of truth within her. She needed him.

She clenched the handles of the spanking bench in a grip that made her fingers ache and her arms quiver. But she wasn't backing down. Damn it, this was for her. She couldn't take her eyes off of the imposing man who glared back at her.

What would he do?

She'd brazenly thrown out the challenge, gone against his command and acted out. Was she deliberately asking to be punished? Yes. God, yes. She was crazy, she got that. But she wasn't thinking right now. Reacting, that's what she was doing.

This was on her terms. She was controlling it. And she wasn't afraid. Not of him. Not Deklan. She did trust him. Completely, or she wouldn't be lying here naked, begging him to spank her. Hit her. Make her forget it all.

But he didn't move. His face was a hard, controlled mask with thin lips and a tense jaw. His deep blue eyes were almost black as he stared at her, his nostrils flaring slightly with each breath that expanded his large chest. The tight, black T-shirt molded to his torso just like his black leather pants hugged his powerful legs and outlined his erection. He was dressed for his Master role and damn it, she wanted him to perform.

But he wasn't a puppy following her lead.

With deliberate movements, he lifted his hands from his hips, gripped the back of his shirt and yanked it over his head in one swift pull. Relief clashed with anticipation as she gobbled up the view of his muscled chest and arms. Her fingers flexed with the need to touch every inch of him. Something she hadn't done yet, but ached to do each time they played. He was a temptation held just out of her reach, which only made him more alluring.

"Safe word," he demanded.

"Lilac." The breathy reply was exhaled on a wave a relief. He was going to do it.

He unsnapped his pants, his eyes commanding her to understand his intent. "Remember it."

She swallowed, barely able to manage the task as he unzipped his pants and hooked his thumbs under the waistband. Was he...? The answer to her unasked question came when he eased the leather over his hips and down his thighs.

"Oh, my..." Her reaction was mouthed, but no sound came with it. He was beyond gorgeous. His dick fell out of its restriction as the material was tugged away. No underwear, of course. He bent to finish removing his clothing, temporarily blocking her view, and she took the second to gather her frayed thoughts but didn't manage it before he tossed his socks and pants aside and straightened.

Holy...crap. Brain synapses sizzled and fried instantly. Her eyes ate up every inch of his displayed body in a second then cruised back to fully savor the sight. The man before her left Eric in the dust. But then, she knew that.

She licked her dry lips, holding her bottom lip between her teeth to keep back the moan that wanted to escape. His legs were as muscled and strong as she'd envisioned. His cut abs tapered to the V-shaped definition of his groin that drew her attention straight to his large, hard cock. The dark nest of hair that surrounded his erection and balls was almost a mocking declaration of what she'd been missing out on.

Her pussy clenched in want, the fire of arousal swamping her in its sudden attack. His erection stood out in a glorious declaration of his own need. She wanted to lick that too. If he let her. A slim smile formed at that thought. Would she get the chance tonight?

His lips thinned into a grim line and he turned his head to stare at the wall, his fists clenching at his sides. Without a word, he shifted and strode around the front of the bench she was on, moving past but not sparing her a glance or a touch. She swiveled her head to follow his movements. What was he getting? Anticipation pumped up her adrenaline, all thoughts of being afraid or angry gone.

He stopped beneath a spreader bar that hung from the ceiling. Lifting his arms, he grabbed the long metal pole before stepping back to the wall and adjusting the chain that held the bar, tugging it higher. The rattle of the chain clanked loudly in the quiet Dungeon.

Confusion made her brows pull down. "What are you doing?"

Ignoring her, he went back to the bar, tested the height once again then kneeled. Her view was blocked by other equipment and she resisted the urge to lift herself up to see what he was doing. A moment later his hips came up, he bent at the waist as he spread his legs wide and worked at something at his ankle.

Was he…? No. She pushed up, kneeling on the bench as he straightened and met her eyes. He lifted his left arm to the bar over his head, the slow, precise movement challenging in its own way.

"What…" She couldn't finish the question, too stunned to grasp what he was doing.

Gripping the bar, he used his other hand to buckle his wrist into the attached cuff. No. He couldn't be. This wasn't what she wanted.

Bolting upright, Kendra dodged the obstacles to halt before him. "What are you doing?"

His feet were buckled into the spreader bar attached to the ground, one wrist bound to the bar over his head with his last hand gripping the other side of the bar, unable to buckle that one on his own. He stared at her, conveying more in his eyes than he'd ever done before.

"I'm yours." His voice was steady and he dropped his gaze to the ground. "Do with me as you wish."

"No!" She flew at him, her anger blinding her. She pushed him, her palms slapping his hard chest, forcing him backward until he halted with a jerk at the limits of the bars. "Damn you. I don't want this."

Why was he doing this? It made no sense. He was the Dom.

"You insist on having a Scene. This is what I can give you." His voice was solemn, resolute. "I trust you, Kendra."

Her chest constricted, the anger clouded by confusion. He was letting her master him. "Why?" She backed away, her hands trembling where they rested over her stomach.

"The tools and toys are in the cabinets along the wall." He spoke to the floor, the submissive pose not flattering on him at all. Yet there was something appealing about seeing the powerful, dominant man at her mercy.

"Look at me," she ordered, stepping forward again. His head snapped up, obeying immediately. Her sense of power flared at that one simple move. His eyes held no challenge. No worry or apprehension. "You want this?"

"Yes, Mistress."

The honorary sucked the breath from her right before the warmth flooded her. He was in her total control. She'd never had this kind of power over anyone.

"Fine," she snapped. Reaching up, she went on her tiptoes, grabbed his one free wrist and buckled it into the cuff, completing his bondage. Dropping back to her heels, she let her fingers drift down the length of his arm, reveling in the feel of his skin beneath her touch.

If this was what he wanted, she wasn't backing down. If it was a bluff to get her to quit, she was calling his.

"Safe word?" she asked.

"Lilac."

She shook her head. "No. Yours."

"Lilac," he repeated.

The flash of anger hit again. She didn't understand the point he was trying to make and she was sure there was one. Whatever, he could have her word. She pinched his nipple, getting only a small flinch as a reaction from him. He wanted to play games? Fine, she'd play.

She placed both hands on his chest and used one of his tricks. Turning her fingers into claws, she ran her nails down the entire length of his body. Over his pecs, down his ribs, around his dick and along each leg until she reached his toes. The shudder that followed her descent was only mildly satisfying.

At eye level now, his cock stood out proud and tall; his erection hadn't flagged a bit. It bobbed before her, mocking her. She leaned forward and sucked him down. He was smooth, hard silk in her mouth. His groan echoed through the room and his hips thrust forward, as if he couldn't control the reaction. She hummed her approval, grabbing his ass to hold him still when he jerked again.

She pressed her tongue against the underside of his shaft, stroking up and down over the ridge of the thick vein that bulged from the base to the rim. He tasted like man and she inhaled, the light sent of soap and sandalwood driving her mad. She pulled back, sucking hard before stopping at the rounded tip to run her teeth under the flared head. Teasing, taunting. Hurting.

He sucked in a long draw of hissing breath, his muscles clenching beneath her hands. He was at her mercy. She smoothed her tongue over the soft top, tasting the first drop of pre-come as it leaked from the tip. The taste of salt and him was heavenly.

She released her prize and looked up the length of him to find him staring at her. "Do you like pain, Deklan?"

His jaw worked. "Yes."

She dug her nails into his ass cheeks. "Receiving it? I know you like giving it, but do you enjoy receiving it?" She kept his gaze locked with hers as she released a trail of hot breath down the length of his erection. Snaking her hand between his legs, she clenched and tugged his sensitive balls, watching his eyes widen and his mouth fall open. She squeezed until the orbs compressed within her palm. "I'm waiting."

"Yes, Mistress." His reply was gritty with pain and something else.

She released her hold and bent her head to suck the tortured balls into her mouth. The light covering of hair tickled her tongue as she took turns soothing first one then the other. Did she really want to hurt him? It was so tempting to just love him. To savor the feel of him under her palms and enjoy the smooth glide of his skin, the scent of his arousal, the moans of approval as she pleasured him. She slid her hands down the backs of his legs, the softness of the hair there contrasting with the rougher curls under her tongue, tormenting her with a driving need for her man.

Her Dom.

Damn it. Why is he doing this? There had to be a lesson involved. Doms didn't give up control for no reason. And he'd never come across as a switch, as a man who'd be comfortable in a submissive position. Everything he did and presented was about being in charge. Always in power.

Yet here he was, willing, at her mercy. It had to be fake.

Instantly her anger returned. The fury mounted until it consumed her passion, leaving her cold and hurting. Snatching her touch away from him, she pushed back and rose to her full height. Her gaze scoured upward one more time before she spun around and stormed to the cabinets he'd indicated along the wall.

She whipped open each and every one until all five units exposed their hidden stash of whips, floggers, crops, canes, paddles, ropes, clamps, cuffs, condoms, lube, dildos—and the list went on. She'd never seen so much BDSM equipment displayed and available for use. It was a blatant reminder that this was all a business for Deklan.

She was a client.

The reality stabbed at her heart and she squeezed her eyes closed in rejection of what she felt. What was between them could never be more. She didn't *want* it to be more. Eric had shown her this stuff didn't belong in a good relationship. It could never coincide in real life. It was a lesson she had to remember.

In a haze of denial she yanked tools off the shelves and hooks at random. A flogger, a crop, a paddle, it didn't matter what exactly. Maybe she'd try them all. They'd all been used on her at some point and it was past time she used them on someone else.

How would it feel to strike Deklan with these tools of *his* trade? Yeah, she nodded absently, grabbing another heavier flogger from the cabinet. *Let's see what makes him writhe and moan.* Scooping up a ball-gag for good measure, she turned with her collection of toys and sauntered back to him. *Let's play, Deklan. You wanted this? You got it.*

He didn't move, but he followed her every step with intent eyes. Was he nervous? Anxious? Excited? His appearance gave away nothing. She'd change that.

Dropping her collection on a cart within his full view, she kept her back to him as she ran her fingers over them all. She grabbed a riding crop and swished it back and forth in the air, testing the weight, savoring the low whistling sound as it broke through the air.

She spun around, tool in hand. His erection had softened some and the sight made her pause. "Are you sure?" she asked, her conscience invading. This wasn't something she'd ever desired to do. By nature, she was the receiver, not the giver in this world.

"Yes, Mistress." His even, controlled voice spoke of his lie. There was no pleasure or even willingness portrayed. Only resolve, a commitment to continue even if he didn't want to.

"Damn you," she growled, stepping forward and swinging at the same time. The square end of the crop smacked him right below his ribcage. The slap as it hit his skin vibrated up the tool and resonated under her palm at the same time the sharp sound reached her ears. He winced, but only slightly. "I'm not your Mistress."

She hit him again, lower, just below his bellybutton. She knew from experience that the licks of stinging pain would shoot straight south. If he liked this, she would know. Shoving her hair out of her eyes, she watched his cock harden once again. He might not want to do this, but there was a part of him that liked it.

Raising the crop, she brought it down on his erection. The organ bobbed under the strike, his hips jutting forward as he bit back a sound. His face was screwed up in a grimace, but he kept silent despite the pain that had to be screaming through him.

"Let it go," she demanded, frustrated at his restraint. She needed to hear his pain. Wanted his agony to match her own. "You wanted this." She struck another blow on his groin area. "Let me hear you." A smack on each thigh. He hissed. "Will you scream for me?" And the kill stroke, an upward strike against the underside of his cock.

"Fuck," he roared, back arching, arms pulled tight against their restrictions.

Satisfaction curled through her, the little red squares from the crop standing out on his skin. But it was chased by a niggling thread of disgust. *No. He asked for this.*

There was a part of her mind that grasped she wasn't acting rationally. That the events of the day had piled up to this point where there was no way for her to process it all. But she wasn't backing down. She was done running away.

She threw down the crop, grabbed a flogger and struck. The tassels smacked over his abdomen before she brought them down on his chest. Over and over again she hit him, his skin coloring with pink stripes before flushing to a deep red. Vaguely she noticed the ache in her arm, the drop of sweat that ran down her temple, the strands of hair caught on her lower lip. But her own torments were nothing compared to the ones she'd wanted him to feel. For reasons she couldn't process, she needed him to experience the hurt and pain that clawed within her.

She paused, panting from the exertion, her fingers clenching the leather handle of the flogger until they ached. His skin was red where she'd struck him and based on the coloring, there weren't many places she'd missed in her frenzy. From the undersides of his arms down to his calves, he was marked in varying shades of red and pink, the stripes taunting her with her deed.

She'd done that to him. Her blood roared in her head, her pulse racing with adrenaline. Her eyes flashed to his face and she froze. He was staring back at her, his breathing as heavy as her own. His eyes were dilated but focused and what she saw there almost made her crumble.

Devotion.

She shook, refusing to see it. Refusing to understand what she saw. "No," she snapped. "You can't look at me like that."

"How?" he demanded. "What do you see?"

She struck him again, the leather strands whipping across his nipples. He sucked in a breath but didn't look away. "Don't," she cried.

"Don't what? Care about you? Want you? Love you? Which is it, Kendra?"

"Damn you. You have no right." To what, she didn't care or even know. He just didn't.

But he didn't back down. It didn't matter that he was at her mercy. He came at her with his words. "Why not? Because you don't want me to? What do I have to do to prove myself to you? This is me. Here. For you."

"But I didn't ask you to be."

"Didn't you?"

"No! I don't need you."

"But you do need this," he snarled, his arms jerking in their hold. "You told me that, and I listened."

She reeled back, his verbal blow like a punch to her gut.

Rejecting everything, she clung to her anger like the shield it was. *Ass. Oh my God, he was as much of an ass as Eric. How could she have been so blind? Twice.*

She spun away, unable to look at him anymore. More importantly, she didn't want him to see how much his words hurt. How true his strike hit.

Grabbing the other flogger—the one made with hard leather and knots at the end of the tassels—she stalked around to his back. The new tool quivered against her calf where it hung from her hand, the strips of leather teasing her skin as if it couldn't wait to be put to use.

He was as muscled and perfect from the back as the front. She swung the leather strips to smack over his rounded ass. No preamble, no warning. He didn't deserve the courtesy. When he didn't react or move an inch, she hit him again. And again until his butt muscles clenched and tensed, betraying his resolve.

"You going to safe word?" she taunted, almost wanting him to give in. But even before he responded, she knew his answer.

"No, Kendra." His reply was flat. Emotionless after the passionate exchange just moments ago, making her anger simmer and boil over. He made her feel irrational when she didn't want to be. Damn him. It didn't matter that a part of her knew that's exactly what she was. Instead of facing that fact she took aim at him.

"What are these?" She cracked the flogger over the list of names that reached from the crease of his butt down the back of his leg, stopping halfway down his calf. "Huh, Deklan? Why the names? Are they your victims? A list of kills?" She knew he'd been in the military. Were these the names of the people he'd taken out? The thought of that sickened her more. She really didn't know him at all.

"No," he gritted out, the anger back in his voice. His head

hung between his raised arms, but he didn't try to turn around or look at her.

Sensing she'd struck a nerve, Kendra honed in, needing to see him break. "I don't believe you." She flung the flogger over his leg again and again, wanting to scratch out every name on the limb. "Jessie McCall, Alex Stover, Juan Veracruz," she read off, striking him after each name. "They mean nothing to you?"

"No, damn it."

"Then who are they? Past lovers?" She laughed at the thought. All of the names except the very last one were male. But then maybe that explained why he'd rejected all of her offers for release.

"Drop it, Kendra." His muscles were pulled tight, every one bulging under his skin down the length of his arms, shoulders and back.

"Answer me." Her voice sounded shrill, the resounding echo scraping off the walls, making her wince. This wasn't her. What was she doing? She thrust back the doubt and hit again. The back of his leg was bright red from the repeated strikes, the black ink of each name appearing even starker. "Did you kill these men?"

"Yes," he roared. "Is that what you want to hear?"

Struck numb by his answer, she couldn't move. Their labored breathing competing for air was the only sound in the large room. "No," she whispered, not wanting to believe him.

His limbs went slack, as if the admission had sucked the strength from him. "They're the ones I couldn't save," he said so quietly she almost missed it. His guilt was intertwined with each word and reached out to choke her.

"Couldn't save? How?" There was something there that grated against her and she grabbed at that. Who was he saving?

"They all died under my watch." He took a deep breath but said nothing more.

"Is that what I am?"

His head snapped up, the tension returning. "What do you mean?"

"Someone to save? A project to make you feel better?"

"No," he denied, venom strengthening his words.

But she didn't believe him. Maybe she didn't want to believe him. She didn't want to feel for him. Couldn't let herself feel anything for him except the anger that kept her distant. Separated. "Is this just another sacrifice you're willing to endure to appease your guilt?" she snarled, grinding up the bitterness and beating it into him. "Well, consider me a failed project."

"You're not a project."

"Wrong." She struck him between the shoulder blades, his back arching away from the bite of the tassels. "Every client is a project for you."

He gasped for air, his words pushing out between the breaths. "You're more than a project. Isn't that what this is all about?"

"No, damn you."

"Then what is this?"

"You *asked* for it."

She streaked around his side to see his face, needing to see his expression. He stared back at her, his eyes dark and fierce with emotion. A vein bulged at his temple, pulsing with the beat of his heart. Another snaked down his arm, the blue-purple trail contrasting with the red blush of his skin. He reminded her of a savage warrior, defiant even in defeat.

"You demanded a Scene. I gave it to you." The hoarse tenor of his voice was the trigger that finally broke her.

"I am not a project," she screamed, losing it completely. She didn't want to see the concern in his eyes or hear the conviction in his voice.

Launching forward, she beat at his chest with her fists, the flogger dropped in her need to release her anger on him. Her pain. "I'm not a project," she insisted, the tears streaming down her cheeks.

In one leap she was up him, scaling his body until her legs wrapped around his waist, her hand gripping the longer lengths of hair at the top of his head. She hugged him tight with her thighs, the hot span of his erection taunting beneath her wet pussy. He clenched his teeth and watched her, his pupils consuming his eyes, leaving only a thin circle of blue around the black.

"I am *not* a project." Her voice was rough with emotion, her breath hitching with her struggle.

"I told you that."

"I'm not broken," she croaked, her hips moving to rub his cock over her spread and aching sex. "I don't need to be fixed."

"No, you're not. You don't," he agreed. "You're perfect as you are."

He was lying, had to be. She was so far from perfect it was funny. This had to be another one of his games. He wasn't going to win.

"Is this what you want?" She wiggled her bottom and was rewarded with a grimace and stifled moan. "What you've been waiting so patiently for this whole time?"

"No, Kendra." The fire was back in his eyes, the tendons popping along the sides of his neck. "This was never about sex."

His cock was rigid against her aching pussy. She rocked her hips, riding his hardness, letting it tease her clit. "But you want it."

"No," he gritted out, shaking his head in denial. "Not like this."

"Don't lie to me," she demanded. All men wanted it. Her muscles were shaking with the strain of holding herself to him and she shifted her grip, lifting herself higher. His stiff dick followed her slight rise until the tip was resting so very close to her entrance.

"God, Kendra," he groaned, his head dropping back to hang limp. He swallowed, the point of his Adam's apple bobbing with the movement. "I want you so fucking badly. But don't do this. Not here. Not like this."

"Why not?" Her voice broke and she squeezed her eyes closed against the show of weakness. He was denying her. But he wasn't in control here. She was. "It doesn't matter," she countered quickly. "This is my show."

His head snapped up, his eyes pleading with her. "Don't do this, Kendra. Stop and think for a second. Who is in control here?"

"Me," she fired back, her point proven.

"Right," he said, conviction flashing in his eyes. "So whose show is this?"

Slowly understanding dawned, clearing her fog of denial and forced resistance. She was in charge, but it wasn't her show. It was his. She was supposed to care for him. Listen to him.

Be there *for him*.

The small keening sound that leaked from her mouth was pulled from the depths of her humiliation. She had the power and by ignoring him, she was abusing it.

She was abusing him.

Oh, God. She shoved away from him, the horror of what she'd done, of what she was about to do ripped at her heart and tore out her soul. Her feet hit the cold floor, dumping her back into reality. Her hand shook against her lips as she edged away. "I'm so sorry…so sorry. Oh, God…" The tears flowed freely, leaving wet trails of her shame on her cheeks. How could she have done that? What kind of monster was she?

"It's okay," he soothed. "Baby, it's fine. It's okay."

"No," she whimpered, shaking her head, refusing to be forgiven. "I…what did I do?" She was no better than Eric. Her actions were appalling. Disgusting. She'd become everything she despised. Worse. "I almost," she choked, bending in half, her arms wrapped around her waist as a sob escaped. "I almost forced you…" She couldn't finish. She couldn't say it out loud.

Her knees hit the floor as she crumbled under the weight of her actions. What had she done? She curled into a fetal position in an attempt to hide. He'd said no and she almost forced herself on Deklan anyway.

"I'm so sorry," she moaned into her arms. "So sorry." The words repeating over and over around the tears that refused to stop. She shook with it all. The fatigue, pain, shame, shock—it was all there in every sob and tear that fell.

After years of running, hiding and dodging, she'd finally hit rock bottom. And she'd done it to herself.

TWENTY

The low, mournful cries filled the Dungeon, flaying Deklan raw with their tortured echo. He jerked at the bonds, not caring if he ripped his fucking arm off. He needed to get to Kendra. Her pain flayed at him worse than the flogging she'd given him. She was huddled in a ball, her face hidden behind her hands and hair, her whole body shaking with each gasping sob she expelled.

He didn't know what he'd expected to happen when he'd started this Scene, but it wasn't this. Hurting her like this was never his intention. Now he couldn't even comfort her. He was such a shit. Growling, he gave another yank on the bonds, knowing it was useless.

Never in his life had he felt so helpless and exposed. And he was the one who'd caused this.

The creak of a door opening had his head snapping around. He met Seth's cool stare as the other man strode toward him. Deklan looked away, unable to deal with the judgment he saw there. Not now.

Not with Kendra's pain-filled cries fueling his guilt.

Seth undid his wrists cuffs without saying a word. The second his hands were free, Deklan bent and went to work on his ankle bonds, but his fingers were numb and fumbling, his hands shaking. Pushing away his bumbling efforts, Seth completed what Deklan couldn't seem to manage.

He growled, accepting the help with grudging reluctance, and waited for the last cuff to be undone. Even before the leather was completely freed, he was moving. His knees slammed against the hard floor and she was in his arms.

"I'm so sorry, Kendra," he whispered against her temple. He clenched her to his chest and she didn't resist him, wonder of wonders. Threading his fingers through her hair, he cupped the back of her head and tucked it into the crook of his neck. "You're safe. I've got you."

His heart cracked with each tear that hit his skin. She placed her hand over his shoulder and he almost broke when she tugged him closer. Skin to skin, she pressed against him, completely naked for the very first time and in more than the physical sense. She'd bared everything to him and in turn stripped him raw.

At that moment he knew with certainty he was never letting her go.

He lifted her up and carried her out of the Dungeon. The long trek back to Jake's loft was made in complete isolation. He didn't know if everyone was truly gone or just smart enough to stay out of sight.

The light from the kitchen showed his way as he moved through the silent loft to the guest room, where he sometimes crashed. He worked at the covers one-handed until he could crawl under them, Kendra still tucked safely in his arms.

His heart pounded out the significance of the moment. This was the first time he'd ever allowed himself to just hold a woman in bed. His Scenes took place in the Dungeon, his aftercare on a chair or a couch. Beds were intimate. Personal. Then again, everything with Kendra was personal. It had been since the very beginning. Seth had been right about that. Tonight hadn't crossed the line because he'd trampled that boundary long ago.

She eventually stretched out, wrapping herself tightly to his side, one leg wedged between his. The sting and bite where she rubbed against his skin still tender from her flogging were fit reminders of how he'd failed her. Her cries slowed until they became soft sniffles and finally deep, breathy sighs. And still he held her, rubbing his palms over her soft skin in motions meant to soothe.

Outside the wind continued to hammer at the windows, making them rattle in their frames and declaring that the storm was still going strong. She swiped at her cheek with her fingers then tugged up the edge of the sheet to dry the rest of her face. Her breath hitched a few more times as she settled back into his arms, never once looking at him.

"I'm sorry," she whispered, her lips fluttering against the hollow of his collarbone. "Please forgive me."

The vulnerability in her voice had him pulling her closer. If he could he swore he'd take her right inside of him, where he could always keep her safe. "Already done," he told her. "If you'll forgive me."

"But…I'm the one who hurt you."

"And I hurt you." He ran his fingers down the line of her jaw, feeling what he couldn't see. "Sleep now. We'll talk more later." Neither one of them was in the right frame of mind for the discussion they needed to have.

She shook her head, her hair tossing against his shoulder. "How can you forgive me that easily? I was horrible to you."

"You were honest with me."

"I don't understand," she croaked, another sniff betraying her struggle for composure.

He stroked her hair, his fingers straying to the smooth contours of her cheek. "You don't have to. It's been a long day. Let it go for now. I'm not going anywhere."

"Why?" She sniffed. "Why aren't you running?"

He wrapped his arms around her, holding her tight, her chest firm and comforting against his own. "Because I'm yours, Kendra. You own me."

A small gasp was her only response. Her hand fisted where it rested on his ribs, her legs tensing around his. But she didn't pull away. She didn't run.

Slowly she relaxed, the stiffness leaving her muscles until her breathing flowed in a consistent pattern and her body twitched as the exhaustion pulled her into slumber. It was a long time before he followed. The simple pleasure of holding Kendra wasn't something he wanted to relinquish. Ever.

He had no doubts about his declaration. Kendra owned him, heart and soul. He'd do anything for her. Even let her go if that's what she wanted come morning. If he'd failed her that miserably, hurt her that badly, he'd let her run.

And it would kill him.

Deklan woke to the howling echo of the wind, the warm press of skin on skin and the soft tickle of breath against his neck. Fully awake an instant later, he took in his surroundings in the dim light of morning. Jake's place.

Dropping his head back to the pillow, he took a calming breath and hugged Kendra closer. He'd been out of the service for over five years and he still couldn't shake the paranoid alertness that'd been drilled into him.

Kendra shifted and murmured, "You okay?" Then as if she'd just realized where she was, she pushed away to prop herself up and stared down at him with wide eyes. "Oh…" He could almost see the memories as they flooded her, the events from the night before replaying in her head.

"It's all right, Kendra." He cupped the back of her head, tugging her down. She resisted only slightly before resting her head on his chest. "We're fine."

"Yeah, right," she said with a sarcastic edge. "How can you say that after what I did to you?"

"And what did you do that was so bad?"

The quiet settled around them and he focused on the tingle of sensation that trailed behind the light touch of her fingers as she traced the outline of his tattoo. "I used you," she said softly.

"How do you figure?"

"I took my anger out on you. I almost…" She wiped at her cheek. "I was as bad as him."

He pulled back, shocked at her words. "What? As bad as who?" He couldn't see her face, but the tension had returned to her body and told him everything.

"Eric," she whispered after a moment. "My ex."

"How in the hell do you figure that?"

"I didn't listen to you. I beat you and then almost forced myself on you."

He flipped her over so fast she could only gasp and gape at him in surprise. He pinned her to the bed, careful to keep his morning erection away from her. "But you didn't," he ground out, his eyes drilling her with the force of his words. "You stopped. You did listen to me. You are nothing like that bastard."

She searched him, the remnants of her breakdown still visible on her face. Her eyes were red-rimmed and puffy, her lips swollen, making her appear soft and vulnerable. "Why? Why'd you do it?"

"What? Bind myself? Submit to you?"

"Yes."

"I told you." The answer was so simple for him. He brushed her hair away from her face, his fingers lingering on the shell of her ear. "You needed it. I didn't trust myself to be the Dom, so I let you."

She shook her head. "Wrong. I was never the dominant in that Scene. You might have been bound, but you were still in control."

He couldn't deny her words. "Does that make you angry?"

She was silent for a moment, her face giving no hint to her thoughts. "Not really. It probably should, but I don't have the energy to be mad." She gave him a weak smile that didn't reach her eyes.

"I don't want you to be mad. That wasn't the point."

"And what was the point?" She looked so earnest as she waited for him to reveal the answer. The urge to kiss her senseless made his cock pulse where it was trapped against the bed. Damn, how he wanted her. Last night she'd driven him to the very edge and he'd almost thrown it all away just to be in her hot, wet pussy. She'd been right there, rubbing her wetness over his dick, and he'd been seconds away from thrusting into her and fucking up everything.

She'd turned the tables, called his bluff and had almost won. She was a fighter, even if she couldn't see that in herself.

He pulled on his restraint and brushed a chaste kiss to her forehead. "To help you."

She sucked in a breath but didn't respond. He could sense her shutting down, resisting him and his words. It was time to back off before she ran.

An outline of light peeked in around the blackout curtain and he rolled away before the temptation drove him to do something they'd both regret. Being naked with Kendra in bed was a fantasy he hadn't fully acknowledged until it was reality. But now wasn't the time to do anything about it, even if he ached to do so. He refused to take advantage of the situation or her.

"How does coffee and a shower sound?"

She groaned, the longing clear in the sound. "Like heaven."

Chuckling, he gave her shoulder a shove. "Go and shower. I'll start the coffee."

When she didn't move, he turned to look at her, raising his brows in questions. The flush that crept over her cheeks was so fucking cute it almost made Deklan forget his resolve to be good.

"I know this is going to sound stupid, given all that we've done together, but…" She bit her lip and peeked at him out of the corner of her eye. "Would you mind closing your eyes? I'm kind of naked here and…"

He laughed. Her sudden shyness was a complete twist in character but somehow it was endearing. "Got it." He made a show of placing his hand over his eyes, his grin filling his face. "Go."

He bounded out of bed as soon as he heard the bathroom door click shut. Pushing back the curtain, he took his first look at the damage from last night's storm. The rooftop across the alley had a good foot or more of new snow covering its surface. A glance to the street showed the same, the pristine covering unmarred by car tracks or a plow path, confirming his suspicion that they wouldn't be going anywhere soon.

The sound of the water motivated him to get moving. Using Jake's bathroom, he took a quick shower, pulling on a pair of sweatpants and a T-shirt hijacked from Jake's dresser when he was finished. A quick hunt through the drawers, and he found a pair of yoga pants and a sweatshirt that he assumed were Cali's and left them on the guest bed for Kendra to find when she came out.

He flicked on the TV to the local news station and watched a few minutes of updates, confirming his earlier assumption that they were pretty much grounded for the day.

The coffee had just finished brewing, the fresh-ground smell filling the loft when Kendra emerged from the bedroom. He glanced up and pointed to the bar stool. "Have a seat." He grabbed the pot, set a mug down on the island bar and filled it with coffee. "Cream or sugar?"

"No, thanks." She sat on the stool and took a long drink, her eyes closing as the liquid hit her system. She sighed and smiled, her shoulders slumping, releasing the stiff posture she'd held. "That is pure heaven. Thank you." Her eyes opened and a real smile curved over her lips. The first he'd seen on her since before the Eric incident. "For everything. The clothes, the coffee, the help. I don't get it, but thank you."

He took up a position across the kitchen, leaning back on the edge of the counter next to the coffee machine. "What don't you get?" He picked up his own coffee and took a sip.

"All of this." She waved her hand in the air as she set her coffee down. "Why you're being so nice when I was so awful to you."

The shower had taken care of most of yesterday's damage, but her eyes still showed the remains of a good cry, and the weariness was etched into the tight lines around her mouth. Her hair was damp where it hung past her shoulders, leaving wet marks on the pale yellow sweatshirt.

"I thought we talked about this." He waited until she looked at him. "Yesterday was about you, not me. You did nothing wrong."

"Then why do I feel like I did?"

"Don't know." He moved over to lean his forearms on the bar, his coffee mug hugged between his palms. "But I don't see it that way."

She stared at her fingers, lost in thought as she traced the random patters swirling in the marble design. "Why are you being so nice?"

He smiled. That one was easy. "Because I like you."

Her mouth dropped open to form a small O and he resisted the urge to laugh at her stunned expression. He'd keep repeating that sentiment until she got it.

His stomach rumbled and he used the excuse to give her room once again. He opened the fridge and checked out their options. He took his time digging around in the crisper drawers, letting his words sink in. He'd never shied away from what he wanted and he was done hiding that he wanted Kendra. "Looks like Jake has the makings for an omelet. Cali must be rubbing off on him." He grabbed the veggies, cheese and eggs and set them on the counter.

Kendra took her coffee over to stare out one of the large windows. It was a dance he was doing now. An undefined one that had him stepping forward and back to keep her from sprinting the fuck out of there.

Deklan was more at home in Jake's kitchen than the owner was, and breakfast came together quickly. The low sounds of the local TV station highlighting the aftermath of the storm played in the background, while the smell of the sautéed vegetables and eggs added that intimate morning vibe that was cozy and downright homey.

"Omelets ready," he called out, setting the plates on the bar. Wiping off his hands on a towel, he grabbed two forks and set them out. "More coffee?"

Kendra wandered back to the kitchen from the sitting area where she'd been watching the news and set her empty mug out for refilling. "You're constantly surprising me," she said with a shake of her head as she sat down.

He choked back a snort and turned away to replace the

coffee pot. He'd been surprising himself a lot lately as well. "Why do you say that?"

"Savior, Dom, chef. Is there anything you don't do?"

He shrugged, looking away, the praise feeling awkward on his shoulders. "Windows?" That got the laugh he was looking for. The full sound helped to ease the ache in his neck that hadn't quite relaxed since he'd pulled Eric off her yesterday.

"So you are human," she joked, picking up her fork. "That's good to know." She moaned in appreciation after taking a bite of the omelet. "Wow. You really can cook."

He ducked his head under the guise of picking up his plate to eat. "Thanks," he mumbled.

"Is that…" She tilted her head, leaning to the side for a better look. "Is that a blush I see?" Her face lit up, a smile beaming. "It is. Oh my God, the mighty Deklan can blush."

Scowling, he shoveled a forkful of eggs into his mouth. Her laughter was almost worth the embarrassment.

"Sorry," she giggled. "I shouldn't laugh. I hate it when people laugh at me."

He shrugged. Normally he did too, but it wasn't such a big deal with her. "I guess I earned it after last night." He winked, letting her know he was teasing.

She returned his smile before taking another bite of her eggs. Gesturing with her fork, she motioned toward the window and swallowed. "It doesn't look like we'll be getting out of here this morning, huh?"

"Nope." He watched her reaction. "Does that bother you?"

"Not really. I didn't have to work today anyway."

"It doesn't bother you to be stuck here with me?"

She eyed him as if trying to judge if it was a trick question. "No. Why do you ask?"

"Just making sure," he answered honestly. He collected the empty plates and took them to the sink to rinse off. The dirty dishes were stacked in the dishwasher before he turned back to find her studying him. "What?"

"Nothing," she said, a glint in her eye hinting she was bluffing. He started to comment but got distracted by the glimpse of her midriff as she stood and stretched her arms over her head. "So what should we do today?"

There was a whole truckload of shit they needed to talk about, but it was obvious she wasn't ready to do that yet, so he took a side step. "Movie?"

"Sure." She headed toward the television. "What's Jake got?"

"He has Netflix. Pick something out and I'll finish up."

Deklan wiped down the counters and sent off a few quick texts to Seth and Jake before settling down on the couch next to Kendra. She'd curled up at the far end in a kinked-up way only females seemed to manage. A blanket was tucked around her legs and she'd crammed a pillow under her arm propping her head on her hand.

That wasn't going to work. Opening his arm wide, he motioned to her. "Come here, Kendra."

She hesitated for a moment, her eyes cautious. It was another long second before she shifted to snuggle against his side. He wrapped his arm around her and scooted down on the couch until her head rested on his chest. Her sigh as she relaxed within his hold was perfect.

She was perfect.

The movie was a recent action-adventure that held no interest to Deklan. He couldn't think about anything but Kendra. Her hair had dried and the soft ends caressed his arm every time she moved, like the teasing brush of a feather. Her deep, even breaths indicated she was relaxed but also reminded him of her firm breasts, the barest hint of her nipple jewelry rubbing his side through the material of their clothing. Maybe that was his imagination or wishful thinking, but it didn't matter. He knew it was there.

The urge to keep her curled within his protection forever was so strong he almost sighed in contentment. There was a quiet in him that he only had with her. The clean smell of the standard bar soap in Jake's bathroom was wrong on her and he hungered for the faint lilac scent that was Kendra.

She smoothed her fingers in random patterns over his abdomen, making him inhale against the desire that flared. He bit back a curse and laced her fingers with his, halting her movements to keep his cock from tenting the sweatpants. The ache to have her was reaching an almost unbearable point. Where were the goddamn snake pits when you needed them? The mechanical disassembly of his gun replayed in his mind once again, a task he knew better after his many weeks of abstinence than he had when he'd actually done it every day. He played with her hair, letting his hand thread through the locks, the silky texture running past his fingers in mental time with each gun part that came off.

She was so close, exactly where he'd wanted her. Not in a Scene or under contract. It was just her and him without the pretense or excuses. And now it wasn't hard to imagine keeping this or to see a future with her. This, right here, was what he never let himself imagine having. Yet the barriers between them were still so huge.

Walls never stopped him before, and his shoulders tensed at the thought of kicking her when she was down. But they had to tackle the issues now or they might never overcome them.

And losing her wasn't an option. Fuck what he'd said last night.

She was his.

TWENTY-ONE

"Why lilac?"

The out-of-the-blue question yanked Kendra out of her thoughts and tore open the door of the cozy haze she'd been drifting in. There was so much she owed Deklan—words, explanations, apologies, thanks. All morning she'd taken the chicken way out of avoidance and he'd let her. Until now.

The coffee she'd consumed earlier churned and burned in her stomach as she mentally prepared for the conversation to come. Deklan had shown her nothing but patience and kindness since that very first night she'd begged him to spank her. Would that still hold after they talked? She wanted to hope so, but purging her demons would mean she had to risk losing Deklan.

And that was so much more than she'd risked by running away from Eric.

She'd kept her shame hidden from everyone for so long and now she was going to bare her soul for the second time in two days. It should be easier the second time around, but it wasn't. There was so much more riding on this discussion than yesterday's.

She waited, pretending to watch the car barrel off the edge of the parking deck, tires squealing, to magically land unscathed on the neighboring rooftop, escaping the bad guys who chased them. If only real life could be choreographed to land without bumps, bruises or scars.

"It's a good memory," she answered Deklan, knowing it was just the start. "Every year when I was younger, my family would take our yacht from Chicago up to Mackinac Island for the annual Lilac Festival. We'd spend the week there, stay in the Grand Hotel and ride our bikes around the island. And the lilac bushes were always in full bloom." A sigh escaped as she remembered the sense of security and closeness she'd felt during those trips. "It was the one time my father would take time off just for us."

"How many siblings do you have?"

"Three. Two older, one younger." She turned down the volume on the television now that the noise was an unwanted annoyance neither of them cared about. The remote bounced down the couch where she tossed it and she turned her face into his chest to hide from his perceptive eyes. "Jane is the oldest, then Christopher, me, and Emily is the youngest."

"Is your family close?"

"Not really. That's what made that trip special. On the island we were a family. Otherwise, we were mostly raised by nannies. My dad's life is his company, and Mom's purpose is to support him. Social circles, image, presentation—it's been hammered into us since we were born. It's all about what people think and see, not what's real."

His fingers returned to her hair, the gentle strokes both calming and tantalizing as the light tingles danced over her scalp before shimmering down her spine. "And Eric is friends with Chris?"

She closed her eyes, absorbing Deklan's presence. The softness of his old T-shirt, the slow rise and fall of his chest, the hint of laundry soap that didn't mask the unique scent that was him even without the sandalwood. This was real.

"They're best friends. They graduated from Harvard together, and Eric came to work with Chris at my father's company."

"Your brother didn't mind him dating his little sister?"

"It didn't matter what Chris thought." The depth and truth of the words stunned her for a moment. "Dad was overjoyed at us being a couple and that trumped any objections Chris might have had. Or me, for that matter."

"Even though he abused you?" Anger roughened the edges of Deklan's voice and warmed an icy place in her heart.

"No one knows," she said softly, the embarrassment making her shy away from the words. "Remember, it's all about image and the one everyone saw of us was of a happy couple. For once in my life, my mom and dad were proud of me. I wasn't the daughter who chose to go into social work instead of finance or law. Or the one who avoided the parties and they dismissed as eccentric. For once, I was the one they beamed and gushed about."

"I'm sorry."

"For what?" Confusion marred her brow as she tried to understand.

His lips brushed against her forehead as he answered. "That they were proud of your actions but completely missed the fact that there was this courageous, strong, independent woman who deserved their love, regardless of what you did."

A gentle kiss landed on her temple. Every time he did that she melted a little inside. It was almost like that spot was for him alone. Each kiss opened a little bit more of her heart, making her believe in love once again. She blinked rapidly at the thought, swallowing back the rising emotions. She couldn't dare to love Deklan.

But a part of her knew it was already too late.

"What were your parents like?" she asked him, changing the subject.

He made a scoffing sound in his throat before shifting away, his head dropping against the back of the couch. "Exactly opposite of yours."

"How so?"

"You talk of yachts, nannies and image. Think the other side of the tracks." His voice was tight and filled with loathing.

She turned then to look at him, wanting to comfort him as he had her. But his eyes were closed, his face shuttered. "Was it that bad?"

"Worse."

"Is that why you joined the service? To get out?"

A ripple of remorse or maybe shame crossed his face. "Not exactly. But it worked." He took a deep breath and blew it out, the frown smoothing from his brow. "I'd just turned eighteen, two weeks away from graduating and being out of that shit hole when I came home one night to find my step-dad beating the shit out of my mother."

She inhaled but stayed quiet, wanting him to continue. There was pain buried under the deadpan tone of resolution that came from someone who'd long ago accepted the events for what they were.

"It was nothing new," he continued. "But that night I snapped. The bastard wouldn't stop hitting her and she was letting him and there were my two little sisters huddled in the corner, afraid to move. I reacted." His hands tightened into fists, the one in her hair tugging just enough to make her wince, but she said nothing. "I almost beat him to death before the cops ripped me off him. My mom had called the police on me. Not the bastard who used her as a punching bag, but me."

His chest expanded with a deep inhale and he rubbed at his eyes as if that would eliminate the image from his mind. "The court saw the family history, the documented cases of suspected abuse and foster homes and went lenient on me, even though my mother backed my stepdad. I could graduate from high school and join the army or go straight to jail. I picked the first one."

This time it was her offering comfort. "I'm so sorry."

Puffing out a laugh, he lifted his head to look at her. "Just goes to show life can suck with or without money."

She smiled, giving a soft laugh to match his. "Suckiness has no boundaries." They were both undermining their experiences, but there was no need to dwell on finished history. What was done was done. "What happened to your mom and sisters?"

Another sigh. "She's still with the asshole. I haven't spoken to her since I entered the army. But with the money from the service, I was able to get my sisters out. They both live back in Sioux City with good husbands and families."

"Is that where you're from? Sioux City?"

"Yeah."

"Do you ever go back?"

"I try to, but not often enough."

She sat up, tilting her head back and forth, the cramped muscles stretching but not loosening. She shifted around to set her feet on the floor, the cold surface refreshing against her bare feet. Her elbows dug into her thighs as she leaned forward, kneading the ache in her shoulders. A second later her hands were brushed away to be replaced by his. She moaned in appreciation, leaning into his strong touch.

"I should be doing this to you," she told him.

"Why?"

"Because I'm the one who took advantage of you last night." She bit her lip, the shame returning as she thought of her actions. There's no way she could ever justify what she'd done.

He gave her a rough shake. "We are not going over that again." His voice was stern, his grip firm on her shoulders.

She squeezed her eyes closed, her lip stinging where her teeth held it, but she nodded. They might not talk about it again, but she'd never forget what she'd done or the shame that came with it. "Can I ask you something?"

"Shoot."

"The names on your leg. Are they really people you lost?"

He went still and she turned, searching his face for the answers that hid there. His lips thinned before he gave a tight nod. "They were fellow soldiers who died in the line of duty." He rubbed absently at the back of his leg, as if talking about it triggered the action.

"But why?"

There was pain in his eyes, his memories flashing almost vividly enough for her to see them too. His voice was rough when he spoke. "It started as a way to honor them. But it was also a reminder of my failures."

"They're all male except the last one. Does that mean something?"

The bare whisper of words reached her. "Samantha J. Boyd." He paused, his jaw working before he continued. "I left the military after her death. Every loss hurt, but hers almost broke me. I failed her, just like my mother."

"You were telling the truth last night." His silence was her answer. Her hand shook as she reached to run her fingers along his jaw, the scruff of his beard abrading the tips. He held perfectly still as she touched him, his eyes filled with remembered hurt and…trust. He trusted her enough to share this truth that was so personal. "And I dismissed it."

His half-grin returned, his dimple appearing with the shift in his mood. "You had other things distracting you last night. My hang-ups weren't important."

"But they are," she insisted. She spun around and straddled his lap. It was suddenly essential that he understood her. She cupped his jaw, forcing him to look at her. "They are just as important as mine. They matter to me. You matter to me."

She captured his lips in a gentle kiss, needing to feel him but also to hide. She poured her emotions into the brush of moist softness, holding back while aching to dive in. There was so much contradiction in this man. Hard and soft, rough and gentle, strong but fragile. And she wanted every part of him. She shouldn't, God, she shouldn't. But she did.

How had this happened?

The trembling started in her shoulders, running in a wave down her arms to her fingertips. She loved him. Damn it. No. It couldn't be.

The crash of realization scared her worse than the thought of being beaten again. She eased back, taking shortened breaths, trying to keep it together. The crook of his neck was the perfect place to escape and she tucked her head there, seeking the safety it offered. He stroked her back, long caresses that teased her breasts against his chest but loosened the constriction in her throat that threatened to cut off her air. The smooth consistency that was him pushed back her panic before it completely formed.

That was Deklan—a pillar of consistency there for her. There for everyone around him. "So who's there for you?" she asked, her fingers playing over the short stubble of hair at the back of his head. "If you're there for everyone, who's there for you?"

His hand hesitated on her back for a second then resumed. "Seth and Jake have been there since we were kids." No mention of his real family. "What about you? Is that why you ran? Because you had no one who would understand?"

She gulped back the sudden gasp that emerged at the direct hit. He was so right. Even among her family, all of the social acquaintances and superficial friends, she'd been so alone.

"It's all right," he murmured, pulling her even closer. "You have friends now. People who care. You have me."

"How? Why?" The pleading words sounded anxious and pitiful but she needed to know. Her history wouldn't let her just believe, even if she wanted to.

"How not? Why not?" he countered. He lifted her head, making her shift until she was forced to look at him. The intensity of his eyes made her blink, her chest winding into coils that were too much like hope. "You have to know by now that this, us, is more than a contract. That I care about you as more than a client. That I want more than submission and dominance with you."

Her pulse raced until her heart rammed against her ribcage. So many thoughts and doubts fled in and out of her mind that she couldn't capture and hold any of them. Was this possible? Her fingers shook as she dared to trace the edge of his hairline along his forehead, the action giving her something to focus on besides his dark blue eyes.

"I want all of you, Kendra." He leaned forward until she had no choice but to look back at him. "I meant what I said last night. You own me."

She shoved away, only he wouldn't let her run. He held her tight and she shook her head in denial, her doubts crashing forward once again. "It won't work. It can't. That doesn't work in a relationship."

Annoyance flashed in his eyes under a heavy scowl. "What doesn't? What we do in the Dungeon? Haven't I proven to you by now that it can work?"

"That's there," she shot back. "It's separate. It has nothing to do with love and commitment."

"Doesn't it? Isn't that the ultimate in trust? When it's done right, it's all about caring and sharing. About giving each other what we both need and want. Isn't that the very foundation of love?"

Love? Oh, God. He'd said it. She couldn't breathe. Her chest tightened, the brick pressing down until the pressure was too much, too intense. "No," she whispered, her voice trembling. "It's all false."

"How?" he asked, the demand so gentle that she strained to hear it around the roar within her head. "Is this false?"

His lips were hot and insistent when they touched hers. She didn't want to believe, but he was so warm. Alive. His tongue traced a path over her bottom lip, tempting her mouth open to claim the warmth within. The faint traces of coffee lingered on his tongue, his advance both cautious and demanding, making her want more. The soft bristles of his hair coursed over her palms as she ran her hands up the back of his head, seeking the longer strands on top that she could hold tight and anchor herself to him.

"Tell me, Kendra," he said against her lips, his mouth teasing hers with each word. The hot, coarse touch of his palm smoothed under her sweatshirt to scorch over her ribs before surrounding her breast. She arched into his hand, her head falling back, his lips trailing wet kisses down the exposed skin of her neck. "Is this false?" His breath tickled the sensitive area just below her ear, the softness countered by the rough scrap of his beard.

Air raced into her lungs, the constrictive vise of fear receding to allow her a gasp of breath. He circled his palm over her nipple, a fire of arousal shooting straight to her aching core. Her hips bucked, her pussy rocking over his hardened shaft. Her low moan rumbled into the quiet and she held his head to her neck, savoring the feel of him. His breath on her skin, the wet trail of his tongue around her ear, the press of his hand on her breast, the length of his erection pressing against her needy sex.

This was so real. Primal.

She didn't resist when he pulled her sweatshirt over her head, baring her breasts to him. He lifted them until her nipples pointed high and wicked toward his mouth. Her nails dug into his shoulders where she held on to him, her chest heaving with each breath she took.

He stared into her eyes, the desire making his black and endless. "Do you want this?" He passed his thumbs over her aching nipples; her inhale at the shot of sensation was husky and harsh. "I'll stop now, if that's what you want." The torture of doing that showed in the low grit of his voice. But she believed him. He would stop if she said to.

Deklan would never force her to do anything she didn't want to do.

He wasn't Eric. She knew that. Deklan had proven that repeatedly and still she resisted, letting Eric's evil spill over to taint this. But it was her choice. She could run again or take the risk and trust the man before her. With everything.

He slid his hands down her sides and started to pull back, but she grabbed ahold, jerking his mouth to hers. "Don't stop," she breathed against his lips, her heart breaking open. "Don't ever stop." She kissed him, all the passion erupting from her tight hold. Her tongue stroked his, plundered his heated depth and sought everything he offered.

The growl that erupted from his chest vibrated against her lips, raising her desire. His hands dug into her hair and he yanked her away, his breath panting with hers. He closed his eyes and swallowed before locking his gaze with hers. "I want to make love to you. No whips, chains, bonds, toys. None of that. Just you and me." He ran his hand up her side, the heat trailing behind it. "And this."

Inside, she turned to mush. He was so passionate, open where he was usually shuttered. And he was offering it all to her. There was only one thing she could say. "Yes."

She wanted him. No matter how scared she was to move forward, she couldn't deny her need for him any longer. Fusing her lips to his, she poured everything into that kiss. He returned her hunger, his teeth nipping her lip, his hands rubbing her everywhere, leaving her skin tingling and hot wherever he touched.

"God, Kendra," he rumbled against her neck. "I've wanted you for so fucking long." He dove his hands beneath the back of her yoga pants to grip her ass, the hard squeeze bucking her hips up, forcing a long, slow moan to pour from her lips. He lifted her up to devour her nipple. He sucked the hard peak between his lips, his teeth worrying the flesh around the loop, his tongue playing with the charm.

The whimper that escaped sounded as impatient as she felt. After waiting so long, she couldn't get enough of him. Like a person starved, she wanted to touch every inch of him. Feel him under her palms, taste him, bite him. Consume him whole.

He moved to her other breast, teasing and working the tip like he'd done the other. She couldn't think anymore, didn't want to for that matter. Thinking would make her stop, let the fear enter, and she didn't want that. Holding his head to her chest, she ground her hips into his lap, feeling his erection and wanting it all.

Groaning, he pulled away to capture her mouth in another scorching kiss. One she returned until her lips were bruised and they were both gasping for air.

He scooted forward, yanking her tight against him. "Hold on," he said right before he stood, her legs automatically locking around his waist. "I've waited too long to do this on the couch."

She had to kiss him again; there was nothing else she could do. His lips were an addiction now, his taste her craving. She loved his strength—the feel of his hands gripping her ass and holding her tight as he walked to the bedroom drove her wild. It didn't make sense, she should run from so much power, but instead she longed for it.

She pulled back as they entered the cool darkness of the bedroom. The curtains were still drawn over the large window, leaving the space dark and intimate. Glancing back, she spotted the rumpled bed, the covers still askew, reminding her that she'd slept naked next to him last night. And he'd been a gentleman. He could have pushed this then or even this morning and she probably wouldn't have objected. The fact that he waited until she felt stronger, until she could agree without guilt or pressure meant so much.

It showed how much he really cared about her.

He eased her down, her body sliding along his until her feet touched the ground, not an inch of space separating them. Her arms were wound around his neck and he leaned down to kiss her softly, tender caresses of his swollen lips countered by harder strokes of his tongue that made her toes curl into the cold floor beneath them.

Her hands found their way down his chest to ease under his

shirt and she reveled in the feel of his hard muscles beneath her palms. His skin was as warm and smooth as she remembered from last night, and she wanted more. More skin, more him.

Tugging his shirt up, he broke away to help her remove the interference. The instant it was gone, her lips were on his chest, tasting the hard line of his biceps, tracing the outline of his tattoo, grazing the hardened nub of his nipple. His breath hissed between his teeth when she sucked the tip between her lips, working it with her teeth.

"Kendra," he groaned, his hand weaving into her hair to hold her close. He ground his hips against her, pressing the length of his cock into her lower stomach. "I gotta have you."

Humming her consent, she leaned over to suck his other nipple into her mouth before drifting to kiss each ripple of muscle down his abdomen until her tongue could swirl around his bellybutton in sweet temptation. He tasted of clean with a hint of salt and she wanted more.

She dropped to her knees and smoothed her palms under the back of his sweatpants to cup the firm globes of his ass. There wasn't an ounce of fat on him. It didn't matter that he was ten years older than her. He was as fit and lean as a man in his twenties.

And he was all hers. A possessiveness she'd never felt before swamped her with the need to claim him before he got away. To mark him. She rubbed her cheek along the hardness of his erection still hidden beneath the cotton of his sweats and earned a growl of approval from above. Gripping his ass cheeks, she tugged him closer to suck hard and fierce on the skin just over his hipbone.

He thrust against her mouth, his hips jerking in response to her actions. But he didn't pull away or make her stop. It was another long minute, his hips rocking before she pulled back to admire her mark. She released her tight hold on his ass to trace her fingers around the already darkening red and purple bruise she'd made. God, it looked perfect.

She tilted her head, scanning up the hard lines of his body to meet his eyes. What she saw made her whimper, but she bit her lips to keep the sound from escaping. There was so much emotion communicated in his eyes, more than she could process, or maybe it was what she was able to accept.

His focus shifted to where her fingers circled the mark she'd made. "If I could, I'd make that permanent." His voice mirrored the emotion she saw in his eyes.

She sucked in a breath, wanting more than anything to keep that look forever.

Before she could dwell on that feeling for too long, she yanked at the waist of his pants and tugged them down his legs, freeing his erection to bob heavily before her. She let him finish kicking the pant legs off his feet as she grabbed his velvety length and swirled her tongue over the heated end of his cock. The taste of his pre-come danced on her taste buds and she hummed in appreciation.

She consumed the length of him in one long swallow, unable to go slow. His groan of approval vibrated along his shaft and rang in her ears. Her actions became almost frantic in her need to get more of him. She sucked long and hard, moving her mouth over his shaft. He was thick and long, in proportion with the rest of him, and she savored every inch.

She cupped his balls, working them between her fingers before reaching back to rub the area behind them. He gripped her head, his knees bending as his hips jerked forward with his low moan.

"Fuck, Kendra," he grunted. "That feels so good."

She smiled around his cock, pulling back enough to lick the tip once again, collecting the new drop of come by dipping the tip of her tongue into the small hole. Pleasing him, making him feel as good as he made her feel warmed her like nothing else. She wanted this. She loved seeing his look of ecstasy, feeling his legs shake, his hands quiver and knowing it was because of her.

"Come here," he growled, hooking his hands under her arms and yanking her up before she could protest. The next second his mouth was on hers, a frantic mating of lips and tongues that turned her wild. She'd never, ever felt so crazed, so desperate for anything, anyone.

He shuffled them backward until her legs hit the bed, then he pushed. She tumbled onto the mattress, the springs giving as she bounced lightly, her mouth gaping in surprise. His eyes traveled over her as she spread her arms wide, returning the appraisal.

"You are so gorgeous," she murmured, still in awe of his physique. She could get lost staring at him.

In the next instant, her pants were yanked from her hips, the soft material stripped from her legs. Her back arched, her hands clenching into fists at the shock of flames that seemed to scorch her skin from the outside in.

He stood tall and proud between her knees before he slipped his rough palms up her legs, stopping at the juncture of her thighs, his hands cradling her sex, his eyes on hers. "I want to do everything to you," he said, his voice so low it sounded as if it was coming from somewhere deep inside of him. "Touch you, kiss you, worship you as you deserve. I fucking ache to be in you, yet I can't stop looking."

He dipped his head and pushed her legs wide to swipe his tongue up her pussy. He hummed in appreciation. "Tasting." Her abdomen was covered in soft kisses and her legs went naturally around his waist as he eased them up until they were both on the bed. He claimed her nipple with his mouth. "Sucking," he murmured, his prize held tight between his teeth. He bit down until her nipple throbbed in that pleasure-pain state that she loved.

"Deklan," she cried, her hips thrusting up to ride her wet pussy down his shaft. She ground her clit into his rigid length, helpless to stop. He snagged her nipple ring, the light clank of metal against teeth giving her just a moment's warning before he pulled back, extending the tender bud until her back arched in an attempt to ease the tension. She loved it.

She felt wild, sexy, adored.

His lips were back on hers, his fingers sliding over her wet sex. He groaned, and she swallowed the sound as her own burst forth when he found her heat, the hard, urgent stabs up her canal making her insane with need. He rubbed her clit in time with his thrusting fingers and she almost came that quickly.

She wasn't sure if she said something or if he just sensed her need, but a second later Deklan was reaching for the night stand, grabbing a condom. He sat back on his heels and tore the square with his teeth, the protection rolled on faster than she could suck in a breath. Then he was back over her, his erection prodding her entrance, his eyes holding hers.

His breath caressed her cheeks and he tucked his arms under her until she was cradled close to him. She wrapped her legs around his hips, urging him forward. No words were said, but so much was communicated through his eyes as he entered her, his hard cock filling her. She dug her fingers in his hair and leaned up to take his mouth in hers, unable to process what she saw in his eyes. Afraid to believe, while knowing it was real.

He tore his mouth from hers, cursing. One hard lunge had him fully within her. Her back bowed, her head falling back at the pure sensation of fulfillment. She gasped his name and cried out in pure joy. Her entire focus was on her lower body, on the way his shaft rubbed against the sensitive walls of her vagina. Of how damn good he made her feel.

There was no grace in their movements, no choreographed anything. Kendra dug her fingers into his shoulders, her nails streaking down his back. He pumped into her, hard, firm demanding. Like him, their coupling was wild and harsh. It was exactly how she imagined it would be with him.

Tucking his knees up, he sat back, using his strength to pull her up with him until he was resting on his heels with her riding him. The new position made it feel as if his cock was impaling her, going so deep that she sobbed with the pleasure. He plundered her breasts with his mouth, gripping her hips to guide her in a rhythm that seemed almost slow, leisurely compared to the urgency building within her.

She cradled his head against her breast and rode him. Taking everything he offered and making her own demands. Her clit rubbed the base of his dick with each downward plunge until she whimpered, the high sound blending with his low grunts and the slap of their skin in their own erotic song.

"Fuck, Kendra," he swore against her neck, skimming his teeth over skin. "You're perfect." He managed to work a hand between them, finding her clit.

She gasped, her nails clawing his soft flesh.

"You're everything to me," he growled, biting down on the juncture of her shoulder and neck.

The cry that left her mouth said it all. She exploded, a burst of white and yellow lights flashing behind her eyelids as every nerve in her body lit on fire. Her stomach muscles tightened and she ground against him, seeking more. He thrust one more time, hitting her clit just right to prolong her release before he roared his completion.

She clung to him, heart thundering, breath huffing as she let the world float around them. Distantly, she felt herself being lowered back to the bed, Deklan stretching out beside her, holding her tight.

Curling against him, she drifted in a hazy cloud of contentment. "Thank you," she mouthed against his chest, knowing he wouldn't hear her. Knowing he wouldn't understand how grateful she was to him for everything.

In his arms she'd had one of the most amazing orgasms of her life. Something she'd been convinced she couldn't have without pain, whips and bonds. But Deklan proved her wrong. She wasn't broken. There was nothing wrong with her.

With Deklan she was whole. He'd shown her repeatedly that she was stronger than she'd thought. He'd willingly shared his own strength until she believed in herself once again.

For him—no, for them, she'd do what she so desperately didn't want to do. And hope that he was still here for her when she returned.

Then maybe, with Deklan, she'd find her home.

TWENTY-TWO

Deklan rolled over stretching out his arm, searching for Kendra in half-sleep. They'd spent the previous day lazing in bed, passing away the time in a bubble of sex, talk and laughter. Being with Kendra was everything he thought he'd never have.

Love. God, he really did love her. Now more than ever.

The high-pitched *beep*, *beep*, *beep* of a plow backing up jerked him completely awake with the subtlety of a cold dump of water. Groaning, he flipped to his back, rubbing his hand over his face and eyes. Where was Kendra?

The empty space beside him was cool, letting him know she'd been out of bed for a while. He couldn't remember the last time he'd slept so soundly. Deklan cranked his neck looking for a clock, only to remember Jake's spare room didn't have one. He should get one.

Flopping back down, he listened for the shower but heard nothing except the grind of the plow working outside. The city would be getting back to business that day. The sun had come out yesterday afternoon, starting the snowmelt and assisting with the cleanup. The spring storm might have been fierce, but it wasn't lasting.

He forced himself to get out of bed with one last groan as he shivered in the chill of the room before slipping on the clothes he'd borrowed from Jake. The scent of coffee made its way to him, putting a grin on his face. A quick trip to the bathroom, and he was shuffling out to find Kendra. He'd ribbed Jake more than once for the stupid smile that must cover his own face, but he couldn't make it go away.

Until he saw Seth sitting on the couch. He had one ankle resting on his other knee, a steaming mug of coffee in his hands. Deklan's smile flattened right along with his mood as he quickly scanned the rest of the loft.

"Where's Kendra?" he demanded, his anger rising as fast as the realization that she was gone.

Seth set his mug down on the low coffee table before leveling a hard stare at Deklan. "She left."

"What?" Deklan searched the area again, not wanting to believe what he heard and his own eyes confirmed. "When?"

"About two hours ago." There was no emotion displayed on Seth's face, but his shoulders were tense, his hands clasped tightly between his knees where his forearms rested, like he was forcing himself to stay still.

"Fuck." The curse rang sharp and hard from Deklan. He jerked his hands over his hair as he stumbled back against the wall, the wind sucked from his chest. She left. The words nailed him harder than the impact of a bullet. No. She couldn't have done that. Not after yesterday. After all they'd shared and done.

He scoured his face, his hands rubbing insistently as if he could wipe away the shock. The hurt. A second later, he sprang up, stalked toward Seth and let his frustration loose on his friend. "Why'd you let her go?"

Seth sat back, lifting his shoulder. "It wasn't my place to stop her."

"You know what happened to her, why I brought her here."

Seth nodded.

"And you let her leave anyway?" A part of Deklan knew he had no right to accuse Seth of wrongdoing, but it didn't make him stop. "What if her abuser's waiting for her? What if he hurts her again?"

"What if?" Seth asked so casually Deklan almost vaulted over the couch to pound the other man. "She wanted to go. She's an adult free to make her own choices. I assumed she knew what she was doing."

"And what if she doesn't?"

Seth's head snapped back. "Wow. So you're saying she can't think for herself now? Make her own choices and judgments?"

"No," Deklan insisted, his hands fisting on the back of the couch as he tried to corner his fragmented thoughts. "Of course she can think for herself."

"Oh, I get it. You trust her, but not her judgment."

"What? No. Fuck." Deklan spun around and headed back to the bedroom. He didn't need Seth's shit. Not when Kendra could be in trouble.

He changed into his own clothes in rushed, brisk motions. It was then that he noticed the neat pile of borrowed clothes Kendra had left on the dresser, a folded piece of paper resting on top. He'd found their own discarded clothing waiting outside Jake's door yesterday and assumed Seth had brought them up from the Dungeon.

Snatching the paper off the clothing, he flipped it open and read her short note. *I have to go, Deklan. I'm so sorry to run out like this, but I have to do this on my own. There are things I need to finish before I can move forward with you. You showed me that yesterday. Thank you. For everything.*

The paper crumpled in his fist as understanding dawned. She was going back.

Storming into the main room, he headed for the door, ignoring Seth's presence. He ran a hand over his beard scruff, scratching along his jawline, hating it when it started to itch like that. His wallet went into his pocket as he grabbed his coat from the side table. She couldn't have gotten that far ahead. Maybe he could catch her at her condo.

"You can't force her to stay, Deklan."

The low words although spoken calmly struck a sensitive chord in Deklan. "I don't plan on forcing her to do anything."

"Then what *are* you planning to do?" Seth rose from the couch, turning to face Deklan, his arms crossed over his chest. It was still early, not even nine in the morning, which was like the ass-crack of dawn for the late hours they normally kept. But Seth was already showered, shaved and dressed in a preppy-looking black turtleneck sweater and slacks. His hair was pulled neatly into a queue at his nape, leaving Deklan to assume he had a business meeting that morning. "Charge in like her knight in shining armor demanding she let the big, brawny man save her?"

Deklan glared at the other man. Who the fuck did Seth think he was? "I won't let her get hurt again," Deklan gritted out. His jaw gave that all-too-familiar twinge that precluded the ache that would soon throb in the back of his head if he didn't loosen up. Fuck that.

"How're you gonna do that? You gonna put her in a bubble, stop the world from revolving?"

"Don't be stupid."

Seth shrugged. "I'm just asking. People get hurt. People die. That's life, Deklan. When are you going to learn that not everyone wants you to save them?"

"We're not talking about this again." Deklan turned away. "Just drop it."

"No. I won't." Seth strode around the couch, his hands fisted at his sides matching the hard rage on his face. "You can't save everyone. Get that? Sometimes people have to save themselves. They don't want you to do it for them. They need to do it on their own." His chest rose and fell in deep swells as he drilled Deklan with his conviction.

"And if they get hurt doing it? What then, Seth? Am I supposed to just let that happen?"

"Yes, damn it," Seth yelled, slicing his arm through the air. "You're not fucking Superman. Let her do what she needs to do. Trust that she can take care of herself. Trust *her*, Deklan."

"You dick." Deklan pounced, his fist wrapping around Seth's collar yanking him close, his other fist raised ready to strike. "I fucking do trust her."

"Do you?" Seth challenged, not even flinching. "Is that why you're so mad? Because you trust her? Or are you so damn cocky and arrogant to think she can't do it without you?"

Rage, fear, guilt—all of those emotions and more swirled within Deklan as the faces of over a dozen victims flashed within his mind. His hand shook as he battled against the demons of his past. Seth just stared him down, demanding Deklan face what he'd avoided for years.

Slowly he loosened his hold and dropped his fist, spinning away from the one person brave enough to push him. Every swear word he knew flew through his mind; it didn't matter what he was cursing at or who. They were just there battling against what was so plainly laid before him, thanks to Seth.

"You can't save them all," Seth said quietly. "Let her do what she needs to do."

Deklan braced his hands on the wall, his head hanging to

stare at the floor. "How do I do that?" he rasped. "The last person I walked away from is still hurting every day."

"Kendra is stronger than your mother. She needs to face this her way."

"And what if she goes back to that bastard? He threatened her family. What if she caves to the pressure and returns to him?"

"Then it's her choice. But do you honestly believe she'd do that? She was strong enough to walk away from everything once before. Would she really be so weak as to go back now?"

Seth was talking as if he knew what was going on, like he understood Kendra's background even though it hadn't been shared with him.

Deklan spun around, leveling a stony glare at Seth. "You read the file, didn't you?"

He didn't even look guilty. "Yes."

"Why would you do that?" Deklan exploded, angered for Kendra at the invasion of her privacy. "*I* haven't even read that. It was private information. Not something that concerned the club. You had no right," he seethed. It didn't matter that he was the one who'd had the data collected. Seth shouldn't have been snooping when it wasn't his business.

"It was on the computer. It concerned you, and I knew your honor wouldn't let you. So yeah, I looked. I figured if you had someone go through the trouble of getting the info, there must be a reason."

He didn't know if he wanted to kill the man or beg for the file details. Yes, he'd had Rock do a detailed, mostly illegal gathering of Kendra's history, but Deklan respected her enough to not look at the file himself. He'd wanted her to tell him, just like she had. But how much had she left out?

"Fuck." He spun and pounded his fist into the drywall, pulling up just enough not to punch through. Did he trust her completely? That's exactly what Seth was challenging him to confront. Deklan would give his life for her, but was his faith in her strong enough to accept that she'd do the same for him?

That she might just love him enough to fight for him?

They'd never spoken words of love through all they'd exchanged yesterday. He'd assumed it was understood, that their connection spoke for itself and their actions proved it. If that was true, then he had no choice but to believe in her. Trust that she knew what she was doing and she'd come back.

That still didn't mean he couldn't be there for her.

Damn it. He had to do something.

"I pulled all the important info from the file." Deklan turned around as Seth walked back to the coffee table and picked up a manila folder. He flipped through the papers too fast to be truly reading them. "What you need is all here. Including everything about her asshole ex." He closed the file and held it out to Deklan. "You can't help her confront her past, but you can sure as hell make sure the dick pays for what he's done."

Deklan grinned, the vindictive sense of satisfaction settling in his chest. He took the folder, eternally grateful for his friend he called brother. "Thank you," he managed to say around his tight throat. "I'm still pissed. But thanks."

"I got your back. Always have."

"Right." Deklan tucked the folder under his arm, slipped his boots on and straightened to catch Seth watching him, concern marring his face. The bare truth of his words touched at Deklan. There were very few in his life that would dare to challenge him the way Seth had and still be there for him.

Deklan leveled a meaningful stare at the other man. "Sorry. You didn't deserve that."

"No problem," Seth answered after a short pause, a grin playing on his lips. "I could've taken you if I wanted."

"Only if I let you," Deklan joked back, relieved that his irrational temper hadn't harmed their friendship.

"Dream on," Seth chuckled before pointing toward the file under Deklan's arm. "Let me know if there's anything I can do."

Deklan nodded and left, a sense of urgency pushing him to hurry. Having no patience for the elevator, he thundered down the stairwell, the loud clump of his step banging off the narrow walls.

The door of the security room slammed against the wall when he shoved through. Rock's gaze shot up, but the man didn't move other than to track Deklan's movements as he tossed the folder on the counter and sank into the other chair.

Deklan tore open the file and dug into the information Seth had printed. The sound of the papers flipping were meshed with the occasional click of computer keys as the security head resumed his work.

The steely years of military-ingrained focus held him in the chair. His driving need to be with Kendra was only just contained. The tight twist of pain traveled up the back of his skull screaming how fucked he was.

He would be there for her, damn it. This he could do, and fuck if it made her mad. Eric would pay for every sadistic thing he'd done to her.

He was almost through the papers when a coffee cup appeared at his elbow, the scent of the brew breaking into his concentration.

"Thought you could use it," Rock said, indicating the coffee. He took a sip of his own cup, his pale eyes lingering on the folder in front of Deklan. Rock had more than proven his loyalty through years of battle and covert operations, the long scar running from his brow to his jaw proof of his dedication. He'd been one of Deklan's best men while in the service. He still was.

Deklan sat back and picked up the steaming mug. "Thanks."

"Ready to deal with that?" Rock pointed to the papers. Since he'd been the one to collect the data, Deklan didn't question what he meant.

"Yeah." He looked up. "You willing to help?"

"You have to ask?"

"It's not the service. You have a choice."

"What do you need me to do?"

Straightening, Deklan set his coffee down. "Pull up a chair. Let's get this done."

Showing what could at best be called a smile but came across more like a scowl, Rock complied. Eric would be sorry he ever messed with Kendra when they were finished with him.

Of that, Deklan was certain.

TWENTY-THREE

The richly appointed room was as stifling as Kendra remembered. The high bookshelves along one wall were stuffed with leather-bound tomes to impress and, coupled with the large wood desk in the corner, marked the room as the study. There was a gas fireplace along another wall, but it was dark now, leaving the large space as chilled as the cool tones that complemented. An elegant sitting area was arranged in the middle of the room, not that any of the furniture encouraged curling up with one of the many books.

She paced across the plush carpet, running her hand over her cotton shirt in a hopeless pass at smoothing out the travel wrinkles. She'd driven straight to her parents' house, the eight-hour trip great for solidifying her determination, but also allowing for a boatload of nerves to pile up. Having arrived unannounced around six, she was now waiting for her parents to get home.

"Are you sure I can't get you anything?"

Kendra snapped around at the sound of the maid/butler/cook. The older lady had been with the family for years, not that she ever broke decorum with any of them. She took her job seriously, as noted by the severe bun trapping her gray hair, pressed apron and demure slacks.

Forcing a smile, Kendra declined. "Thanks, Susan. I'm good." The thought of putting anything in her stomach only made it tighten and curl in anticipated dread.

"Mr. Morgan is usually home within the hour. I believe Mrs. Morgan will be with him." Susan backed out of the room. "Let me know if there is anything I can get you." It didn't matter to the woman that Kendra could get it herself. That she'd been raised in this house and was perfectly capable of getting her own drink or food. Susan ruled the roost when it came to all things domestic.

The door clicked closed so quietly the sound was only audible due to the complete lack of other noise in the house. The large six-bedroom home felt almost like a tomb. Kendra gave a shake, the chill running down her spine at the sense of foreboding that came with the thought.

Crossing to the window, she pulled back the sheer drapes to look at the street as if watching the road would make her parents appear faster. Then again, she wasn't really sure she wanted them to show up. A lone street lamp provided a pale circle of light in the darkening night, highlighting the fact that the private drive in the gated community wasn't a hotbed of activity. The storm that had hammered Minneapolis only brushed by Chicago, so just a few small traces of the late snow remained on the lawn.

She cursed softly before turning away from the desolate sight. Exhaustion forced her to give in and drop into a stiff-backed chair. She wished like hell for the secondhand eyesore of a chair that swallowed her whole back in her condo. She could really do with sinking into the overstuffed cushions and forgetting everything.

Wiggling around trying to get comfortable in the piece of furniture she was certain cost more than everything she owned only proved to her once again that money didn't guarantee comfort. As if she'd ever believed that. The only thing money had ever guaranteed for her was loneliness.

And didn't that sound as pathetic as it was. Poor little rich girl—a story told and retold too many times to make it endearing.

Stop it. I'm better than that, she admonished, her hands fisting until her nails dug into her palms. Deklan had helped her to see that. He'd helped her to see a lot of things. Namely what she had to do tonight. There was only one way to stop Eric, and that was to take away the power he held over her. The man wasn't going to stop unless she stopped him first.

Taking a deep breath, she pulled out her phone to check for messages one more time. Nothing. She'd expected Deklan to leave some kind of remark. He couldn't have taken her disappearance well. He wasn't the kind of guy to just sit back, which was why she'd had to leave in the first place. Confronting her parents was something she had to do on her own. Even if the thought froze her to the bone.

But complete silence from the formidable man was more unsettling than an angry voicemail or confrontational text. She could only hope that she hadn't ruined the one good thing she'd found in her life. Well, not the only one. She'd never be that dependent on a man for her happiness ever again. But Deklan was definitely a solid component in her future. One she didn't want to lose now that she'd found him.

Her pulse increased just thinking about the day before. The connection she had with the strong Dom was nothing compared to the love she had for the man. It was hard to determine exactly when she'd fallen in love with him. Maybe it was that first night, when he'd been so patient and understanding.

Or it could have been during their long runs together, when he was simply there by her side, their breath and pace matching as if they'd been running partners for years. More likely it was during one of the many Scenes they'd done together, where he'd shown her repeatedly how submission was about power, not weakness, and her masochistic desires were okay. Maybe not normal, but not wrong.

She couldn't analyze it down to a specific moment or event, didn't want to. It was the whole man she loved. The man she was pretty certain very few people got to see.

Now she just had to get through the evening so she could tell him that and hope he understood why she'd had to run from him before she could run to him.

Deklan shifted his truck into park and turned off the engine, the silence of the night settling around him. The little clinks and pings that emanated from the cooling engine were the only noise to break the darkness. The urge to shift in the seat was easily squelched by years of training. It didn't matter if his ass was numb from driving for seven hours; he'd endured much worse without fidgeting.

He would have made it in six hours, but he'd forced himself to slow down after sneaking past the first cop. Getting thrown in jail for speeding wouldn't help Kendra.

Scanning the quiet street, he waited another minute before finally grabbing his phone. The last text from Rock let him know that their plan was underway. Having extended connections in the Chicago area was one of the benefits of his military service. Calling in favors had been an easy decision to make. There wasn't anything Deklan wouldn't do for Kendra.

A vindictive smile curled over his lips when he saw the pictures that were waiting for him. Bet Eric never saw that coming. Bastard. He deserved far worse than being subjugated to his own cruelty. The series of images showing Eric blind-folded, bound, gagged, whipped and humiliated still weren't enough to dull his anger. Deklan would be sure to send a special thanks to the club owner for letting his men show Eric exactly how it felt to be abused by someone stronger under the guise of dominance and submission.

Deklan sent off a quick response then sent another text to Rock, inquiring on the status of the other task. The man might come across as a dumb jock or a muscled meathead, but Deklan had yet to meet anyone who was a better computer whiz than Rock. He could hack his way into the White House and get out without being caught if he wanted to.

Temptation had his fingers poised over the phone ready to send one more message before he curbed the urge and tucked the object back in his pocket. He exited the truck, keeping his goal in mind. Ducking into the shadows, he scanned the tree-lined street, double-checking for unseen eyes before leap-ing up to grab the top of the metal fence enclosing the pri-vate community.

Vaulting over the supposed security barrier was incredibly easy for a guy who was used to sneaking into terrorist camps. According to the maps he and Rock had analyzed, the guise of safety the rich and privileged paid for within the confines of the metal fence and guard house was really nothing more than the pretense they all hid behind.

It didn't take him long to reach the house of one Thomas and Eleanor Morgan. The tightness in his chest eased a little when he spotted Kendra's old-model blue sedan, completely out of place in the long driveway. The meticulous landscape and oversized house couldn't be further from his upbringing. The two-bedroom shack with paint-chipped siding and an overgrown yard that cultivated more weeds than grass that he'd once called home could've fit in the Morgans' garage with room to spare.

He could never give Kendra this kind of luxury. But he could give her the security and love she'd never felt here.

Stepping into the glow of the lone streetlight, Deklan pulled out his phone and finally sent the text he'd been wanting to send since he'd found Kendra gone that morning. He leaned against the cold, metal pole, preparing to wait. He'd stay out there all night if that was what Kendra needed. Waiting, he could do. Even if it killed him to stand outside, knowing what she was facing inside.

No matter what happened, he wasn't leaving until he was positive she was all right. And he could only hope that she'd be leaving with him.

TWENTY-FOUR

She wasn't certain how long she forced herself to sit in the god-awful chair, the sense of time having slipped away from her as she tried once again to form the words that she would say to her parents. It didn't matter that she'd been doing that exact same thing since she woke up that morning; the words still weren't there.

The click of the door opening rocked through the room like a bullet. Kendra jumped and stood, clasping her hands before her to keep them still.

"Kendra." Her mother's excited voice filled Kendra with a brief dose of warmth before she took in the stilted smile and sharp reprimand that was forming in the woman's eyes.

"Mother," Kendra said stiffly, her gaze scanning to the man entering behind her well-groomed mother. "Father."

He shut the door without responding, the slight scowl in his brow the only giveaway to his feeling on Kendra's surprise visit. Her mother glided over to give her a light hug and peck on the cheek, like she hadn't been basically missing for the last ten months.

Stepping back, her mother executed a slow appraisal over Kendra, every critical judgment showing on her face before she pasted on a stiff smile and patted Kendra's arm. "It's good that you're home. We can go shopping tomorrow. I'll call Mel and get you in for an appointment, too." She lifted her hand but stopped, as if Kendra's hair was too ugly to actually touch. "Yes, well. That man can do wonders."

Kendra suppressed a sigh and stepped away, reminding herself why she was there. She'd given up on gaining her parents' acceptance or approval back when she'd decided to run from Eric. Now she was here for herself. And them, once they understood why she'd had to come back at all. Maybe that would garner some favor from her parents, but it wasn't likely to make up for the humiliation she'd have to endure first.

Her phone buzzed in her pocket and her heart skipped a beat. She warred with the instant desire to yank it out, but she couldn't handle it now if the message was bad. Losing Deklan right then would crush her remaining resolve.

Her father cleared his throat as he turned from the bar inlaid within the bookshelf on the far side of the room. "Can I get you something?"

Kendra shook her head while her father didn't even ask her mother. Eleanor always had the same glass of Pinot Gris, as if altering the choice would disrupt her smoothly laid-out life. As for Thomas, his preference was scotch on the rocks, a man's drink for the hard-cut businessman image he always projected.

"So what brings you here?" her father asked as he handed the glass of wine to his wife. No *are you okay*? or, *where have you been*? just, *why are you disturbing our evening*? She shouldn't have expected anything different, yet she'd still held out a slim hope that they might actually care enough to ask.

A weak smile curved over her lips at her own foolishness.

"I need to talk to both of you," she said, taking a seat in the torture chair from earlier. She had little option, since they'd taken seats on the matching sofa across from her. It was expected that she'd sit, so she did if only to make the conversation easier. Like sitting down would do that.

"After ten months of silence, you decide now is the time to talk to us?" Her father arched a brow, but it wasn't really a question as much as an accusation. The sprigs of gray that had dared to overtake his black hair a few years back only made him appear more intimidating and seemed to complement the prominent creases at the corners of his eyes.

"I needed the time to find myself." She looked down at her hands. "I told you that when I left."

"And did it work?" The doubt was heavy in her mother's voice. Her pointed scan over Kendra indicated that her mother didn't think so.

She resisted the urge to pull the quilted vest she wore closed, like that could hide the discount label on her clothing. Plowing ahead, she swallowed back the angry retort with a slow breath, pleased that her voice showed none of her inner turmoil when she spoke. At least she'd learned one thing of value from her mother. "Yes. In fact, it did." Just saying the truthful words made her spine straighten, her chin coming up with pride. "For the first time in my life I can honestly say I accept who I am. It might not be who you want me to be, but *I'm* happy with who I am."

Her father took a sip of his scotch before continuing. "So when will you be returning to Eric? We did our best to pacify him when you left, but I'm not sure if he's still willing to take you back. I could throw in a promotion and raise if you need the help."

He couldn't have shocked her more if he'd slapped her. She knew her mouth was hanging open, but there was no way she could close it. They didn't get it at all. The pain of their latest betrayal hurt deep in her chest, making her suck in a breath in an attempt to ease the ache that seemed to grow with each shallow inhale she was able to take.

"Kendra," her mother snapped. "Your father is trying to help you. You could at least thank him after the way you muddled up the best thing you had going in your life."

Kendra snapped back, her focus returning with the biting words of her mother. "Really? That's what you believe?" The cool, hard tone of her voice and rigid set of her shoulders must have alerted her parents that they'd said something wrong. She didn't even try to hide her disgust, knowing her face showed everything she was feeling. "I had no idea you really thought that low of me."

Her father sighed, one of those deep-chest ones that suggested he was searching for patience. "You know that's not what your mother meant."

"No? Then tell me, what did you mean, Mother?" Kendra cocked her head, nailing the woman with a glare that challenged her parents in a way she'd never done before.

Eleanor ran her hand over her perfectly coiled hair, superficially smoothing the blond strands back to the sleek French twist that looked as perfect now as it had when she'd left the house all those months ago. "Of course I don't think poorly of you, dear. I just want the best for you, and you and Eric look fabulous together. Plus, he was very generous after you quit that awful school counselor job to lounge around his penthouse all day. You wouldn't even help me with any of my charity events when I asked."

"That's because he wouldn't let me!" Kendra shot out of her seat, her anger venting at her mother's blindness. But then, she was the one who helped to hone that blindness. It was past time they saw the truth. "Eric made me quit my job that I loved. He held me prisoner in his penthouse, taking away everything that was mine until I had to depend on him. He beat me until I was afraid for my life. That's why I ran."

Her final words hung in the stunned silence, her parents staring wide-eyed and ashen at her. She choked back a sob and sank back to her chair, the outburst having sucked the strength from her legs. Her hands shook in her lap, her stomach cramping as the tension in the room rose until the air practically crackled with suppressed energy.

Her father cleared his throat, the ice cubes clinking in his glass as he shifted on the ill-fitting sofa. His brows lowered, pairing with the disgruntled line of his lips. "I don't understand why you need to make up these lies. We raised you better than that."

Just when she thought her parents couldn't disappoint her further, they did. She slumped back in her chair, not even bothered by her mother's frown of disapproval at her poor posture. "They're not lies," she said, resting her head in her hand, the defeat morphing her voice. "For the first time in years I'm telling you the truth and you still don't believe me." She brushed at the errant tear that slipped from her eye, annoyed at its untimely appearance.

"B-but," Eleanor stammered, showing the first hint that the conversation unsettled her. Only Kendra didn't know in what way. "I don't understand. If Eric was really abusing—" her lip curled in disgust at the word, "—you, why didn't you say something before?"

Kendra bolted up, her arm swiping toward her parents. "This is why. I didn't think you'd believe me. In your eyes, Eric is perfect and I, your daughter, am nothing without him. The only time I have ever had your approval was when I was with Eric—and then, it was because of him, not me." She thrust to her feet, too agitated to sit.

"That's not true, dear," her mother said, but there was a trace of doubt in her voice. "We love you. Now sit down."

Ignoring the command, Kendra paced to the window to get some distance. She couldn't breathe being that close to them. She hugged her arms across her chest and leaned against the window frame, the defeat sinking her low. "Then why don't you believe me?" She spoke to the lacy sheer curtain, unable to stand the disappointment that was plastered across her parents' faces. The slight waft of cool air coming off the window was refreshing as she absorbed the chill into her numb bones.

"What do you expect us to do, Kendra?" her father asked. "He's never been anything but respectful to all of us, and out of the blue you claim he beat and abused you. This is after you just up and disappeared with barely a word to anyone for the last ten months. Do your actions warrant our belief?"

Ever the logical one, even when it came to family. She shouldn't have expected more from her father, yet she did. "I thought the fact that I was your daughter would be enough."

The silence that fell was long and uncomfortable. The clink of ice cubes was the only sound that echoed in the room as they each waited for the other to say something.

She stared through the sheers at the hazy pool of light cast by the lone street lamp until the vague outline of a shape took form. Yanking the curtain aside, she couldn't believe what she saw. Her breath caught in her chest and she blinked just to ensure she wasn't imagining it. The tall strong form of Deklan leaned against the light pole, waiting out there for her.

He was there.

She blinked rapidly, her throat aching with suppressed emotions. His head was turned in her direction and he pushed away from the pole before giving her a nod. That was it. His hands were stuffed in the pockets of his leather jacket, his breath appearing in a white cloud to float over his head with each exhale. He made no move to come toward to the house, only stood there all stoic and male, staring back at her.

She didn't know how he knew she'd be there, but right then it didn't matter. She hadn't realized how much she'd needed his support until she'd seen him. Yet he wasn't charging in to save her; he was simply there. Remembering the buzz of her phone from earlier, she jerked her phone from her pocket and read the text message from Deklan. *I'm here for you.*

That was it. No admonishments or anger, just support. What she needed. The smile that lit her face must have seemed completely out of place to her parents. She read the needed words one more time then returned her phone to her pocket.

She would finish this.

Kendra addressed her parents with her newfound strength. "I guess being your daughter isn't enough after all." She walked back to the sitting area, knowing what she had to do. "I was hoping my words would be enough for you, but I see that they aren't. You want proof, so here it is."

She turned then, lifting her clothing to expose her back. The soft inhale from her mother, the muttered curse from her father let her know that they saw the scars Eric had left on her. She lowered her shirt and eased around to face her parents.

"Kendra," her mother said softly from behind the hand that hovered against her lips. There was a shine in her eyes that made them appear bluer than usual. "We didn't know. I'm so sorry."

Her father cleared his throat once again, but this time there was a dryness to it that he chased with the last of his scotch. He looked to Kendra, the level set of his gaze showing the beginnings of a rage that made grown men cower. "Eric did that to you?"

"Yes," she said, keeping her voice flat. "Those scars are

from the last time he whipped me. I left as soon as they were healed enough for me to move."

The brows over her father's deep brown eyes dropped into a menacing scowl.

"Why didn't you come to us?" her mother asked, the confusion and hurt showing.

Kendra's shoulders sagged, whether from exhaustion or relief she didn't know. "I was too embarrassed and ashamed," she told them honestly. "I didn't want to lose your respect."

Thomas shoved to his feet and stalked back to slam his empty glass on the surface of the bar, making Eleanor jump. "Now it's my turn to ask you, do you really think that low of us?" He braced his hands on the edge of the bar, his suit jacket pulling tight across his shoulders.

"No," she answered quietly. "But you didn't believe me now until I showed you proof." She sucked in a deep breath for courage. "And there's more."

Her father turned around, his face a mask of suppressed fury. "More?" he asked coolly. "What aren't you telling us, Kendra?"

Here came the hardest part—admitting her own guilt. "Eric will tell you I—" She faltered, swallowing down the nerves that threatened to stop her. "That I asked for it. That I like the pain." She rushed out the last words, squeezing her eyes closed to block out her parents' reaction.

"Why would he say that?" her mother asked.

"That's ridiculous," her father barked. "Why would we believe something like that?"

Kendra opened her eyes and forged on. "Because he has copies of my membership to a local BDSM club." The heat crept up the back of her neck to engulf her face in a warm flush. She never in her whole life wanted to admit that to her parents. There were just things your parents didn't need to know. Ever.

"A *what* club?" Baffled, her mother shook her head, her brows raised in question. "I don't understand."

Kendra almost smiled at that. Almost. Of course her mother wouldn't know what that acronym meant. "A sex club, Mother. BDSM stands for Bondage, Dominance, Sadism, Masochism."

Eleanor's eyes widened as understanding dawned. "Oh," she breathed. She licked her lips and attempted to collect herself. "Well…umm, okay. I still don't get the connection."

Dropping back into the chair, Kendra kept her eyes on the floor. She couldn't look at her father. "I'm a submissive. If you ask Eric, he will tell you that I asked him to hit me."

Her mother gasped. "That can't be true. Can it?"

God, how did she answer her mother's plea, especially when the answer wasn't what her parents wanted to hear? But she had to continue. There was no turning back now.

"Unfortunately, it is." Kendra dared a glance at her mother to see the disappointment she'd expected. "But I never asked to be abused. What started out as consensual quickly turned into something dark and controlling that I didn't know how to get out of." She picked at her cuticles, reverting back to the small flicks of pain for focus.

"Tell me exactly what he did to you, Kendra." Her father growled from across the room in his "you must obey" voice that brought her instantly back to her childhood. He'd always held an authority that none of them had ever dared to buck when that voice was used. Kendra wasn't shocked to realize it still worked even now.

"You don't want to know all of it," she answered, keeping her head down, her confession told to her hands. "The real abuse didn't start until after I moved in with him. He took away all of my credit cards, forced me to quit my job by threatening to show the school pictures of me bound and naked." She sucked in a breath. "He made me his slave. I wasn't allowed to wear clothes in the house. I couldn't do anything without his permission and was punished for infractions. If I really made him mad, he would beat me then chain me to the bed until the bruises and marks healed."

The harsh curse that left Thomas jerked Kendra upright. He father rarely swore. "I'll kill the bastard," he growled, storming to the desk.

"Thomas. What are you doing?"

Her mother's inquiry went unanswered as her father picked up the phone and dialed.

Kendra wiped away the tears that fell at her relief. Her parents believed her. Her father was angry *for* her. They might not always show it, but this proved that they really did love her. As did her father's next actions when he ordered Eric barred from the company, his termination effective immediately.

Afterwards, her father walked over to her and bent on one knee beside her chair. "Kendra, my daughter," he said, his voice thick and gruff. "I am so sorry. I had no idea."

"Oh, Dad." Kendra dove into her father's arms like a child, seeking his comfort and love. "I'm sorry too," she mumbled into his suit collar. The spicy scent of his aftershave brought back the instant memories of times when the hugs came more freely and she hadn't doubted his love.

"We would never want that for you," her mother said from behind Kendra, having left her seat on the couch. "We just didn't know."

Kendra eased out of her father's embrace, using the back of her hand to wipe away her tears. She stood to be engulfed in another hug from her mother. "I know, Mom. I didn't let anyone see what was happening."

Her mother pulled back, swiping at her own tears. "Are you okay now? Are you coming home?"

Kendra sniffed, and her father was there with a box of tissues. She gave a low chuckle, thanking him as she cleaned her face. "I'm doing good now," she answered. "But I'm not coming back. I'm happy in Minneapolis. I'm going to stay there for a while."

"Are you going to press charges against Eric?"

She looked to her father, his brows still drawn in a stern frown. "No. There's no point. I just want him out of my life."

"Why are you telling us this now?" her mother asked. "After all this time, what happened to make you come to us now? Did he hurt you again?" The sharp bite of fury that crossed her face with the question warmed Kendra. Even delicate Eleanor was ready to charge to her defense.

"No and yes," Kendra answered, gathering her courage for the last admission. "Eric found me in Minneapolis. It's okay," she reassured them when the anger flashed across both of their faces. "I have friends there who stopped him before he could physically hurt me. But he threatened me with something that would hurt our entire family. I couldn't let him do that."

"What?" her father demanded. "What else does he have on you?"

Shocked, she stared at him for a moment before asking, "How'd you know that?"

"Because that's how weasels like him work. They only have courage against the weak or by gaining leverage by some other means. There had to be another reason why you'd stay with him for so long. What is it?"

She paced back to the window, taking strength from the outline of Deklan through the sheers. "Eric has a damaging video of me that he took without my knowledge. It shows me as a submissive bound and begging to be…hit."

Her father cursed again, and she smiled at the window. The perverse satisfaction at her father's anger was something she didn't try to analyze.

"For years he's threatened to show it to you. Now he's upped the ante and demanded I return to him or he's going to sneak it into the video montage Chris is creating for your anniversary party."

"He wouldn't," her mother snapped. "That would be beyond cruel."

"Eric is not a nice man, Mother. He has everyone fooled by his aristocratic front, but it's all a show that hides his true character." A chill shuddered through her at the memory of just how cruel he could be.

"I just never imagined…" Eleanor trailed off.

"No one did." Kendra turned to her parents, wiping her damp palms on her jeans. "I'm not going back to him."

"Of course you're not," her father growled. "That's not even an option."

She nodded, giving her father a smile. "I realized the only chance I had at stopping Eric was to take away the power of his threat. By telling you my shame, he can't use that anymore."

"But will that stop him?" Her mother looked as horrified as Kendra felt at the prospect of the video being aired at the party. "How do we get the video back?"

Kendra had thought about that long and hard during her drive to Chicago. She didn't have the leverage or ability to do it herself or she'd have done it a long time ago. She'd torn the penthouse apart looking for it, knowing Eric would never leave it where she could find it. "I don't know, but I know someone who might be able to help us with that."

"What do you mean?" Thomas narrowed his eyes at Kendra.

This was supposed to be the easier part, but Kendra's pulse

raced once again. "I met someone in Minneapolis who has helped me through a lot of things. Most of all he's helped me accept who I am. He's ex-military with connections that could help us."

"I have connections." Her father looked affronted by her suggestion.

"Not his kind." She held up her hand at his rising outrage. "Deklan isn't bad. Don't worry. He just…" Crap, she wasn't explaining this well. Taking the last and final plunge, she met her father's hard stare. "Would you like to meet him?"

"He's here?" Her mother looked over her shoulder, as if Deklan was going to jump out from behind the couch and knife them all.

"He means something to you, doesn't he?" Her father ana-lyzed Kendra, leaving her feeling completely exposed.

"Yes. He means a lot to me."

"Where'd you meet him?"

"He lives in my condo complex." She smiled at being able to tell the truth about that. There was no way she was going to divulge all of her dirty, dark secrets to her parents. They already knew too much.

"And he's here?"

"Outside. I'll go get him." She left the room before they could object or grill her further. Kendra hurried down the hall, anxious now to see Deklan. She had no idea if he could really help them with the video issue, but that didn't even matter. After the last hour of soul-bearing exposure with her parents, she needed his arms around her.

She wanted his strength beside her.

Opening the door into the chilly night, she stepped onto the porch. Deklan was already moving toward her, crossing over the lawn with long, sure strides. If she'd doubted before, she knew now with certainty that she loved him more than anything.

He stepped onto the porch and a second later she was embraced in his arms, his warm breath heating her temple as he squeezed the breath from her. She was okay with that. In fact, she reveled in the honesty that one action showed and she held him just as tight.

Deklan was here for her. That was all that mattered.

TWENTY-FIVE

The ache in Deklan's chest eased the instant Kendra was in his arms. It had almost fucking killed him, standing outside just waiting for her. The cold air hadn't even registered when all of his focus was on the one small window where she'd appeared. Thoughts of charging the castle and damn the consequences had almost forced his hand. It was only Seth's calm logic replaying in his mind that kept Deklan's feet firmly planted under the streetlight.

He took his first deep breath in over twelve hours, the scent of lilacs seemingly enhanced by the crispness of the air. Or maybe it was just the relief of having her back in his arms. Of knowing she was safe. If he had anything to say about it, she would never doubt that again.

He pressed his lips against the small curl at her temple, the one that always drew him in with its teasing softness. Easing back, she cupped his face, her blue eyes shining in the dim light of the porch.

"Thank you, Deklan." She didn't need to say more. He

got it. Thank fuck Seth was stubborn enough to make sure Deklan had gotten it too. He owed that man something big.

She lifted up to capture his lips in a kiss that was as possessive as he felt. The groan that left his chest was filled with every emotion that he'd locked down since she'd left. Her mouth was hot and sweet, filled with the lingering flavor of spearmint and her that he wanted to taste forever. Her nose rubbed over his cheek, warm against his chilled skin, smooth against his beard stubble. She pulled back to trail kisses down his jaw until she nuzzled her face into his neck. Her slow sigh caused an avalanche of goose bumps to chase down his neck and over his chest.

Holding her tight, he simply felt her, the length of her firm, lean body pressed as close as they could get without being inside each other.

"I love you, Kendra," he whispered into her ear, the rough tightness of his voice making the words sound as raw as he felt. Exposed and bared to her in a way he'd never permitted with anyone else.

"Oh…" she breathed against his neck, her lips skimming over his skin. Her hands fisted on his back before they drew his head down for another consuming kiss. Her tongue searched out his, caressing and telling him silently how she felt. She nipped along his bottom lip, sucking the flesh into her mouth then soothing it with tender licks.

Pulling back, she searched his eyes, every ounce of vulnerability displayed in her own. "I love you," she said. Her admission almost brought him to his knees. He'd hoped, been pretty damn certain she'd felt that way. But hearing it shattered the wall he'd long ago built around his heart.

"I'll never harm you," he insisted, brushing a stray piece of hair away from her face. He wanted her to understand how much he meant it. It wasn't just words for him.

"I know." She blinked a few times, her thumbs stroking along his jaw. "I know. You're the one who taught me the difference between hurting and harming. Between play and abuse. Love and control. I trust you, Deklan. In all ways."

He tugged her close, overwhelmed by her openness. "How?" he asked, his voice still rough with emotion. "After all that asshole did to you, how can you trust again so freely?" He laced his fingers in her hair, his lips pressed back to her temple.

"Because it's you." She kissed the sensitive spot right below his ear. "Only because it's you."

The deep rumble of a throat clearing had them stepping apart, but he kept his arm tightly around her shoulder. He wasn't letting her go.

The stern expression from Kendra's father met them, his broad frame filling the doorway as he assessed them both. Deklan recognized the man from the photos that had been included with Rock's research. Thomas Morgan appeared every inch the formidable businessman he was. And right now, he was displaying the protectiveness of a papa bear over his cub.

"Father," Kendra said. "This is Deklan Winters. He's the man who helped me find my way back."

"Mr. Morgan," Deklan said, stepping forward to offer his hand in greeting. He sensed it was only well-ingrained manners that made Kendra's father accept the handshake. The stony stare that reminded Deklan of Kendra confirmed the suspicion.

"Mr. Winters," Thomas said, his hand still gripping Deklan's. "If I ever find out that you've harmed my daughter, I will hunt you down and make you beg for a mercy that doesn't exist."

Deklan smiled. He understood the man perfectly. "I would expect no less, sir."

They separated, a tenuous truce achieved. He knew, however, that it would take years of proof before Kendra's father truly believed him. Just one more thing the bastard Eric stole from Kendra's family.

Kendra led him down the long hallway of the grand house, his wet boots squeaking on the hardwood floor. Every step a reminder of just how far outside his realm he was.

The introduction to her mother didn't go much better than her father. The woman was smaller than Kendra with a delicateness that would never apply to her daughter. Eleanor could have easily walked off the pages of a magazine, her clothes, hair and makeup making her appear years younger than what Deklan knew her to be.

Her parents displayed the full intimidation of a prominent power couple. The fact that they were still together in a time when divorce was the norm said something about the strength of their marriage. Maybe it was all about image as Kendra had said, but the one they projected was pure unquestionable authority.

Kendra squeezed his hand, their connection solid despite the overtures of distaste that emanated from her parents. "Mother, Father," she said, her voice strong and sure. "Deklan helped me in more ways than I can explain. He doesn't come with the pedigree that Eric had, but he has a strength of character that Eric will never come close to."

Deklan was humbled by her conviction as much as her declaration. "I love your daughter," he told her parents. "I would give my life to protect her, and you have my word that I will never harm her." He held each of their gazes in turn, communicating with his eyes what he felt to his soul.

Her father inclined his head. "I'll hold you to that." Clearing his throat, he dove into the next topic. "Kendra tells us you may be able to help us get that..." He looked to Kendra, as if seeking confirmation that it was okay to proceed. She gave a nod, her lips thinned. "Video that bastard Eric has on her."

"It's already done, sir." There was a small bubble of satisfaction that Deklan couldn't deny as three faces stared at him in stunned surprise. There was always pride in a job well done. This was no different. Years of military efficiency and delivering reports came back as he recited the facts. "All copies of the file have been retrieved and destroyed, including the one locked in his penthouse safe and the one held by the bribed employee of the video company creating your anniversary video. Eric's computer has been wiped, a nasty virus destroying the hard drive. Any possibility of remaining copies should not be a threat, considering the pictures and video we now have on him."

"T-the what?" Kendra stammered, her eyes wide. "What did you do?"

"Personally, nothing," he reassured her. "But trust me when I say he'll never dare to harm you or your family again. He's been treated to a taste of what he forced you to submit to." He cupped the back of her neck, tugging her close, her parents forgotten. "Cowards like him run when faced with a stronger opponent. I made sure he knew who was stronger."

"You did that for me?" The wonder was clear on her face.

"Don't you understand?" He gave her a soft kiss. "I'd do anything for you."

The hesitant, soft smile that filled her face flushed him with a peace he never wanted to lose.

"How can we thank you?" her father's deep voice interrupted once again.

Deklan kept Kendra close, but turned his head to address Thomas. "None required, sir. I told you I'd take care of her. I mean that." Every word. The only reason he hadn't gone after Eric himself was because he'd have been hard-pressed not to kill the bastard.

"Are you sure you're all right now?" Eleanor asked her daughter.

Kendra looked to Deklan, a wide smile on her face. "Yeah, Mother. I'm okay now."

Deklan understood exactly what she meant. Okay was not even close to defining how right it felt to have Kendra by his side. In his life. But that simple word said it all.

They were okay.

TWENTY-SIX

The music wound in the background, a jazzy tune that blended with the low chatter and clink of silverware that fit the posh surroundings. All around them people decked out in designer gowns and name-brand tuxes laughed, smiled and posed to impress. Kendra didn't bother to figure out who they were impressing. It wasn't important to her.

"What's that smile for?"

She looked up to meet the deep blue eyes of the man she loved. "Because I don't care." She ran her fingers down the smooth line of his jaw, marveling at how soft the clean-shaven skin could feel when it was usually a little abrasive. Resting her hand on his chest, she enjoyed the slow sway of their bodies as they moved together across the dance floor.

"About what?"

"Anything. Everything." Kendra laughed, a deep, refreshing freedom consuming her. She tilted her head back and let Deklan spin her around before he tugged her in for a long, slow kiss that almost made her forget where they were.

It was the small giggle off to their side that finally forced her to ease away from the hypnotic kiss. A quick glance to her left revealed the source of the small laugh. Her four-year-old niece covered her mouth at having been caught and dashed away between the legs of the other dancers.

Kendra rested her head against Deklan's strong shoulder, inhaling the sandalwood scent that was just so him. "Thank you for coming with me tonight."

He hugged her closer, even though there was no room left between them. "I wouldn't have missed it."

"Right," she chided. "This doesn't really seem like your kind of an event."

"For you, it is." He kissed her temple, that one spot that was now his.

Melt her heart. Her Dom was constantly surprising her with his tenderness. A girl could get spoiled. Something she was a hundred percent fine with. "Have I told you how handsome you look in your tux?"

"Yes," he growled, nipping her earlobe. "Which is the only reason it's still on."

She chuckled, twisting her hand around his tie. "I can take it off you if you'd like."

"Any time you're ready."

Kendra pressed her hips closer to slowly rub over his growing erection. His low groan made her bite her lip to keep her laughter hidden. Teasing him was fun. It was just one more thing she was remembering about having a real lover in an honest relationship.

Yeah, relationship. That's what they had. And it didn't even scare her to say that. Not with Deklan.

"Should we say goodbye to your parents before we leave?"

She leaned back to look at him then swung her hips one more time, his cock rising hard and firm within his pants.

His arms tensed, jerking her to his chest. He cursed into her ear, his warm breath sending chills down her neck straight to her nipples. "You asking for something, Kendra?"

Lifting up, she whispered into his ear. "Please, Deklan."

"Fuck."

The breathy growl made her laugh again. It felt so good to do that. To be here at her parents' anniversary party with Deklan. To have the support of her family after all she'd been through. Telling her brother and sisters hadn't been any easier, but it'd helped that her parents had agreed her siblings didn't need to know all of the details. Chris had been just as angry and hurt by Eric's actions. Eric's poison had touched her entire family.

But no more. No one had heard from Eric since Deklan's little intervention. Deklan had offered to show her the incriminating pictures of her ex submitting to Deklan's dominant friends, but she'd declined. There was nothing of Eric she ever wanted to see again.

"Come on," she said, leading him off the dance floor. She glanced back, scanning down before leaning back to whisper, "Don't worry. No one can see your boner under your jacket."

He covered his cough behind his hand and nailed her with a look that could only be classified as a promise of retribution. A pale shade of pink touched his cheeks. Yup, that was her big, bad Dom blushing.

She spun around, cupping his face. "I love you. So much." She planted a fierce, hard kiss on his lips then quickly pulled away before he could respond. This whole love thing was so new it still made her feel vulnerable at times when she realized just how much she wanted Deklan in her life. How grateful she was that he was in it.

"Hey," he said, tugging her back around. "I've got you. Remember that." He ran the back of his fingers down her cheek in the softest of touches.

She closed her eyes and simply absorbed the feel of that light caress.

He leaned down to once again nuzzle her ear. "And later I'm going to have you bound to the headboard on that luxury bed in that ritzy hotel, spread eagle and begging for me to take you."

She inhaled, her pulse fluttering with the image he created. She swallowed. "Yes, Deklan."

His chuckle tickled her ear before he nipped her lobe and finally leaned back. A devilish grin covered his face, his dimple on full display. "Two can play at that game."

"Come on," she said, tugging his hand again. "Let's find my parents and say our goodbyes. Then you can keep all of those promises you made to me."

"Always."

She smiled at the low reply that reached her even over the din and chatter of the room. That one word said it all. Deklan had taken the time to prove that he meant it. That despite how he looked and came across to most, he was the kindest, most giving man she knew. She had no doubt that he would be there for her.

And she vowed to be there for him too. Always.

Deklan shut the door behind them, the low click settling in the room. He leaned against the door, content to watch as Kendra moved into the large, overpriced hotel room her father had insisted on paying for. She was beautiful. The sleek, black dress hugged her body, showing off exactly how fit she was, and her heels made her legs look longer than sin. Her sandy blond hair was pulled into a fancy arrangement that let long curls hang down, tempting him with every move of her head.

Tonight she was all sophistication and elegance. She'd blended beautifully with the posh crowd at the party. Laughs, polite inquiries and appropriate replies, she'd managed them all with ease. And it had been so superficial.

He twisted his fingers around the chain in his pocket, wondering again if it was the right move. But damn it, he wanted to see it on her. He wanted it with an urgency that should've scared him, only it didn't.

She looked back at him as she removed her dangly earrings and froze, her eyes going wary. "What?"

He went to her then; it was impossible not to. He cupped the back of her neck, urging her closer. Her body softened as she molded herself to him. The sigh that lifted her shoulders and flowed over his neck said it all.

This was so much more. More than he probably deserved. More than he imagined. "I love you." After never saying that to anyone, he couldn't stop telling her.

"Thank you."

He should be thanking her, and he would for the rest of his life if he had his way. He eased down the zipper on the back of her dress, savoring the low purr of foreshadowing that came with the action. She wiggled against him, and he chuckled at her devilish play. Thank fuck that bastard Eric hadn't stolen that from her. He'd tried, but Kendra had been stronger than that weasel ever hoped to be.

The prick had high-tailed it back to Boston as fast as Daddy's private jet could take him. If he was smart—and that was questionable—the man would never return. Deklan didn't care what he did as long as he stayed away from Kendra.

The dress slid down her body to pool around her feet in a glossy pile of silk. He ran his hands around her trim waist, savoring the outline of muscles that rippled beneath his palms. He'd only returned from Minneapolis that morning. Kendra had stayed with her parents all week, using the time to repair old wounds. Seth had insisted The Den would be fine without him, but Deklan had plans he'd needed to put in motion.

Neither Seth nor Jake had objected to moving Marcus, one of their most trusted Doms, into the role of training submissives. Deklan would continue training new Doms, but the connection required to properly train a sub wasn't in him to give anymore.

His only connection was with his only sub, Kendra.

He'd already terminated most of his client contracts, so there'd only been a few of those left to cancel. Kendra had ruined his desire to master anyone but her weeks ago. But she was so much more to him than just a sub.

"What are you thinking about?"

Did he tell her? Never one to doubt himself before, he was now full of indecision when faced with the possibility of losing her.

Her bright blue eyes were filled with curiosity and she tilted her head, studying him intently. "Hey, what's wrong?" She ran her fingers over his brow, smoothing away the frown that had formed. "You're starting to scare me."

"What?" He snapped out of his thoughts, angry at himself for making her worry. "No. Nothing." He kissed her lips to reassure her. But he should have known better. He couldn't do with just one kiss from her. One turned into two then three before he had to yank himself way, panting.

Her lids were heavy, her smile silky with the same lust that pooled in him. The need to claim her completely pushed him forward, hurdling past his doubt and fears.

He lowered himself down, dropping to one knee to kneel before her. Her eyes went wide, the confusion forming. He kissed the soft skin of her abdomen, holding her hips firm as his tongue swirled around her navel. She hummed her appreciation, her hands coming to rest on his shoulders.

The moment was as gentle and quiet as the room and Deklan wanted to cherish it like he did her. There was more to them than the whips and wild passion that had first brought them together. There was this too.

"Deklan." Kendra ran her fingers through his hair, sending chills over his neck and shoulders.

"Yes," he mumbled around the kisses he left on his way down to the low line of her lacy black thong.

"I love you."

"I know." And he did. Sucking in a breath of courage, he slipped his hand into his pocket and removed the slim chain. He kept it hidden in his fist and looked up so she could see how much she meant to him. "I don't know how or why, but I don't doubt that you do."

She smiled, her eyes dancing. "I could say the same."

He smoothed his palm over her flat and toned stomach, marveling at each muscle that showed. "I have something for you."

"Oh? What's that?"

The heater clicked on in the background, filling the room with its low purr, and Deklan took one more breath. This couldn't be wrong, not when it felt so right. Plunging forward, he circled her waist, the chain dangling from his hand where she couldn't see. Keeping his eyes on hers, he brought the ends of the long gold chain around her slim hips and held it together in front.

"You're mine, Kendra. As much as I'm yours."

Her eyes shimmered, the blue sparkling in the light as her chest rose and fell in long breaths. His leg shook, his nerves getting the best of him when they'd never once beaten him, even during his most dangerous mission.

"Will you?" He held the ends together in one hand so he

could run his free hand over her stomach once again. "Can I claim you like this? In a way that is just between us?"

"Oh." The breathy sound trembled, just as her hands did where they rested on his shoulders. "I swore I'd never wear a collar after...him. But this." She ran her fingers over the gold links pressed to her side. "This. For you. Yes."

His breath expelled in a wave that had him tipping forward to rest his forehead on her ribs. "Thank you," he said against her skin.

He managed to make his fingers work, fumbling the tiny clasp until it was finally secured. The chain settled low to rest on her hipbones, forming a sleek golden ring just over the line of her thong.

It was perfect.

He rose and claimed what was his. Her lips yielded under his, letting his tongue in to taste her sweetness. The lingering flavor of the champagne blended with her heat and tempted him to seek more. She was all warmth and goodness when he'd thought he'd never have either.

She pulled back, one hand grasping his arm as the other dropped to stroke the chain. She looked down and he followed to watch her sleek red nail click over the tiny links. "It's nice. Perfect." Her eyes met his. "How'd you know?"

Finally something easy to answer. "Because I know you, Kendra. This is about us. This chain is stronger than any cuff that could bond me to you. But only you need to know that. Every time you feel it against your skin, you'll remember how much you mean to me. You're my love. My life. Forever."

"Deklan," she breathed. She skimmed her fingers over his lips, the soft tips leaving a trail of longing behind. "I am yours. Make love to me."

Like she had to ask.

"Every day," he growled and swooped her into his arms to carry her to the large bed in the adjoining room.

He set her down on the silky bedspread before shedding his monkey suit. She laughed when he fumbled with his tie, and he shot her a devious look as he tossed the object to land across her waist in a taunting promise. Her laughter died and she squirmed against the covers.

"Strip, Kendra."

A seductive smiled curled over her lips. "Yes, Deklan."

She lifted her hips, the chain sliding toward her navel as she took her time easing her tiny thong down her long legs. He stalled on his own task, his hands immobile on his zipper. He was too entranced by his sub's provocative striptease. She knew exactly what she was doing.

Fuck. How in the hell did he get so lucky?

Her little lace bra smacked him in the chest, firing him back into motion. He was naked in two seconds flat and was sprawled over the top of her in the next. She laughed, her joy filling her face and dancing in her eyes.

She was warm and supple beneath him, and he couldn't get close enough. He grabbed her hands, holding them over her head in one of his so he could run his free hand down the length of her arm. He tweaked her nipple, playing with her beautiful jewelry. Someday soon he'd add to that collection. There was so much that could be done with a simple chain attached to each loop.

She moaned her pleasure, arching into his touch, and he gave her a smile of promise. "Soon."

"Now," she demanded, winding her legs around him to ride her moist pussy over his erection.

"Fuck." He couldn't argue with her. Not tonight. Instead he kissed her, showing her exactly how crazy she made him. She kept up her slow grinding motion until he pulled back, diving for a condom. "Keep your hands up." He looked back to see her obeying, her wrists crossed right where he'd left them over her head. She was a vision of submissive splendor.

He couldn't get the condom on fast enough. Not for her.

Settling between her legs, he lifted her hips and sank into her. Finally. His head dropped back as the tight, hot wetness that was her surrounded him. She felt so damn good.

"Deklan," she breathed.

"Kendra," he said back, easing down to hold her close. He rocked against her, loving the way her mouth parted and her eyes darkened with each slow thrust. He wanted this to last. "Fuck. This is perfect." It was so much better than that, but he didn't have a word for it. Or maybe he did.

Home.

With Kendra, he was home.

★ ★ ★ ★ ★

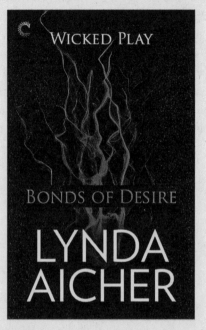
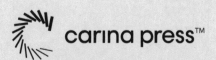